Tales from the Water's Edge

Moorhead Friends Writing Group

MOORHEAD FRIENDS WRITING GROUP

Copyright

Contents

Introduction

MELISSA PRUSI AND STEVEN
HOPSTAKEN

"Water does not resist. Water flows. When you plunge your hand into it, all you feel is a caress. Water is not a solid wall, it will not stop you. But water always goes where it wants to go, and nothing in the end can stand against it. Water is patient."

Margaret Atwood, the Penelopiad

THERE'S SOMETHING THAT HAPPENS whenever we're on the edge of a large body of water. Well, 'happens' might be too strong a word; it's more a feeling, an urge to simply...sit, to just be primordial, instinctive. Where do our thoughts go in those times? Sometimes to ponder a personal issue or to work out a plot point in something we're writing, but often they go nowhere, really. (Honestly, it's probably the closest to meditation that Melissa ever gets.)

We don't think we're alone in this. For many folks, there is something about water that draws us in. It's a necessity of life, of course, and the need for water has been a driving force in human history, determining where cities and towns spring up, motivating feats of engineering, and inspiring the plots of several Mad Max movies. But even when water is plentiful and we can get it simply by turning on a tap, we're still inexorably pulled to the nearest lake, river or ocean.

Water sustains us, irrigates our farmland, transports our goods. It's where we make some of our fondest memories: think family picnics by a lake, tubing down a river, the romance of any ocean voyage.

But it can also be treacherous. What happens if a child wanders away from that family picnic and into the lake? If you veer down the wrong branch of that river towards the rapids? If that romantic ocean voyage is on the Titanic?

We're drawn to the water, yes, but we would do well to be wary of it.

The list of ways water has been used as a symbol or metaphor could fill an ocean. (See what we did there?) It means depth and mystery. "Still waters run deep," you might say about the quiet but intriguing person at the edge of a party. In the old Disney movie, Pocahontas sang about the river as a place of change and rebirth. More recently, another Disney princess, Moana, saw the sea as a pathway to adventure and discovery. She doesn't know where it will bring her, but who wouldn't want to find out?

Myths and folklore are full of stories about water, from Narcissus becoming entranced by his own reflection to Paul Bunyan's footsteps creating Minnesota's 10,000 lakes. Because water cleanses and purifies, vampires are said to not be able to cross running water, a trope we played with in the second book of our *Stoker's Wilde* trilogy.

For those of us who live in Minnesota (and, as in both our cases, grew up in Michigan), we're never far from a body of water, and that proximity becomes ingrained in our psyches, part of who we are. From the big lake they call Gitche Gumee to the headwaters of the mighty Mississippi to the city lakes we might stroll around on a quiet Sunday morning, our lives as Minnesotans are tied to water. And, if we have a creative bent, those lakes and rivers might also inspire flights of fancy.

You can take some of those flights within these pages. Join a teenage boy on a fight for survival in the wilderness of northern Minnesota. Eavesdrop on a couple taking a weekend getaway that might turn deadly. Try to solve a true-crime story about a murder on a lake. And look out – there's something in the water that can scare a scuba diver to death. In genres that run the gamut from inspirational essay to horror, you'll read stories tied together by the theme of lakes, rivers, and oceans.

We don't know about you, but we can't wait to get started. After all, a book is like a lake. It might look serene from the shore, but you don't know what's under the surface until you dive in.

♦

Steven Hopstaken and Melissa Prusi are the co-authors of *Stoker's Wilde*, *Stoker's Wilde West*, and *Land of the Dead: A Stoker's Wilde Novel*, published by Flame Tree Press. Their first novel was on the preliminary ballot for Superior Achievement in a First Novel for the Bram Stoker Awards. Steven is also the author of *A Man Among Ghosts*.

There's a First Time for Everything

SUE QUINN

THERE SHE STOOD, ANKLE-DEEP in the water, lost in her own tears. Happiness and gratitude coursed through her with overwhelming power.

♦

Cindi had been divorced for almost three years and had just celebrated what she dubbed Freedom Day, the day she had grown a backbone and decided to stand up for herself.

It hadn't been an ugly or difficult divorce. How could it have been when Cindi gave up almost everything to gain peace? She didn't fight for the house, the truck, or either of the boats. She took only a couple pieces of furniture and let him have the rest. If he needed the control and the power, well, he could have it.

In the past, Cindi wanted to see more of the world, craved it, but was married to someone who refused. There was little chance she would ever lay eyes on more than her own backyard. She needed permission to go anywhere and just seeing her family had turned into a fight. Cindi would get up before the sun, drive four hours to her mom, help out as best she could with appointments or paperwork, get her mother's errands run, then turn around and drive back in order to have supper on the table. She didn't do it because she wanted to. She did it because it had somehow become necessary to save the marriage. Friends would comment on her strength and stamina but, in reality, Cindi was defeated and exhausted.

After years of mental, financial, and verbal abuse, Cindi packed a bag one day, took the dog, and walked out. Freedom Day. No plan. Nowhere to go. No one even knew what she had just done. She made some calls and found a friend who took her in while her not-yet-ex demanded she start divorce proceedings.

It hadn't been easy, emotionally. She grieved. She lost her home, way of life, time with her daughter, friends, and mostly the man she thought loved her. Her heart didn't break. It was torn from her chest. Things were better now, but healing didn't happen overnight.

Oddly enough, in the middle of this whole process, Cindi's mom fell ill and passed away. Now there would be no need to fight for household items. She would be able to outfit a new apartment with her mother's belongings. Less fighting was always good. He pushed and pushed, and three months later, he had his divorce.

As things started to calm down and Cindi began to find her new 'normal,' her job started to fall apart. It was a place that thrived on drama, and when there wasn't any, management created some. She decided life would be better somewhere else and started putting in applications.

♦

One afternoon, she met a friend, Jennifer, for lunch, who asked her how the job hunt was going.

"Good, I guess," Cindi replied.

"Well," Jennifer continued, "did you see the one for a bookkeeper?"

"I did. I'm not familiar with the organization."

"You know how to look things up." Jennifer smirked. "Google them. It sounds perfect for you."

After Cindi promised to do that, the subject spun to family events, things happening in life, and with friends.

The next day, Cindi looked up the company and it spoke to her inner hippie. This organization promoted environmental change and growth around the world. At least that's what she took from it. She applied, interviewed, and got hired. That was back in August.

By May, Cindi was standing on a beach in Australia. Turns out her new job involved international travel. She had a new life, a dream job for the past nine months, and new friends. Life was so much better than ever before.

🌢

Cindi hadn't ever been out of the country, much less all the way to the other side of the globe. Yet here she was. She'd been in this glorious place for almost two weeks. She walked all over the city of Brisbane, held a koala, petted kangaroos, and saw them in the wild. Today, Cindi and two of her coworkers were booked on late flights home and had the better part of a day at their disposal. They booked a tour to explore the fourth largest sand island in the world, Bribie Island, and spent the day on the beach.

Cindi walked up and down the shore picking up shells and luxuriating in the feel of the warm water on her feet. Their guide pointed out things she would have never noticed, such as snail trails. He even taught them about little clam-like creatures called Pippies that would dig themselves back into the sand with a long tongue as soon as you let go of them.

Cindi's pockets were almost as full as her heart.

Her coworkers were off with the guide when Cindi wandered into the surf. Lost in the feel of the tide sucking the sand from around her feet as it pulled back out to sea, reality hit her. Three years ago she would not have been allowed to take a job that took her out of the country, out of range of three mandatory phone calls a day, and where every time she used her debit card, it pinged her husband's phone. This trip would not exist. These people who were so supportive would not be part of her life. And she would definitely not be standing in the bubbly surf, crying.

Cindi was grateful for all the things that happened to get her to this place, both the good and the bad. Her life was dramatically different. She was in Australia! Her paychecks were her own. She controlled what she spent and where she went. She made her own decisions. Best of all, she had a safe space at home where walking on eggshells didn't exist.

And she cried. Tears of joy and gratitude. Cindi thanked the Universe and the Powers That Be for all they had done to protect her and help her move forward, for the good people in her life, for her girls, and for the opportunity to be right here in this moment. Tears streamed down her face, her pockets were wet, sandy, and stuffed with shells, and her feet were in the ocean for the very first time. Cindi was the happiest she had ever been.

●

Susette Quinn writes everything from poems to short stories, romance to humor. She is a long-time member of the Moorhead Friends Writing Group and has lived in the Fargo Moorhead area for over thirty years. While she does not have a slew of published works, she can claim ownership of "Stronger" published by the *Potato Soup Journal* and short stories in *Tales from the Frozen North* and *Welcome to Effham Falls* with the Moorhead Friends Writing Group. Ms. Quinn maintains a busy lifestyle that includes working for an international nonprofit, a local bookstore, and volunteering at a local dog rescue.

The Sandpit

Suzi Wieland

THIS VACATION COULD'VE BEEN so much better.

Marty could've stayed with Lizzee in a cozy one-bedroom cabin on the adults-only side of the lake resort. They could've spent the days fishing and the nights at the lounge enjoying adult beverages… with other adults.

But no, Lizzee had insisted her two kids come with. So they had a cabin on the busy family side, and they only fished for two hours before the boys grew bored and wanted to return to play on the beach with all the other kids. And their evenings were spent cuddling on the lumpy sofa while the boys went to bed in the loft.

Calvin was seven, old enough to stay with five-year-old Sawyer while Marty and Lizzee had a few hours to themselves, but she refused to leave them alone even though she could have left her phone with them.

Marty finished applying another layer of Lizzee's cocoa butter sunscreen—tropical resort in a bottle—and glanced toward the glassy lake waters as Lizzee splashed around with her sons. She waved to him, her smile bright. At least the beach wasn't busy today since a large chunk of people had left Sunday night, and the new ones hadn't made it out yet.

The beach would fill up after lunch. "Don't forget your life jackets," mothers would screech. "You're in too deep. Come back." And shrieking children would ignore the haggard women, kicking sand up everywhere as they played or fought with their siblings and got in Marty's way.

He waved back to Lizzee.

The resort needed to toss the faded, scarred plastic lounge chairs. In fact, the whole place needed a facelift, including the 1980s-style lodge and restaurant. He should have checked out the place before Lizzee called in the reservation. When they married, he'd take over making the reservations so they wouldn't end up at shitholes like this. He hadn't popped the big question yet though.

If they'd come alone, he might have done it this weekend. Please, please, please, let's just the two of us go, he'd begged. Lizzee's ex was an okay guy, and he would've switched days to give them the much-needed alone time.

No, she'd said the first time he asked. No, she'd said the second time. And no, she'd said the third time. The boys had never been to a cabin at the lake, never been to a beach, never fished before—which again, they only did for two hours before whining about being bored.

Calvin dunked Sawyer under the water in the roped-off swim area, and the younger boy bounced up, sputtering.

"Good dunk, Calvin," Marty called, and Lizzee's icy look across the water about froze him. She waded through the water to rescue Sawyer, her face stern like she was the fun police. But Sawyer was laughing, and he flung himself at his older brother to try to get him back, so she didn't scold them.

Lizzee didn't grow up with brothers and didn't understand boys even though Calvin was already seven.

Marty wanted to close his eyes and take a little snooze in the warm sun, but the laughing boys and the lawn mower droning somewhere behind him kept him from drifting off. He scooted to the end of the chair and put his feet in the hot sand.

"Mommy," Sawyer called. "Watch this."

Calvin knelt, and Sawyer scrambled up to sit on his shoulders. Calvin straightened, and Sawyer counted down three, two, one, then flung his arms in the air like he was reaching for the clouds. They toppled back together into the water, hit with a splash, and jumped back up to do it again.

Calvin was patient with his little bro, and Marty hoped they'd both be that way when he and Lizzee had a child too.

A child. Was he really ready?

Yes.

Even though those stupid doubts appeared now and then, Marty knew he'd marry Lizzee. She wanted more children too, and since she was a physician assistant and he delivered furniture, they both agreed that he'd be a stay-at-home dad. Which would be super fun. No more getting up at six every day, and no more stupid-ass bosses or having to work with idiots.

"Marty, did you see what we were doing?" Sawyer ran up, showering Marty with sand. Then he stepped on Marty's toes—the boy always did have problems with getting into people's personal space.

"Yeah. Watch the toes, buddy. You're getting big now, and you might crush them."

Sawyer jumped back with a giggle. "We fell backwards into the water, and then I was jumping from Calvin's shoulders. Maybe we can jump from your shoulders. That'd be like super high. Like jumping from a skyscraper."

"I'm in." Marty gave Sawyer an enthusiastic two thumbs up.

He might have to endure a few kicks to the face, but he could tough it out. Just like he did in their many professional-style wrestling matches on the living room floor, where Lizzee would shake her head as the boys jumped on him and tried to take him down. They rarely succeeded, even when double-teaming him. Those wrestling matches and the football games they played were Marty's favorite times with the boys, and they didn't get that with their dad because he was a stuffy college professor who preferred art and music and other things that required the boys to sit still and listen. At least Lizzee's ex was in their lives and paid attention to them.

Marty's dad hadn't been around, but he had an uncle who'd babysat him. They shot BB guns at paper targets tacked to a tree and climbed up into the treehouse at his grandmother's and played endless games of hide-and-seek and tag and soccer.

Calvin dropped onto the sand behind his brother. Lizzee took her seat in a lounge chair and tossed the blue starfish sand mold onto the ground next to the dump truck, the other molds, and the shovels.

"The water is so beautiful. You need to come swim." Lizzee pulled her long hair behind her head and squeezed the water out. The woman was beautiful and intelligent. Smarter than Marty even, although he'd never admit that to anybody.

"Marty said he'd let us jump from his shoulders." Sawyer waved at Marty, his face bright with anticipation.

"We should also play *Toss the Elf,*" Marty added.

"What's that?" Calvin's big brown eyes widened.

"That's where I look for sneaky elves, and if they get too close to me, I grab them by their arms and legs. I spin around and toss them into the air."

"I want to be an elf. Can I be an elf?" Sawyer practically bounced on his feet.

Lizzee crossed her arms, probably thinking that someone was going to break an arm or end up in tears. "As long as the elves are in deep enough water."

"Yay." Sawyer clapped his hands together. The boys had so much energy, and although Lizzee took them on bike rides and to the park, she preferred reading, telling stories, and doing art. All that was good, but they needed more roughhousing in their lives.

"I think it's time for food, Liz." He checked his phone, not really knowing the time, but lunch had to be coming soon. Eleven-fifty. "You said we'll get lunch from the cantina today, right?"

"Can-tin-a. Can-tin-a," both boys chanted, waving their arms back and forth. Despite there being a full restaurant, the bar food in the lodge, and the BBQ food truck that showed up every day, she had brought groceries along, and they'd only enjoyed one meal out. And *enjoy* was a strong word. The boys had gobbled down their food and grown bored. Marty barely had time to finish his one beer, let alone order a second one.

Lizzee's face wrinkled. Although she'd already agreed to lunch on the beach—the boys just didn't know it—she had to put on an act like she was considering it. She played that game too often, and the boys would figure it out soon. "Okay, let's do it. It is our last day here."

She brought up the menu on her phone, and the boys looked it over. He wasn't sure why. He knew what they'd get.

"Chicken strips and fries," Calvin requested. His back was covered in sand.

"Me too," Sawyer said. "Don't forget the ketchup."

Marty could've staked his life on that exact order. They never varied, never tried anything new no matter what Marty or Lizzee suggested. "I'll take the smokehouse burger."

Sawyer scooted closer to the water and filled up his bucket with wet sand. He smoothed off the top, carefully flipped it over, and then started with a second.

"Got it." Lizzee typed into her phone, then tossed it on the colorful beach towel she'd bought just for this trip. Ugly pink flamingos for her towel, Sawyer had dinosaurs, Calvin's sharks, and Marty's was crabs.

Crabs, for pity's sake. Ugly red, big-eyed crabs. He wasn't sure why she couldn't just get a plain towel, something without ridiculous cartoons on it.

"When will it be ready?" Calvin stretched out his legs and dragged his heels along the sand to make small trenches.

"Maybe twenty minutes. The app will text us when it's ready." Lizzee raised her face to the sun and closed her eyes, and Marty took a minute to appreciate her beautiful curves. He'd tried talking her into a bikini, but she denied him that too. At least behind closed doors, she wasn't so modest. His eyes stayed on her until a gull squawked above them, breaking his stare.

Marty pushed up to his feet and scooped up some sand toys. "I'm going to help Sawyer build his sandcastle. Want to help, Calvin?"

"Sure," Calvin said and followed Marty. They plopped down next to Sawyer, and Marty dropped the sand toys, studying the pathetic sandcastle. The boy was only five, he reminded himself.

"You need a moat." Marty snatched the shovel and started scooping out a moat along the front of the castle.

"Can we fill it with water?" Sawyer blinked his big eyes up at Marty. He was a sweet kid, most of the time. He'd just turned five and should be going to kindergarten at the end of the summer, but Lizzee insisted he wait until next year because his birthday was in early June. She said he needed more socialization and had to learn how to sit still better.

Marty had argued how dumb that was—the boy was old enough and was ready, and Sawyer's dad was okay with him going to kindergarten. Not to mention she'd save so much money on daycare, but she wouldn't listen to him.

"Of course, buddy." Marty scooped out the perfect ninety-degree corner and dug across the side.

"I'll get the back of the moat." Calvin used his hands to drag an uneven line behind the castle. It was wider in some places and narrower in others.

"We need to use the shovel. Otherwise, it'll look weird. Let me fix it." Marty crawled around the castle and filled the moat line Calvin had created. Then he pulled his shovel along the back to create a new one. Calvin stayed out of the way, and Marty's line was straight and clean.

Much better.

Marty didn't have a ton of happy childhood memories, but playing at the beach at the state park was one of the few. His mom helped him with sandcastles and buried him in the sand. Then she'd pretend she couldn't find him even though his face was showing. He always stuck close to her because his big brothers were supreme assholes who liked to shower him with sand in the face or pretend crabs or fish would bite his toes if he stood still too long on the beach or in the water.

He'd been waiting for karma to get Shane and Daniel after all those years of torture, and now Shane had two spoiled shits that he constantly grumbled about. Marty would remind him: like father, like sons.

Marty paused from his work and glanced at Lizzee. "I've got a fun idea, boys."

"What?" Sawyer's head popped up, but Calvin was suddenly Mister Mopey.

"When your mom leaves to get the food, you should bury me. I'll let you completely cover me. Even my face."

"Your face?" Calvin perked up slightly.

"Yes, but I'll have a towel over it. I don't want sand in my eyes or mouth." If they worked super-fast, they could probably do it. Marty would have to do the heavy digging, but the boys could cover him quickly. Lizzee would see the obvious hump in the sand and hopefully play along. Calvin was old enough to understand the game, but Sawyer might really think she couldn't see Marty.

Sawyer jabbered on about how this was such a cool trick to play until finally Lizzee called out that the food was ready.

"I'll help the boys clean the sand off while you get the food." Marty waved at the two sand-covered creatures next to him, then glanced at a boat whose motor started up on the dock down the beach. Someone probably going out fishing. Lucky guy.

Lizzee stood, pulled her white cover-up over her body, and slid on her blue flip-flops.

"Okay, boys," Marty whispered. "Here's the deal. As soon as she walks away, we start digging."

They waited until Lizzee was about twenty yards away, and the three of them ran to their spots, dropped to their knees, and started shoveling sand with their hands. Marty was moving over double the amount of sand they were.

"Faster, boys. Your mom will be back soon. Now don't say anything, Sawyer. Don't ruin the surprise." The boy was a bit of a tattle. Calvin, on the other hand, knew how to keep his mouth shut when Marty let out a swear word, and he never ratted Marty out that time he had come home early and caught Marty with the neighbor from down the street.

Of course, he hadn't seen Tomi on her knees between Marty's legs.

They'd heard the door slam, and she'd shot into the recliner just before Calvin walked in. Luckily, she was still fully dressed, and Calvin didn't notice her red face or disheveled clothes. Nor did he question why Marty had a blanket over his lap when their air conditioning was running.

He'd never even told his mom Tomi had been there—it was a normal enough occurrence for Tomi to stop by when Lizzee was home, so nothing had seemed off to him. They'd been more careful since then.

Sand flew this way and that, and soon the three of them had a long trench dug. Marty scooted into it and shoved his feet into the sand at the end. The coolness was a relief from the hot air.

He spread sand over his legs. "Okay, I'll hide my face with this towel, and you guys can cover me up. Sawyer, you just follow Calvin's lead when your mom comes back. Don't tell her where I am."

"I won't." Sawyer raised two fingers like he was doing his Cub Scout oath. "I promise."

Marty's phone rang with a text message, and he told Calvin to check it.

"It's Mom. Do you want me to open it?"

"Yes. 1-2-1-1-2 is the code." Marty didn't worry about Calvin reading any of Tomi's messages because they were in another name, and they used code words. Plus, her naked pictures were saved in a hidden folder. He wasn't stupid enough to leave those ones in his texts.

"She needs help with the food." Calvin's shoulders drooped. "What should we do?"

"Perfect. We won't have to worry about her coming back before we're done. Pretend you're me and tell her I'm sending you. Then let's get me buried, and you can grab the food and hurry her back." The only part he was unsure about was breathing under the towel. If the air became too stifling, he'd just move his head to get fresh air.

Marty grabbed the towel and lay back in the sand. He bunched up the end of the towel and folded it. Best to make a little pocket of air. Double protection, too, from sand getting into his face.

"Mommy's never going to find him." Sawyer giggled as he filled his bucket with sand and dumped it onto Marty's waist.

"If she can't find him, you can tell her." Calvin patted Sawyer on the back and returned to the sand, which was now almost up to Marty's neck. They only actually had two to three inches on top of him, which felt refreshing under the strong sun.

"Nope. I'm not going to ruin it." Sawyer shook his head vehemently just before another bucket of sand hit Marty. "Will you bury me after we eat?"

"Maybe. If we have time. We'll see what your mom's plans are." Marty ignored Sawyer's sad face. He should've just told the boy yes. It's not like it'd take long to bury him anyway. But they'd be washing sand out of his hair for days.

"'Kay, boys. I'll put the towel over my face, then you can cover my arms and head. Like I said, make sure you hurry back."

Marty laid the towel over his head and adjusted the part over his mouth and nose. His arms went to his sides, and the boys scooped sand over him. Lizzee would definitely know to play the *Where's Marty* game.

Usually it wasn't a game, at home at least. She always scolded him when he forgot to tell her he was leaving, and she'd go all over the house looking for him.

She sometimes forgot that he wasn't a kid and didn't always need to check in with her.

The weight of the sand pressed into his face. His air pocket steamed up quickly, but it wasn't anything he couldn't handle. His whole body was encased in a tomb of sand now, but it felt just like the weighted blanket Calvin had.

"Going to get Mom now." Calvin's voice was lightly muffled, and soon their voices trailed off.

The towel had definitely been a good move. The crab towel.

Marty let out a laugh. He remembered learning as a kid about how the ocean crabs dug into the sand, and you wouldn't even know they were there. His mother had assured him that was only the ocean and that crabs didn't live at the lake beaches. They liked salty water.

He'd never questioned her as a kid, but now he wondered if that was true. Not that he was afraid of the small creatures. They'd be more afraid of him.

Marty wiggled his fingers, wishing he had a picture of his grave. The pit he was in was only really about the depth of his body. If he was in the middle of the beach, he might worry about someone stepping on him, but he was right next to all the towels and lounge chairs. Not to mention the towel over his face was halfway uncovered too. Someone would have to be an idiot not to realize he was under the sand.

Other than the heat of the air pocket, the sand was cool, and his muscles relaxed. He could almost take a nap out here. These boys were exhausting at times.

At the sound of voices, Marty concentrated, but it only took seconds to recognize Sawyer's jabbering.

"Now, where's Marty? I don't see him." Lizzee's tone was

light, and Marty imagined her standing there pretending to look around—everywhere except for the mound of sand the length of a body.

"He was here when we left," Calvin said. There was a thump and crackle of plastic off to the side.

"He was, Mommy. I saw him when we left. He was sitting on his towel." Sawyer couldn't contain the excitement in his voice. "Maybe you should look for him."

"Look for him where? I'm looking everywhere, but I don't see him." Lizzee let out a little huff.

"I'm hungry. Can we eat?" Calvin asked. "Maybe Mom should sweep away all this sand so we can have our picnic here."

"Yeah, Mommy. Can you clean up the sand? Me and Calvin tried to make a sandcastle, but it didn't work. We can sit right here in the sand."

"That's one long sandcastle you were trying to make." Lizzee pretended like she was impressed. "Maybe when Marty comes back, he can help you too."

Sawyer giggled.

"Calvin, you get the food, and I'll make us a little table over here."

Movement next to Marty made him certain that Lizzee had knelt down. The sand above his chest stirred, like she was wiping it away. Then he felt the sand moving above his legs, but she hadn't uncovered any part of him.

He wiggled his toes, expecting the sand to fall away, but she was obviously making a big show and barely scooping off the sand.

He waited. And waited.

And then the motion stopped.

"Where's Marty?" Sawyer squeaked.

"Yeah, where did he go?" Calvin's voice grew louder, and Marty felt a pressure against his body. "He was here when we left."

The sand stirred above Marty again, this time in two places. Above his shoulders and his chest. More urgently, like the boys were looking for him. Somehow, though, the scent of the greasy goodness of the burger Lizzee had brought made its way to his nose, and his stomach rumbled. He wanted to dig into that smokehouse burger with its melted American cheese and four slices of bacon.

Okay, this was getting ridiculous. How long could they string this out? There was only a few inches of sand on top of him.

"Where did Marty go, boys?" Lizzee asked.

"I'm right here, for pity's sake," Marty muttered.

"He was here, Mom. We buried him right before we came to the cantina." Calvin sounded as confused as the others.

Time to end this charade.

Marty lifted his shoulders to sit up, but he couldn't move. He tried to raise his arms, but the most he could do was wiggle his fingers, which got him nowhere.

Same for his feet.

His face heated, and his muscles tightened. The three inches of sand felt like concrete, but that was impossible. Had they thrown a weighted blanket over him without him knowing? But Calvin's blanket was back at the cabin, and they didn't have time to get it. And Lizzee would never allow the boys to bring that blanket to the beach.

"Enough, boys. Let me out of here," Marty barked. He was all for pranks, but this went too far. He tried to crawl out again but couldn't.

"I swear, Mommy. He was here when we left." Sawyer's voice grew timid, and the sounds of frantic shoveling grew louder.

"Marty," Lizzee called.

"I'm right here." Marty strained upward, but the sand locked him into place. The air pocket grew even hotter, and Marty gasped for air, his chest tight. The weight on top of him seemed to grow even heavier.

Settle down. They're playing a stupid joke on you. Or Lizzee was. But big practical jokes weren't her style, especially ones on her children. And from the way Calvin and Sawyer were speaking, they didn't sound like they were in on it.

Sawyer would've been giggling by now. No, they weren't a part of her joke, and it had probably been her pretending to dig those other times.

Marty attempted to push himself up, to even just slide his arms or legs to the side. He grunted and tried folding his legs back, but nothing worked. He was locked in a sand coffin and couldn't get out.

Settle down. You're not locked in. Take a deep breath and relax.

His heart raced when the sand suddenly shifted beneath him. He sunk lower into the earth, the sand chilling his arms.

"Lizzee, get me out of here now," Marty demanded at the same moment she called his name.

"He must have got up and filled in the sandpit when we left," Calvin suggested.

"I'm right here. Right. Here," Marty screamed. The sand smelled dank, musty, and his skin prickled like bugs were creeping all over him. Or... or...

Crabs?

No, not crabs. They lived by the ocean. It was just the sand brushing his skin, not hundreds of bodies with eight spindly legs crawling all over him, their claws searching for the perfect skin to pinch.

"Maybe he ran back to the cabin to use the bathroom." The disapproval in Lizzee's voice rang strong. "He should have told us he was leaving."

Her theory was ridiculous. He never would've walked all the way back when they had public bathrooms at the beach.

"I'm right here." Sweat beaded on Marty's forehead, and despite the chilly sand, his temperature rose. He was still breathing, but it wasn't enough, like he had a cold and couldn't get a full breath. He moved his arms, and the sand shifted around him.

Thank God. It hadn't done that before. They must've stopped doing whatever they'd been doing to hold him down.

"Let's just sit down and eat. All of our food is probably cold now." Lizzee sighed.

In seconds, the smell of fried food permeated Marty's nose again, and he salivated. "Don't eat my burger."

He started tunneling upwards. When he got out, he'd tell Lizzee off. They were probably sitting right next to him this whole time, pretending to dig him up.

"Not funny, Lizzee," he shouted.

The hot sun hit Marty's face, and he took in a deep breath of the clean air. He was free.

He glanced over to Lizzee and did a double-take. She looked like a giant perched on a giant lounger, sitting next to a giant Sawyer.

"Lizzee," he called as he headed toward her. He must be dehydrated—that was it. The sand sucked all the moisture out of his body and weakened him.

He scuttled forward.

Marty froze and sucked in a breath. He looked down with his beady black eyes, at his small mottled brown body with eight legs and two massive pinchers.

He was a crab.

A sand crab!

"Lizzee," he howled and sprinted to the monstrous feet in front of him, his bodying sailing over the sand like he was flying. "Help me!"

He was so close.

I'm hallucinating. This isn't happening.

"Mommy, look. A crab." Sawyer jumped up and clapped his hands.

Lizzee let out a squeal that burst Marty's eardrums. Except he didn't have eardrums anymore. She whipped up her flip-flop from the sand and swung at him.

Whack! Marty's front claw twisted into an unnatural angle.

Whack! Marty's left eye squished into mush.

Whack! Marty's front legs cracked from the force.

"Lizzee, stop," he yelped. His legs seemed wet, like they were dripping with blood. *Do crabs have blood?* God, he didn't even know. All he knew was that he was losing strength, and his legs wouldn't hold him up anymore.

"Lizzee, you're killing me." He tried to get her to stop, but she took another swing at him. He soared through the air, farther and farther away and landed on his back in the sand. He floundered around, trying to right himself, but it was impossible with his broken legs.

Had Lizzee found out about his misdeeds? Had Calvin told her? But she couldn't have done this—it was impossible. There were no such things as witches and magic.

Whether it was Lizzee or karma, he had no clue, but as the sun beat down on his squirming body, he knew this would be the end.

◆

Suzi writes in a variety of genres and has published horror and suspense stories under Suzi Wieland and contemporary young adult novels under Suzi Drew. When not writing, she spends time with her family and friends and her sweet and fluffy dog. She works as a freelance editor and has the privilege of editing fantastic stories for her job. You can find out more about her writing at SuziWieland.com

Three Bridges

Dan McKay

She always brought a wedding dress when she traveled, just in case. She'd received several proposals of marriage, none of which she accepted. Some men had been handsome, others had been rich, but Ellie was not ready. Not yet. Usually, there were extenuating circumstances that required she leave town, sometimes in haste. *Veni, vidi, vamoose.*

The porter hauled her travel-worn steam trunk off the train and onto the platform. Its brass corner caps wore dents and tarnish, and the sides had scrapes from rough handling. The sign on the platform read "Three Bridges," one of which she could see from where she stood. So this is where he had planned to come back to.

"I take it the town has three bridges," she said to the porter.

"Yes, ma'am," he said. "All cross the same river. That one's called North Bridge. A fellow can drive a cart across it unless you meet another. Main Bridge—now that's a right proper bridge. I seen a cart meet the stagecoach on it, right smack-dab in the middle. That's a four-horse coach, mind you."

"What's the river called?"

He met her gaze and paused. She was accustomed to people's reactions when they noticed her eyes. One was blue and the other hazel. Heterochromia, a doctor had told her. He had assured her it was normal and not a symptom of any malady. In prior times, people might have considered her someone special and worshipped her, or, in other times, a witch and killed her.

"Deer Creek," the porter said, staring at her eyes.

"That's two bridges," she said. "Where's the third?"

"Oh, that's East Bridge on the other side. A lot smaller. It's just for people on foot or horseback."

She turned around and pointed. "Doesn't the railroad cross a bridge back there?"

"That it does," he agreed.

"So why isn't the town called Four Bridges?"

He removed his cap and rubbed his head. "Well, I don't rightly know. Maybe on account of the railroad bridge is just for trains. Or it's too far outside of town."

She reached into her purse, showed the porter a coin, and looked pointedly at her steam trunk.

"Where to, ma'am?" He hoisted the trunk.

♦

Once the trunk had been delivered to her hotel room, Ellie went next door to the saloon. All conversation stopped when she walked in. She surveyed the people at the tables and bar. Simple, small-town folks wearing outdated fashions, unlike the modern white dress with lavender trim she wore. Since she held their attention, she thought she might as well take advantage. "I'm looking for Big Jake."

Judging by the way everyone's eyes bugged out, she'd hit a collective nerve. "Ain't no one here laid eyes on him in nigh on a month," the bartender drawled.

She knew that to be an accurate statement. The last time she'd seen Big Jake, more than two weeks ago, he had been nearly a hundred miles away, lying dead in the dirt with a bullet hole in his chest.

One of the saloon girls walked over. "What business do you have with my Jake, sister?"

Sister? That sounded somewhat aggressive. The saloon girl stood a head taller than Ellie's petite frame, but she knew it wasn't the size of the cat in the fight. "Your Jake? Is he your brother?"

"You don't have to take that from no stranger, Rose!" a man called.

Rose pursed her lips and fire shone in her eyes. "Jake is my man."

Ellie raised an eyebrow. "Don't see any ring."

A couple of men at a card table whooped. Rose stood, arms akimbo, and called over her shoulder to the men. "Go soak your heads! And get your own damn beers." She sized up Ellie. "We ain't formally hitched just yet, but that day's a-coming."

Here she was in the flesh: Rose, the woman who'd claimed Jake's heart. Ellie met Rose's angry stare. "I knew Jake from long ago. He wrote me a letter and asked me to meet him here."

Rose shook her head. "You must be mistaken."

"How many towns called Three Bridges could there be?" The ruse was risky, but Ellie needed information. Big Jake was in no position to contradict anything she claimed. "Although, truth be told, I counted four bridges."

A couple of men at a nearby table counted on their fingers.

"I don't know what you're talking about, but Jake loved me, and I loved him back. If you know anything about his whereabouts, I..." Rose looked around the room for support. "We would all appreciate to hear it. Ain't that right, boys?"

A murmur of approval swept the room. Ellie gave a tight smile. Her ploy hadn't gone well, but she still had cards she could play. Somebody knew something more, and eventually they'd approach her. She smoothed her dress, feeling the derringer hidden in a pouch she'd sewn inside.

●

Ellie walked through the town, crossing the bridges from one side to another in search of anyone who had been Jake's partner or confidante. She's already burned the bridge with Rose, but Rose wasn't going to share anything, anyway.

After the first day, she stayed out of the saloon. It was no place for proper ladies, and she wanted to keep a clean reputation.

The sheriff's office was quiet, but Three Bridges was a quiet town. The sheriff was out of town on official business and had left gray-haired Deputy Johnson in charge. He eyed her suspiciously and kept tight-lipped about the sheriff's whereabouts.

The barber always had someone in his chair and usually two or three waiting their turn. The strange looks she received when she entered told her the barber shop was no place for women. Those kinds of attitudes hadn't stopped Ellie in the past, but she needed to use a subtle approach, so she excused herself and left.

She stopped in the dry goods store and bought some licorice and hard candy to hand out to children. Newspaper boys told her stories they'd heard about Big Jake, and sometimes had witnessed personally. There was no doubt everyone in town adored him.

The mercantile store had handkerchiefs in pastels, and she selected a few to buy. She took her meals at the busy hotel restaurant, always sure to compliment them on the food. Everyone in town had seen her somewhere. Everyone had a chance to re-consider keeping secrets.

●

During Big Jake's short time in Springdale, it hadn't taken Ellie long to figure him out. With some subtle and not-so-subtle applications of womanly charms, soon she was his traveling companion on an expedition for hidden gold.

He had studied a map, which he'd kept for his eyes only at first. Gradually, he let Ellie see glimpses as he surveyed the bends in the river they followed. He told her there were two pages to the map, and he only had one. The missing page had more information, including a city or railroad depot. No one knew who had the other half, although there was no shortage of speculation.

Ellie asked how he knew the river they followed was the one on the map. Jake said he had a strong hunch based on a place he and a partner from Three Bridges had trapped muskrats years ago. The river's shape, as he remembered it, matched the map. She knew better than to ask for his buddy's name, and Jake never mentioned it again.

◆

Ellie's hotel room was stuffy, and she couldn't sleep, even with the window open. The night sounds of the river called to her. She pulled her dress over her summer nightgown and slipped out the hotel's back door. She walked the short distance to Deer Creek's bank in the starlight.

The river appeared black and impenetrable. She stepped out of her shoes, hung her dress over a branch, and waded into the cool water, which elicited a shiver down her spine. Silt squeezed between her toes, and the current flowed around her calves, wetting the hem of her nightgown. If she were somewhere more private, she would have left it behind and swam. While it was still tempting, what she was doing was already scandalous enough should anyone see her.

Her original plan was to come into Three Bridges and charm the information she needed from the locals. Unfortunately, her plan wasn't working. There was gold hidden out there somewhere, a lot of gold. Rumor had it there were a hundred pounds of buried gold, or possibly more, depending on the drunkenness of the person talking. Enough for people to kill over. She would have to tread lightly.

Once she figured out who had the other half of the map, then what? Could she do it without help? Without a trusted partner, it would be the only way. She would need supplies and a packhorse.

Then there was the matter of spending it. A hundred pounds of gold ingots would attract a lot of attention at a bank. Even one ingot would raise eyebrows and invite questions. That was a problem for another day. First, she had to find it, which brought her back to her situation in Three Bridges. She shivered as she waded out of the water and back to the tree where her dress hung.

She was reaching inside her dress to slip it on when a man's large hand clamped over her mouth. His brawny arm reached around, pinning her to his chest. A coarse beard scraped her cheek as the man whispered in her ear. "You been pokin' your nose where it don't belong. I'm going to find that gold, not you." The sour odors of whiskey and chewing tobacco brought bile to her throat. "Now keep yourself quiet while we go someplace else. You hear?"

She nodded against his iron grip while her fingers frantically searched the contours of her dress. His hand left her face and tugged on the fabric while he loosened his grip enough to pull the dress out of her arms. "You won't be needing this no more." It fluttered into the shadows.

She cocked her derringer and pressed it against his thigh. It was only .32 caliber, but it still bucked in her hand as she pulled the trigger.

The sharp retort silenced the frogs. Dogs barked nearby. The man fell to the ground and grasped his wound with both hands. She pulled his pistol from his belt, pulled the hammer back, and held it behind her back. The spreading pool of blood shimmered in the dim light. She'd seen similar wounds and judged he would not last long.

She kneeled by her attacker's head and whispered. "You need a doctor quickly, or you're going to die. Do you know where the other half of the map is? Tell me."

He squinted at her. "Go to hell."

Ellie stuck the pistol barrel against the wound on his leg and pulled the trigger. The second shot was much louder. Ears ringing, she dropped the pistol out of reach, slipped out of her blood-spattered nightgown and threw it into the river. It briefly reflected the starlight as it floated downstream, slowly sinking under the surface.

The man stopped writhing, but blood continued to spurt from his leg. She wiped her hands on the grass, donned her dress and, satisfied she was alone, hurried back to the hotel.

Back in her room, she quickly changed into her dressing gown. Voices came from the hallway. "I heard something, too," one man said. "I'll go get the deputy. The sheriff's out of town. Nothing like this happens when he's around."

She stuck her head out of her door and found Tom McCready, the hotel manager, with Mary, who had a room down the hall. "Was that a gunshot I heard?"

"Nothing to worry about, Miss Ellie," Tom said. "Probably someone drunk. I am sure Deputy Johnson will handle it.

The next morning, Ellie joined Mary for breakfast in the hotel dining room. News of the death along the river spread through the town like a prairie fire. Ellie marveled at her story of a shoot-out with an unknown number of men.

Deputy Johnson walked in, removed his hat, and stood by the

counter. The conversations stopped, and all eyes went to him.

Mary set her coffee cup down and craned her neck. "Good morning, deputy. What can you tell us about poor George's untimely death?"

"Now, Miss Mary," he drawled. "You know I can't say too many particulars about it." He grimaced, shifted his boots on the wood floor, and motioned for coffee.

"Is it true there was a shootout?" Mary asked, eyes shining.

"I didn't find evidence of that," the deputy said, shaking his head. "I found a drunk who shouldn't've ought to pull his pistol in his inebriated condition." He let out an exasperated sigh.

Mary fidgeted with her coffee cup. "Well, something caused him to draw."

Deputy Johnson turned his gaze to Ellie. "Miss Ellie, you're mighty quiet this morning."

"I find I hear more when I am not talking," Ellie replied. She tried not to show her annoyance at being singled out. Just what she didn't need, crabby old Deputy Johnson casting a suspicious eye toward her.

He continued to stare. "Where were you last night?"

Ellie leaned back in her chair. "I was in my room. I opened my door and spoke with Mr. McCready in the hallway after I heard the commotion. He assured me it was safe in the hotel, and I believe it was he who went and found you." She glanced behind the counter at Tom, who nodded in agreement.

An older man with bloodshot eyes walked in. Tom came out from behind the counter. "Now, Trampus, you just get right along to wherever it is you're going."

"Hold on," Deputy Johnson said, raising his hand toward Tom. "Trampus here witnessed something last night, and I want to ask him some more questions about it."

Trampus hooked his thumbs in his drooping suspenders and stood taller. "That's right, I seen a ghost."

"You saw George's spirit?" Mary gasped, half-raising from her seat.

"Naw," he said. "I think I saw what ol' George was fixin' to shoot at."

"Tell me again what you saw," Deputy Johnson said.

"Now I was half in the bag, but I was sober enough to know what I seen. I heard some gunshots. First one and then the other. Then I seen the ghost scootin' away from the riverbank. Was all dressed in white, like a ghost usually is. Pretty light on its feet, too."

"Feet?" Mary said. "Ghosts don't have feet."

"This one sure did," Trampus insisted. "Scurried right along, staying close to the buildings." He used his hands to imitate feet running. "Hopped down the alley right next to the hotel."

"Look around the room, Trampus," Deputy Johnson said. "Do you see your ghost anywhere?" He took a sideways glance at Ellie.

Ellie bit her lip and tried to act casual, despite sitting in her white dress. Was Deputy Johnson thinking what Trampus had actually seen was someone dressed in white?

Trampus rotated his head left and right. "No, sir, these here people are alive. I told you it was a ghost I seen."

Deputy Johnson gritted his teeth and escorted Trampus out of the hotel. Mary turned back to Ellie. "If that isn't the strangest thing I've heard in a month!"

◌

Ellie had dug Jake's grave using a shovel she found strapped on his packhorse. Six feet down was a foot taller than Ellie herself and, true to his name, Big Jake was a big man. After sharing a bedroll since leaving Springdale, she felt she owed him a proper burial. The air was muggy, and she threw the dirt out of the hole while clad in her underclothes. Less to wash later.

She kept a close watch on the surroundings, not expecting any further trouble, but the situation called for caution. Once, when one of the horses had nickered, she leaped from the hole, brandishing both pistols. A small animal rustled in the brush as it ran away. She wiped sweat from her brow and returned to digging.

Dawn was peeking over the east horizon as she struggled to roll Jake's stiffened body over to the hole. By mid-morning, she had filled the grave and spread the extra soil around to disguise the location, even though they were miles off any traveled road. She led his horse and packhorse to a nearby stream, tied them to a tree, and bathed.

◆

Ellie strolled down the streets of Three Bridges, wishing she had a parasol. Her sunbonnet provided enough shade for her face but was not as stylish. She walked onto East Bridge, heading for the other side. The rails were low and offered a view of the river below. A boy sat on the rail, dangling his bare feet. He held a fishing line with a cork bobber, which formed a small wake in the current. Ellie stopped to watch.

She didn't recognize him as one of the boys she had already talked to, and she reached into her purse. "How's fishing?" She offered a stick of licorice.

The boy took the licorice and smiled. "Ain't caught nothin' yet."

"What's your name?"

"Freddy."

"Pleased to meet you, Freddy. I'm Ellie. What do you usually catch?"

"Perch and bullheads. Sometimes a trout. Hooked a pike once." His eyes widened. "It fought hard. I had to lean way over and almost fell in."

Ellie eyed the distance to the water. "Is it deep? You must have gone swimming in the river."

"It's pretty deep in the middle. I can dive off this here bridge. Little Joe and Matt are too scared. They jump in feet first."

She pulled out another stick of licorice. "I hear Big Jake likes to fish. Did he fish with you off this bridge?"

Freddy took the licorice, and his head snapped to attention. Ellie held her breath. What crucial piece of information did he know? She waited as he stared off into the distance.

After a moment, she followed his gaze to a cloud of dust. Soon she heard what the boy had heard—the faint sounds of horses running hard and men's shouts. Soon the group came into view. The men rode low on the horses' necks, urging them on.

Ellie scrambled to stand on the outside of the railing where Freddy had already climbed. She glanced nervously at the river flowing below them, the current seemingly faster than before. Could she swim wearing her petticoats, or would they weigh her down and drag her under?

The horses thundered by in a blur, and their hot breath mixed with the aromas of dust, sweat, and leather wafted across her face. She nearly lost her grip on the rail as the bridge shook, and splinters pierced her white gloves.

The group continued down the street, scattering chickens and stray dogs.

"Who were those riders?" she asked Freddy as they climbed back over the rail.

"Walter and his men, ma'am," he replied.

Her curiosity piqued, and she followed the dust trail until she found the horses tethered at the saloon. Some boys from the livery crossed the street to retrieve them. One man called to them to take the horses and cool them down. He then patted his horse and dashed into the saloon.

Ellie lingered near the doors and listened. The riders talked excitedly, and Big Jake's name came up several times. She slipped inside and sat at a back table. One man seemed to be the leader and did most of the talking.

If Freddy was right, that man was Walter.

The men had ridden hard for two days to get back. There were rumors of gold. Ellie leaned forward; her eyes locked on Walter. Big Jake had found a map, but no one knew where Big Jake or the map was at the present. Ellie knew approximately where Big Jake lay in eternal rest, and the map lay hidden inside the lining of her steam trunk.

"This here's Jonathon." Walter used his thumb to indicate a man at a front table. "He rode back with us. He was there at Springdale with Big Jake."

Jonathon stood and scanned the room. "That's right. Jake told me about some gold stolen during the war. The men who stole it were deserters, and they were shot before the army knew anything about the gold. It seems the men drew a map but cut it in half so a fellow would need both pieces to find the gold."

Jonathon reached for his beer mug and whispered something to the others at the table. "Jake thought he could figure it out with just the part he had. He told me he was pretty sure he knew who had the other half. A couple of weeks later, a guy showed up with the packhorse I'd sold to Jake. It wasn't just the packhorse. He had the new boots and some of the gear I'd sold to Jake, too."

A murmur swept across the saloon.

Jonathon nodded to someone at the back. "The thing is," he continued, "Big Jake wasn't alone when he left town. There was a woman with him. The man with Jake's horse said he bought it from a woman with different colored eyes. Right then, I knew he was tellin' the truth."

Ellie pushed her chair back and started to rise, but rough hands grabbed her and lifted her off her feet. She opened her mouth, only to have her protests muffled by a dusty bandana. She twisted her arms, trying to get reach her derringer, but the men were strong and held tight.

"Like that lady back there," Walter said. "Keep a hold of her, boys, but let her explain herself."

One of the men pulled the bandana out, and Ellie spit the dust from her mouth. "Jake and I were going to get married. He told me to meet him here in Three Bridges and—"

Jonathon cut her off. "That's not what Jake told me. I warned him about you. I could tell you were trouble from the first time I saw you."

She locked eyes with Jonathon. She had seen him in Springdale when Jake picked up his packhorse. "Liar! You lousy son-of-a—" The bandana cut off the rest of her diatribe.

Walter gathered his men around a table where they held a hushed discussion with frequent glances at Ellie. She kicked and squirmed but to no avail. Walter banged his beer mug on the table. "I've heard enough."

As the men carried Ellie out of the saloon, she met Rose's eyes, which burned with cold fury.

◊

Jake drew the revolver from his gun belt and leveled it at her. "Sorry, Ellie, but you've seen too much. I got to take care of loose ends."

"You don't have to do this." She put on her sweetest smile. "We make a good team, you and me."

"Yeah, but it ain't you and me." He clenched his jaw and pulled the hammer back with his thumb. "I got a sweet rose back in Three Bridges." The hammer snapped onto an empty chamber. He yanked the hammer back and pulled the trigger again. Another empty chamber. Eyes wide with realization, he reached for his knife. Ellie fired the revolver she'd taken from his pack.

◊

Walter and his men rode out of Three Bridges to the hanging tree, leading the horse carrying Ellie slung over its back. Walter pulled a rope from his saddlebag. "Frank, tie this off."

Frank climbed the tree and lowered the noose from a large branch perpendicular to the trunk.

The men untied Ellie's feet and forced her upright on the horse. As they cinched the noose around her neck, she remembered the look on Jake's face when she'd shot him. A look of astonishment that changed to realization.

She'd always managed to escape even the direst situations. If her charm and wit weren't enough, she used her derringer. But even if she could stretch her bound hands to her derringer, it only held two shots. All the men were armed and once the horse spooked, she'd be hanged anyway.

"Such a shame to snap a pretty little neck like that," Jonathon said.

Walter pulled the bandana from her mouth. "Got any last words?"

"I demand to see the sheriff!" she sputtered. With the sheriff out of town, they would have to wait, giving her more time to think. It was her only hope, and a long shot at that.

Walter pulled a badge from his vest pocket. "You're looking at him. If there's nothing else, may the Lord have mercy on your soul." He stepped back and reached for his hat. The other men removed theirs, as well.

The rope scratched against her neck with her terrified shaking. Her mind raced frantically for any other options and came up empty. She wasn't ready to die, yet her life would come to an undignified, abrupt end in a godforsaken little town. Lips quavering, she whispered a bedtime prayer from her childhood.

A dust cloud came on the trail from town, a horse galloping with the rider bent low on its neck. The men stopped and watched. Rose rode up screaming, "Wait!"

Ellie's hopes faded. Rose had every right to watch Ellie hang. After all, she had lost her lover to Ellie. Maybe he had promised marriage. But now he was dead, and Ellie had killed him. In cold blood, as they had claimed back at the saloon. How else could such a petite woman get the best of a man like Big Jake?

"It's true," Rose gasped. "I found this in her trunk." She reached into the saddlebag and pulled out an ivory wedding dress, complete with beading and fancy lace.

Walter narrowed his eyes and studied Ellie. "Is that yours?"

Ellie nodded as tears poured down her face. Did she dare hope to be spared?

Frank whistled. "We almost hanged an innocent woman."

"I wouldn't say she's entirely innocent," Rose said. "But I believe she and Jake were going to get married. There's no way she could have killed him."

The men had a loud discussion, and the horse snorted and pranced. "Get her down from there!" Walter ordered. Frank ran back to the tree and swore as his boots slipped on the bark. The horse shied and side-stepped, pulling Ellie onto its rump. Walter rushed over and caught her when the horse bolted. She sat piggy-back on his shoulders while Frank sawed the rope with his knife.

Back at the saloon, Ellie requested whiskey, specifically the best damn whiskey they had, and Walter stepped in to pay for it. After downing the first glass, her hands stopped shaking. She sipped the next glass, relishing the calm it brought.

Rose approached Ellie's table. "I am sorry I looked through your steam trunk."

Ellie laughed and a few tears trickled down her face. "No apology necessary! If you hadn't, well, I wouldn't be talking to you right now."

Rose stuck out her hand. "Sisters?"

Ellie shook Rose's hand and nodded emphatically. "Sisters." She brushed her fingers over her derringer, still hidden under her dress. Sisters. For now.

Dan McKay has had several short stories published in anthologies, including the *Fark Fiction Anthology,* the *Talking Stick*, the Fargo Library's *Northern Narratives,* Moorhead Friends Writing Group, and Pixie Forest Publishing. Dan is active in local writing groups and lives with his family in Fargo, ND.

Sea Change

Justine Cadwell

"I don't even know why I am here."

Ari's fierce blue eyes darted between her boyfriend Greg and their couples' counselor, Candace, attempting to gauge a reaction. As usual, Greg's shaggy dark hair obscured the left side of his face, but this didn't stop Ari from witnessing his exasperated eye roll. Candace straightened the white-framed glasses on her weathered face as she cleared her throat and leaned forward.

"You are here because Greg is worried about you and the state of your relationship."

Ari sighed. They had been dating for over two years, and she loved Greg, but in the only way she knew how— at a slight remove. Since childhood, Ari exhibited a shallow ability to attach herself to anything or anyone above sea level. She warned Greg about this gnawing within. He insisted upon counseling, convinced he could change her mind despite her unwavering stubborn nature. Why prolong the inevitable?

"No, I mean, I don't know why I'm still living on dry land at all."

Greg's dark-rimmed eyes welled up with tears. Ari should have let him go before it got this bad. He wanted a 'happily ever after'. Watching her mother coast through marriage on autopilot didn't set the best example, but even without it, Ari viewed the relationship escalator as a trap. What happens when you finally reach the top floor? Where do you grow from there?

Ari's sister Waverly now waded through the tedium of marriage with the same sad acceptance they witnessed their mother endure. Waverly also suffered from infertility and had put herself through various rounds of IVF to no avail. Ari suggested Waverly's struggles stemmed from their mermaid heritage, in which external fertilization was the norm. Waverly wouldn't even entertain the idea and insisted on blaming herself instead. Typical female humanoid. Was Ari the only sane person in her family?

Why did so many people waste their lives pretending to be satisfied instead of wandering off into dangerous unknowns? Ari craved adventure, harboring a low tolerance for stasis. Surely, she inherited this tendency from the grandmother she was named after. But Ari could never relate to her grandmother's decision to give up a life under the sea for the cesspool of human life on dry land. For what? Rumors of an immortal soul Ari didn't believe in? Or the alternate version repeatedly recited to her and Waverly while growing up—to marry a handsome human she barely knew who liked her singing voice? Obviously, her grandmother had been looking for a way out too.

"Where does this desire to run away to the ocean stem from? Perhaps your fear of commitment?" Candace inquired, eyebrows raised.

Fucking Triton. Of course, everything must be blamed on relational ineptitude if you steep yourself in family conflict every day. How did it always boil down to these simplified accusations? Modern medicine loved to twist her discomfort and dissatisfaction into pathologies, reducing them into evidence of cultural non-compliance.

Doctors deemed Ari's ability to breathe underwater a "birth defect." She deemed it an evolutionary adaptation. What they diagnosed as "depression," she diagnosed as homesickness. What they called "restless legs syndrome," she called a phantom fin. Her legs ached for movement, craved fluidity. Confining clown fish to an aquarium likely induced the same affliction. Not that anyone cared about the discomfort of fish—or unruly women for that matter.

"No. It's because I don't belong here."

Would everyone be making this big of a fuss if she was a man with the same desire? Ari recently read an article about a male scientist embarking on a record-breaking experiment to live underwater for one hundred days. Was he a traitor for leaving his family behind? No, he was a hero. And what about Thoreau? He trudged off into the woods to live alone, free to write and exist outside society's magnifying glass. But sweet feminine Ari? She was a social pariah for wanting the same luxuries in a different environment.

"What makes you say that, Ari? You have a beautiful home, a doting partner, and a thriving career in marine biology. You seem to be doing a fine job of living above the surface."

Like pure breeding animals to the point of suffocation. How many counseling sessions had she tolerated throughout her life? Was anyone even listening to her? Candace seemed desperate to convince her by presenting facts any automaton could accomplish. Never mind that Ari was born with achromatopsia, a severe form of color blindness in which the world above sea level appeared to her in shades of gray, black, and white. Never mind that when she swam in the ocean, the ability to see all colors magically returned, with hues so brilliant they made her weep with joy. She was a living, breathing example of an antidepressant commercial. Yes, why give up this seemingly perfect life on land for something so trivial when she could star as the femme fatale in her own film noir?

"Anyone can fake being a successful human with the right balance of pharmaceuticals, pleasantries, and a modicum of intelligence," Ari replied.

During Ari's long, luxurious swim sessions in the sea, her body would finally relax. The deeper she dove, the better she felt. Her chronic pain melted into the water like an ice cube released on the surface of the sun. She was alive, she was free.

"You seem to believe that living a life under the sea would be easier, more satisfactory, but how can you know this for sure?"

No one in Ari's family had attempted to live in the ocean since their grandmother's bold transformation. They all knew the ocean was their heritage but didn't trust they possessed the skills or knowledge to navigate such an existence in modern times. The realities of increased pollution and rising sea level temperatures only deepened their uncertainties.

"I don't."

These unknowns stood as daunting obstacles to Ari's family members and to Ari too—until recently. Something had shifted in her, her attraction to the ocean was now resembling withdrawal.

"Hormones?" her doctor suggested.

"Midlife crisis?" Waverly offered.

How about a refusal to stop denying her internal compass?

"Be careful," Waverly had warned. "Change one vowel, and the whole equation changes: Drawn becomes drown."

Life on land had grown so mundane, stifling. At work, Ari channeled her obsession with the ocean into meaningful projects, but she had endured discrimination and sexual harassment during her climb to mainstream success. This sullied the experience, and living on the periphery failed to satisfy her anymore. Ari's love life was an ongoing battle. Greg demanded affection and reassurance, morphing her inability to settle into a life on land into a personal attack. Out of obligation, Ari attempted to relate to her friends' desires and interests. How many more times could she coo over the picture of a newborn baby who looked more like an alien than a human being? How many more diamond rings could she fawn over while imagining the harm their production caused? How many more home renovation projects could she fake giving a single fuck about?

Ari's daily fantasies threatened to morph her into a human beyond functionality. Despite the pills her doctor prescribed, an infinite stream of thoughts blasted through her on a constant basis, making it impossible to focus on anything else. Under the sea, endless possibilities enticed her. Would she run into old relatives? Discover a new sea creature her marine biology contemporaries could never find? Her favorite fantasy involved starting a mermaid rebel group, sparking storms, and sinking cruise ships full of rich, corrupt politicians.

Perhaps she wouldn't find any other mermaids at all. Her field loved to dismiss the possibility of their existence. Ari accepted that true merfolk may have gone extinct years ago. She was an introvert anyway. But what if they did exist? Would other mermaids reject her for looking different, for her strange past on dry land? Could merfolk be as bad as humans? Worst case scenario, she could find herself a giant coral reef to live in. She didn't mind the idea of being a hermit the rest of her days.

Candace glanced at the clock. "I'm afraid we're out of time for today, but this seems like a good stopping point. Ari, you prefer to live in this fantasy world where the ocean will solve all your problems, but you just admitted this might not be the case. Admitting this to yourself is the first step. Why don't you reflect on this knowledge a bit before our next session?"

Ari offered a slow nod. *There will not be a next session.*

After piling into Greg's car, Ari removed her sandals with the vigor of a toddler. Footwear was not a technology she would miss. A salty summer breeze whistled in through the partially opened passenger side window as Greg fastened his seat belt. He reached for the ignition button, but Ari grabbed his forearm.

"Greg, I can't do this anymore."

"Go to counseling?" Greg's hesitant tone was heavy with false hope.

Ari's heart ached for him, but her spirit's siren song threatened to deafen her. Silence simmered between them for several minutes as Greg's defeated figure and the looming sunset nearly altered her decision. He was such a romantic, just like her grandmother. *He will make a nice husband for another woman.*

Ari threw her arms around Greg's warm neck and planted a kiss on his stubbled cheek. She would miss his scent, a mixture of cedar and sweat.

"I'm sorry," she whispered. "It's over."

♦

The next morning, Ari arrived at her favorite secluded swimming spot at the crack of dawn. She opened her car door and stumbled out onto the deserted strip of sand, intoxicated with yearning. She searched beyond the horizon, cool waves brushing against her toes. The wind flung strands of wild red hair across her face. Scattered, gleaming white seashells decorated the sand beneath her feet, reminding her of the prison she longed to escape. A sense of peace overwhelmed Ari as her body coursed with assurance.

Ari undressed and glided into the water, submerging her entire body beneath the waves. Dark green and burgundy seaweed tickled her feet near the shoreline. As she swam, the water grew colder, invigorating her to dive deeper. She encountered iridescent jellyfish and radiant fish: neon yellow, bright orange, and powder blue. The farther she ventured, the faster she swam, her legs fusing into a single unit. She spotted new landmarks, numerous sea caves, and canyons to explore, indicators of unchartered territory.

A cozy euphoria enveloped Ari alongside the rippled waves her body created. Would the ocean heal her or slowly dissolve her into sea foam? Irrelevant. Ari's limbs tingled with ecstasy as she reflected on a single certainty: In this moment, she was alive. She was free.

Justine Cadwell is the author of *The ABCs of My Neuroses: Tales from an Anxious Life.* Her work has appeared in *The Collapsar, Adelaide, Living Crue Magazine,* and elsewhere. When she's not writing, she's working as a clinical dietitian at a long-term care facility, playing music as "Channeling Merlyn" on her YouTube channel, or volunteering at hospice. Justine lives in Minnesota with her husband, daughter, and feline friends. To see more of her work, follow her on Twitter @JustineCadwell.

Little Cannon

NEAL ROMRIELL

THE BOY PAUSED, AS if trying to determine the best place to make his cut. The razor-sharp knife hovered tantalizingly close to the soft, supple flesh. Letting out a slow breath he made the first tentative cut. The blade sliced all the way to the bone, and a look of surprise crossed his face.

"Great job, son," Kyle said.

Jacob smiled at his father's compliment. He then began carefully peeling apart the fish, filleting it just as he'd seen his father do a hundred times. Upon completing the work, he gently placed the prepared fish on the family's outdoor grill.

Kyle tussled his son's hair. "Now don't tell them, but your first fish looks much better than either of your brothers' first tries."

Jacob beamed as he hugged his father, filling Kyle with appreciation for the one-on-one time. While the two older boys had favored their mother, Jacob looked like a young version of his dad.

"Can I go play football now, Dad?" Jacob asked enthusiastically.

"Go ahead. Tell your brothers dinner's going to be ready in fifteen minutes."

Kyle's youngest ran two houses down to join with the other neighborhood kids. Chuckling to himself, he dusted the fish with his personal blend of seasonings. Despite the heat, firing up the grill always put him in a good mood.

"A beer for the cook?" Stephanie slipped an arm around his waist.

"What's it going to cost me?" Kyle took the long-necked bottle and kissed his wife's cheek.

"As soon as you shower, I'll tell you," she teased. Looking at the kids playing, she asked, "Have you told them where you're taking them this year?"

Kyle took a sip of his beer. "Not yet, I figured I could keep them in suspense at least one more night." He flipped a couple of the fillets. "This might be Trent's last trip for a while. He's going to be varsity this season, and he's already planning to attend football camp next year to meet with the college recruiters."

Stephanie smiled. "I guess it's good you've got something special planned then?"

Kyle put down his beer and took his wife in his arms, swaying back and forth. They danced for a moment to a song only the two of them could hear. "So what do you and your sister plan to do while the boys are away?"

Stephanie stepped back, stealing a sip of his beer. "Oh, you know. We figured we'd call a few strippers. Maybe head down to Salt Lake and deflower a couple of innocent Mormon boys. The usual."

"Well, as long as you take pictures," he said.

"You're terrible." She giggled.

Kyle gave her one more kiss. "You want to call the boys back to wash up? These fish should be ready soon."

Stephanie took another drink, then headed to the edge of the yard. "Stone boys, supper's ready!"

◆

Trent turned nine in the summer of '88. Before school started that year,

Kyle took him on a camping trip to Red Fish Lake. Two years later, when Mark turned nine, he joined the now yearly expedition. Five years brought Jacob to the appointed age, so Kyle would be taking all his boys on this year's excursion.

Each summer Kyle chose a different location, and the boys were eagerly awaiting the news of their destination. After breakfast on Sunday morning, they began the process of cleaning then packing the family's van. When they broke for lunch, Kyle called them together at the dinner table.

A map lay open, and the boys quickly began studying it, trying to guess which spot of blue they would be hiking to.

"Okay you three, step back." Kyle waited as the boys took their seats. "I know you're all anxious to know where we're going, but I want to tell a quick story first."

Make sighed. "Are we talking quick in normal terms, or dad terms?"

"Very funny and, to answer your question, normal quick. So, one of the guys at the Agency has a daughter who works for the forest service. Last summer she helped with some helicopter surveys in and around the Seven Devils Mountains. Randy's daughter took a picture during the survey of a lake that's not on any map, right in this area." Kyle placed an X on the map to the west of Cannon Lake. "So what do you say, boys, are you up for a real adventure that includes finding a hidden lake?"

Trent and Mark let out a tandem whoop then gave each other an exaggerated high-five. "Do you think we can name it? The lake, I mean," Jacob asked.

"I don't see why not." Kyle patted Jacob on the shoulder. "But this is going to be a much more grueling hike than what we normally tackle. You boys sure you're up for it?"

"We've got this!" Make flexed his arms, and Jacob quickly imitated the motion.

Trent stood and gave his dad a hug. "Now I get why you've been holding out on us.

♦

They set out at four in the morning on Monday. The drive to the Twenty Lakes Trailhead took a little more than seven hours, though the boys slept through the first several.

A steep and rocky road made up the last leg of their journey. At its end they found a dirt parking lot with a wonderful view of the meadows at the base of the tightly clustered mountains. Reaching Cannon Lake required a five-mile hike—not a taxing distance, especially on a relatively level trail. The cool mountain air felt refreshing compared to the long, hot summer days back in the valley.

While Kyle and Trent double checked the packs, Jacob and Mark began exploring the immediate area. Only two other cars shared the lot, one of them being a forest service truck. A communication board sat directly beside the trail's starting point. Warning about keeping fires controlled and carrying out one's waste were posted alongside maps and black bear notices.

Mark noted three different missing persons posters thumbtacked to the board. He threw a pebble at one of them, hitting the paper but not the man's face where he'd been aiming. As he reached back to launch a second rock, Jacob began shouting about a dead rattlesnake. Mark quickly dropped the handful of rocks and ran to examine Jacob's find.

Soon, the four of them were heading down the trail, Trent in the lead and Kyle at the end. The trail passed through beautiful terrain, full of lush ponderosa pines and even the occasional snowbank hidden in a shadowed creek bed. Halfway down the trail, they came to a small park ranger outpost that included a horse corral and latrine. No rangers could be seen, likely out on patrol, and after a short break, they continued.

Mark let out a long whistle when they finally crested the last ridge that brought them to the shores of Cannon Lake. The emerald-green water cast a perfect reflection of the towering mountain peak behind it. A fish jumped, marring the reflection but bringing a smile to the boy's faces.

"Great call, Dad," Trent said. None of them moved, instead taking a moment to enjoy the view.

"Okay, boys, let's find a good spot to camp. And remember, keep your eyes peeled for tracks or other evidence of wildlife. We don't want to plop our camp down right in the middle of a bear's walking path."

Finding a good spot took some time, picking their way through the underbrush and avoiding muddy patches, but eventually they settled on a flat, grassy clearing on the north shore of the lake. Soon, a cozy fire burned a safe distance from the sturdy tent.

"I'm going to catch the biggest fish," Jacob declared as they enjoyed their dinner.

"Not if I catch it first," Mark countered. As if in response, a fish jumped nearby, delighting them both.

"You think there'll be fish up in that hidden lake?" Trent asked.

Kyle nodded. "Seems likely, especially with fish being present in this lake. The forest service may have stocked it, but these fish likely came down from a higher lake during spring runoff."

The younger boys smiled as Trent responded, "Cool, so what's our plan for finding it?"

"Based on where Randy's daughter indicated the lake would be, I'm guessing it's up over that ridge to the west. Hopefully, we'll be lucky enough to find a stream or dry creek bed, something that'll lead us right to it."

After dinner they roasted marshmallows, and Kyle told a couple of ghost stories. He climbed into this sleeping bag, thinking of the strings of rainbow trout the boys and him would be cooking for dinner the next day.

Long after everyone else had fallen asleep, Mark lay awake, the cold night air and anticipation of the next morning's hike keeping him on edge. He closed his eyes to make a final attempt at getting some rest when a sudden boom echoed through the mountains. Startled, he tried to wake his father, but Kyle continued to snore soundly. Mark lay awake for an hour longer, until finally he fell asleep, the boom fading from his mind.

◆

"Trent, lift him up on three. One. Two. Three."

Trent lifted Jacob so that Kyle could get hold of him. Once Jacob had been moved up to the rocky outcropping, Trent cupped his hands and gave Mark a boost.

Kyle's suspicions of a dry creek bed had proven correct, and for the first mile and a half of the journey they moved with relative ease. But the creek appeared to be fed by a steep waterfall, ending their progress and forcing them to move out around the ridge, rather than going directly up. Kyle, Trent and Mark could scale the boulders and get over fallen trees without trouble, but Jacob often needed assistance.

Once everybody made it onto the shelf, they redistributed their fishing poles. Kyle checked the Glock he'd brought along on the off chance they needed to scare away a bear or cougar. Satisfied that everything was still secure, the group restarted their climb. Luckily, they were now near the top and, after pushing through a last stubborn stand of bushes, the crystal-clear hidden lake came into view.

"It's just like in a movie." Jacob stared in wide-eyed wonderment.

"It's better than a movie," Mark corrected.

Stretching out to the west and north, this body of water was much bigger than Cannon Lake. Three peaks surrounded the lake, their granite faces standing sentinel over the hidden gem below.

"Boys, look!" Kyle pointed as a foot-long trout swam close by the shore. Farther out, another fish jumped, creating a great splash as it fell back to the water.

"We could fish off those rocks over there." Trent motioned to a series of boulders that made a natural pier of sorts.

Kyle nodded. "Lead the way, son."

Rocks and smaller boulders littered the landscape close to the lake, making the footing tricky as they approached their chosen spot. Trent called them to a halt short of the rocky outcropping. "Dad, are these bear tracks?"

Kyle kneeled to get a closer look. "Those do look like a bear, but these tracks are older. See how they've had time to dry out? I think we'll be fine." He patted his holster to help reassure the boys. "Way to keep your eyes peeled, son."

When he stood, Kyle noticed something. A small clump of tangled fishing line wedged in some rocks closer to the water's edge. The boys hadn't noticed, and he decided to keep the discovery to himself. No need to spoil the sense of adventure.

They marched out onto the rocky pier in single file. Once they reached the end, they fanned out, giving each other room to work.

While setting up their gear, Mark noticed several fish swimming up to the rocks, then slowly moving away. "It's almost like they've never seen humans before," he said with awe.

A large, dark-colored fish swam by, and Trent said, "Maybe they haven't. What if we're the first people to come up here?"

"Well, in that case, what do you boys think we should name our lake?" Kyle smiled as he carefully set his bait.

"It's so clear, but Clear Lake sounds kind of dumb," Mark said.

"We could name it Stone Lake," Trent suggested, then scrunched up his face like maybe he didn't like the name once he'd spoken it aloud.

"What about Little Cannon Lake?" Jackob asked, grinning.

"But it's way bigger than Cannon Lake," Trent replied.

"That's why it's funny." Jacob laughed.

"You know what, I really like that, son." Kyle stood, preparing to cast. "Little Cannon Lake. What do you think, Mark?"

"Yeah, I could see that."

Trent nodded. "Little Cannon it is."

Kyle cast his lure far out into the lake. He had barely locked his rod when a fish struck, causing the pole to bend. "Holy cow." Kyle cranked his arm, countering the sharp pull of the fish.

The boys quickly finished their preparations and cast out their own lines. Each quickly hooked a fish. Kyle hauled his trout in, secured the pole, then went to help Jacob bring in his own.

"Dad, have you ever seen anything like this?" Mark raised his pole, a fat crappie hanging from the dripping line.

"I've been fishing for thirty years, and I've never seen fish biting like this, son."

Trent cast again, waited a full minute this time, but still hooked a fish. Mark hooked his second soon after. Kyle and Jacob brought their second casts all the way back in without a bite. Nonetheless, catching six fish in less than ten minutes was nothing short of amazing.

Kyle decided to try a lure with a bit more weight, hoping to cast out into the deeper water. As he dug through the tackle box, Mark patted him on the shoulder.

"Dad, check out that boulder."

The huge egg-shaped rock didn't match the color of any of the granite formations around or above. It resembled rusty metal more than anything. The initial beauty of the lake and its surroundings must have distracted Kyle from noticing it sooner.

"Huh, good eyes there, son. See how rusty it looks? Probably has a lot of minerals running through it."

Trent had taken notice. "You think it might be valuable?"

Kyle laughed as he removed his old lure. "Could be, but it'd take a lot of heavy machinery to crack a rock that size, let alone move it."

They settled into a steady rhythm of casting, reeling and, on occasion, catching something. Mark threw back two runty fish, and Trent lost a lure after getting it caught on something under the water.

"What do you think, boys? Time to find a new spot?" Kyle asked.

Trent nodded. "Let's make one more cast each, then we can move onto dryer land and eat some lunch."

His brothers nodded. They each took turns, trying to cast out the farthest. Jacob's distance was particularly good considering his size and experience. Almost immediately, the tip of his pole began to jump up and down.

"Check it out, I've got a nibble," Jacob announced. The others had barely acknowledged him before his pole bent hard. The youngest Stone nearly lost his grip as the fish began diving.

"Dad, help!" Jacob struggled to keep his balance.

Kyle dropped his rod and hurried to Jacob's aid. Trent shuffled over, gathering his father's fallen pole.

"Jacob, I think you might just get the biggest fish after all," Kyle said as he helped to steady his son, allowing the boy to put all his efforts into bringing in the prize catch.

The fish jumped, trying to throw the hook. Only then did Kyle realize just how far Jacob's line had extended. "You'll need to take it slow, bud. Let the fish be the one to get worn out, not you."

Jacob pulled the base of the pole closer to get more leverage over the fish's strength. Inch by inch, the line came in, the fish exerting a bit less pull with each dive than the one before. "I'm doing it, Dad."

"You sure are, son. Good—"

The pole jerked out of Jacob's grip with tremendous force. The rod and reel flew twenty feet out into the lake and landed with a splash, but the pull of the fish was so strong, the pole skipped along the surface.

"What the hell?" Kyle hadn't meant to swear in front of his kids, but a better phrase escaped him in that moment. The fish must have been a true behemoth to exert that much force.

Jacob shuddered, trying to hold back tears. Kyle turned the boy around and gave him a wink. "We'll get you a new pole, bud. You did great fighting that fish. He must have been bigger than we realized."

Jacob sniffed, wiping his runny nose on his sleeve. "I know. I just wanted to catch the biggest fish."

"Umm, Dad?" Trent's voice quivered from nerves.

Kyle looked back at his oldest staring out into the lake. "What's wrong, Trent?"

"The pole, its coming back," Trent's right arm shook as he pointed at something.

Kyle's skin broke out in goosebumps as he looked out over the water. The pole had gone clear across the lake and was now bouncing back in their direction.

"Boys, get back to the shore now." Kyle picked up Jacob, Mark and Trent dropped their poles, and all of them turned away from the water.

Mark tripped over the tackle box and fell hard on the rocks, scraping the skin from his hands and elbows.

"Go!" Kyle told his youngest son, putting him down. They only had seconds before whatever was dragging the pole made it back to the rocks. He unlocked his holster so that he could quickly draw his pistol, then pulled Mark up before waving him onward.

Trend and Jacob reached the shore with Mark and Kyle close behind them. Tears were streaming down Jacob's face.

Kyle felt a moment of relief as Mark reached the end of the pier. Kyle planted his foot and jumped the remaining distance to the shore, landing hard. Rolling over, he whispered a silent prayer, thankful to have gotten everybody back to land in relative safety.

Trent began checking Mark's wounds. They looked unpleasant and probably burned fiercely, but he'd recover. Kyle stood and drew his pistol, turning to the lake.

Nothing moved. The pole had disappeared, the surface of the water once again calm and serene. Even the forest seemed to have gone quiet. No flies buzzed, no wind rustled in the pines. The only noise came from Jacob, who stood whimpering by his father.

Trent looked up from tending Mark. "Dad, what was that?"

Kyle shook his head. A small part of him felt foolish for the panic he'd been in moments earlier. He'd overreacted and scared the kids over a dumb, albeit aggressive fish.

Jacob squeezed his father's hand. "Is it gone?"

Water erupted at the halfway point of the rocky pier when a form flew out of the lake and landed twenty feet from the assembled Stone family. Kyle's breath caught in his throat as his mind processed the tall, hulking, nearly translucent being with bright purple veins standing before them.

"Run!"

Kyle grabbed Jacob's hand. They all broke into a sprint, trying to put distance between themselves and the creature. A gurgling cry echoed through the basin as the group attempted to navigate the difficult terrain.

Trent tried to jump over a downed tree, but his foot caught and he fell shoulder-first onto the rocky ground. When he let out a cry of pain, Mark stopped.

"Keep running," Kyle yelled. "Follow your brother, Jacob. Don't stop running."

The youngest Stone took off when Kyle stopped beside his oldest child. Trent's shoulder appeared to be dislocated, his right arm sitting askew, preventing him from standing on his own.

"Dad, go," Trent said.

"I'm not leaving you." Kyle scanned the area, lifting his pistol with a shaky hand. Even as his mind raced for an explanation for what was happening, he tried to play back the previous moments.

They had all seen it, whatever it was, and yet it was nowhere to be found. Kyle caught sight of their gear, sitting abandoned on the rocks. As he continued to watch the shoreline, the faintest glimmer of hope crept into his being. Maybe the whole exchange was over.

A splash and a scream from behind him shattered any thoughts of relief. He pivoted, nearly hitting Trent with the pistol. Several yards away on the lake's shore, Mark struggled with the creature. Stands of a milky substance held his legs together as the beast applied more to his arms and chest.

"No, Mark!" Kyle brought his pistol to bear on the creature and fired two shots. The bullets struck below what could only vaguely be called the monster's head, causing an explosion of purple fluid. The thing emitted another gurgling cry before shoving Mark aside and jumping into the water. Kyle quickly lost sight of it in the clear waters of the lake.

Trent began picking his way towards Mark, who lay unmoving on the rocky beach. Kyle quickly overtook his injured son, keeping one eye on the lake and the other on Mark. Several agonizing moments later, he reached his fallen child.

Mark's eyes were rolled up into his head. Most of his body was covered in a sheen of milky goo. Thin purple tendrils extended from the edges of the slimy coating, probing the boy's skin and drawing tiny red beads of blood. Kyle forced himself to breathe, as fear raced through him.

"Come on Mark." Kyle placed his ear over his son's mouth, but he was unable to hear the child breathing. Horror gripped him as he realized Mark's mouth had become clogged with the substance now turning more and more translucent. Panic drove Kyle to tear at the coating with frenzied hands, but the substance was hardening, preventing him from getting any kind of grip. Somewhere behind him, Trent let out a cry of pain.

Kyle pulled hard on a section of the coating. With a sickening sucking sound, a long stretch of Mark's face, including his lips and nose, tore free.

Mark spasmed, and blood gushed over his cheeks and onto the rocks.

Kyle and Trent both screamed, though Trent stopped with an unnatural suddenness. Kyle let go of Mark and pivoted, certain of what he'd see. The beast had Trent. Half a dozen pulsating strands extended from the creature's body and wrapped around Trent's head and shoulders. As the monster stepped from the water's edge towards the pair, the strands were simultaneously pulling Trent inward.

Kyle fired multiple shots directly into the right side of the nightmarish form. Purple blood and cottage cheese-like gore burst from the wounds, splattering the beach. In response, strips of goo lashed out at Kyle. His skin went numb when the substance touched it. He fired the pistol wildly but dropped it as his fingers became unresponsive. A string of the foul-smelling slime landed on his face. His eyes crossed as the muscles used to control them stopped working. His last thought before he lost consciousness was, *I hope Jacob's okay.*

♦ .

Barely fifty feet from the shoreline, Jacob Stone lay on his stomach, listening to the gunshots, the screams, and the horrific gurgling sound the creature made. There was a final gunshot, then the basin became quiet.

Jacob stifled his tears, then slowly raised his head to look over the edge of the stump he'd hidden behind. He watched transfixed as the monster slowly covered his father and both his brothers in gooey secretions.

The thing had no eyes or mouth to speak of, just clear skin over pale muscles with bright purple streaks. Several times, the beast paused, as if testing the air before going back to work. Jacob barely breathed, refusing to put his head down even after seeing the being pick up the bloodied body of his brother Mark.

The creature let out another cry before jumping into the water, holding the cocooned Mark. Jacob wasn't sure what to do. For a moment he wanted to run, but his movement would surely attract the monster's attention. He considered trying to free his father before the thing returned. While preparing to move, something drew his attention to the far side of the lake.

Still holding Mark, the monster rose from the water near the opposite shore. It walked a short distance to the strange, rust-colored boulder Mark had pointed out earlier in the morning. Jacob's eyes widened when a hatch opened, and the beast carried Mark inside. The interior of the rock glowed a strange blue color, obvious even in the afternoon sun.

Shortly thereafter, the thing emerged from the boulder and jumped back into the lake. Jacob's tears flowed as the process was repeated with both his father and Trent. But the creature didn't return once it got Trent into the rock. Instead, the strange door closed.

For several long minutes, Jacob watched, unsure of what to do. He slowly became aware of a low humming sound. The huge rock rose from the ground and began to slowly spin. With each rotation, a blue light pulsed from within. The humming grew louder and louder as the boulder spun more and more quickly. With a sudden bright flash, the rock lifted high into the air. The spinning became a blur, the inner light now constant. A boom echoed back and forth between the mountains as the boulder zipped into the sky and disappeared within seconds.

Jacob, now alone at the lake, buried his head in his arms and cried like he'd never cried in his life.

❦

Two park rangers on horseback trotted down the Twenty Lakes Trail, kicking up dust. They wanted to make it to the outpost before the sunset.

They clicked their tongues, encouraging the horses to hurry their pace.

Ever since the missing persons flyers went up, people were reporting strange lights and noises every other day. Three days earlier, a hiker reported hearing several gunshots, followed later by a louder boom near Ogre Peak. Events like these kept the rangers and their horses busy day and night.

The rangers reached the junction where the trail from Cannon Lake joined the main trail. They each spurred their horses again, knowing the outpost was nearby. As the building and coral finally came into view, the horses became skittish, whinnying and kicking at the trail.

"What the hell's gotten into you two," the first ranger said, trying to calm his ride.

The second ranger put a hand on the first's shoulder. "Hey, is that a kid?"

Sitting just to the side of the outpost's padlocked door, a huddled form shivered.

The first ranger leaned towards his partner. "That father and his boys, what were their names? Strom or something like that."

"Stone," the second ranger said. She dismounted and instructed the other to take care of the horses. Approaching the child, she noted the tattered clothing he wore. The face that turned towards her was malnourished and haunted.

The ranger kneeled, offering a hand. "Hi, sweetie, are you alone out here?"

The wide-eyed boy shivered and, without blinking or looking at the ranger, slowly nodded his head.

"Where are your parents, honey," the ranger asked, inching closer to the child.

The boy stood, retreating a couple of steps before wiping his nose on the back of his arm. "Mom's at home. Dad's gone. And my brothers too."

The ranger retracted her hand to put the child more at ease. "Gone?

Where did your dad and brothers go?"

A tear ran down the boy's cheek as he looked up at the sky and pointed.

Neal Romriell was born and raised in Idaho and enjoyed hiking and camping with his father and brother. The locations featured in *Little Cannon* are real places that Neal and his family visited within the Seven Devils Mountains. These days, Neal lives with his wife in South Carolina, where he continues to enjoy the outdoors. Neal's debut novel *Site Alpha* was released in 2022, and his short story "The Top Prize" was included in the anthology *Welcome To Effham Falls* in 2023.

The Pond

Matthew R. Clark

When she woke in the frigid, gray dawn, she felt for the chick. The down of the little creature was warm against her beak, and she felt at ease. The hen rose from the nest, careful not to disturb the sleeping hatchling. She hoped her little duckling was dreaming of some place warm, where the sun was shining and life thrived. With a sudden pang in her chest, the hen realized the chick had never experienced those things. All the chick knew was the silence and the cold.

She cautiously peeked out from the corroded tin of the storm drain perched above the pond, the rust-flaked edges framing her view. Her long neck craned out and she scanned the expanse, checking for any movement in that decaying wasteland. But the world was still. Even the gray clouds overhead refused to move. The leafless trees rose from the cold ground like bones, their bare branches clawing at the sky, pleading for the sun. The air was thick with silence, each sound swallowed by an unseen abyss. Her breath was visible but mute in the ash-covered barren land that had once been her home.

She hopped down and ventured out into the lifeless dawn, the air rank with the acrid scent of smoke. Ash coated the pond's once clear surface like thick scum, rendering it gray and still, a distorted mirror of the sky above. The once green tapestry of nature was now a gray canvas, each element bearing witness to the destruction wrought upon it.

Determined, the hen slowly glided into the frigid water, her feathers tinged with gray as the ash clung to her. There she swam. Alone. The water lapped at her, the only sound for miles. She took a deep breath and plunged under the water. The ash stung her eyes as she looked for any signs of life at the bottom of the pond. All she saw was gray murky clouds and the decayed flesh of those long gone.

As she hunted, she thought of the past. It was a day in late spring in the time before. The clouds were sparse and a shade of pink high above. When the hen broke the surface, the setting sun enveloped her in its fading glow. He was there, standing by the nest, keeping the unhatched brood warm. This drake wasn't like the others she had mated with. He was nurturing, protective, and willing to let her hunt while he kept the eggs warm and slowly starved.

With a flick of her head, droplets of water came raining down around her like stars. The drake watched her from the large tin cave where they made their nest. Honking softly, she swam towards him, eyes locked, droplets of water dripping from her beak. His answer was full of assurance and understanding.

With that, she swam on, looking for her meal. Before she dove under the green water, she caught a glimpse of him as he nestled down onto the nest, being sure to cover the eggs with his feathers and keep each of the oval shapes warm.

The cold water cut deep and shook her from her daydreaming. She rose to the surface, the water dripping from her beak freezing the moment it touched the air, a testament to the unforgiving cold. The chick's chirp echoed from the elevated storm drain. She was awake and she was hungry. The hen debated on whether to sooth the hatchling or continue her fruitless search for food. But as the icy water seeped past her feathers and chilled her skin, she knew it was time to get out.

The hen's feathers began to freeze as she hopped up into the drain. The chick tried to nuzzle her, but the chill of the water drove the young one away. The hen tried to shake off the ice but the thick coating of ash on her feathers made the action futile. She would have to drip dry, and that could be a problem.

The wet ash was like mud and weighed her down. It was hard to move and even harder to fly. She would have to stay in the storm drain to dry off before venturing out in the gray silence again.

She retreated to a drier section of their cylindrical tin home and settled down. With a soft quack, she called for the chick to come to her. They huddled but didn't touch because of the cold chill that clung to the hen. They stayed like that for a long time and slept.

When the hen opened her eyes, the world was black. The chick was standing at the mouth of the drain, its white feathers a defiant contrast to the darkness that engulfed the world. The hen stood and shook the dried ash from her feathers. Together, they watched the darkness, a shapeless abyss from inside their cylindrical home. Then came a muffled crunch from the water's edge, the sound of footsteps in the ash. The hen nudged the chick behind her, both unable to see what lurked beyond. Voices rose from the darkness, the unmistakable cadence of human speech. She couldn't understand what was being said, but the familiar sound stirred a memory.

Human children, smiling and carefree, would toss morsels of soft bread into the pond, their laughter resonating in the air as they clapped in delight watching her and the drake feed upon their gift. Oh, how she yearned for the taste of that manna once more.

The night stretched out like eager hands to embrace them in a chill that even fire couldn't thaw. Sleep eluded the hen. She watched the starless sky, as if her will could summon that familiar black silhouette again. But the drake was gone, and she knew he wasn't coming back.

The morning was jarring and colder than before. The hen quacked at the chick, warning her to remain inside as she waddled out to hunt. But the world mocked her, for when she ventured out into that silent dawn, she saw the gray pond frozen, the water still. She couldn't see through the ice, the ash coating hiding what morsels that might be lurking beneath. With a rebellious grunt, she pecked at the gray sheet of ice. The futile gesture only served to rattle her brain and exhaust her. When she looked up to the ever-grasping trees, she noticed a black crow alone on a barren branch, watching her with unblinking black eyes.

As the morning wore on, the ice relented its grip on the pond's edge, and the hen and the chick were able to sip the ash coated surface. The hen coughed. Sudden and violent. She tried to stifle it as best she could, but the action left her disoriented. At first, she attributed the cough to a lack of food and the quality of the water, but when she saw her feathers, now tainted with a shade of pink, she understood her reality. She had to get the chick ready.

They spent the morning waddling around the pond, both of them pecking at the shore edge or under the ash for any seeds or insects. By the time they had looped around the pond, it was close to noon. The chick was fortunate enough to have found a few dead beetles and a snail. The hen went without.

That afternoon, they haunted the frozen edge of the pond like little ghosts, disappearing into the drain at every sound. The smell of smoke and charred flesh was still thick in the air like a pollen cloud, a constant reminder of the carnage that befell the world. Yet, the two were content for the time being.

The chick was still a few days from being able to fly, but the hen decided it was still in her best interest to show the chick the proper technique. She would demonstrate by flying low around the pond's surface, careful not to go above the tree line and catch the eye of anything watching. It was then that the hen noticed a second crow sitting beside the first on the withered branch. Both were watching her.

By the evening, the pond was frozen again, and no amount of pecking would break the surface. They would have to wait until the next afternoon for another drink of water.

The air was suddenly pierced by the jarring sound of gunfire, echoing around the pond for the first time in what felt like another lifetime. The hen, heart pounding, herded the chick into the safety of the elevated storm drain.

From inside, they could see a pale human run towards the pond, in his arms a small child with hair made of gold. A long black gun was strapped to his shoulder, the barrel still emitting wisps of smoke in the cold air. Spotting the drain, the human ran towards it with desperate uneven strides, each footfall an ominous beating of dread.

The hen panicked and dragged the chick deeper into the depths of the drain. The man approached and, with a grim urgency, stuffed the small child inside the pipe, destroying the hen's nest. Yet, in spite of all the commotion, the chick remained silent, her innocent eyes following the man as he abandoned the child.

The little girl's voice pierced the cold air, "Daddy! Daddy, please don't go! The deers. Daddy, what about the deers?" Her words reverberated against the tin walls of the drain, but the man ignored her as he receded into the desolate landscape, past the pond and back towards the woods.

Driven by innate curiosity, the chick attempted to waddle past the hen, her tiny eyes focused on the human girl. The hen had to quietly nudge the chick back with her beak, trying with all her might to keep their presence hidden.

The man suddenly stopped his trek and threw up his hands. The girl let out a tearful squeal as three more men came out of the woods. The middle man, with an air of authority, aimed his long rifle at the girl's father. The hen heard a short exchange of words, the meaning unknown to her but the tone harsh, and dread washed over her. Suddenly, a deafening blast roared through the pond, reverberating in the small drain. The girl's father crumpled to the ground, sinking into the ash.

The girl's sobs, a haunting sound full of despair, filled the narrow space. Her hands covered her mouth, the muffled mourning known too well in this land. The hen watched on, feeling the noose tighten around her. This girl was a beacon for searching eyes and destruction. She would bring their ruin via plucked wings and cooking fires.

The three men moved with a hungry determination. The leader of the three, distinguished only by the smoking gun barrel, took the black rifle from the dead man and the bag strapped to his belt. With a harsh bark from him, the other two men spread out and began to patrol around the pond, their eyes searching the gray landscape like predatory birds.

The men called for the girl in mocking tones, as if they could coax her out of hiding.

The hen's instincts told her to hide, to protect the chick, but she also knew that no matter what she did, the girl would still be the harbinger of doom. She had to do something to rid the nest of these intruders. She quietly dragged the chick farther back into the drain and into the shadows, then began to peck the tin walls.

As the metallic echo filled the otherwise silent expanse, the girl's head snapped around and saw the hen, her blue eyes wide with surprise then quickly full of fear. But before she could react, she saw the three men quickly making their way towards her, closing in like predators towards wounded prey.

The girl, overwhelmed by terror, tried to scramble out of her confines, but the men were too quick, and they dragged her to the ground as she tried to fight them off. The middle man raised his gun and struck her in the head. The crack of the blow sounded like a branch snapping. The girl fell limp onto the ash. With their prey in tow, the men skulked away, leaving behind unbearable silence. All that remained was the hen, her chick, and now three black crows that sat on the high branches, watching all that had transpired.

A thick fog rolled in with the night, bringing with it a chill like death. The three crows flew down from the void, as if crafted by it. They landed on the ground, kicking up plumes of ash with each flap of their wings. They hopped upon the dead body of the girl's father, cawing at each other in deep guttural tones that frightened the chick.

The hen remained silent, her gaze unblinking. She figured the crows had come to feast upon the dead, but they simply looked at the body and cawed at each other. They hopped along the pond edge, towards the drain. The hen nudged the chick behind her, and she puffed out her chest, ready to defend her last gift from God in this godforsaken world.

The crows stopped right before the mouth of the drain and looked up at her, their obsidian gaze a window into the very void itself. Their stares were a look of pity, as if the crows knew of her plight, and what was to come. The hen felt a sense of dread and her chest began to hurt. Time froze, as if the word suddenly succumbed to the deathly cold that ravaged it night after horrific night.

The middle crow's caw cut through the silence, a harbinger's call that drew out a gruff reply from its twins. Then as fast as they appeared, they flapped their wings and ascended into the night sky. Their pure black forms became barely visible silhouettes against the black and gray.

The air seemed to grow colder, as if their wings had stirred the abyss into action, redoubling its efforts to turn the world into ice. The crows were swallowed whole by the night, leaving no trace other than the ominous echo of their calls.

With the destruction of the nest, the hen and the chick slept uneasily through the night. The piercing cold gripped the chick, causing her to shake uncontrollably. The hen's cough came with a sudden ferocity, each bout hitting her chest like a hammer. They huddled together, desperately looking for warmth where there was none.

The hen dreamt of the past, before the cold and the ash. She rose from the nest and stretched her white wings, letting them catch the soft breeze of the spring evening. Above her, the pink and purple clouds of dusk slowly sailed over the pond, casting the lush greenery in shades of orange.

The red sun dipped behind the tree line, revealing the yellow glow of fireflies.

The drake swam in elegant circles on the green surface of the pond, his rhythmic splashes a soothing cadence in the stillness of the coming night. His beak dove in and out of the water, trying to catch his first meal in days. She knew he would leave soon and that their time together would come to an end. She would be left alone to care for their offspring, and then she too would leave them to fend for themselves. And the cycle would repeat until the end of her days. But for now, she would enjoy this moment.

With a mother's diligence, she tended to the clutch of eggs, rolling them gently with a nudge of her beak, making sure each were receiving adequate warmth. Yet, as she fussed over the unborn, the heavens lit up with fire as an apocalyptic thunder roared overhead. An ever-expanding plumage of flames licked at the sky and burned away the tranquil clouds. The earth heaved and shook, threatening to swallow them all whole.

Oak giants groaned and came down with a cracking moan before crashing into the pond in a deafening splash. The drake let out a honk in alarm, flapping his wings fervently, as he tried to dodge and weave under the falling debris.

Ash and ember rained down on them, coating the ground in glimmering shades of red and orange. Instincts took as the world began to burn. The hen rushed to get on top of her eggs and protect them from the falling heavens. The drake quivered, flapped his wings, and took to the fiery sky, becoming a silhouette, a shadow to never be seen again.

When the gray dawn greeted the hen, it did so with silent mourning. The hen rose from the nest to check her brood, but to her horror, in her haste to protect them, she had doomed them. Before her lay the broken prodigies, yellow yoke running down cracked shells like tears from the unhatched. She let out a wail, a deep guttural sound joined by a chorus of others that echoed around the world.

In the aftermath, with the sun's warmth a memory, beneath the oppressive grayness, she found promise in the ruin. In the wreckage of the nest sat one last gift of a merciful God. This was the fragile life she protected from the cold and the darkness in the drain. Her one last duty before she could allow the world to claim her.

Sometime in the morning the hen ventured out with the chick. She wanted to inspect the man's body to see if it held anything of use. She was hoping to find some wool, or loose fabric, anything that she could use to rebuild the nest. There was no smell to the corpse. The frigid night had almost frozen the body solid, a statue to commemorate the fall of man.

The chick, a silent sentinel, observed the hen closely as she conducted her investigation. Amongst the faded fabric and stiff pockets, she found a plastic bag and a single golden dinner roll inside.

The hen tore at the baggy until the manna was free. Slow and ceremoniously, she nudged the piece of bread towards the chick, beckoning her to eat. The duckling gave it a cautious peck before snapping at the bread viciously.

The roll had almost been devoured when the chick tried to get the hen to eat it as well, but she declined and let the youngling have it all.

As they slept later that day, a deep rapid sound like rustling of dead grass startled the hen awake. She peeked out to see an emaciated dog, ash clinging to his paws and legs, sniffing at the dead man near the pond edge. The chick waddled up beside her, giving the dog a curious look before looking up at the hen. The hen just watched the dog, wondering how long it would take for him to devour the body.

The dog glanced right and left, as if he felt guilty for what he was about to do and wondered if anyone was looking. The dog licked the body, seeing if the man would move, but the dead don't move. They rot and turn into bones. He cautioned a nip at the dead man's hand and when the man didn't react, the dog bit the arm and shook his head violently, tearing red flesh from white bone. He backed up with a chunk of meat in his jaws and began to chomp down on the meat.

After the dog was satisfied, he lay down beside the feast, as if afraid the body would get up and walk away. The hen stomped her webbed feet in anxious anticipation. She couldn't hunt with this dog here. She quacked angrily to herself as the dog slept in the ash. She paced in the drain, trying to think of how she could go out into that unforgiving country and get the chick food. The dog had turned the pond into his territory and there was nothing she could do.

A few hours passed and the hen had meticulously remade the nest. The chick nestled within it peacefully like a statue, the last holy relic in hell. The duckling began to shiver, and the hen gently nuzzled her in an attempt to keep her warm.

The hen wondered how long they could last with the dog here. He hadn't sniffed them out yet, the ash covered their scent well enough, but it wouldn't be long before they were found out. The chick needed to learn how to fly so they both could leave this place.

The dog didn't get up again until the afternoon. He sniffed the body before going to the pond to lap up the ash-coated water. His head suddenly snapped up, ears pointed, eyes sharp and searching. He raised his nose to the air, taking deep pulls, each snuffle filling the hen with dread. Why was the dog so tense? Did he smell them? His ear perked again, and he turned to face the ghostly tree line.

The hen couldn't hear anything, but the dog was visibly agitated, haunches raised high and his head low. She couldn't help but peek her head out from the drain to look at what the dog was snarling at.

Across the scorched clearing, a lone buck, his majesty long gone, slowly limped out from the tree line. His antlers, once a crown, were marred with remnants of flesh that hung down like tattered banners. He had an open sore along his neck and another on his haunches, blood traveling down brown fur in thick globs, puss oozing from the sores.

Even from inside the drain, the hen could smell the buck's decay, like a corpse walking. Whether from the flesh on his antlers or his infected wounds, the smell enveloped the pond, overpowering the scent of smoke and char.

The hen watched with despair as the buck approached the pond. She thought that surely the dog would kill the buck, giving him another source of food. He would starve them out, condemned to wither away to feathers and bones.

But the dog didn't attack. In fact, the dog began to back away from the buck, as if he were a larger, more ferocious beast. The buck lowered his head, the ragged flesh on the antlers dangling just over the ash-covered ground. The lone deer meant to charge the dog, his back legs firmly planted, his right front hoof stomping in rage.

The attack was as quick as it was devastating. As the buck charged, a tempest of ash flew in the air, a testament to the violence of it. The dog's yelp, full of terror, rang out around the pond. The buck's horns sank deep into the side of the dog, penetrating flesh and sinew. The hen, from the protection of the drain, could see the blood of the dog seeping into the ash, covering gray with red.

The dog snapped ferociously, a last act of defiance, but only managed to claim the buck's ear. It was a hollow act for the buck didn't seem to care. He began to move forward, pressing his head down, pinning the dog against the ground as his antlers dug deeper into his adversary's flesh. He pushed forward, dragging the dog, ash piling up against the canine as he screamed in agony. The buck picked up his pace, a death march into the woods, leaving a long streak of red in its wake.

In the trees, the antlers caught on something, and they bent back towards the buck's snarling face. Yet, the deer kept his pace and with a sickening crack, the antlers snapped like dried wood. If he felt any pain from the act, the hen couldn't tell. The dog, however, was long dead, his flesh torn away in ragged chunks.

The chick let out a quack as she waddled up beside the hen. The buck must have heard it, for his head snapped up, the splintered shards of his antlers still caked in the dog's gore, and he looked towards the pond. They all stood in silence for a long time.

By the time the buck moved on, the gray skies were slowly giving way to blackness. The hen couldn't help but cough throughout the night, droplets of red sprinkling her dingy feathers. When the chick was awakened by one of her fits, the hen nuzzled her back to sleep before waddling out the drain and into the cold darkness of the night. She looked up towards the sky as if something would penetrate that ever still grayness. She imagined the stars as she remembered them, millions of glowing specks in the sky. The moon, a giant ball of white, the pond reflecting it in its murky green waters. It was then that she realized she would never see them again and sighed before returning to the drain.

It was the chick that woke her up, her small beak pecking at her left wing. The hen's chest and head hurt, a dull pain radiating from them that made her want to close her eyes and never open them again. The chick had other plans however and excitedly quacked at her to come with her outside. With a monumental effort, she opened her eyes, the mocking dawn filling her vision.

Together, they left the refuge of the drain. The hen was anxious, her nerves taut as a bowstring. Her eyes scanned the desolate landscape for any signs of doom but only the grayness filled her vision.

As she surveyed the charred landscape, a sudden movement caught her eye. She looked down at the chick, whose small frame was quivering, wings unfurling with eagerness. The hen watched as the chick beat her wings and launched into the air, finally escaping the ashen ground.

For a moment, as the chick ascended, the hen remembered her first flight. The air was clean, the sky blue, the gentle lap of the pond against the shore. The weather was warm, and her belly was full. She wished the chick could experience her first flight as the hen had. But now there was a chance for them to find something new together. Each flap of the chick's wings was a testament to that possible future.

The chick skimmed over the frozen water, never daring to crest the treeline. The hen quacked softly, a sound filled with praise and hope as she watched the last angel take flight.

When the chick touched down, her small body was filled with exhilaration. The hen allowed a cautious optimism to spread through her. They could finally escape this frozen graveyard and head south, where life may have carried on and they would too.

The hen wanted the chick to rest a while before they moved on, so they walked around the pond one final time for food. As they rounded the forest edge, the hen noticed a familiar figure staggering out of the woods. A shambling shadow coming back to haunt them.

The little girl was covered in streaks of red and ash, her once golden hair plastered with mud. With the help of a long, curved piece of wood, she stepped into the clearing. With each labored step, the hen's heart seemed to beat harder. The girl was a mirage of life, hollow eyes and a silence about her that was more chilling than death. She was an omen, a storm full of vengeance, the calm before it quickly fleeting.

With an almost ceremonial slowness, the girl caressed the corpse of her dead father, his solitary mourner. She put a hand over his face before hugging his neck. She rose with the help of her piece of wood and, with the look of a wounded animal, locked eyes with the hen.

Her next movements seemed methodical and practiced. She pulled something from her back and put it against the long piece of wood. The chick, innocence incarnate, watched curiously at the actions of one who was once like her. The hen, though, felt an unexplainable fear, an instinctual dread.

A ripple pierced the air, and something tugged at the hen's chest. She suddenly felt like she had to cough. The chick, as if warned by the wind, ran and flapped her wings, taking to the air. The hen turned around and flapped her wings too, ready to finally leave this pond, but something bit at her chest, something sharp and hard. It was difficult to run with this pain. She cast her gaze downward. A long shaft made of wood protruded from her chest. Slowly, almost in denial of it all, she realized the truth of the arrow.

The ground rushed up to meet her as she collapsed, the impact snapping the shaft and sending a jolt of pain through her. In that moment, the pond, the ash, it all faded away. Only the cold remained, caressing her as the darkness gathered around her. The chick, the light of her world, called for her, a soft bellowing honk high in the sky, but that too slowly began to fade.

The hen's vision turned into pinpricks, blackness enveloping the edges of her world as it began to crumble away. But, for a fleeting moment, she could see the vision she had longed for. The chick soared high above, wings beating defiantly against the cold and the ash. And in that last, lingering gaze, as she watched that black silhouette fly into the unknown, the gray clouds parted, and she saw the sun.

For Cormac McCarthy. Rest in Peace.

Matthew Clark currently lives in South Carolina with his wife and soon-to-be two daughters. He is working on finishing up his debut novel and plans for it to be released by the end of this year.

If I Never Told You

ALEXANDER VAYLE

HANSON'S LAKE WAS CARVED deep into the iron-kissed earth of northern Minnesota. Her cold waters were filled with bass and trout and surrounded by Balsam fir and towering red pine. Beyond the picturesque shoreline, a vast wildlife reserve stretched into the surrounding hills.

Public access was limited to a narrow, unmarked strip of land. Those who knew about this paradisiacal secret kept it well. So, on a tepid day in late September, only a single canoe, piloted by a teenage boy, floated over the massive lake.

The boy, Jerud, first came to Hanson's Lake with his father at age six. At fourteen—a year after his father's fatal heart attack—his mother allowed the first of many solo adventures. He was a responsible kid, after all. A scout. An outdoorsman. Truly his father's son.

Now fifteen, Jerud lay in the belly of his canoe as it drifted lazily in the calm water. He whispered quick, desperate words to his father, as he often did in times of stress and fear, and held pressure—oh, so tight—on the gunshot wound in his abdomen.

He'd been in the bow seat, eating a turkey sandwich and imagining his father sitting astern, when the roar of a rifle echoed out of the woods.

An invisible force blew apart the binoculars hanging from his neck and knocked him back over the thwart and into the canoe. His head bounced off the aluminum hull, and the blue sky above him momentarily turned stark white. However, before he could reach for his throbbing head, his stomach announced a sharp ache below his left ribs.

With trembling hands, Jerud popped the clasps of his life jacket. He slid his fingers under his sweatshirt and found a slick layer of blood. Then he felt a barb of pain as his middle finger poked into a ragged hole.

His brain spun into a nauseating whirl of questions and fear, eventually seeking refuge in a memory of his father. He cried out, "Dad, I've b-b-been shot!"

Another resounding *KOOM* rocked the canoe, and a hole appeared in both the starboard and port sides a few inches above him. The grounded part of his mind spoke in his father's voice: *This isn't an accident, Jerud. Someone's trying to kill you. MOVE!*

His thoughts sprinted again. He stuttered, "N-no shield. No cover. No weapons. Open water. I'm ah-ah fish in a barrel. Please help me, I'm a fish..."

Another shot ripped through the starboard side. His old metal tackle box jumped, and the lid sprang open, spraying out hooks and spinners.

On the still water, the impact was sufficient to send the canoe into a gentle bobbing turn. With Jerud lying to stern, the next round would have a chance of hitting the top of his head. Even if he readjusted his position, there'd be no safety here. He had to get out of sight.

Jerud wrestled out of his life jacket—prompting a hook of pain in his gut—as another shot tore a four-inch gash at the waterline.

The lake invaded the old canoe. Jerud pressed both hands over his wound, then kicked the yoke once, twice, and broke the support out of his way. He rolled to starboard. The canoe leaned. Water fountained through the hole. Then he quickly rolled to port, flung himself over the edge, and splashed into the frigid water.

His skin erupted in goose flesh as he coiled into a ball. His heavy boots and clothes countered the buoyancy of his lungs, and he hovered a few feet underwater. A terrible thought came; he'd not be able to make the surface. He'd drown. He *was* drowning. He—

Count to five, his father said.

One...two... The initial shock of the plunge began to abate. *Three...four...* His arms loosened, legs stretched out. *Five...* His eyes opened to the crystal-clear water.

The pebbled shoreline wavered fifty feet ahead, sloping steeply in the abyss below. He was neither rising nor sinking. A small effort with his arms rewarded him with forward motion. He was in control. But his breath wouldn't hold forever.

Debating direction was pointless. The dock was across the lake—a twenty-minute paddle by canoe. An impossible swim. The only choice was the closest shore, where the shots originated. If he could swim parallel to the land a ways, he might have a chance to hide.

As if in defiance of that thought, a round struck the water. The bullet cut a line toward Jerud but slowed quickly, arced downward, and sank. He wondered if the gunman saw him beneath the surface, or if it'd been a lucky shot. Either way, time to move.

Jerud let go of his abdomen—sacrificing blood for efficiency—and swam west. Hiking boots made his feet clumsy. Every stroke brought fresh, tearing pain to his wound, but his lungs held fast.

Since his first swimming lessons, Jerud had measured his ability to hold his breath. His was three and a half minutes. As he swam, he counted.

At seventeen seconds, another round zipped into the water. He didn't turn to see how close it came. He concentrated. Kicking, pulling, trying to ignore the pain and forget the ribbon of blood in his wake.

Two minutes and ten seconds. The chilled water didn't bother him anymore. It felt clean and invigorating—a welcome counterpoint to the grating pain in his abdomen. His lungs, however, were burning.

A short distance away, an old pine lay half-submerged in the water—as good a hiding place as he could hope for. Jerud swam to the tree and cautiously broke the surface.

Above water, the tree's branches had shed their needles and fallen in a broken jumble against the trunk. Jerud crouched in the shallow water and worked his way into the clutter.

The hiding spot offered a decent view of the shoreline. No beach here. Only a two-foot buffer of rust-colored stone and clay transitioning into tall grass and reeds. A hundred feet downshore stood a rocky outcropping—the place he'd been near when shot. His heart sank at how short a distance he'd covered.

Jerud heard the sound of wind stirring the leaves, then realized the *shush* was localized, coming from the woods and approaching the lake. He tucked in close to the fallen tree and listened.

●

"...dead. Gotta be. Let's split." A man's nasally voice.

"Better be. Why the hell didn't you aim for his head?" A second voice. Gruff, bassy. Easier to hear.

"I always go for the heart. Even if you miss, you blow a lung apart. Still dead. You miss the head, they get away scot-free." He sneezed, snorted, and spit. "I hate nature. Pave it over, that's what I say."

"So, you hit his chest?"

"You bet. Left side. That's the good side. Heart leans that way, you know?"

"Everyone knows that."

"Yeah, sure. So, let's split."

"Keep your pants on."

The two men stepped into view above a line of high grass, thirty feet from Jerud. The closer man wore a black coat stretched across his square shoulders, hair buzzed to an ashen shadow, and a bushy mustache sat beneath a boxer's nose. His eyes were dark lines squinting over the water. "We'll give it a minute. Keep scoping the shores."

"Piss on that." The second man hawked a glob of snot. Pear-shaped, he sported a mop of brown hair and wore slacks and a dress shirt that fit like hand-me-downs from a big brother. "I checked the shores. He ain't there. Nobody holds their breath this long. I'm out."

"We leave when I say so. Now get on your damn scope."

"You nuts? Somebody might'a heard my shots. Somebody might be buzzin' over here on a jet ski right now. The kid's dead, okay?"

The big man turned to his partner. "Wud you say?"

His partner averted his gaze and fidgeted with his rifle. "I said he's dead."

"Naw. You said 'the kid' is dead. What kid?"

"Look, let's just scat. We'll talk about it in the car. Alright?"

"Straight answer." The big man pointed a thick finger at the lake. "Was he our guy or not?"

"I...look, what are the odds of somebody else showin' up, right place, right time? Had to be him. Didn't it?"

"Ah, fer the luv'a Mary..." The big man rubbed his temples in hard, slow circles. "You just killed a kid, didn't you? You goddamn dummy."

"He looked like our guy! I was already squeezin' the trigger, you know? Point 'a no return. Then he lifted his chin a little and he looked...young." The fat man shrugged. "Doesn't matter now, right? If he was our guy, he's dead. If he wasn't, that means our guy knew this was a setup."

"Or it means you scared him off. Either way, you screwed us, Bert."

"Hey, hey..." Bert shot a look over his shoulder. "No names. You know that."

"We're in the middle'a nowhere, ya fat idiot. Besides, that rule don't matter anymore." The big man moved with practiced speed as he drew a pistol from within his coat and shot his companion in the neck.

Bert's body went limp and he collapsed with a choppy gurgle.

The big man stretched his neck from shoulder to shoulder, then tipped his head back and watched a flock of Canada Geese pass by. "I hit your spinal cord, Bert. Lucky shot. I'm not gonna bury you. The animals out here do pretty good work, an' the blood bubblin' outta your cake hole is like a dinner bell. Maybe they'll clean up that poor kid you shot, too." He sighed and shook his head. "What a mess."

The big man tucked his hand in his sleeve and wiped down the pistol. "I liked this gun. Can't get attached to things, though. That's the key." He hurled the weapon into the lake. "Boss ain't gonna be happy. You being dead'll help. Still, she ain't gonna be happy." He started back to the woods, listening to the last of Bert's life bubble out and running a palm along the swaying grass. "You're incompetent, Bert. Always knew I'd kill you. Should'a done it years ago and saved the headaches."

◆

Jerud's adrenaline waned as his blood leaked out. Still, he held pressure the best he could. The cold water might have helped. Like putting ice on a wound to keep the swelling down. Maybe it had, but not enough.

Breathing hurt. Moving hurt. And, man, he was tired. He could lie down in the mud and be asleep inside a minute. His eyelids drooped. Head sagged. That's when he heard the big guy say, "That rule don't matter anymore." And a gun went off.

Jerud jumped, tore his scalp on a jagged branch, and yelped. He slapped a hand over his mouth.

The man hadn't heard him. Not over his buddy's final, gargling hack.

Jerud's fatigue whisked away, and he whispered, "He killed him, Dad! He killed him!"

It's alright, Jerud.

"No, it's not! He's dead and I'm, I'm—"

Alive.

He breathed a little slower. "But I'm bleeding. Our canoe's gone. There's no way out of here."

Are you sure? He's getting out.

Jerud watched the big man walk out of sight, hands empty. The rifle had been abandoned. And why not? He probably considered it a murder weapon for a murder he didn't commit.

You know what you have to do.

"I can't, Dad."

You can, because there's no other choice.

Jerud grabbed a branch and pulled himself onto the slick, rock-strewn bank. Cool air drew out goosebumps on his wet skin and his brain went fuzzy, like he'd stood too fast. He shook his head to combat the encroaching shadows.

You'll need both hands free. Bind your wound. Hurry.

Jerud peeled off his sweatshirt and spun it into a twisted length of cloth. He snugged it around his midsection, double knotting over the injury.

You're teetering. Grab a stick.

He selected a broken branch from the heap and, using it as a staff, scrambled forward.

He spotted a pair of polished dress shoes in the reeds. White socks, brown slacks. White dress shirt over the soft mound of the man's torso. Streaks of red dripping down...

Don't look, Jerud. Focus.

He pulled his eyes away and searched the grass. There was the rifle, fallen at the man's side. Jerud claimed it. Then he turned to the woods.

Tucked into the treeline fifty feet away, the big man stared at him in wonder. "Well, ain't you somethin'? Thought I heard nature's cleanup crew. Sure as shit wasn't expecting this."

The two eyed each other. Jerud's heart thrummed, but he heard his father's mental encouragement.

You have the gun. Be brave.

Jerud dropped the branch and brought the rifle across his chest. He stepped forward, trying to keep a steady gait. His dad had been an extraordinary shot with every firearm he'd picked up. Jerud, on the other hand, had never taken to hunting. He needed to get a little closer. Just a little.

"Thought you were done for, kid."

"I need a hospital." His voice wavered, but only slightly.

"You sure do. That liar said he hit you in the chest. Still, a gut shot's a bugger. You know what's happenin' right now? There's shit leaking into your body. That's the trouble with gut shots. They keep you around. Give you hope. Meanwhile, the infection of a lifetime is brewing in your belly. It's a miserable death. I could speed things up if you want. Show you a shortcut to the finish line."

The big man advanced two steps. Jerud's legs tightened. He fought the instinct to retreat and, instead, brought the rifle to bear, wobbling against its weight. "I said I need a hospital. If you have a four-wheeler or something, I'm taking it."

The big man's mustache widened as he smiled. "What kind of gun you got there?"

Jerud glanced at the weapon. "It's a...a deer rifle."

"What you got in your dainty little mitts is a Winchester thirty-thirty with a custom walnut stock. I believe that particular gun is over sixty years old. Now, I forget, would that hold five rounds in the tube or seven?"

Jerud glanced at the gun. He couldn't remember how many shots were fired. He didn't know how many it held anyway. His hands tingled. Dark waves flowed against his consciousness. From the bottom of some mental well, his father called out, *Never mind what you don't know.*

Concentrate on what you DO know.

He wasn't familiar with how to check "the tube," so forget it. There was no bolt, no pump. This looked like Uncle Orrie's gun. Lever action. It worked like—

Jerud pushed the lever down and back. A casing ejected from the chamber. He tucked the stock into his shoulder and peered down the sight. At the other end, the big man's confidence took a momentary leave.

"I need your car, or whatever you have. I'm not gonna argue. If you don't help me right now, I'll shoot you and leave you for the bears, just like you did to your friend."

Hard lines deepened around the big man's eyes and downturned mouth. "Sure you got a shot left?"

"You sure I don't?"

"Your skin's white as paper. Drip, drip, drip. There she goes. I'll bet you can't hold that gun up for another thirty seconds."

"Then I guess I shouldn't wait. Last chance."

"Fuck you, kid." He started forward.

Jerud's vision blurred, but the man's chest offered a wide target. He told his Dad, "I don't want to shoot anyone."

That's because you're a good kid. And you'll still be one after this. Now do what you have to do.

Jerud squeezed the trigger.

The report thundered through the woods as the big man backpedaled into a tree. For a moment, his stunned eyes focused on nothing. Then he looked down.

At the last second, he'd raised his arms. The round had struck both bones in his left forearm, leaving his hand hanging by torn flesh from a new, traumatic joint between his wrist and elbow.

The big man stuttered and babbled. He reached for the mutilated limb, hesitated, then rerouted to his shoulder. A touch came away with a palmful of blood from where the bullet had continued and hit him a second time.

Jerud worked the lever again, aimed, and squeezed. The rifle offered a solitary *click*. Just to make sure, he tried again.

The big man turned away from the wreck of his arm, and his shocked countenance tightened to a dark, malevolent mask. He advanced again, building into a charge.

Jerud gave a fleeting thought to using the rifle as a club, but his strength had failed. The weapon fell from his hands as he backed up.

His father screamed, *Cover your wound!*

Jerud brought his arms across his abdomen in time to feel knuckles, like a row of stones, pound hard enough to fold him over. A solid knee came next, dead center in his chest, followed by an elbow dropping like a brick onto the back of his skull.

Jerud vaguely registered that he'd fallen. He shielded himself with his arms, only to have them knocked away, but he feebly raised them again. He heard the big man, who seemed to speak from a mile above him.

"Feed me to the bears, huh? Gonna feed me to the bears?"

Jerud ignored the words and concentrated on his father's voice. *I'm coming. I'm coming. Hang on, Jerud. Please, Son, just hang on...*

◆

"Detective Mulick? We found the boat." A portly deputy with a friendly, round face stood near the public docks at Hanson's Lake. "Detective?"

Kently Mulick, a toned forty-something man of middling height, gazed over the water. A five o'clock shadow covered his cheeks and jaw, whose sharp angles and pallor spoke of long-term hunger, perhaps illness. His grubby sweatshirt and roll-cuffed jeans might have come from a lost and found. "Bring it in."

Minutes later, a skiff bearing the crest of Itasca County Sheriff's Department neared the shore with an aluminum canoe in tow.

The men dragged the boat ashore and lifted it to the back of a flatbed trailer. As they secured it, the skiff operator, a deputy with gray hair and a wizened squint to his eyes, spoke to Mulick.

"She drifted o're ta the east slough. She's the one, though. Bullet holes. Blood. The whole works."

Mulick stared into the boat. Scraps of a sopping, half-eaten sandwich floated over a few inches of blood-tinged water. The meat and cheese had lingering dashes of cracked pepper and green flakes that might have been oregano. Something a mother would do. "You take pictures?"

The old deputy snugged the final strap. "Few dozen, before I set a finger on her. Not my first rodeo, detective."

"'Course not. Sorry."

"Don't worry 'bout it. I'll tarp her an' head back to town. Need a lift?"

"No. I gotta get back across the lake. Talk to the crime scene guys. I'll keep your skiff if that's alright. I ran my boat into the shore pretty hard."

"Sounds good. Deputy Fentzer can help ya out."

"Thanks." Mulick didn't look him in the eyes as they shook hands. When he tried to release, the deputy held fast.

"Don't go blaming yourself, detective. We can't control the world, much as we'd like to."

Mulick nodded. The deputy let go, gave the detective a clap on the shoulder, then returned to his duties.

The amiable Deputy Fentzer walked over. "Well, at least we found the canoe, huh? Surprised it didn't sink. Looks like it started takin' on water, then I guess it stopped."

"When the kid jumped out or fell out, the boat rode higher, and the hole wasn't a threat anymore."

Fentzer nodded and shook a finger at the detective. "That's why they pay you guys the big bucks."

"Yeah, well, the bucks ain't that big."

Fentzer tipped back with a laugh. "All aboard, detective." He held out a hand to the skiff. "I'll get you back over there. Don't get to take out our boat much. They won't let us use it for fishing. Seems like a waste."

All available evidence had been processed and cataloged. The sun had set, and a drizzling blanket of gray clouds hung over the city.

Mulick drove a black SUV through the slick streets, squinting at the glare of digital billboards and streetlights reflecting off every smooth surface he passed. Driving at night was like taking a sedative. Driving at night in the rain made his head hurt.

He parked and killed the engine.

The rain trickled outside, getting heavier. He patted his suit coat, already sure of what he'd find: badge, wallet, phone, pocketknife. His fingers drummed on the wheel as he tried to summon another reason to delay. Eventually, he whispered, "Get up, you wuss."

And he did.

At the front desk, an elderly receptionist informed him the family was done receiving visitors for the night. Mulick nodded, thinking he'd been saved by the bell. However, when he turned to leave, she asked, "Unless you're Kently Mulick?"

He sighed. "Yeah, I'm Detective Mulick. But if it's too late..."

"Jerud's mother has been asking about you for hours. If I let you leave, I'd never hear the end of it. Fifth floor, detective. Room five-thirty-seven."

Lights were dimmed on the fifth floor. Most patient rooms were closed. He walked by a single open door and glanced in. A privacy curtain within the room left a small gap, through which he saw an elderly man lying in his nakedness save for a thin blanket bunched up over his groin. Tubes and lines ran from a dozen places on his body. The most prominent of which extended from a large gray machine, then snaked over his bed and arched into his mouth.

Kently looked away as fast as he'd looked in, though he knew the scene would stick in his head. Maybe forever. He silently hoped the old man would defy everyone and die before sunrise.

Five-thirty-seven's door was slightly ajar. Just enough to let people know they wanted privacy, but there were always exceptions. He tapped a knuckle on the glass. A chair squeaked over the floor, then a woman slipped through the curtain. Mulick stepped in.

Jerud's mother was petite. The kind of petite that probably forced her to stand up for herself as a kid, maybe learn how to throw a jab with her wiry arms and hard, little fists. But even tough girls who grow up to be tough women have a breaking point. Like when their baby is lying in a hospital bed surrounded by monitors and machines.

She sniffed, brought a well-used Kleenex to her nose, then momentarily studied his face. "Are you—"

"Detective Mulick. Sorry about the wait. We had to..."

She watched him intently. Her quivering mouth told him she had something to say, was *dying* to say, but she'd wait out of respect. She was the kind of citizen who thought of all law enforcement as heroes. Given the situation, he couldn't think of anything worse.

"We just had a lot to do. How is he?"

Her trembling lips struggled to form the word. "Alive." Then tears fell, and thin lines bunched her face into a web of worry and exhaustion.

Mulick wasn't the hugging type. Although, for this tiny woman who'd already lost her husband, then come within an inch of losing her only child, he'd make an exception. His arm encircled her shoulder.

She fell into him, whispering between sobs, "Thank you, thank you..."

The crying subsided, and she took the tissue to her eyes and nose before stepping back. "I'm Abby, Jerud's mom. You probably guessed that." She smiled and rolled her eyes.

"I'm pretty good at that type of stuff."

"I bet. He really wants to meet you. Come in?"

"Is he awake?"

Abby slid the curtain over.

The thin fifteen-year-old lay in bed, looking too small and too young to be in such a place. He gazed at Mulick with sleepy, brown eyes and a quiet smile. Like the old man in the other room, he had his share of tubes and lines. His arms had thick steel pins sticking out every few inches, attached to what looked like an erector set. He'd defended himself to the end.

"Hey, Jerud."

Jerud blinked away a little sleep. "I was waiting up."

"I see that."

Abby offered Mulick her chair. "I need to stretch. Maybe I'll let you boys talk a minute. Will you be alright, hun?"

"I'm fine, Mom."

"Okay, I won't be long." She kissed the top of his head, whispered, and kissed again. Then she departed.

Mulick sat, unsure of where to start. He wasn't uncomfortable with kids, but not having any, he wasn't practiced either. Thankfully, Jerud broke the ice.

"So you're the one who saved me?"

The detective turned away from the kid. The monitor near the head of the bed displayed numbers, waveforms. The detective could figure out what they meant if given a minute but, at a glance, he deduced—with no flashing and no tones going off—the kid's vital signs were in the green. "I didn't save you."

"But the other cop said—"

"I know what he said." He glanced at Jerud, then stared at his shoes. "What he didn't say is that I'm also the one who damn near got you killed."

"What?"

Mulick suddenly found the proximity to the kid intimidating. Jerud's openness contrasted too starkly with the closed door of his own personality. He walked around the bed and stood before the large floor-to-ceiling window. There, he could see Jerud's reflection, and Jerud could see his, but the intimacy was broken.

"I've been working undercover. I was supposed to meet those guys. In fact, I was supposed to get there ahead of them."

"What happened?"

"I was lazy. Showed up an hour early. Should've been two, because they were already there, waiting..." He found the courage to turn from the reflection and face the real deal. "I had no idea those guys were on to me. None. I'm a good detective, but I don't make a great undercover. You gotta be an actor. Have a better imagination than me. I don't know why the hell I let myself get talked into it."

"So, they were waiting for you and—"

"And I should be the one who got shot. You saved *me*, Jerud." Mulick returned to the window. He didn't want to look at the kid anymore. The wires. The machines. He didn't want to know if the surgeon cut out a length of his intestine and Jerud was currently shitting into a plastic bag. He wanted to be lying there instead.

"It's okay," Jerud said.

"Don't tell me that."

"But it is. I saved you, and you saved me. That makes it okay, doesn't it?"

Mulick wanted to agree, but he couldn't.

The kid watched him in the window. "Can you at least tell me what happened?"

The reflection in front of Detective Mulick faded as his mind projected a memory from earlier that day, on his way to Hanson's Lake. "I was a couple miles from the public access..."

♦

Mulick's junky Ford Escort zipped down the road. He'd arrive almost an hour early, enough time to scout around. Just like the other meetings. No sweat.

A nine-millimeter sat tucked into his belt, hidden under a baggy sweatshirt. A handheld radio was stuck beneath the dash. He wondered if Bert would come alone or bring his bruiser friend. Mid-thought, a gunshot echoed in the distance.

"Ah, shit." Someone was duking it out with the assholes he was supposed to meet. DNR, maybe, sticking their collective nose where it didn't belong. Yet...

More shots thundered. All from the same direction. All sounded the same caliber. No overlapping fire.

This is one person. A warden would be firing back. Who the hell are they shooting at?

The turn snuck up on him. He hit the brakes and cranked the wheel, momentarily lifting two tires before hissing across the gravel of the public access road and slamming back down to all fours. The Escort fishtailed down the short road and, in minutes, came to a split. A boat launch to the left. Dead ahead, a half-dozen wooden bollards separated a turn-around from the dock. The brakes locked, and the car slid over leaves and gravel until it smashed into the heavy posts. Pain in his legs, ribs—all background noise. Easily ignorable in the face of a half year of undercover work that appeared to be falling apart.

Mulick snatched his radio and bailed out. He ran down the dock, leaped, and crash-landed inside an old fishing boat he'd arranged the day before. In seconds, the moorings were cast off, and the outboard chugged to life.

In the water, he radioed for backup, then there was little he could do but wait—one hand on the tiller, one gripping his gun—as he darted toward the opposite side of the lake. After three minutes, he spotted Bert's large friend on the shore, hunched over and yelling into the weeds. Someone was at his mercy.

The man reached down and came up with a rifle, held backward, making the stock the business end. Mulick fired wide, fearful of hitting whoever lay in the grass. The man looked up, hesitated a second, then raised the rifle one-handed and brought it down on his victim.

Mulick shouted, "FREEEEZE!" But the command did nothing to slow the attack, and the rifle slammed down again. He released the tiller and tried to sight up his target, still fifty yards out, but with the boat jouncing through the water, the shot seemed impossible. Still, he held his breath and readjusted his grip. To his disbelief, he realized—*My God, the shot's there. I can hit that. It's right...*

He fired. The man reeled back and dropped the rifle. Mulick aimed again. His second shot caught the man's flank and spun him backward. The final round homed in and sent a spray of blood from the top of his target's head. Then the man dropped forward and disappeared into the reeds.

The window once again showed a reflection of the hospital room and the teenager who watched him with rapt attention.

"When I found you, you were barely conscious. Your arms looked pretty bad. But to go through what you did? You're tough, Jerud. Damn tough."

"Yeah, I guess." Jerud scanned the framework around his arms.

Mulick made his way back to the chair. "They'll heal."

"Will they? I can't fish anymore. Not for a long time, anyway. It's what me and my Dad used to do. It's...it's kinda what we still do."

"Maybe this will cheer you up." Mulick pulled out his phone, gave it a few taps, and showed it to Jerud.

Jerud's eyes popped open. "Dad's canoe? I thought it sunk!"

"Nope, just drifted away. Shouldn't take much to patch up. Unless you're considering a proper fishing boat. Not a lot of people fish off canoes."

"I do. Kayaks, too. I even fished off a paddle boat when I was a kid."

"Way back then, huh?"

"You bet." Jerud stared at the image for a few seconds, then his eyes drifted toward the detective. "Do you fish?"

"Long time ago."

"Why'd you quit?"

Mulick turned away. In the window, a man bearing an eerie resemblance to his father spied on him from the dark reflection. "My old man and I, we...fell out."

"Oh." For a moment, the boy's patience filled the space between them.

The detective cleared his throat. "Wouldn't mind picking up a rod again. Probably be all thumbs, though. End up with a hook through my finger."

Jerud brightened and waited.

"Know any good teachers?"

The kid's smile stretched open. "Serious?"

"You instruct. I'll cast. Deal?"

"Yeah! I've never taught before, but I think it'd be easy. You can use Dad's old gear. I'll show you how to clean, too. Some people think it's gross, but you probably see all sorts of stuff..." He rambled on for a few minutes, then his excitement heightened even more when Abby came back and he got to share the news.

The three of them talked until the nurse came and offered a nighttime dose of pain meds. Not long after, the medication and the day's trauma overrode Jerud's enthusiasm. He fell asleep and—Mulick hoped—saw his father in a dream somewhere between heaven and Earth.

◆

By the time Mulick left, the drizzle had given way to heavy rain.

He wondered what he'd gotten himself into. Fishing with a kid. Good as a promise after the excitement Jerud displayed. Maybe it wouldn't be so bad. God knew he needed a hobby, something relaxing where the largest threat he'd face might be a largemouth bass. He entertained himself with the idea for a couple minutes, then called it what it was: a distraction.

His mind shifted to the story he'd told Jerud. And yet, not the story. The page he'd left out.

He hadn't told Jerud about the panic he'd felt when the first gunshot sounded. Like a mental alarm, infinitely more potent than the heightened awareness he'd felt on the job a hundred times. In fact, the only comparable sense of urgency he'd ever felt was when he was eleven, in charge of his little brother at a park, and his brother had vanished. At that time, the dread had been justified, but now, in the car, the origin of such a dooming sensation was a mystery. Mulick hadn't crashed into the bollards due to a misjudgment. In truth, he'd found it almost impossible to take his foot off the gas. There'd been an overwhelming impression that the sands of time were falling and falling fast.

On the boat, he should have been analyzing the situation or planning the best approach to the scene, but his anxiety had spiked to a horrible crescendo. There was no concentration to be had, so he closed his eyes in an attempt to level himself. In those few seconds, his life changed. Without thought, his dry lips had whispered, "I'm coming. I'm coming. Hang on, Jerud."

He'd known the boy's name.

Mulick sat at a stoplight, deliberating as the intersection blurred and focused with every swipe of his windshield wipers. *The name was a guess. But it wasn't, I knew. That's bullshit, though. I couldn't have known...*

He thought about the shots he had fired. Beyond his skill. Luck could explain one. Not two. Certainly not all three.

But it was luck. Luck and a healthy dose of adrenaline. His brain countered itself, using memory as evidence.

I felt hands guiding my aim. Didn't I?

The arms of Mulick's cognitive scale bent downward with the weight of the argument.

In the end, the name was inconsequential. What it represented was paramount—the knowledge had been gleaned from an unknown source. And if that was possible, then the world had truly opened a secret road for him.

The light turned green. A driver honked, then pulled around, calling out an obscenity as he passed. Mulick remained still, pondering possibilities.

If he indeed had been touched by something or someone, who else had the ability to reach out? Worse, was this an isolated incident, or only the beginning of something much more grand?

He wanted to put his car in reverse and drive backward through time. Undo the hours and forget the mysteries they held. *Just give me murderers and thieves,* he thought. *Isn't that enough?* But there was no way back. That road was gone. The world it led to, gone. There was only the surreal night around him and the unmapped morning that would follow.

♦

Alexander Vayle is a writer of supernatural suspense, thrillers, and crime fiction. His short story collection 'Among the Stray' was published by All Things That Matter Press in 2021. He is a long-time member of the Moorhead Friends Writing Group and has contributed stories to each of their anthologies. Alex resides in Fargo with his wife and four children.

She Calls to Thee

Logan Richard West

"Mankind was not absolutely alone among the conscious things of earth, for shapes came out of the dark to visit the faithful few."

H.P. Lovecraft, The Call of Cthulu

Archibald Tedsworth lurches as the clipper tilts backward. And his eyes are drawn skyward.

A raging tide rises like a great dragon from the sea; a rippling wall of water some twenty strides high, white crest seeming to touch the storm black firmament. It hangs there for what seems an absurd amount of time before—

Lightning crackles between the iron clouds.

The thunder rumbles in reply.

The old, grey planks groan and creak.

Then, as if on cue, the sails catch a dying wind, and the ship starts down the back of a great surf, wind and spray crashing over the prow. They come to a slow, yet dramatic stop.

Archie's eyes flit in all directions.

The massive wave, if it were real and not some figment, is nowhere to be found. The waters quiet, the rains calm, the occasional flash of light filling the air with apparitions and haunted faces, adding a foreboding surrealism to the already ominous surroundings.

Archie has to willfully peel his fingers from the rail and rope. Then everything hits him all at once, the shivering cold, the chafing wetness, and a more curious sensation, a warmth in his trousers. "I...I believe I've pissed myself."

"Heh-heh," Briar, the rig-master, lets out a wheezy chuckle. "I do it all the time." He starts up the ropes to the topsails. "Nobody to know you made a mess when there's water all about yeh', yuh' dandy landlubber."

Archibald can only blink in dumbfounded revelation at that.

"Anchor down!" His grating old voice echoes over the calm sea.

Archibald spins round.

"The wind's east!" The captain scuttles by with a real sense of command—if scuttling can be done with a sense of command that is. His left leg drags from an old cannon wound; his right hand is an arthritic knot. Still, he points here and there, shouting. "The wind's east, and we're west. Turn 'er round, boys. Anchor down and make hard fer' starboard 'afore the next crest comes." The captain spins young Lucian the lantern boy around by his frail shoulders. "Starboard, lad, starboard."

Archibald can only stare, cold and wet, body rigid with shock, and terror, and ...exhilaration?

Yes, that's what it is. This is exhilarating.

So thrilling in fact, he's soiled himself; so shocking that he's been put into a kind of voyeuristic stasis. It feels like his spirit has left his body, and all he can do is watch on in amazement as greater, or at the very least, braver men than he, work to survive the next wave, the next onslaught.

And to think, it started so serenely.

The voyage thus far had been a rather pedestrian affair indeed, a calm crossing from Fort Vyer's Gulf of Dorado to Puerta Preciosa in the Antilles Sea. Six of seven days it had been, and there'd not been an incident to speak of; a lonely storm cloud passed by without shedding a single tear; a grey blanket hovering far off in the blue sky sent a light sprinkle spitting sideways, giving the crew a mystical and welcome reprieve from the sweltering summer sun; but as night drew on the sixth day, in the far distance, a dark front approached. The tempest spanned as far north as it did south—or east to west—Archibald was never very good with directions truth be told. Regardless, the sun turned black as the dark front edged closer, hour by hour, until it swallowed them whole and started tossing about and battering, what had seemed a mighty vessel, with waves great as God's fists.

The clipper tilts suddenly sideways with a sound like breaking timber.

Archibald lets out an effeminate yelp as he reaches out for some handhold, anything. He catches a rope, tears a fingernail, body slamming into the rails, leaving him half hanging overboard.

A heavy fist lands on Archibald's shoulder.

Oh, no.

He's thrown backward onto the deck, flopping like a landed fish.

"Get ye' back on board, yuh' dandy landlubber." The captain scoffs before thumping up the steps to the quarterdeck. He takes the spokes, gives the wheel a spin, and snatches it in both fists, straining with the effort. "Catch the wind, boys! Eastward by hook or by crook!"

Three things happen in sequence: the sweaty men 'round the capstan grunt and heave, the anchor chain rattles, and the canvases flutter as the ship makes its arduous about-face.

Archibald watches all of this from the flat of his back, trying to gain his bearing.

'Dandy,' the captain calls me—the ingrate! Just who does he think he is?

The answer is obvious, however. Black Jack Drake is the captain of the Sierra O'Hara, one of the few ships willing to sail the Antilles on account of it being swarmed with pirates. Mind you, they were one of the few ships willing to sail the Antilles because they *were* pirates. But that seemed beside the point. The crew of the Sierra O'Hara had seen several naval conflicts, a few territorial skirmishes, and had outrun and outgunned the fastest ships in the New and the Old World. There was no ship finer, no crew better— despite their presentation—and Archibald always had the finest of everything. So why not the finest *former* pirate crew?

Archie rises unsteadily and dusts himself with a backhand. He takes a few wobbly steps until he gets his sea legs again.

I hate the ocean, detest the water. And yet, this is truly exhilarating, the stuff of legends.

And that was why he had ventured here, after all. He'd journeyed far and wide in search of stories, folklore, myths, all good fodder for his floundering writing career.

If only I could recapture the glory of my first novel, 'A Portrait of Power and Corruption.' He lets out a heavy sigh. *Maybe then I could stop running from the debtors, repay what's owed, and return home.*

"How 'bout it, Captain," first mate Terrence McMarth states through his thick mustache.

The captain gives no reply.

Archie puts his back to the cabin door and peeks round the corner, up the steps.

"Seas eerily calm," McMarth tries again.

And again, the captain gives no reply, just a scoff.

A good man is McMarth, by Archie's account anyway. He is the stalwart caretaker of a most contemptible crew and the reassuring and levelheaded calm to Black Jack Drake's uproarious drunken rage.

The captain produces a small bottle from his sleeve, as if in testimony. He pops the top with his thumb, tips his head back, downs the whole thing in one swallow. "Sea's calm..." He side-eyes the world around as if everything is out to get him: the wind, the water, his own crew even. "Sea's calm...but it's making me nervy."

"If I may," McMarth says. "That's the drink talking, Captain."

"Oh, aye," the captain replies absently. "The drink speaks, she does." His expression and voice turn cold. "She whispers to me, tells me secrets. She shows me where buried things are hidden. Tells me where hidden things are hoarded away. She points which way the wind will blow. And I follow her...Like a lovely lady lying on a bed of silk, she beckons...And I let her lead me."

It's McMarth's turn to give no reply.

Very well, I shall have to do this myself.

Archibald presses his clothes flat before ascending the steps to the quarterdeck. "You didn't say anything about storms, Captain," he says coolly. "Will this throw us off course, and if so, how far?"

"Aye, we're on course, yer' majesty." The captain openly scoffs before producing yet another bottle from his opposing sleeve. He pops the top with a thumb, takes a long pull, then wipes his whiskery mouth. "We've a storm to defeat first. But we'll have ye' to Precious Port in three days' time, I promise ye' that."

McMarth stands at brisk attention, twirled mustache fluttering in the breeze. "Three days is optimistic, Captain." He thinks it over. "I count...five days, yes, five days to Puerta Preciosa."

The captain hawks up something gross and spits into the empty bottle.

Archie scrunches up his face.

I say?

The captain pulls back his sleeve, revealing a small scar on his pale wrist. He digs a gold-bladed thumbnail into the old scar, drawing blood without making a sound.

Archie is momentarily lost for words, a bad look for any author. Then it all comes pouring out at once. "I say, sir, what the hell are you doing?"

The captain lets the blood drip off his wrist and into the bottle. "Making an offering 'o peace to the deep." He produces yet another bottle from his coat's inner pocket, rum judging by the smell, and he pours half into the bloody, spit-filled bottle. The rest he obviously drinks. "You're some sort 'o quill-driveller, aye?" He holds out the bottle. "Speak these words, then toss the offering off the poop of the O'Hara."

Archie arches one finely plucked brow. "Off the what?"

The captain snatches Archibald by the collar. "Saint beneath the Seas. Dweller in the Deep. I offer blood, life, and spirit in exchange for peaceful waters and safe passage."

Archie blinks.

But the old man's bloodshot eyes never waver. "Say it." His breath reeks of booze and rot.

Archie's lower lip wiggles. "Saint of the—"

"Saint *beneath*," the captain corrects.

"S-S-saint beneath the seas, d-d-dweller in the deep," Archie stammers. "I offer blood, life, and spirit in exchange for peaceful waters and safe passage."

"Aye, that'll do." The captain lets go of Archie's collar with a shove. "Say it. Then toss the bottle off the back 'o the ship. Speak the words, then off the aft."

Archibald takes the bottle with a shaky hand, turns, and shuffles to the back of the boat. With stomach pressed against the railing, he holds the bottle out over the waves, and—

The bottle slips from his fingers—*Plunk*—and it sinks into the strangely serene black waters.

Archie gawps, speechless for a moment. Then he spits the words out all at once. "Suh-saint beneath the waters, dweller in the—sea—I offer spirit, blood, and life in exchange for peaceful waters and safe passage." He flinches, expecting the worst.

But nothing happens. No divine lightning cracks the sky to split him in twain, nor do the seas rise to swallow him whole. In fact, by all appearances, the ritual is exactly what it seems: a bunch of superstitious bullshit.

Archie shrugs and straightens the collar of his fine coat. "Well then. That's that." He turns and walks to the wheel. "I've done it."

"Good lad," Captain Drake says with a sly smile.

McMarth takes Archie by the shoulder and skirts him aside. "You said the words?"

"I did."

"You said them just as the old man told you?" McMarth casts a skeptical brow.

Archie takes his time to nod. "Yes...of course."

McMarth shines a whiskery grin and adjusts Archie's collar with his big hands. "Then there's nothing to worry on, lad." He gives him a kindly nod and takes his leave, but not before calling over his shoulder, "While there's a lull in the storm, you should come below deck and have a bite...might be the last for a while."

"Yes, yes," Archie replies absently. "I will." His attention is drawn elsewhere.

There's this angelic whisper in the distance, in the darkness beyond, a barely perceptible, phantom sound that feels as if it's on the edge of his hearing. Without even thinking he walks toward the starboard rails, staring off into who knows where.

A rolling mist creeps from the outer darkness, settling over the black waves as they lap-lap-lap the side of the ship. Planks creak, rigging groans, and the ropes hiss in the ebbing breeze.

The angelic voice rings out again, clearer this time, and closer.

'Hoo-ooo. Hoo-ooo.'

It is beautiful, yet sad, beckoning, yet haunting, not quite a cry, not quite a question. It is many things and more, but most of all, it is powerful, resonating, a tangible thing that reaches deep into the very heart of Archie and stirs some unsolved and primal emotion. It is terror, shock, melancholy... exhilaration?

Am I going mad, or is this some siren that calls out to me?

Archie shakes his head as if from a daydream.

"You hear her now, aye."

Archie jumps aside, one hand to his drumming heart.

"She calls to thee." Captain Drake has this long, accusing look, the creases round his eyes like ancient bark, the lines round his dry lips like striated stone. "You hear her now, same as I do. I can see it on ye." He reaches in his boot and produces a fifth and final bottle. "This here's the only thing that'll cure what ails thee. This here...and dry land o' course."

Archie takes the bottle, examines it, and sniffs the cork stopper. "What is it?"

"Liquid courage." And with that, the captain makes a shambling about-face and leaves.

What pray tell do I need liquid courage for?

Archie looks to the bottle. He looks to the waves.

'Hoo-ooo,' the haunting voice calls out.

Archie tries to pop the cork with a thumb, but his fingers are trembling—his whole body is shaky honestly, and he simply doesn't have the strength. He has to use two hands and all his might—*Thwop*—the cork comes free, contents spilling onto the deck.

Archie gives it another sniff.

'Hoo-ooo.'

It smells like piss and vinegar.

'Hoo-ooo.'

Archie upends the bottle, and drinks. *Ugh! It tastes like piss and vinegar!* He coughs, sputters up spirits. "That's strong." He takes another generous sip and is forced to clear his throat again. "Very strong."

Silence.

Then sound returns, as if from a great distance. The lapping waves, the creaking planks, the groaning rigging, the fluttering sails, the common commotion one might expect from a sailing ship. And slowly, a merry din drifts up from below deck, the chatter of the crew, the uproarious laughter of the drunkard, the poorly sung songs of the sailor.

Archie is drawn like a moth to flame. In a daze, he makes his way down the quarterdeck, across the main, then down again into the guts of the ship.

The crew's chatter is made hollow within the hull of the great clipper. The galley glows orange with lantern light, shedding shadows over forty-nine filthy, half-dressed men as they eat, play cards, place bets, every man accustomed to the subtle sway of the ship; they use their arms as rails, their feet as handholds, and those resting in hammocks creak from side to side—or port to starboard rather.

A new silence washes over the crew, and the ship truly feels hollow now.

That's when Archie notices everyone staring, staring at him, a hint of apprehension and accusation in their eyes. "Carry on," he says.

Like that, the tension is broke, and everyone returns to what they were doing: eating, chatting, playing cards, placing bets.

As Archie moves through them, the faces are nameless mostly, lost, or unknown but for the chosen handful who were willing to speak. To be fair, most pirates weren't interested in chatting with a 'quill-driveller' as men of the pen were called in those days.

Regardless, the crew had some colorful characters.

Garthry the galley mate, Thornton the rig-man's apprentice, and Lucien the lantern-boy are hunched over a crate, tossing dice.

Garthry is a tall lad made of bones, which is the exact reason he was cast in the kitchen as a matey. The lad was barely able to lift a crate of apples, much less haul a rope, or hoist an anchor.

Thornton is a stump of a lad, though this was not his defining feature. His arms are as long if not longer than his legs, all meaty forearm and boulder-like shoulders, leading to a bullish neck, a peanut of a head. It was as if he were made for the sole purpose of hanging from masts and ropes and the like, but his normal gate was something akin to an ape.

Lucien the lantern-boy is a sorry sight if ever there was one. His white hair is thinning. His limbs look frail as glass, the joints of his elbows and knees, almost childlike. Every part of him appears ready to break in fact, except for his heavy, steady hands, his long spindly fingers, which are only good for holding lanterns or lighting tapers and candles, thus cementing his name: lantern-boy.

The three look up and give a subtle nod as Archie passes by.

A sickly cry breaks the common commotion, almost sounds like someone saying, 'Help!'

Archie turns.

Four piss-soaked sailors are furiously burping, hands on the hull to steady themselves. The drunker of the four blows chunks down the hull, 'Yelp!'

So that's what that sound is. How foul.

Archie snatches the kerchief from his breast pocket, holds it to his nose, and keeps onward, cursing to himself.

The damned ingrates! Heathens, the lot of them!

The captain occupies the head of a long, proper table, its four iron legs securely fastened to the floor. Upon seeing Archie, the captain holds up his cup, and another, more reverent silence washes over the galley. "Those of you who are drunk may sleep," he says.

Half the room moans, half of them cheer.

"Those of you still drinking, must stop. You've the first watch, boys." The captain pauses to sip some wine. "Sleepers, you've the second watch."

Those who'd cheered let out a unifying groan.

Captain Drake yanks a knife from the table and points round the galley. "My word's the law on this ship. Don't likes it, ye' can take a long walk off the prow." He spits on the floor. "Fathoms have ye', yeh' faithless mongrels."

McMarth waits several seconds before bellowing, "You heard him, lads. First watch on deck, second watch bunk down. Grab your scraps and get to work."

All at once, the crew clear the tables, stack the barrels, tuck loose food-scrap into their pockets, and, as commanded, first watch marches to the top deck, while second watch wanders toward the aft of the Sierra O'Hara.

The three mateys all saunter by, heads hung low.

What a rough life. Shame they chose to sail the seas I suppose. Tough luck that.

Archibald plucks out a fresh-looking apple before using the barrel as a seat. He takes that first delicious bite. While he crunches into the thing, expecting the crisp texture to turn into sweet mush in his mouth, while he chews, juice dripping from his lips, he comes to realize...he cannot taste. Or rather, he knows he's chewing, can feel he is eating, and yet, there is no pleasure in it, no sweetness, just dull, drool on his palate.

How odd?

He examines the red apple for blemishes or worms, turning the eaten side over to red, the red side to eaten, up then down.

No, nothing wrong, nothing—

That's when the faint lines on the apple's pale flesh bulge like purple veins, then the flesh erupts like many tiny wounds. Trickling at first, blood begins to leak from the apple, spilling down Archie's hands before dripping onto the floor. His mouth feels suddenly warm. He puts a finger to his lip, sees the crimson on his trembling fingertips, and...

The apple hits the floor with a wet *thud.*

"Ha, ha, ha," comes a mocking, grating laugh.

Archie turns to see the captain still seated at the head of the table. And when he looks back to the apple on the floor, it's perfectly fine, half-eaten maybe, but definitely not rotten and certainly not bleeding.

"Har-har-har," the old seadog laughs again, though there is little joy in it. "You feel it now, aye? The thirst. The hunger which cannot be sated. It is a terrible thing." He stands and scuttles over to Archie, until he is inches away. "It gets easier in time. I promise ye' that. It gets easier in time, if…" And he whispers, "Ye' are willing to give in to the sea…"

Archibald arches his nearly famous brow. "The sea, you say?"

"Yes."

"Easier, you say?"

"Aye," the captain purrs.

Archie puts on his most skeptical frown. There is a decisive finality to the word 'easier' which he does not like.

Note, the good captain did not say better. But rather, easier…in time?

"Soon," the old seadog whispers. "Ye' will see, and ye will know the truth in my words." And with that, once again, the captain shambles away.

The ship's usual sounds settle in, a silence in which the vessel spoke its wizened words, a tale of long voyages and heavy hauls, of rough seas and daring escapes. There is the unifying creak of hammocks if Archie really listens, and beyond that, there is this calling, like…

'Hoo-ooo.'

Archibald's eyes go wide as a wave of nausea threatens to topple him, but he holds fast to his barrel seat and breathes, in, out, in, out. And again. And again. His shaky hand finds its way into his breast pocket where, without realizing it, he's stashed the captain's bottle of spirits. He pops the cork with trembling effort and takes a swig.

'Hoo-ooo.'

Another swig.

'Hoo-ooo!'

Louder now, she calls louder.

He takes another swig and another.

The world turns black as night.

But from that darkness a vision descends, a figment like smoke, reaching and writhing from the recesses of Archie's mind to the fore, and a voice beckons, beckons.

"Who!" the darkness screams.

Archie feels his face torn by long nails, along his cheeks, across the bridge of his nose. Only...no...he's lying face first on the planks in the galley.

How did that happen?

He gets groggily to his feet.

I must have fallen asleep.

He absently kicks the bottle of empty spirits at his feet.

Or dare I say, drank too much.

The galley is dark as a crypt but for the sallow moonlight piercing through the open stairwell. The ship sways smoothly from port to starboard, port to starboard, and the familiar creaks and groans all persist. Nothing unusual.

Archie gathers some courage before forging ahead, knocking into this thing and that on his way toward the top deck, the moon's light guiding him like a beacon.

That's when the pale glow of the moon begins to fade to a false light, a vanishing candle flame in a long tunnel. Slowly, slowly, the light morphs from a waning orange to a burnt brown before taking on an altogether darker tone: the deep red of blood.

Archie turns to stone—a trembling stone, but still. He wants to move, but he simply can't. He wants to run, but it's dark behind him, red light before him and, in truth, he's far more afraid of the dark. His legs begin to move, and this terrible, wonderful, awe-inspiring sensation he can't quite put into words overwhelms his heart.

Thrilling.

Yes, that's what it is. Terrible, but thrilling. He didn't want to see, but he had to look. He didn't want to find out, but he had to know. The part of him that was always searching for inspiration and stories; the curious part of him had to know, had to see, had to...

Archie ascends to the top deck in a daze.

A full moon, red as a ruby, hangs in a clear sky black as pitch, and even the stars themselves seem to bleed crimson light. Along the deck, candles are lit, and men in black robes kneel in offering, hands raised.

They pray? But to whom?

A prayer, that's what it is, or something akin to it. But it's not words they're speaking. Rather, it is a chant: a sweet, sad coo.

'Hoo-ooo...Hoo-ooo'

Archie puts a hand to his breast, feeling for his absent heart, but it's there, thrumming like a rapid drum. He finds himself drawing closer rather than retreating, moving forward instead of away. He can't help himself.

I must know...

A hunched figure cloaked in black stands at the prow, back turned to face a big iron offering on a pedestal. An offering whose orange flames slowly begin to change, orange hue turning to blue, then green.

Three youths, if only judging by their sizes, are kneeling before the cloaked figure. The one on the left is tall and thin. The one in the middle is broad at the shoulders and thickly necked. And the third is misshapen, sickly almost.

"Lady of the Sea," Captain Drake grates out the words. "We call to thee."

The hunched figure in black turns and stands tall, revealing a bloody dagger and a twirled mustache. First Mate McMarth holds up his free hand, a bloody hand, and in his palm is carved two crude symbols: an eye and, above it, a wave. "Lady of the Sea, we call to thee," McMarth repeats, and he lays his hand upon the crown of the first boy. "Garthry of Fort Vyer." And the next. "Thornton of Delfin." And the last. "Lucian of...parts unknown."

"Children." The captain shambles from behind the altar to stand next to his first mate. "We condemn your souls to our Lady of the Sea."

The three boys jolt up, backs arched. A light begins to emanate from their faces, and it grows until it burns white as a star. The three boys stare at the captain and at McMarth, and the two of them stare back into that blinding light with expressions of pure amazement and some other intensely troubling emotion—relief maybe?

As the light emanating from the boys' faces dwindles, they fall onto all fours in pain, heaving like rabid animals.

"Now..." Captain Drake shines a fiendish grin. "Children of the sea, bring the lady her offering. Bring me the landlubber who's never held a rope nor pulled taut a sail. Bring me the one who has never sullied himself with the toil of the sailing man."

Archie realizes with sudden clarity just who the offering in question is. "Me?" He takes an instinctual step back. "You mean me!"

The three boys get up from their hands and knees, only they aren't hands and knees. They are changed, morphed into strange shapes, hard to define under the blood moonlight. In unison, the three turn and they shamble, shimmy, scrape closer.

Archibald takes several more steps back, but it feels like the whole crew is closing in around him. "What is the meaning of this? What the hell do you plan to do with me?"

There is no reply. No reply but for the heavy breathing of the sneering crew, the grinning sailors, more like cutthroats, more like...

Pirates?

A shiver runs up Archie's spine; his whole body uncontrollably shakes. This is not exhilaration; this is fear, and it only deepens as the three misshapen figures, once boys, draw closer and closer.

Garthry's long limbs have been replaced by slithery, slimy tentacles that drag along the planks. His face, once rather pointed, is flattened out, nose replaced by two holes that open wide, then close to furious slits, and his giant, amber orbs for eyes never blink.

Thornton's face is longer, pointed, and oddly smooth. His eyes are black, emotionless balls, and on either side of his neck are thin folds of skin that vibrate with his every breath. As he inches into the candlelight, Archie can see the boy is grinning, only his grin is too wide and too sharp to be a man's. The monster opens its maw, revealing row after row of serrated fangs. Looks like he can swallow someone whole.

What the hell is this madness? This cannot be real—stories, myths, fables, legends—it wasn't supposed to be real!

But Archie was beginning to see that stories and fables, these are often parables, spoiled by time and lesser minds in the retelling.

No, no, no, this simply cannot be real. Dreaming, that's it, I'm dreaming.

The last of the three limps into the light, his every step making this heavy, hollow *clonk-clonk-clonk* across the planks.

"Oh...Heavens, no..."

Lucian, or what's left of him, is covered in shells, barnacles, tiny beaks that gnaw at the air. A tiny crustacean skitters across his chitinous chest, and he snatches the critter up with a long-clawed hand, then feeds it into his mouth, a tiny orifice with tiny limbs that make this awful crunch and click.

Archie stares in wild-eyed horror. He sees but he does not believe. He sees, and he knows now. Myths come from somewhere. And legends, legends never die. Out there in the great beyond, if one goes searching, stories exist beyond the imagination. Problem is some stories are tragedies...some stories are beyond nightmare.

In the night sky, the blood moon begins to wane.

The shadows close in, the crew constricting around Archie, reaching. Archie takes a final step back and smacks against the wall of the captain's cabin. Nowhere left to run...

"Our time is short." The captain jabs at the air. "Seize the dandy, set him on the offering."

All at once the shadows collapse. Archie is dragged up by his limbs, and the mob carries him to the prow of the Sierra O'Hara where a bold, green flame burns beneath that big iron offering.

Even from this far, the heat licks at Archie's face, at his body, sweat pouring off him to leave a trail on the planks. Maybe that isn't sweat come to think of it. "No, please?" he cries. "Please, stop this madness, no!"

But no one hears. Or rather, no one cares.

Archie is hoisted high over the offering plate, arms wrapped up by sticky tentacles, body held by sharp shells, legs squeezed in a vicelike grip.

"Lady of the Sea," the captain calls out. "We offer this land-dweller to you in exchange for power, eternal life, and the mariner's blessing. Power, so that we might master the storms. Life, so that we might serve forever in your briny grace. And the mariner's blessing, so that we will always know the course and never drown at sea."

There is a moment of reverent silence in which even the wind seems not to blow.

Archie hangs in the air, shivering with terror but hot as the hells.

Please, wake up.

He glances over his shoulder.

Not like this, please, anything but—

"Drop 'em."

Everything falls away. Archie reaches for something, someone, anything. "Ugh!" He lands on the iron offering. It takes two seconds for him to realize... "Ahh," then he's screaming, writhing in agony as his body burns. "Please, no, nah—" His voice turns to a garbled plea, an incoherent cry which would go unheard, though it echoed across the dark waters of the Antilles Sea...Where, even to this day, some say you can hear the cries of the many offerings of the Sierra O'Hara.

The skipper sits on a crate, twirling his limp whiskers while the campfire crackles between him and his three apprentices. The surf makes a shushing sound as it sweeps the beachfront. The wind whispers salty lover's secrets. And the night sky is a violet cloth pinpricked by diamond stars.

"So," Skipper says. "What did we learn?"

Of the three boys, Garth and Thor sit in horrified silence, but the boy in the middle, Luca, licks his lips before replying.

"N-never trust a pirate?" he offers.

Skipper makes a face, scratches the back of his head, and stares out at the sea before letting out a long sigh. "Aye, lad, never trust a pirate. You've got the gist." But what Skipper is thinking is...

Some stories are lies. Some stories are bent truths. But stories come from somewhere. Myths aren't born of ignorance alone, no matter what the wisemen might say. There's a reason that legends never die. They're a part of us, burned into our very bones. And sometimes...sometimes the fables touch on truths you're better off trusting than experiencing firsthand.

"S-S-Skipper?" Luca stammers.

The old ship's captain startles as if from a daydream. "Aye, lad, what is it?"

The three boys sit in wild-eyed silence. Luca jabs a finger, pointing somewhere down the distant shoreline.

Skipper glances over his shoulder.

Where the sand meets the surf, a glowing specter in a flowing, white gown stands watching the waves crash. Her dark hair swishes in the breeze, covering her face. Then she turns and she stares at Skipper, black eyes like the deepest fathoms of the sea.

And he knows...

Skipper can't find his voice. Mouth suddenly dry. "God's sake...Not yet...Not now."

The lady in white lifts a bony finger and she points.

'Hoo-hoo...Hoo-ooo...'

Skipper swallows the rising knot in his throat, for in his heart and soul he knows who the lady means to summon. "You will know not the time, nor the place." He lets out a shuddering breath. "But in the end, she calls all to her briny embrace. In the end...she calls to thee.

♦

Logan Richard West is a father of three and a writer of things and stuff.

The Shrinking Coast

Michael Pickell

Nathan clutched his sack lunch tight, so the gale forces wouldn't blow it away. Water sprayed on him from the crashing of waves against rock. Or was it rain? He couldn't be sure. It may have been a mistake to visit the lake on this day, but he had to. Therapists told him the visit would make him feel closer to his old girlfriend. It would help him find closure, whatever that meant.

As he strolled down the path leading to the beach, his hand tightened over the last note she ever wrote him. It said: *Will be back soon, need to clear my head.* His glasses fogged over from breathing as he huffed his way to the beach. His black matted hair clung to his forehead as if pasted on by glue. His wet black denim shirt clung to his chest. And now, his black Columbia jacket soaked, he wished he had brought his raincoat.

After minutes of walking along the beach, he found a clearing. An indent in the cliff that could provide some reprieve from the bombardment of rain. It wasn't a far walk from the park-n-ride to the waterfront, but long enough in the pouring rain to get him soaked. Why he had taken his lunch from his backpack before he got off the bus was a mystery. A sign of his absent-mindedness. He thought he could escape the rain before his sack lunch got wet.

In the cove, he pulled out the sandwich consisting of sourdough, potted ham, and gouda cheese. It tasted of salt water, like someone's tears, the hardened bread now soft from rain. Would she have liked the sandwich? Maybe. Though she would have complained about its plainness. Would they have still been together? He could never know for sure. She was taken away from him far too soon.

Nathan met Gina in his first year of Uni, when he studied to be an architect and she a poet. Now it was twenty years later, and he had never married.

The brown paper bag, tattered from the rain, fell apart when he took out the bottle of Coca-Cola. He washed his sandwich down with the soda. A gust of wind sprayed his face with rain and lake water. The lake was so large and close to the ocean that he often thought of it as the sea. And in the rare moments when he talked about Gina, he said his girlfriend had been washed away by the sea.

He finished his sandwich and Coke and put the trash in his backpack. Then he set out against the rain. After twenty-odd years, the cabin they rented was still there. He gravitated towards it, though he had no desire to ever be there again. It was supposed to be a fun getaway. Instead, they had gotten into an argument. Bile rose in his throat at the thought of the fateful weekend. And he couldn't remember if it had been as stormy as it was now.

Cold rain pelted his eyes. He reached into his backpack for the packets of antacid he carried for the occasion. Then he ripped them open and popped a couple into his mouth. His boots marred the sand as he strolled against the wind.

Up at the cabin, a red light flashed. He wasn't sure where it came from since it appeared that no one had rented the cabin. Because of the clouds and rain, there was no sun to reflect off the windows. His curiosity got the better of him as he trekked along the beach towards the vacation rental.

♦

Gina's chest heaved as she unleashed a flood of sobs. Blotches of mascara ran down her cheeks as she tried to utter a sentence towards him. His lips were pressed hard, and he imagined they looked white by now. In a normal situation, he would have run his hands through her copper hair, told her that it would be alright, but she had upset him.

"I saw you talking with my sister."

"Don't be ridiculous. I feel nothing for her."

"She looked interested."

"Didn't you hear what I just said? I feel nothing for her."

She turned her gaze away from him. Scoffed at him with her hand.

"Can you tell me what's really wrong?"

His girlfriend returned her gaze onto him.

"I'm pregnant and you're making moves on my sister."

"Finally. Let's talk about it."

"I can't talk with you now." Gina picked up her coat, then slammed the door of the cottage behind her.

Later that night, she returned, subdued. They didn't speak much, but just held each other until they fell asleep. In the morning, he woke, alone in his bed. And when he scrolled towards the kitchen, he found her note.

◆

There were no signs of life as he combed the half mile of beach, save for the seagulls looping above. He trudged up the stairs leading to the cabin. When he reached the top, tears rushed down his cheeks, or was that rain? The place where Gina tripped and fell over the railing, marked by her scarf they found. Days later, her body was found with bruises on her head where she had hit a rock on the way down. The police had questioned him for a day or two until they determined he couldn't have made those blows.

Nathan slipped on the last step. He caught the handrail to stop himself from falling off the cliff and in the motion, banged his head against the post. Pain seared at the back of his skull, but he held firm. Gale forces picked up. A splatter of raindrops stung as they hit his cheek. The clouds above rushed across the sky. It may have been day, but it was tough to tell as the sky drew darker.

He grabbed the rail with his other arm and pulled himself back up, like doing a pull-up. Was this how it happened twenty years ago? He couldn't quite say, but he guessed she must have slipped the way he did.

A flood of memories surfaced. The fight, the good times they had on weekends and between classes. His doodles of her. Then there were her ghost stories. He missed everything about her, even after the twenty-odd years since her passing. No question, Gina had been his one true love. And then she slipped out of his life.

On that fateful morning, he grew nauseous at her disappearance. An hour after he woke up alone when she still hadn't shown up, he worried something bad had happened to her. His love would often go out on walks alone when she was upset. It helped her think.

At the top of the cliff, before him, were evergreen bushes. He couldn't remember if they were there before. They were shaped like skeleton hands and reminded him of bonsai trees, only larger. A dirt path followed the cliff, then curved towards the little house. He forgot how cool the place was.

"You should stay." A disembodied voice said. Or was it the wind?

"I can't." He yelled back to whatever entity said that, knowing it was his mind playing tricks on him.

He turned around and surveyed the dreary landscape. The grass leading to the cabin was sparse. Forest and mountains filled out the background. A flicker of something red. The sky darkened and Nathan knew he should turn back. An unseen gravity pulled him towards the window where he saw the flickering. Something howled off in the distance. A wolf.

As expected, there were no signs of life when he reached the cabin. The inside was dark, but he could make out the furniture inside. His memories of the place had faded, and he couldn't tell if it remained unchanged.

To prove to himself that he wasn't chicken, he peered into the window. All was quiet, and everything was still inside. The owners had covered the furniture between guests. Then a movement. An apparition. His heart raced. He jumped at the sight, which looked like a woman. He couldn't tell because his vision blurred. Tears ran down his face.

Across the room, a bright red dot floated, moving like a firefly, zigging one way, then zagging in a different direction a moment later. The ghost woman drifted away from the red specter. Nathan couldn't take his eyes off of it. The thing grew in size and morphed into an old man, a zombie. He knew he didn't want to be anywhere near it and yet, he couldn't move. It laughed and howled. A finger pointed at him.

The thing growled at him. "You shouldn't have dated her sister."

"I didn't."

Though his hands only rested on the window, he couldn't take them off. As he stood fixated, the darkness of the storm enveloped him. The air grew cold. He could see his breath, which looked like a spirit trying to escape him.

Boom. Far away, there was an explosion, or a sonic boom. The ground rumbled. Earthquake. Not too strong from where he stood. He guessed the epicenter was miles away, but close enough to make the ground shake.

He whipped around. This was the moment to listen to his gut, which told him to run. Maybe the earthquake would shift the dirt and the sands, and the cliff would fall into the lake. Certain he didn't know the way from the cabin to town, he ran towards the path and the stairs. He almost tripped on the curve of the dirt path onto prairie grass. Waves crashed against the cliff below. He ran along the cliff.

Without warning, the ground below him sank. Nathan leaped. Out of breath, he stayed ahead of the falling cliff, but falling into the lake with the cliff was imminent. Possibly fatal.

Then he saw her. Gina, his love, whom he missed all these years ago. She stood at the edge of the cliff ahead of him with her hand extended. She hadn't aged. Not that it mattered, she was a ghost.

"Grab onto me," she said.

He ran quicker, unable to say anything.

"You will be fine. You will live."

His breaths were labored. Then he lunged towards her, trying to catch hold of her hand. Cold and dirty, his nails dug into something, and they hurt from the force of hitting something. He hoped his fingernails didn't claw into her. Something wrapped around his hand and he realized she was holding his hand. The sting in his fingers shot waves of pain down his arm. Despite his gut feeling not to, he stared down the side of the cliff. They were clumps of dirt and rock falling over the beach then being washed out into the lake. He gasped. The waves were maybe a hundred feet below him. If he fell, his fate would be the same as his girlfriend's.

And he could do it, just let go. Fall and he would join her. But wasn't that her above him, whose hand he held?

When he looked up, he didn't see his true love. Instead, his hand was held by the roots of a tree perilously attached to the cliff. And even though it hurt, he swung his free hand to grab another part of the skeleton hand.

He pulled himself up, then rested on the ledge. On the other side of the giant bonsai, boards and rock were on the beach where the stairs used to be. The sky lightened above him. His body hurt too much to sit up straight. He winced at the pain and rested on cold wet earth where visions of ghosts slipped out of his mind.

Michael Pickell currently resides in Fargo, ND. He has been published in the Nebraska Writer's Guild Anthologies *Voices from the Plains* Volumes 1 and 2. He has written articles for *Food & Spirits* Issues 21, 27 & 28. His self-published collection of Haiku poems can be found on Amazon: *Across Distant Galaxies*. When he isn't doing web research (job) or writing ghost stories, he enjoys hiking and photography.

Dessert

Alexandra Juve

MIKEY IS DISORIENTED, THE ground shifting beneath him and the sun hot on his face. He pulls apart his sticky lips and sits up, wide awake. *Where am I?*

He scans the deck of the boat—or yacht, rather—looking for something that makes sense. Once standing, he sees he is wearing a white polo, slacks, and loafers. *That's pretty normal, okay.* Mikey touches his face, noting the warmth, and walks into the shade of the cabin. Spotting a mirror behind the bar, he approaches and assesses his face—it's a little sunburnt, but not too bad.

"Hello?" Mikey calls into the cabin. No response. He calls again: "Hello?" then walks through the top deck's interior space before making his way down the stairs to the second level. "Helloooooooooo," he calls once more before entering a bedroom. The room is lavish and well-decorated with fine white furniture and distinguished wall art, all of it illuminated by sunlight streaming in from a rather large window. Simple, clean, and quality–the mark of quiet wealth. "Anybody home?" The boat unexpectedly rocks a little harder to one side and Mikey fights for his balance as a *thunk* and the sound of something heavy rolls across the floor. Mikey finds his balance and an unopened bottle of warm Veuve Clicquot that has landed at his feet.

Shuddering at the notion of alcohol, Mikey picks up the bottle, places it among the pillows of the bed, and keeps moving.

Dragging himself from one room to the next, Mikey encounters soft, pearl-white bedding and fresh linens, as well as a safe, closed and locked. Everything else is bolted down or attached to the ship. During this search, it becomes clear to Mikey no one else is on this yacht with him. Dissatisfied, he makes his way to the helm. A thorough inspection reveals the key is missing, not that Mikey would know how to drive a yacht even if he had it. I bet *I could figure it out. After all, I graduated from Stanford.* The pride in this thought is only slightly dampened by the fog of his hangover. After trying a few switches and buttons to no avail, Mikey peers through the window into the sea ahead.

His stomach sinks. There is no land in sight, and he is alone.

Water. Thirst overcomes him all at once. *I need water.* He makes his way to the nearest bathroom and turns the tap. A trickle comes out, then stops. Mikey jostles the handle back and forth in an attempt to get more with no effect.

Frustrated, Mikey moves quickly back to the bar area and continues his search. A quick scan of the shelves reveal there is alcohol, and lots of it, but nothing that could quench his thirst. Yanking open the cupboards only reveals more liquor bottles, much to Mikey's disappointment.

Slow down. Think. He closes his eyes and takes a slow breath, filling his lungs. *Solve the problem. Gather your resources.* Realizing he left the champagne in one of the rooms, Mikey retrieves it and sits at one of the tables in the bar area. He places the bottle on the table, realizes it might fall if the boat rocks again, then sets it on the seat beside him. Feeling how warm it is, he gets up and places it in the wine fridge behind the bar. The top shelf of the small fridge contains a pizza box. "Yessss!" Mikey exclaims before grabbing the box and returning to his seat.

He lifts the lid of the box, revealing one pizza crust that is stale and hard as a rock. His face falls. *So much for resources.* Mikey attempts to eat it, even though it feels like tree bark in his dry mouth. Nearly choking, he feels every inch of the crust's journey down his throat, and his thirst becomes even stronger.

Where am I? It's that gnawing question again, coupled with a new one...*What happened?* A panic comes over him as he realizes he has no idea how he ended up in this situation. *Breathe, Mikey, breathe. Start with what you know.*

He speaks out loud. "My name is Mikey. I'm twenty-two years old. I graduated from Stanford in 2024 with a Bachelor's in Computer Science and a Minor in Marketing."

Good. Keep going.

"My family loves me," he continues. "I have a mom, and a dad, and a girlfriend..." Does his girlfriend know he's here? He can't remember.

Don't panic. Switch gears.

"I play video games, and I like to party." He stops. For some reason, it's embarrassing to say out loud–in this predicament–to an empty room.

Mikey scans the shelves filled with liquor behind the bar, jogging his memory.

Drinking...we were all drinking. The party...

A patchwork of moments are coming back to him. He knows they drank—hard. Someone suggested a yacht. The boys walked together down to the boat and...*the boys.*

Mikey was invited by one of his college buddies to join their weeklong bender in celebration of their recent graduation from Stanford.

"Invite only," his classmate had said. "And private. Don't tell your parents, and leave your girl at home. Keep it hush-hush." It sounded so enticing at the time.

Where is everyone now? Mikey has no answer.

His gaze travels from the bar to the above mirror, where his name is scripted in an elegant font onto a piece of paper: his diploma.

"Oh, no way! What's this doing here?" Hardly believing what he sees, Mikey jumps up to take the frame off the wall and reads his name and credentials clearly printed under the font of his Alma Mater. *How did this get here?* He doesn't even remember bringing it onto the boat.

Unsure of what to do next, Mikey turns and places his diploma on the counter behind the bar above the wine fridge and takes one more lap around the yacht, exploring all three levels. Stopping by the safe this time, he attempts to unlock it to no avail. Something tickles his brain, giving him the feeling they did something with the safe last night, but nothing really comes. He gives up and goes back to the bar table.

"What do I do?" The rocking of the boat and the sound of the waves are his only answer. He's on his own. In an attempt to curb his rising panic, Mikey reaches deep into his mind to search for something—anything—that will tell him more of what happened or give him some clue on what he should do next. A pang of hunger rumbles through his stomach. Unfortunately, the one pizza crust didn't accomplish much in the way of curbing his appetite.

"Someone has to know I'm here, right?" Walking out onto the sun deck, Mikey observes the gentle waves of the ocean and feels himself calm just a little. *It's actually kind of peaceful.* He stands where the overhang from the cabin can provide him some shade while he watches for any boats that might sail nearby.

"Someone will come." The words don't provide as much comfort as they should, probably because he doesn't really believe them. *I have to hold on to hope. Someone will send a rescue. Eloise knows I'm here...*

His girlfriend. She knows he is here on this trip, but does she know his current state? Does she know to look for him? He watches the water for a while, but as the minutes drag on, his hope recedes. Eventually, the sun disappears on the waves, and night falls.

♦

In the morning, Mikey wakes up on a cloud made of pillows and soft, white sheets. He yawns, his mouth dry, and coughs. His head absolutely pounding, doom descends as he remembers where he is, the reality of his situation setting in with a fresh sting.

"I have to get out of here." Mikey formulates a plan, and his determination is set anew. He climbs to the top deck and checks for any signs that may help. *Keep moving.* The next few hours are spent tearing apart the boat in search of any food, water, or tool to fuel his escape, starting with the cabin rooms. He opens drawers and cabinets, unfolds sheets, and lifts mattresses. The search reveals nothing he didn't find the day before. Sometime around noon, when the sun is directly over the boat, Mikey decides to take a break and sits at the bar table to rest.

"My name is Mikey. I am twenty-two years old. I graduated in 2024 from Stanford. I have family and a girlfriend that love and miss me, and I *will* get off this damn boat!" After only a few minutes, he cannot stand to sit any longer and continues his search.

While picking through one of the other residential areas, Mikey lifts the mattress and hears a promising *thunk* and *slosh* come from under the headboard. Quickly, desperately, Mikey pulls the mattress back from the wall and reaches under the headboard where he grasps a half-full plastic bottle of water.

Relief rushes through him as he quickly unscrews the cap and gulps down the few ounces in the bottle. The water is gone far too soon, but it alleviates some of his thirst. Mikey collapses on the bed, back against the headboard, and revels in the feeling of fresh water cooling his throat and comforting his stomach.

Why would they leave me here? Are they coming back? He wonders about his companions, his so-called "friends." They could have left him here by accident, as a failure to properly dock the vessel before deboarding at the end of the night. Improperly tying it to the dock makes drift a real possibility. But if that were the case, wouldn't someone in the group have noticed he–or the yacht, for that matter–was missing by now?

The alternative, he realizes, is that they left him here on purpose. *But why? As a prank?* His familiarity with the other members of the group leaves something to be desired. They include him and seem to mostly tolerate his presence, but how well does he really know them? Eloise had warned him not to come.

An aching in Mikey's chest arises at the thought of Eloise. *I miss her so much.* She cited his difference from the rest of the group as the main reason against his attending, along with the unsupervised use of drugs and alcohol. "I don't want you to get hurt," she had said. "You're not like the rest of the group, and I don't trust them."

Mikey's breathing constricts in the reality that she is right. He isn't like them. What do they truly have in common? Mikey went to Stanford on scholarship, while none of the other boys in the group needed one. While they partied their way to a passing grade (with a little help from their family's money in a few sticky situations), he threw himself into his studies. The group would hang out occasionally, but for the most part he had to isolate himself and put every spare moment into his assignments.

Obtaining the degree was difficult, but Mikey was smart and put in the hours to make it happen. He kept his grades up to maintain the scholarship throughout his time at school, but understanding the mentality of his wealthy peers proved to be another challenge. Was it possible they would do this to him, even as a joke? Was this their way of letting him know that he was not, and would never be, one of them?

There is no way they would leave me here to die, though, right?

Money can change a person, but to the point that he thinks so little of his fellow man's life? It isn't something Mikey can bring himself to believe.

Refusing to spend any more energy on the thought, Mikey pulls himself back into the present and keeps moving. After completing his search through the last few residential areas, he heads back to the helm. Ignoring the hunger pangs, he searches through the nightstand of the captain's quarters. There's a slide of metal across wood as he pulls out the drawer. *Was that...?*

His heart pounding, he pulls the drawer out farther. It is–it's the key: the key to the yacht's ignition! Mikey jumps up from his crouched position and inspects it, hardly believing his luck has changed. His breath comes quickly and he starts to laugh, stops, then laughs again. He has never been so grateful to see any single object in his life. He wants to cry, but doesn't–he can't spare the water.

"Yes! YES!!" He bellows as he holds the key up in triumph. "I am going home!"

"Shiny things are distracting, don't you think?"

Mikey whips around. A white Persian cat sits on the ship's control panel, its fluffy tail curling around its body.

Mikey stares at the cat, frozen. *Did that just talk?*

"You're being very rude," the Persian cat says. "Didn't your mother teach you any manners?"

Mikey shakes his head. *There is no way this is real.*

"Oh, I assure you I am real," the cat says. "I am as real as you, as real as life itself."

"You're a cat," Mikey says.

"An observant one, you are!" The cat's condescension rubs Mikey the wrong way, "And you are a person—or were, anyway."

Mikey blanches. "Am I...dead?"

The cat says nothing.

"Oh my god, I'm dead." Mikey wails, "This is hell! I'm in hell and you are here to torture me."

The cat stares at him then blinks. "Relax, human, you are not dead. Not yet."

"What are you? What do you want?"

"I am a companion." The cat hops from the control station and exits the helm.

"Wait, wait!" Mikey calls after the cat, then checks to make sure he still has the key. He puts it safely in his pocket and runs after the cat."Don't leave me!"

"Shiny things are a distraction, I told you," the cat says as it continues walking. "Keep up or you will be left behind."

"Where are you going?" Mikey prances to catch up.

"To bed. It's bedtime. I am tired. "

"Okay, well...can I come with you?"

The cat stops, and so does Mikey. The cat cranes its neck and studies him, considering.

"I haven't seen anyone else in days. You're the first...someone I have been able to talk with since arriving on this boat. Please."

"Fine," the cat says. "Come, human."

Mikey's excitement spikes, but then he pauses. *There is a talking cat on this boat with me.*

"I have officially gone crazy," Mikey whispers to himself.

"Are you coming, human?" the cat asks as it keeps moving. "Or are you going to continue standing there, wondering loudly about whether or not you are losing your mind?"

Weighing his options, Mikey decides to accept the cat, at least for now. *Maybe it will be gone in the morning.* He hopes it isn't. Maybe he is losing his mind, but it's a relief that he is no longer alone.

The cat and Mikey make their way to one of the bedrooms. Together, they curl up into the sheets and rest their heads on the down pillows. Mikey checks his pocket again for the key. *It's still there.*

They lie in silence for a while, and Mikey finds himself still reeling from the whole situation. Being stranded on a boat with a talking cat is a lot to process. *There is a talking cat next to me.*

The cat sighs. "What is it, human?"

"Do you have a name?" Mikey ventures.

"Sisyphus. My name is Sisyphus."

"I'm Mikey," he says, and they both drift off to sleep.

♦

When Mikey wakes, the cat is standing over his body.

"I see you have taken to tearing apart this ship. What else have you tried?" the cat asks.

"Good morning to you too, Sisyphus," Mikey croaks as he peels open his eyes, his mouth made of sandpaper and his head pounding.

"You need some sustenance, human. Have you attempted to fish?"

Fishing, of course! Why hadn't I thought of that? "I haven't," Mikey admits. "I haven't found anything to fish with."

"A poor excuse," the cat says. "We cats know a thing or two about fishing, but I have yet to see a human successfully attempt it without the proper tools. How about water, do you have any of that?"

"I found some yesterday, but it's gone now. I drank it all."

"Hmm." The cat studies him for a moment, then leaps from the bed and starts toward the bedroom door. "It's probably useless for you to even try and fish. Without what you need you're as good as dead." The cat turns around at the door. "You'd better get up now. High noon has already come and gone," it says, then saunters out of the room.

I'm not dead yet. No way. Mikey leaps from the bed and moves quickly toward the helm of the ship, but the strained effort combined with lack of food and water takes its toll, and he almost passes out on the stairs. After catching his breath and slowing his heart rate, he carefully climbs the rest of the steps to the captain's area.

The sunlight sparkles and dances across the tops of the waves. The dance continues into the far-off distance where it... *What is that?* Mikey squints, willing his mind to focus on what he thinks he sees. And he does, yes—yes! Land! He can barely make out the trees swaying in the breeze along the shoreline, but the greenery and yellow sand are unmistakable.

Euphoria rushes through Mikey as he reaches into his pocket for the key. He doesn't feel it right away, so he checks the pocket again, then the other. He turns both inside out and quickly looks around the area for any sign of shiny metal. Panic sets in.

"Sisyphus!" Mikey calls out into the ship, "Sisyphus! Have you seen the key?" With renewed energy, Mikey begins a desperate search of the captain's quarters. He runs into the bedroom where he slept the night before and dismantles the bed, searching every corner–every nook where the key might be hiding.

"Sisyphus! Help me, Sisyphus!" Mikey dashes up the stairs, retracing his steps in a wide, mad-eyed view of the ship's main areas. *I have to find that key.*

"This key?" Sisyphus asks from on the rail of the sun deck.

Mikey squints against the harsh, hot sunlight. Sure enough, the piece of metal ensuring his escape is sitting in between the pointed teeth of the cat.

"Oh my god! Thank you, Sisyphus. Where did you find it? Give it to me." Mikey runs toward the cat and slows as he watches Sisyphus open his mouth and drop the key. It lands in the water with a soft *plink.*

Mikey stops, dumbstruck. *Did that really just happen?* He feels a rage begin to build as he realizes that yes, it did. Sisyphus dropped his key.

He is going to kill that cat.

"Why did you do that?" Mikey shakes with anger. His hunger palpable, he recognizes the cat can be eaten. Deserves to be eaten.

Sisyphus lifts a front paw and licks it. "Shiny things are distracting, I told you. You could have spent all morning trying to teach yourself to fish, find ways to get more water, or generally be practical with your solutions. You humans are never good at accepting your fate. Now you have wasted time trying to get to that island, which I happen to know has nothing for you."

The island. Mikey runs to the edge of the railing. Unable to see it, he rushes up to the helm once more. He fights through the tunneling that threatens the edges of his vision, and strains through the window one direction, then another, then another. It is all ocean and sparkly waves for as far as he can see. The island is gone.

Utter hopelessness hits him like a crashing wave, making his limbs feel heavy. He cannot escape, and cannot leave. He's trapped. Unless someone comes...but who is he kidding? No one is coming. Defeated, Mikey ambles into the bar area. "I am going to die here." It doesn't feel real even when he says it out loud.

Sisyphus hops up onto the bar and stretches out on the wood, content. The cat yawns and curls up to nap as Mikey watches with disdain.

He slowly makes his way behind the bar, opens the wine fridge, and removes the bottle of Veuve Clicquot, retrieving his framed diploma from above the wine fridge as well.

Sitting at the table, Mikey removes the diploma from its frame and studies it. He removes the golden foil from the champagne, untwists the cage, hands shaking, and palms the cage and cork together in a familiar way as he twists the bottle. When the cork finally pops, tears roll down his cheeks.

What was my life? What was it for? For this? Never did he think a moment of popping champagne would be associated with his doom. It feels damning and wrong, yet oddly fitting for such an odd predicament. In this strange situation, of course, this is how he will go out. It's what he deserves.

"My name is Mikey," he says, his voice hoarse. "I am twenty-two years old and have been on this boat for three days. I want to go home." His voice cracks at the mention of his home and tears well in his eyes. He looks at his unframed college diploma and a bottle of Veuve Clicquot that he has all to himself. A party of one.

Mikey tears off a small piece of his diploma. Quivering with hunger, he places the stiff paper on his dry tongue, then puts the bottle of champagne to his lips. The cold, bubbly sensation fills his mouth and nose. He forces himself to enjoy what he wishes was water.

He continues, one piece at a time, one drink at a time, until his stomach is full. When he is finished and nothing remains but an empty bottle and frame, he stumbles out onto the sun deck. His vision blurry, Mikey thinks he sees Sisyphus lift his head from the top of the bar.

Mikey turns and stares at the sunset, willing himself to take it in. The glare hurts his eyes, and he remembers his mother's frequent warning not to look at the sun as he grew up. When Mikey cries this time, he has no more tears.

I want my mommy.

A heaviness settles in his chest when he thinks of what he could have done differently. All the time he spent studying for hours and hours, skipping holidays with his family and canceling dates with Eloise...it was all for a degree that can't do anything for him now.

Eloise.

He shakes as sobs wrack his body at the thought of her. He will never get to see her again, never kiss her again. They will never build a family together. He should have listened to her, shouldn't have come. Why did he want to so badly anyway? To celebrate with these boys who think so little of him? For these boys who couldn't be bothered to rescue him on a stranded boat, and left him to die?

Mikey wishes more than anything that this wasn't real, that he was safe at home with the people he loves and that love him. A cold reality overcomes him as he realizes that they won't even know what happened or that he needs to be rescued.

They would be here if they knew.

But they don't know. The people who care, who could do something to save him from this dire state, have no idea that he needs them right now more than ever. The only people who can help couldn't be bothered to even try and save his life, when it came down to it. Never has Mikey felt so powerless, so worthless. No one was coming. He's alone and will continue to be, except for a stupid cat.

"Are you done with your pity party, human?"

Of course, the cat.

"What do you want, Sisyphus?" Mikey's words come slurred and slow.

"You lament all these choices you wish you had made differently and you are always looking for someone else to save you." The cat comes to a rest just inside the cabin, where the sun deck starts.

"Sisyphus, can I please just have this peace before I die? Is that too much to ask?"

"You refuse to take responsibility."

"Look, would you shut up? This is your fault anyway. You're the one who dropped the key, and I'm pretty sure you did it on purpose. So please, just until I'm dead, shut the fuck up."

The cat sighs. "Poor you. Just like I said–"

Mikey snaps. "Shut up! All I have done since I woke up on this boat is try to survive. I've looked for food and water absolutely everywhere and there is none. I have spent every waking hour fighting to stay alive and find a way off of this boat, but you keep accusing me of not caring about my own life enough to try. All I do is try! All I have done, all my life, is try and try and try. And all you do is sit there and make unhelpful comments. Well, you know what, Sisyphus, if you have a real, helpful suggestion of what I should do, I would love to hear it."

Mikey stares at the cat with bloodshot eyes, furious. Sisyphus is quiet.

"That's what I thought." Mikey returns to stare at the sun, which is halfway set below the waves now.

The cat tilts its head, watching him. "When we met yesterday, you asked who I was. Do you know who I am now, human?"

Mikey says nothing.

"I have had many names but, in short, I am life itself." Sisyphus settles onto its back in a playful posture, swatting at a fly above. "You may think I am rude or mean, but the rules of survival exist whether you like them or not. If you survive, life will continue on. If you do not survive, life will continue on. You humans put so much energy, effort, and resources into things that do not really matter. All that matters is whether or not you survive."

Sisyphus looks around, taking in the boat, then returns to the fly. "Just look at this boat. So much opulence and wealth, yet nothing that you truly need is on it. What is all this wealth for if you cannot meet your most basic requirements? Beyond that, what resources you do have are useless, because you lack the knowledge on how to use them. Tell me, human, after so many years of training, how do you not know how to take care of yourself?"

"They left me here," Mikey continues to stare at the sun, gritting his teeth.

"Those boys do not care about you, clearly, but that is not your fault." The cat stands, rapt attention on the fly. "You did not ask to be born into your house, class, or family, and yet here you are. You may have made some mistakes, but that does not really matter."

Sisyphus pounces on the fly, trapping it on the deck's surface under its paw. Lifting the paw reveals the fly is crushed—dead. Satisfied, Sisyphus sits.

"It is impossible to know where every choice will lead you, and the reality is that much of the reason you are here is out of your control. Every life must train their young to survive, and let them adapt. Clearly, your species has an issue with this."

Mikey considers the cat's words. "And when are you satisfied? When have I adapted enough to survive?"

He could swear the cat smiled. "Ahh, my boy, that is the true problem. Everything dies, doesn't it?"

Nausea washes through Mikey and he vomits up the champagne and diploma, hearing the wet, sticky, papery mass hit the deck. He heaves again, then a third time, his stomach empty. He stares at the vomit covering the sundeck of the yacht, relieved and detached.

"It's time for bed, Mikey." says the cat.

Like moving through gelatin, Mikey stumbles his way to the disheveled bedroom where he woke just a few hours before. Hot and sweaty, dehydrated and weak, he collapses onto the stripped mattress.

Buzz buzz, buzz buzz. Mikey shakes his head to get rid of the sound of blood pounding in his ears.

Buzz buzz, buzz buzz. Mikey sits up groggily, finding Sisyphus sitting on top of the metal safe against one of the walls. "Did you hear that?"

Buzz buzz, buzz buzz.

Mikey scrambles off the bed, toward the safe where the sound is coming from. "What is that?" He slurs through his sticky mouth. He feels the side and is met with a vibrating sensation and again the sound: *Buzz buzz, buzz buzz.*

"Is there a phone in there?" he asks the cat, who sits alert on top of the safe.

"Yes, your phone is in the safe. Apparently, we have drifted into an area with cell service. Do you know the safe's combination, human?" Sisyphus looks at Mikey with a mixture of pity, annoyance, and what he can only assume to be a look of challenge.

Buzz buzz, buzz buzz.

It begins coming back to him: The night of the party they had all agreed to lock away their phones. "One night. All memories, no proof." The group members laughed as his friend said it. Mikey was the first to place his phone in the safe, then someone suggested shots.

His heart racing, Mikey frantically tries to remember the lock combination. *I watched him open it, didn't I?* The delirium of liquor and dehydration makes it feel impossible to organize his thoughts.

"I don't know it...I don't remember the combination."

"A shame," the cat says.

Buzz buzz, buzz buzz.

The cat and the boy stare at each other as Mikey kneels on the floor by the safe, the cat perched on top of the metal box.

"Please," Mikey begs.

The cat watches him as his eyelids fall closed and exhaustion takes over. He collapses next to the safe and lies there, thinking of Eloise and his mother.

I'm so sorry.

Mikey continues to think of them, clinging to their memory and feeling the boat rock like a cradle as the vibration sounds carry him further and further away.

Buzz buzz, buzz buzz.
Buzz buzz, buzz buzz.
Buzz buzz, buzz buzz.

◆

Alexandra Juve is originally from Ohio and now lives in Fargo, North Dakota where she currently works in the field of Human Resources. With a bachelor's degree in psychology from NDSU, she plans to continue fostering ideas, challenging beliefs, and comforting the fellow disturbed in any form of art. Her previous works include participation in local productions acting, directing, and playwriting.

Driving Home from the E.R.

SADIE MENDENHALL-CARIVEAU

County Road 20 at Midnight—Fargo, ND

I STARE INTO THE wet darkness, the dim clouds glowing like stretched peach-stained cotton. Fargo is a thin outline beneath the swirl of lowering fog. *Look, Hun,* my husband says, *doesn't it look beautiful out there?* The car slows around the curve. I feel his eyes.

Yeah, I say, *I was just thinking that, like a blurred chalk drawing.* The hospital smell lingers on his clothes, and the blue bandage holds the gauze where they took his blood—looking for enzymes to understand the chest pains that tore us from dinner and into the rain tonight. I'm exhausted. I want him to stop the car so I can capture the night—the glittering of low balls of lights on puddles. The glistening, the blue and green remind me of the stones in the ring he gave me on our first anniversary when we were still only dating. Behind flashing red and white—bright then dim against the clouds, the steady beat mimics the *lub-dub* on the E.K.G. and the other machines too.

The doctor said *lub-dub, that* the *lub-dub* comes before the beat that pushes the blood through the body, and that's what they watch for when they read the jagged lines. *Lub-dub*, bright and dim through tiny beads of rain that cling to the window. I watch lights and silhouettes through streaks of yellow and swirls of orange that turn and bleed onto moving gray clouds against the black canvas. He takes my hand in his, and I continue to stare, trying not to think. *I'm fine*, he says, *I'm here. I'm not going anywhere.*

The Undertow

SADIE MENDENHALL-CARIVEAU

IN THE DESERT, NOTHING beats the feeling of cool water over skin. Though, in temperatures that average over a hundred degrees, nothing stays cool forever. Nothing really stays cool at all. That is unless I count how the very back of the coolers feel after hopscotching through the hot sun from my barely air-conditioned car into the safety of the corner store. I leave their dimly lit rooms, grateful that I need an extra-large bag of ice and a case of cold soda or water, not caring how icy my sweat-soaked clothes feel when they cling to my curves and crevices. More often, I dread leaving the cooler, wishing I could just sit on the neatly stacked cases in the cooler until the sun sets and the temps go lower in the triple digits. Prayers for rain are always on everyone's mind. Still, leave I must and so I do, trying to look like the heat never gets to me.

The air hits me like a blast from the oven, drying up any moisture in my eyes and my mouth. I don't worry about that though. The car is just across the lot at the first pump. The ice and only the ice is on my mind as I race to my car. The sun bounces off the metal accents on the cars, the heat waves moving up through the air and snaking around my skin as I reach for the handle. My hand stings when I yank on the metal, fling the door open, and toss the ice onto the passenger seat. Finally, in my seat, I cringe as my thighs and the back of my knees stick to it. I peel them from the seat and the cycle repeats. That's the joy of the speed at which sweat appears on the surface of my skin here. It's over one hundred degrees and stupid outside of the car. Inside? It's only slightly less stupid as the air conditioning struggles to keep up with heat billowing over the engine that never cooled.

It doesn't matter at this point because now the only thing I can hope for is that the bag of ice survives the trip back home. There, I will pack it into the overcrowded 1990-something freezer after putting a huge handful of it into the largest cup I can find. Call it a driver's tax, or anything really. I just need something to keep whatever liquid I can find cold long enough to replenish the moisture in my mouth.

I slump onto the newish sofa and cradle the cup close as if I can somehow absorb the chill. It's about now when I check the time only to realize that it isn't even noon. No, as luck would have it, the clock reads only eleven in the morning. The morning! That means the day is still young, and I still have the pleasure of going out to the laundry room to quickly switch loads before the washer starts to stink, and the towels are forgotten in the basket of 'To Be Washed' for yet another day.

The damp laundry feels more like warm washcloths from a bath than something that was washed on the cold setting. Cold. There it is again, that one word that evokes longing. The longing for the heat to go away, to feel something other than warm drippy sweat, warm laundry, hot air, dry lips, and dry mouth. The longing to escape the convection oven that is the desert because for all its beauty, from the red rock canyons and tall mountains to the sandstone, shale, and quartz, it is too hot. Too hot for any sensible person to stick around all summer long, trapped in the arid landscape. There's only one thing left to do. I grab one of the few remaining clean towels, fill a water bottle mostly with ice, stuff my bag with a swimsuit, sunscreen, and a book, then I take off to the coldest spot I know in the desert. Surprisingly, it's not the nearest casino or the nearest pool. It's a lake surrounded by some of the hottest rocks I've ever had to drag a cooler over and it's a good distance away. That's okay, though, because I have the same fighting spirit as any West Coast girl raised in the desert.

I make the drive all the way to Lake Mojave, which sits outside of a ghost town once used as a film set. I load up on cold drinks, some snacks, and a lot of ice and water at the last gas station near the state line, the one where people often buy lottery tickets since their state doesn't sell them. From there, I take a left onto a two-lane highway and follow it until it becomes a dusty gravel road. I wave at the caretakers of the frozen-in-time movie set, pausing long enough to watch some startup models and their entourage pose by a wrecked plane and lean in doorways of old wooden buildings. It isn't far now. Just a few miles up the road, around to the right, and then left into a circular ravine.

Were it monsoon season or early to mid-spring, the area would possibly be flooded. I am so close now I can smell the water. I know what wet soil and rocks smell like after living in the desert most of my life. It's an odd earthy smell that almost makes me feel like I can smell the heat. It smells kind of like those saunas people frequent in gyms. I grab the chest cooler and revel in the feel of the cool plastic against my stomach as I make my way over the rocky shore. The pressure of the stones presses into the soles of my feet, and I do what everyone does around here. I pretend that it doesn't matter. The reality is that I feel as though I am walking on Legos. It's the worst sort of foot massage and, occasionally, the point jabs into my arch and I lose my breath and balance. Still, that is possibly the least annoying thing about the ten-minute slant I am hiking down to get to the outlet that I came in search of.

Sunlight reflects upwards and my eyes sting. The same sort of heat tendrils I saw earlier at the corner store are reaching up from the ground. For a moment, I wish I had chosen someplace different, like a cold dark theater, but I shrug it off as the water comes into view.

Lake Mojave is not a clear blue lake like one would expect in other states farther north. No, this is literally just clear. The edge of the water is a little murky from people walking along the softer sands, and there are larger, slippery rocks there. A fine veil of algae skims over some of the rocks where the water is unmoving, left in a sort of tidepool, and it makes a great drinking hole for the myriad of dragonflies and bees in the area. It almost looks like a tan hair net or lace glove that has been left behind. Farther out, there are different river rocks with lines of white quartz and sparkles of mica and other minerals running through them. Between them is clear sand, some shale, and slate stones which are perfect for skipping, or so they appear. These break it up like an unfinished checkerboard.

I set the cooler in moist dirt by a small inlet. This will allow me to grab a drink or snack while I'm in the water. In theory, it will also keep the ice from melting too quickly. With the scorching sun on my back when my ponytail falls forward about my shoulders, I place my keys into the plastic sandwich bag and tuck it inside the chest. Slipping off my now muddy sandals, I place them on the lid of the cooler with my phone. Then I do one of the dumbest things possible, something I warn everyone about when they visit the desert. I know sunblock is important and that it's only a minor protective layer, but the best protection is cloth. Do I listen to the knowledge I spread? Nope. Instead, ignoring the group of college kids doing their rendition of cliff jumping, I take my protective top and pants off to reveal my plain black, open-backed swimsuit. The local box store's special.

I pad slowly into the water, marveling at the cold soft sand that circles the flesh of my feet. It contrasts with the bath-like temperatures of the solar-heated water. As I go deeper into the water, I take it all in, and the cold dissipates into warmth the farther it travels up my body. Finally, I am at a place where I can duck under the clear water and fully soak. I kneel, take a breath, and hold it, then slowly sink below the surface. I stay that way, pushing the length of my body away from where I was standing, then I come up for air. At last, I am not hot. I no longer feel as if the moisture from my body is being dried up by the unforgiving heat. From that point on, I barely drink any water, relying instead on soda, some sports drink, and random bits of ice I crunch on. I only want the cool empty carbs while I sit on the wet rocks near the cooler or swim out until my feet can no longer touch. The water feels like ice closing around my lungs.

It's a strange thing how temperatures of the lakes and rivers in the desert are always so alien. In a pool, or even in the ocean, the temperature is constant, but that's not so here. Here, it's all dependent on the day, the geothermal temperatures of the rocks below the surface, the type of surrounding sand and stone, or even the type below the water. It constantly feels like bathwater in the shallows, but the deeper I get, it changes. Stepping into water in other places, I generally feel the temperature change but it's the same top to bottom. Vertical boundaries mark the various levels of cold I feel. Here, it's a series of what seems like right angles that go forever. It gets colder and darker the deeper beneath the surface I go. That's the horizontal side of it all, whereas the rest of it draws a line down the center of my body, and whichever side is facing the shallows. The sun side is about four degrees or so warmer than the rest.

The weightlessness of deeper waters beckons. I ignore the voices of others who are swimming and playing in their own area of the inlet. I'm not worried about a family enjoying the water on a hot day. The old guys sitting on a small rock ledge with their fishing poles are of little concern. I simply ensure that I avoid their locale so as not to be hooked. Due to the season, it's unlikely that any of the fish would be scared away by swimming or even the splashing and screaming of the children. The cliff-diving college-aged guys wouldn't even be enough to convince the fish to startle and swim away because the food for the marine life is too plentiful here, especially closer to the rocks whose crevices and heat attract insects and contain a small layer of algae.

I continue to swim farther out. Nothing compares to the incredible way the water feels splashing against my neck, my shoulders, and the length of my arms with each stroke. The best part is how the cold feels transitioning along my skin. I turn around and around, remembering my childhood and how I would spin like a ballerina in the pool. That's when I notice him. He looks incredible, standing atop the higher peak of the sandstone ledge. The sun glistens off his tanned, athletic body. I pause my aquatic dance and float in the water, waiting to see if he is going to dive. The more time that passes, the more I wonder if perhaps he is a climber and not a swimmer. I imagine what it would be like to have the strength to free-climb along a rocky cliff.

At some unknown point, I drift farther out, completely relaxed, but the water gets colder. That's when I let my tired legs sink. Righting myself, I try to gauge just how far it is back to the shore. How could I be so stupid? I know better. As someone who grew up in the desert, I know that I need to let someone know when I leave and where I am going. I didn't do that. Instead, I drove to the state line between Nevada and Arizona, to a remote place where cell reception is sketchy at best, and I chose to go swimming in the Colorado River.

Sure, everyone calls it Lake Mojave, but it's not really a lake. It's a river outlet, inlet, runoff, or whatever. I don't know right now. All I know is that my arms are exhausted, and I am kicking with all my might, hoping to get to a point that allows me to stand. To just feel the soft sand beneath my toes would be wonderful.

I continue to chastise myself as I desperately try to keep going, pausing now and then to float, letting my arms float by my side as I continue to kick. I am surrounded by water, my body is sore, my mouth is parched, and I am becoming short of breath.

Earlier in the day, getting to the water and enjoying it was all I could think of. Now, I only want to feel the ground beneath my feet and the dry heat of the sun on my skin once more. It's a vicious cycle of cravings.

The day has been both cruel and kind, but I am unsure which will be triumphant. The unfortunate part is knowing it doesn't matter which wins. It was all surrounded by water. It's water I longed for, water I am surrounded by, and water that I desire to quench my thirst.

A hurried rumble and splashing noises are drawing nearer. My voice is hoarse, a stranger in my own ears, as I call out. My head is barely above water, a bobber that is beginning to fail. My muscles protest when I force my arm up through the surface. I stare up at the contrast of my fingers against the pale blue sky. There is no way to know if I will be seen, or if I will be pushed aside by the waves. My legs are slower now, growing slower still. Their weight begins to tug on me, pulling me under the surface. The water pools in my mouth and I cough. The path for air is barely clear when I once again sink below the surface.

This time, out of necessity for an even deeper need for air, I wave my hand as desperately as I can.

Don't breathe in, don't breathe in.

I chant the new mantra as the waterline creeps higher towards my wrist. The water is colder the farther I sink. Quieter too. The sounds above are muffled to the point of near silence. I strain through burning eyes to see the light above me. I'm no longer able to keep to my mantra. Contractions rip through my torso, forcing me to succumb. Water rushes past my lips and floods my mouth but there isn't strength enough left for it to go any farther.

I am weightless now. Arms floating about me, legs beneath me.

Tired. I'm so tired.

There's a voice. No, several voices. They sound worried, frantic even. I consider asking why, but instead, I close my eyes. The stinging from the water ceases, but the pressure builds.

Suddenly, two sets of arms lift me out of the water. The hot metal siding of the boat grazes my legs just as another set of arms lift me up and over the side. Someone begins compressions. There is a distinct crack.

One rib breaks. Perhaps more. Strange that there is no pain. My head is tilted back, fingers are thrust into my mouth. I want to tell them I wasn't deep enough to have anything stuck in my throat. The thick fingers stop probing my mouth, but it's left gaping open. Plastic covers my mouth. Air is forced into my lungs. The voices grow louder, and the pressure against my ribs begins again.

Dizziness overcomes me as the boat bounds over the water until it skids into the gravel banks along the shoreline. Orders tossed around by stern voices ring out and almost as soon as the boat stops, I'm hoisted up into someone's arms and set on something firm and flat. More orders sound out. Warm, rubber-coated, no, latex-coated fingers press against my neck. My head is once again tilted back, and my mouth pulled ajar, but instead of fingers, a tube is forced down my throat and secured in place. Sticky pads are pressed expertly against my skin moments before a hum turns into a high-pitched whistle. A jolt of electricity sends my body jumping up from what I presume is a stretcher. This macabre dance of convulsions continues with intermittent air being squeezed into me for several more rounds. Then a pause. Silence, save for a long beep that seems to go forever.

My mind wanders and the sounds drift away. I think about the cliff divers and marvel at the luck they had. Everyone in the desert knows that, like heat, there are rules of respect when it comes to water. Just as I don't go anywhere here without taking water, I don't jump straight in. A body can't handle going from one extreme temperature to another. Doing so can create shock, and this is on the news every night here. I avoid flooded roads so as not to be carried away by the undertow, and I never go on an outing without telling someone where I am because the desert can be dangerous. Yet somehow I ended up here, being pulled from the ice-cold, watery depths of the river.

How did I end up here? There's something I can't remember. Why didn't I tell anyone...or did I? I felt the pull of the undertow, but there's no undertow in the outlet called Lake Mojave. Is there? I never felt it before, or it was never this strong or so cold. That's the worst part. I don't remember if I ever felt water this cold. The warmth that should be hitting my skin isn't right. This is all wrong.

There's a sudden elevation of my body, a strange angular one that doesn't make sense. The shores around Lake Mojave are flat. There's a shifting of weight in my body, then an odd sort of numbness. I can't hold on anymore. I want to, but I feel a tugging. The darkness turns to a lucid image, one with trees, green grass, and a steep riverbank. This is not Lake Mojave, but I can't remember where this is.

There is a raft and divers connected to a cable running from one side of the river to the other and even to the ambulance. On both banks, there is fire rescue, first responders, and police. There is a large firetruck on the other side, and a floating dock being let out where the river seems to still after rushing over a myriad of boulders. I try to take everything in. A news reporter on the opposite bank is fussing with his shirt. He even takes the time to check his hair before stepping in front of the camera. The onlookers are pointing and holding their hands over their mouths. A group of college-aged girls is standing near the bank, but their expressions are different. They point and whisper to one another. I see now that they are pointing at my body on the board, being carried up the bank. I see myself. I see them set the board onto the bank.

I somehow move closer to everything. Someone says something in an accent different from my own. I only focus on the accent and what I see. The first responder shakes his head when he is finished looking for vitals. Someone by the river is struggling to help the divers out. I'm horrified as the first responder places a white sheet over my body. It is only minutes later when a black car pulls up and an older man joins everyone. He inspects everything and checks his own watch before writing down the time. He gives a thumbs up and grants permission to the first responders to place me into a long black bag. I want to scream and let them know that I am in the wrong river. I want everyone to know that I am still here, to make them see me, to make them remember me.

The zipper closes and the tugging pulls me away little by little as the bag is loaded into the back of the black car and everyone begins to clean up. I drift further and further away until the darkness overtakes.

Going Under

Sadie Mendenhall-Cariveau

Water causes me to lull with its ebb and flow.
I imagine drifting down deep, deeper still into the milky
depths.
Further and further toward darkness,
all the while looking up through the light-filtered lake.
Running fingers through brown, rubbery river weeds
and soaking in the cold as water fills me, cleanses me.
I drift asleep cradled in soft blankets on the lakebed.
Only the still, quiet floating.
Going under into the silent turbidity.
Closing my eyes, to be present for this moment
of gently rocking, back and forth, until I am one.
No more pain.
Weightlessness.
No more trauma.
Nothingness.
I cease to be and am released.
I am gone.

Since she was a child, Sadie Mendenhall-Cariveau has had a passion for writing. She has won awards, certificates, and scholarships for her essays, short stories, and poetry since sixth grade. After serving in the United States Air Force, she pursued degrees in Creative Writing. She achieved her AA from the College of Southern Nevada and her BA with Honors from Concordia College of Moorhead MN. Her writing has been published in both online and in-print journals, as well as anthologies by the Moorhead Friends Writing Group, *Tales from the Frozen North*, and *Welcome to Effham Falls*. Her goal is to complete her poetry collection, her book, and to never stop writing.

Down by the Riverside

Sarah Adams

The leaves rustled in the trees, indicating that the water should move along towards its destination. Ravens cawed at the sinking sun while beckoning the ascent of nightfall. Humans viewed night as a time for rest and reflection, but it is an unknown concept to night creatures. Deer approached the water's edge for a quick drink and nibbled on the tender grass before disappearing into the wooded shadows. A river otter floated in the water, disrupting the continuous flow of liquid color. Birds landed on the nearby branches to roost for the night as a sense of calm emerged amid the burgeoning darkness.

Shalimar poked her head out from behind a gnarled, old oak tree to watch the fading light as she breathed in the fragrant night air. Red, violet, and orange rays kissed the water. The dappled ripples flowing in the river resembled colorful ribbons floating by. As the darkness overpowered the light, a river of stars began appearing in the Milky Way, twinkling their special magic. Her mounting excitement gained momentum from the fading sun.

Mischief brewed inside her soul when she returned to the cottage she shared with her sisters: Suki and Delilah. The cottage near a small cave was cozy and dry but permeated by the sweet smell of earth and plants. They were nature-loving people living peacefully among the fairy folk and fauna. The nearby townsfolk viewed them as outsiders and labeled them as crones for their eccentric lifestyle.

The mild temperatures and the beautiful, clear sky created a perfect opportunity to explore creative ventures. Shalimar moved past Delilah and headed to the bedroom. She vigorously nudged Suki awake while beckoning her to come outside to enjoy the crisp darkness. Suki glared at Shalimar for disturbing her slumber, but the nudging grew more persistent and forceful the longer she ignored it. "Good grief! Knock it off, Shalimar! Okay, Okay, I'm gettin' up!"

Delilah listened to the growing grumbles from Suki and braced herself for the devilry growing underfoot. Shalimar started digging in the closet connecting the cottage to a small cave, which served as storage for their belongings and foodstuff. She pulled colored sprinkles, wayward glitter, a drum kit, guitars, amplifiers, and a small toy horse with her into the darkness. Delilah grew increasingly suspicious as equipment with cords trailing behind, rocket launchers, light strings, assorted equipment, and toys kept passing her on their way outside to the riverbank.

"Shalimar!" she yelled, her eyes narrowed. "What in blazing sprockets are you planning?"

"Night music. It's a kind of magic, ya know, and that's what we do best," Shalimar mused innocently. "Howling at the moon sounds like an excellent idea also. It's a beautiful thing!"

Suki finished rubbing the sleep from her eyes despite being annoyed by her sister's hyper enthusiasm. Shalimar's plinking of the guitar strings aroused her curiosity. "How are you planning on getting the amps to work? You don't have any electricity."

"Ummmm... We are wonderful, enlightened souls who are extremely creative. There's electricity all around us. We just need to tap into it, my dear sis," Shalimar replied.

Suki helped Shalimar attach a series of large hamster wheels onto a log. Suki ran back to the cottage to locate some old window blinds that she found discarded in the town dumpster. The girls removed the slats and attached them between the spokes of the wheels. After they finished, they launched the log into the river. The log was secured to trees on either side of the bank with bright green and pink jump ropes, and the wheels rotated in unison when the water flowed over them.

The fireflies played among the tall grass and forest shadows as a soft breeze rustled the leaves. The moonlight danced upon the churning ripples from the water wheel, matching the growing hum from the synchronized churning to create electricity for the generator. Shalimar switched on the amplifiers, and they made a loud hum that kept rhythm with the flowing water. The seductive, hypnotic sound encouraged the coyotes to expand their auditory cacophony. The girls smiled at the howling concerto, and it encouraged the potential for a glorious noise.

Shalimar tuned her guitar and waited to see if her sisters would join. Suki grabbed her drumsticks and reluctantly sat behind the drum kit. Delilah studied the arrangement of several large speakers strategically placed for full-sterco sound.

"Shalimar, this array is large enough to wake the sleeping dead," Delilah stated.

"Nah. They'll never notice. The town is too far away. It's only the heavens, the trees, and the creatures of the night who'll notice," Shalimar asserted nonchalantly.

The moonlight's radiance bounced off the toys placed along the riverbank, while an owl hooted its invitation to creatures in the dark forest. A gathering audience with curious eyes peered out from the darkness. The glowing light bulbs on the amplifier grew in power. The water wheels were working perfectly, and the small river flowing over the makeshift rapids provided enough power to generate the necessary electricity.

Delilah suspected that a kind of magic was at play when she switched on her electric piano. The white keys flashed and glowed in the dark, teasing the fireflies when she warmed up her fingers. The sounds steadily rose when the increasing water flow heightened the electrical output. Shalimar cranked the amplifier to full volume. Delilah's eyes narrowed and she nodded at Suki to hit the drums hard. Boom, Boom, thump. Boom, boom, thump. The thunderous noise caused the ground to shake, and the water droplets bounced on the water's surface as they joined the party.

The ravens and owls raised their voices in unison, calling all creatures to join the night's festivities. The beat grew louder and Shalimar smiled widely while playing her guitar. Soon, the fairies tangoed among the toys, allowing them to magically come alive amid the glittering water droplets suspended in mid-air. Stuffed unicorns, teddy bears, dolls, and nutcrackers partied to the night music. The deer, fox, and rabbits drew closer to watch the fun before joining the reverie. Glitter crackers broke open, creating colorful clouds that rained down upon them. The rhythm caused the earth to move from vibrations reflecting joy and life.

Meanwhile, in town, the constable walked in the ever-growing darkness, but he could not determine the originating point of the noise. The shaking ground surprised him, and he looked around for its cause. The town was not located in an earthquake zone. He looked in the well. The water was rising rhythmically with the ground activity. He decided to remain silent about the matter, suspecting that it was only a temporary phenomena. He did not feel a need to worry the town's residents. The light of morning would allow him to further investigate any changes in the landscape.

But the increased shaking of the ground awakened the townspeople from their slumber. The persistent noise aroused farm animals and pets, persuading them to join the concert. Chickens clucked. Roosters crowed. Dogs accompanied the coyotes' howling, and the canid choir sent chills racing down the townspeople's spines. Several people dressed in pajamas or wrapped in shawls poured out of their homes, looking in the direction of the noise and light. One person thought it was unusual for an aurora borealis to be that bright on the horizon, until they realized that it was the wrong direction.

Murmurs in the crowd suggested the presence of the devil or extra-terrestrials seeking to steal their souls. Another thought it was the government hatching an evil plot to eat them. Some wondered if it was a water serpent coming to terrorize them. A child whimpered to its mother that it was Bigfoot tramping through water. In the back of the constable's mind, the idea of Bigfoot would explain the rising water and the shaking earth.

As the song reached its crescendo during the guitar solo, a crow dropped a cinder to light the rocket launcher's fuse. An orange glow inched its way up the cord, foxes and deer watched curiously from across the river in anticipation of the fireworks to begin. Eyes hidden in the forest peered out behind them.

The guitar riff continued building in power, and a maniacal grin appeared on Shalimar's face. Delilah quickly stuffed cotton in her ears, and Suki donned her headphones to drown out the noise. The output from the amplifiers escalated until it reached its loudest note. At the height of the screaming guitar, the rocket launcher and fireworks flew into the heavens.

When the riff slowed slightly, the rocket and the fireworks exploded. Colorful sparkles rained down on them. Popping fireworks dappled the night sky. The Milky Way created a backdrop for the small explosions of blue, red, yellow, and white. The water reflected the colorful outbursts in the heavens, and everyone stopped to see the shimmering show.

The people watched until the light show ceased, and quiet fell upon them. Twilight formed on the southeastern horizon as the townsfolk returned to their homes. The constable continued monitoring the strong water current and elevated levels in the well. Relief grew as the water started to decrease with descending silence.

Suki looked at Shalimar. "That was fun. We need to do this again."

Delilah nodded despite her hesitance to encourage this activity again in the future. The amplifiers whimpered their last notes then blew a fuse, ending their musical endeavors. The animals returned to the woods, and the three crones quickly cleaned up before daybreak.

Later in the day, the constable and two men searched the area where they thought the ruckus originated, but they did not see anything. The soggy, flattened grass, along with random colorful flecks, were the only remnants of the night's mischief. A raven perched on a branch in a nearby tree scowled, laughed, and mocked them.

💧

Sarah Adams lives on the prairies of North Dakota. Drawing on inspiration from nature, genealogy, music, and popular culture, she writes poems, short stories, and is working on her first novel. She has published several poems in local and regional publications. This is her first short story for MFWG. Writing is a kind of magic. One never knows when it will strike.

A Cup of Tea

T.J. FIER

THE YOUNG QUEEN MARGARETTE set out on her best horse with her least favorite lady-in-waiting the morning she decided enough was enough. The time had come to put her house back in order before any more rumors got out of hand. Unfortunately, desperate times called for desperate measures.

"Is this it?" Her Majesty inhaled the peaty, damp rank of the swamp and wrinkled her nose in disgust. The soggy leaf-strewn lane curved around a particularly murky pond. Frogs leaped into its depths, and dark things wriggled beneath the surface. An oak the size of a castle turret stood at its end, a peeling red door built into its trunk.

"Yes, m'lady." The wisp of a lady-in-waiting standing beside Margarette nodded in several trembling jerks, eyes fixed on the ground.

"Yes, what?"

"Yes, Your Majesty—er—I mean, Queen Margarette."

"Yes, I suppose it would be." Margarette gave an exaggerated sigh as she dismounted her mare. Her riding boots sank into the earth. "Uck. Perfect place for an occultist."

"Knock three times." The lady-in-waiting threw nervous glances up and down the swamp's partially submerged path. "As long as you pay her fee, the witch will give you what you seek."

Rose, Margarette's blood bay mare, pinned her ears and blasted a snort into the undulating shadows among the tree boughs. The horse rolled her eyes at the maid, further terrifying the little thing.

"There, there, my darling. This won't take long." Her Majesty cooed and stroked Rose's neck. She threw her reins into the woman's quivering hands. "Hold her."

Margarette's lady-in-waiting opened her mouth to protest, eyes wide as Rose tossed her head and let out another blast from her pink nostrils. The young queen fought back a smirk. Rose would not be happy once her mistress was out of sight.

"That horse is worth more than you, so don't you dare let her go." Margarette hiked up the hem of her skirts, thankful for her tall riding boots as she tromped down the spongey trail toward the witch's abode. Water pooled with each step. Mud sucked at her feet. Several small creatures splashed into the murky water mere inches away, but the young queen held her head high.

The oak trees' roots nearly tripped Her Majesty several times before she reached the crumbling door. She cursed under her breath when the door opened before the young queen could raise her gloved hands. A small woman of uncertain age, wearing a cloak of rags and leaves, peered up at her with eyes as green as the moss covering the unique abode.

"You're late, Your Majesty." The witch pursed her lips and beckoned the queen within.

"Late?" Margarette snorted as she strode into the witch's warm but dim space. "A queen is never late."

A small fireplace made of mud and rock housed a warm, crackling fire. This was the first inviting thing the young queen had seen since she entered the swamp. A rough-hewn table and chair sat beside the fireplace. A moldy curtain hid what must be the witch's bedroom. Shelves holding hundreds of glass containers filled with herbs, insects, earth, and viscous liquids covered the rest of the hollowed tree.

Her Majesty didn't sit when the witch offered her a stool. "I understand you are a woman who can make … certain things happen."

"I can make all sorts of things happen." The witch shrugged and settled beside the short table where a still-smoldering pipe sat in a ceramic bowl. "Need a sleeping potion? A salve to clear warts? A tincture to clean foul breath?"

"Our royal apothecary can produce such things." The young queen rolled her shoulders, still tense from the ride. "I need something … special."

"Such as?"

Margarette cleared her throat. "Make a woman with child … no longer with child."

"Ah, finally getting to the point." The witch's tangled hair nested several wriggling creatures. The young queen caught the flash of a stringy tail. The gleam of a serpent's tongue. The skittering of an insect with thousands of tiny feet.

The witch pointed to a stool. "Sit."

Her Majesty smoothed the front of her cloak. "I'd rather stand."

The witch bent toward Margarette, her luminous skin paler than the moon, and inhaled deeply. She studied the young queen, blue-stained lips pursed. "This is not for you, is it?"

"No, it is not." The young queen lifted her chin. "It's for … another."

"Did your lady's maid get too friendly with one of the grooms?" The witch's eyes glittered as if waiting for the queen to tell the lie.

Margarette's nostrils flared. "Of course not, I would never bother—No, it's for someone trying to undermine me. To steal what is mine."

"Ah." The witch tapped her pointed chin. Her eyes flicked across the shelves and shelves of various concoctions. "Poison is not my specialty."

"No! Not poison!" The young queen slapped the tabletop, red flashing behind her eyes. "There is a woman in my household whose womb is full with a child she does not deserve. A child that should be my own. The nasty little trollop weaseled her way into places she didn't belong and ... and..."

"I understand, Your majesty, say nothing more." The witch turned to her wall of shelves and grasped a thimble-sized bottle between her fingers. A sand-like substance glittered within. "A few grains of this in her tea, and she will miscarry within the day."

Margarette's eyes widened as she took the vial.

"But I must warn you. This is black magic, indeed. If the child is wanted and dies by your actions, your soul will be marred, your spirit fouled for the rest of eternity."

"Then I shall spend the rest of my life making up for it." The young queen shrugged and tucked the vial into a hidden pocket near her breast. "What do I owe you?"

"I will take no payment and dare sully my own self. Think hard. You are still young and have much life yet to lead. Do you want this upon your soul?"

"I have no choice."

"There is always a choice."

The young queen left without another word. Her mare whinnied in relief upon seeing her mistress. The quivering girl gasped in relief when the young queen snatched back her reins.

"Did you get—"

"That's none of your business." The young queen mounted her horse. "Speak of this to no one. Now, let's get the hell out of this awful place."

●

Queen Margarette brewed her favorite tea on a sunny morning while sitting in her salon. She carefully poured two cups of the rich, spicy concoction and sprinkled half the vial into one of the cups.

A knock on the door interrupted her thoughts.

She ran a hand over her gold diadem and called out, "Come in."

The young queen had spent her life with tutors and governesses, learning the graceful arts of being a lady worthy of a king. And yet this woman of no means, no proper breeding, moved and carried herself like a swan among the ducks. Poverty couldn't mark her smooth, white skin, cloud her gleaming green eyes, or flatten the curls of her silky black hair peeking from beneath a mobcap.

Fen, her sister-in-law's lady's maid, walked smoothly as flowing water despite her growing belly. Could the girl never be ugly?

Margarette bit her inner lip to keep from throwing herself upon the beautiful woman and clawing out her eyes.

Fen bowed deep. "You called for me, m'lady?"

The young queen managed a smile. "Come and have a cup of tea with me, Fen."

"Oh, no, I dare not impose. Molly asked me to help with the king's mending—"

"Mending can wait." Margarette's hands curled into fists. "He's out on the hunt for the next fortnight. There's plenty of time for mending."

"Very well, my queen." The maid bowed her head and lowered herself onto the nearest empty chair.

"Here." Her Majesty graciously handed Fen one of the dainty teacups and saucer. "It's my favorite."

Fen inhaled the tea and smiled. "How wonderful."

The young queen sipped her tea, and the maid mirrored the action. A shadow passed over Fen's face for the breadth of a second. Margarette held her breath. It would take more than a small sip to purge the bastard ripening within the maid's belly.

"We've been so grateful for your miraculous work." Margarette continued to sip her tea, hoping the woman would be a gracious guest and follow her liege's actions. "My sister is so very grateful to have you.

She sings nothing but your praises."

"It's my privilege to serve you and your house." Fen took another drink of her tea. "That's such a unique flavor. I don't believe I've had a tea like this before. What is that, that lovely little tingle?"

"Tingle? Ah, that must be the spearmint."

"No, no, it's something else." Fen sipped again. "Something more woodsy. Where did you say it came from?"

"Oh, I save this for special occasions." Margarette couldn't hide the smirk tugging at her lips. This was working better than she expected. Perhaps the maid wasn't as bright as she pretended to be. "A dear friend gave it to me long before you came here."

"A dear friend?" Fen's lips quirked, and she drained her glass. "You know, the last time I tasted something like this was when I was just a little girl. You see, my grandmother was ... was, well, almost a *witch* when it came to tea. She made the most unexpected combinations."

"That so?" The young queen couldn't stop fidgeting. How long would it take for the tea to work its wonders? An hour? A day? She wanted to watch Fen writhe in agony when the baby that should not be was finally gone and out of her life. Margarette would send the maid on her way once the task was complete. Let the striving creature ruin someone else's house.

"Oh!" Fen dropped her hands to her belly. "What a feeling..."

"Whatever do you mean?" The young queen leaned forward, gripping the edge of the table.

The maid shifted in her seat. "A cramp. Just a little pinch."

"Are you ... feeling alright?"

"Yes, I think so." Fen breathed deep, her hands running over her abdomen. She readjusted in her chair several times, soft grunts of discomfort leaving her parted lips as she pressed her palm near the base of her stomach.

"Anything I can do?" Margarette's pulse thrummed in her ears.

"Here, here!" Fen lashed out, grabbing the young queen's hand and shoving it against her round stomach.

"How dare you touch—"

"Can you feel it?"

"Feel what?"

"The beginning of everything."

A flutter moved beneath the young queen's fingers. The bulge of a hand or a foot pressed against her palm. A growing spark of life murmuring, "I'm here. I'm still here."

"Wormwood sugar is notoriously dangerous." Fen shoved the queen's hand away, her cheeks flushed and eyes blazing. "Causes miscarriage. Paralysis. Sometimes death. Except for those who have been drinking it their whole lives. It gives us strength."

"What are you talking about?"

"How is my grandmother doing? I haven't seen her in over a year. She must be so lonely out there with only the frogs, snakes, and miserable, desperate women to keep her company."

"Grandmother?"

"And soon I shall return to her, my daughter in my arms—a child of old power and new. The one to bring in the next era."

"I don't...I don't..."

"Stop sputtering, you silly thing." The maid's voice deepened, filled with a preternatural richness. "I had planned to leave anyway. I got what I wanted from your husband and tire of this charade. I only stayed because the cook makes the loveliest broth when my stomach needs settling. Well, all good things must come to an end, I suppose."

The young queen's hands flitted about her. "How—""

"This was foreseen." Fen fixed Margarette with eyes the same color as the swamp witch. "There was nothing you could do to stop me. And your lascivious husband made it all too easy. However, this," —the maid tapped her teacup—"was unexpected. I applaud your ... dedication, but you should have heeded my grandmother's warning."

Margarette paled, knotting her fingers together, but said nothing.

"You live in the new ways of manipulation and ambition, cutting down your enemies without seeing the marks it leaves on your soul. Even though your attempt to harm me and my child was folly, it doesn't wipe away your sin."

"Sin?" The young queen spoke barely above a whisper.

"The harm you bring upon others will visit you three-fold. You will never bear a child for the king or any man. Your king will continue to rut around with other maids, ladies-in-waiting, and the occasional prostitute. His bastards will fill this castle, and you will recognize the pale blue of the king's eyes throughout the city."

"No!" The young queen spat, rising from her chair. Her sudden movement upset the table, sending cups and saucers shattering upon the stone floor.

"Yes." Fen smoothly rose from her seat, surveying the mess with sparkling eyes. "And you can only blame yourself. If you had left me alone to go on my way, you would have been blessed with many, many heirs." She bowed her head. "I shall take my leave now. You will never see me again."

The young queen clutched her throat as Fen strode from the salon and met a kitchen maid at the room's entrance. The small woman paid Fen no attention as she hurried into the room with a tray and a rag.

"I'll have this mess cleaned up right away, Your Majesty," the kitchen wench muttered, her red, cracked hands gathering the broken teacups and mopping up the spilt tea.

The young queen turned and walked to the window. Thick clouds gathered in the sky to the west. She shoved away the dark thoughts spinning through her head and clutched her narrow waist.

What did a swamp witch and her wretched granddaughter know? She was a queen. And not even her blackened soul would stand in her way of having everything.

♦

T.J. Fier's short stories appear in numerous anthologies, including but not limited to *Welcome to Effham Falls, Seasons in the Dark, Tales From the Frozen North, The Colour Out of Deathlehem,* and *Nothing Short of Horror.* Three Little Sister Publishing released her debut novel, *The Bright One,* in December 2022. By day, T.J. is an associate professor of set design, a professional scenic artist, and a freelance set designer for theatre.

Unsettled Heart

Silvia Villalobos

With the Pacific Ocean before her, the cool afternoon air kissed Carmen hello. She stepped onto the sand, absorbing the salt-tinged breeze that tousled her hair.

They always met by the water, where the endless ocean touched the sky, because Mira would not allow weaseling out. She'd push and pout and plead until Carmen rearranged her life to be here, where worries vanished, once a month.

The surf pounded against Carmen's legs, leaving a sticky film of salt on her skin. She'd arrived early to let her mind wander. Ten years ago, in senior year, Mira had talked their group into skipping classes and driving from L.A. to Ventura Beach for a Peter Gabriel concert. The same weekend Rey came along. Rey, a whirlwind of passion Carmen couldn't keep up with that summer. Who knew where they'd be today if things played out differently—sinking beneath the waves or riding the current?

The gentle breeze caressed Carmen's skin like a whisper from days gone by. She tore herself away from its comfort and navigated the sand, her feet sinking into the soft surface. No use revisiting the past, but peeling herself away from it was like trying to unravel a tightly wound ball of yarn with no end in sight. Better cut through the entanglement and be done.

Mira sat waiting on the sand, steps from the painted rocks balanced into a triangle with a summit of pebbles. Story had it a homeless man would paint and arrange the rocks into a unique work of art. When the high tide knocked them over, he came to rearrange them during low tide. A symbolic dance between the ocean's chaos and the enduring message of peace. That was Mira's favorite spot.

For a while, they sat and chewed over the same old topics—dream jobs that were anything but dreamy, losing their hearts to gorgeous hunks who turned out to be bores, life moving too fast.

The ocean made talking easy. It saved them from having to look at each other, with the vast expanse of water right there, a natural mediator between words and emotions. Easy letting gazes and thoughts wander far and wide.

Then Mira threw out the question. "Was there a phone call?"

Sand found its way into Carmen's mouth. She clenched her teeth and took a moment. "Brief texts. Just 'hey' ping-pongs."

"Hell of a thing for Rey to do," Mira said. "Write a letter and hide it in a book. Could've been your grandkids finding that letter fifty years from now."

Carmen's recent move, all the cleaning and packing, brought to light what might have remained forever hidden. Rey's letter to her from ten years ago. But he hadn't hidden the letter; he'd slipped it between the pages of *The Age of Innocence*. Carmen's incessant talk about the book must've rendered it her singular corner of solace. A sure place to find the letter. Except that it was a well-thumbed and memorized book, no longer a refuge but admired from a distance.

"People are strange, aren't they?"

Carmen shook her head, more to Mira's tone than her curiosity. "Or romantic."

"He could've dropped stronger clues."

Carmen may have been blind to all the clues. Blind to everything after her mother's passing that year. Too wrapped up in calling herself an orphan. Too lost in the maze of her own emotions.

There wasn't much Mira agreed with, ever. A miracle their friendship remained steadfast despite their different ways of looking at life. "A testament to your chill, Carmen," Mira said on the odd day.

A testament to their long bond, really. Their friendship went back to high school when Carmen, a late arrival, had joined the Social Justice Club, the only one still taking members. She counted the membership and found that it consisted of four, but Mira had scared the other three away when they skipped a social justice march. Fine with Carmen. They were to write letters and raise awareness about environmental concerns and poverty. The school shied away from deeper social issues.

Kids gave Mira a wide berth in school. She was touchy and exploded more times than Carmen could count, bombarding girls with swear words and snide remarks for staring at her. Most girls steered clear of her, like she was radioactive. Carmen's hunch was boys were baffled by Mira or she scared them off. With Carmen, it was different. Maybe because they were the only real members of their club, but mostly because Carmen had never judged Mira. Their friendship evolved over writing letters about world struggles and eating Doritos Chips straight out of the bag.

"People are an enigma," Mira said against the roar of the waves.

Or as uncomplicated as their fragile hearts.

When Carmen's father had passed, Mira found Carmen sitting on the old swing in front of the neglected theater on the edge of town. Mira sat with her, just a comforting presence. Then there was Mira again, sitting with Carmen in the schoolyard amidst the sea of indifferent faces. Her caring was a wild faith, an impulse seizing Carmen's throat. There were no words. There was only the extent of the outstretched hand, the shoulder to cry on.

The following year, Mira had found a box in the attic with pictures of a birth mother she'd never known existed. That day, they sat on the old swing in silence for hours.

Mira had grown into somewhat of a bossy-boots since. "Because control is something I've never had," she'd said, "my life at the whims of others."

Control—a concept so human, the mocking laughter of the ocean would resonate, if able. Meanwhile, seagulls glided overhead, their cry carrying in the distance. The perfect backdrop for small talk, but Mira didn't do small talk.

"Rey is probably a different man now," Mira said. "Ten years is a long time."

"Not when you consider an entire human lifespan."

"What if he's a recluse? Or a nomad, struggling to find inner peace in a world void of activism."

"Nothing wrong with either."

Mira shot Carmen the look only she could—raised eyebrows, tight lips, in the corner of her mouth, the hint of a smile.

"What if he's a sexual healer? They're said to elevate pleasure to unimaginable levels." Mira elbowed Carmen, her faint smile now an ear-to-ear grin.

Their laughter mingled with the cry of seagulls. "Gosh, it's been a long time," Mira said, her voice nostalgic. "But I'll admit. That was one hell of a summer."

The summer of Peter Gabriel, they drank beer that seemed to evaporate through their pores into the heat, swam in the ocean, and watched Rey surf ten-foot waves with a gaggle of surfers. They'd all paddle out with the determination of seasoned daredevils and ride the swelling forces over and over. She'd strain to follow Rey's moves as he disappeared into the waves, only to reemerge triumphant moments later, his fist pumped, his laughter echoing along the shoreline.

When done surfing, Rey would sing and ask everyone to dance. No one in their group took Rey seriously about his singing, but everyone took him up on his offer to dance. Because Rey could dance. Not just make the right steps at the right time, but he could float. He could defy gravity. He danced and sang anything and anytime. He knew how to engage and how to love.

"Life is all about risks," he'd say, "and what's riskier than love?"

Rey's warmth knew no bounds, burning a blaze of intensity in Carmen's life. That year, more often than not, she felt like a stranger to herself. She'd wanted to wallow in self-pity while he exploded with life, leaving Carmen searching for a cool respite.

She'd craved his attention, but from a distance—a hunger for something Carmen couldn't quite name, for she was in search of a missing piece of her soul.

"Adoration without commitment is the slow poison that kills," Rey had written in his letter. He'd put the letter in the old book on Carmen's shelf and walked out of her life.

◆

Beneath the blue sky, the ocean stretched, undulating, filling Carmen's view, falling off at the horizon's edge. Surfers carved through waves in solitude, moving with determination, their silhouettes etched against the sky. A rush of memories hit her like a gust of wind. Each ride out there was an escape from the world, where the only rhythm that mattered was the one set by the ocean waves. Carmen envied the surfers that absolute sense of freedom.

"Are you curious about Rey?" Mira asked.

"A little, about the chapters of his life he's written so far."

Mira scrunched up her face. "I'm not curious," she said. "I've read that some birth mothers don't want to be found. Why would they, if giving up the baby was the better option?"

"You don't know what happened thirty-four years ago."

"Just like I didn't know something was different all that time? My adoptive parents are tall with thick, long hair. In photographs, they loomed over the small, thin hair me."

"Our brains disregard what's obvious to protect us from pain," Carmen heard herself say.

Like she'd done with Rey, casting aside his wishes. Or like how he'd disregarded her pain.

Carmen shook her head, banishing the debilitating thoughts. The past had already unfolded. The present and future were all they had.

Waves crashed against the shoreline, resonating with energy in a tempo shift, the earlier whisper now an assertive murmur from the deep. The ocean sure moved as if attuned to the constant struggles of the human heart, speaking by coming closer, cool and calm, or furious at times.

"Not knowing is fine with me," Mira said, her gaze fixed on the water. Then in a barely audible voice. "In fact, it makes me happy."

Mira challenged the perception of happiness, running away from joy, searching for a hidden truth about what it meant to be content. As if joy was a challenge, an ocean to cross without ever reaching the other side. Maybe that was the real reason they'd remained friends, two souls in constant conflict with themselves, like the ebb and flow of the tide.

"I hate to say this." Mira snapped back into the moment. "Rey had what I would call a rose-color illusion about life."

"Who's not dropping clues now?"

"Excessively optimistic to the point of delusional."

"He had no balance, you mean."

"His approach to life was charming but laughable."

And so Mira kept banging on about it like she was hammering a wobbly nail into a particularly stubborn wall. Going on about Rey's idealistic ways and impractical nature. Much easier dissecting someone else's problems, and, for Mira, a convenient distraction from the chaos within.

Carmen looked out into the ocean at memories revealing themselves piece by piece—being so close to love, getting scared, and pulling back. They crashed upon her, all those memories, bringing it all back too fast. She rose to her feet, not ready for introspection, and waded into the ocean to wash sand off her legs. She'd never seen such sticky sand before. It clung like flour. In her clothes and in her hair and to her skin. She washed and washed, and grains still clung.

◆

The second night, as Peter Gabriel sang, they all knocked back Rebel Ales, danced with abandon, and sang like carefree spirits unburdened by the weight of the world, their hearts light.

After the concert, they stumbled onto the beach, where the moonlight painted a silvery path on the water. They kicked off their shoes and felt the cool sand beneath their feet. The movement of the waves spoke in a language deliberate in its cadence. Carmen could feel it between her toes. *Come closer, child. The water awaits.*

There was laughter—so much laughter that it seemed to meld with the sound of the waves. The music and alcohol had lifted the tension off Carmen's shoulders that night.

The whole group ran into the ocean, then back out. Over and over. Then they all went for a proper swim. Splashed and swam and sang. The water was razor-sharp cold, but Carmen didn't care. It washed over the pain of having lost her mother, and the old and duller pain of having lost her father. It washed over Carmen like a cleanser of the soul, the colder the better.

Eventually, everyone swam ashore, except for Carmen and Rey. They chased each other through the water and laughed as if life had granted them sudden freedom. They jumped through the waves until she ended up in his arms, his mouth to her ear.

"Marry me," he'd said.

The swim to the shore was long, and no one spoke. On the way home, Carmen lay across the back seat, watching the stars through the roof-top window as Mira drove. She fell asleep and dreamed her parents were singing in front of her. But when she woke, the car radio was playing Peter Gabriel's *Tell Me the Truth, You Got Nothing to Fear.*

The world fell apart that summer.

◦

Carmen sat back on the blanket. One wave washed close to the rock triangle but didn't touch it yet. More waves kept coming ashore, swirling, retreating, then crushing again.

"I dreamed I was stuck on the second syllable of my haiku about discarded baby elephants," Mira said. "And I don't even write haiku."

The hurt within always had a way of creeping into our words. It was like a wounded specter, a ghostly presence that refused to be ignored.

"Your subconscious, telling you something," Carmen said.

Mira had been concealing her fear of rejection any way she could. It had been her mantra for the past two decades, since finding her birth mother's picture, her way of coping. She'd lived as a supporting character in someone else's story. Not an easy discovery. Once she'd learned the truth, Mira had conjured up every reason not to investigate further. How would she endure the weight of a snub, carry it through the rest of her life? How could anyone?

"Some nights, I lie back and close my eyes," Mira said. "I think about light and the speed of light. I think about black holes, and how there is no right-side up or upside-down in outer space, there is no sound on the moon. I think about everything, except what I would say to the woman in that picture whose dark eyes mirror my own."

Carmen hugged her knees to her chest, pondering what she might say to Rey.

It's been ten years … where do I even begin? Wondering what might have been, or maybe, what was never meant to be.

The water picked up steam, its waves gaining momentum as they surged toward the shore. They would engulf the rock triangle soon, but it would take some doing to knock it over. Carmen wondered if the man in search of Zen was watching from a hidden spot, waiting for the breach, then for the calm. Anticipating both chaos and serenity.

"We're part of a demographic, you know?" Carmen said. "Women in their thirties, split in two. I wouldn't say shattered. We're not in pieces across the floor. It's more like fractured, I would say, like cracked."

Mira snapped open her eyes. "What's the name given this demographic? Thirty-something wanderers?"

"The nostalgia-prone pals."

A quick laugh passed between them, a wordless connection of bittersweet joy.

"I remember that night, between me and Rey," Carmen said. "The long swim to the shore. How we didn't talk much after because I resented his moving so fast on my pain, and I was scared. How within days he was gone again, that time for good. How I spent too much time wondering what if. But I was split in two that summer. Shattered. Fractured, cracked. I wanted to spend time feeling sorry for myself. Joy was too much to bear. Too offensive a concept."

A wave fizzled past the rocks and reached their feet, washing over like an unexpected embrace from the ocean. The cool, foamy fingers of the water caressed Carmen's skin. A fleeting connection to the vast world.

"You're going to call him, aren't you?" Mira asked.

For once, Carmen wished the ocean could answer for her. All that power out there, capable of touching places she couldn't phantom, altering the essence of the shore and sculpting the coastline over millennia. Why couldn't its current read minds and shape the contour of answers with simple yesses or noes? Save humans from their internal dilemma.

"I know one thing," Mira said, looking up at the sky. "The universe is still expanding, and maybe that means there is always room for new beginnings. For finding the missing pieces of our stories and putting them together."

Carmen clapped. "Optimism. That's new, and it suits you."

"I once tried to explain these things in detail to my parents. You know what I got back?"

"A 'we raised a smart one, honey'?"

"Got a text with a phone number and a message that read, 'She can be reached here.'"

"You've had your birth mother's phone number all this time?"

A subtle nod and a fleeting glance.

They sat in silence for a good five minutes, each with their own thoughts. Just the two of them, the artsy rock triangle, and the waves. Everyone else had left.

"What would you ask her?" Carmen faced Mira.

"Aside from why choose adoption, just one thing: Has she thought about me all these years?"

The chill in the air arrived abruptly, cutting through the coastal air. Ready to chase them off the beach.

"What would you ask Rey? Aside from chapters of his life he's written so far."

"About chapters of his life that remain unwritten. What would he write in them?"

The words spilled out of Carmen before she could grasp them. Was she eager to join Rey's unwritten chapters or merely curious about the story's course? She couldn't say for sure.

"Does anyone really know that?"

Carmen let out a long sigh. "Not know but imagine." She reached into her pocket and squeezed the phone as if ready to break it. A call held the answers.

The moment passed, spilling out onto the sand, onto the beach, into the ocean. Like all the times before, she and Mira wrung every ounce of feeling from every evening spent at Ventura Beach.

Still, the inner debate raged within Carmen, so many questions. To call or not to call?

She looked out at the water and struck a deal with the ocean. If the next wave reached her feet, Carmen would make her phone call and convince Mira to make hers. Carmen's gaze locked on the horizon. Her heart quickened as the ocean inched nearer. The wave surged forth with anticipation, closer and closer, yet at the brink of touch, it receded just as fast.

In the distance, another wave formed, coming with more promise.

If it reaches the artsy rock triangle, this time.

The wave died out before it touched the shore, dissipating into ripples. A fleeting ache, teetering between regret and relief, settled in Carmen's heart.

All right. The ocean had spoken. No phone calls.

Mira stood and helped Carmen up. They'd do this again next month and the month after, two old friends, here for each other's pain and joy, only to return to a relentless cycle of news stories about world conflicts, buyouts or selling shorts, then make dinner and buy wine.

As they waded through the sand, Mira began humming to herself. Carmen picked up the tune to Peter Gabriel's *Washing of the Water* and bobbed along in time with the music, singing loudly. Shamelessly.

Before they stepped off the sand, Carmen sneaked one last look at the waves, now piled onto the shore, knocking over the rock triangle and washing over the very spot where they sat a minute ago.

A delayed answer to her call or do-not-call question?

Swept up in the moment, Carmen allowed herself a smile. Considering the ocean's whispers was like entering a cool current and flowing through the warm water. She lingered there for a second while Mira sang.

Thank you for changing your answer to my question, or giving me that illusion.

Illusions were often necessary daily companions.

Carmen picked up the tune again, singing alongside Mira like countless times before.

Slowly, the singing lowered to a hum, growing quieter. The last chorus dissipated into the evening, until Carmen could hear the street traffic. She considered applauding, but the silence was so comforting she couldn't help but leave it to bloom.

Their days were always their own. Other friends came and went, some giving them a chance to say goodbye, some simply disappearing without a word. Like Rey, who'd left the scene before Carmen could recognize the changes in his eyes, putting his words down on paper rather than face-to-face. The way his posture had shifted over the last few days together, more erect and contained. She should have recognized the signs but read about it all instead.

A symphony of moments, he'd written about their time together. *A melody of shared affection without striking the final chord.* The finality of it hadn't immediately registered, as Rey would often take off for days, then reappear, until he'd left for good, his exit an inevitability in retrospect.

Now, Mira's breath caught in a sob. Carmen wrapped her arm around her friend and told her not to speak, that it didn't matter right now, that crying was just fine. She should cry.

There was much that Carmen feared in matters of the heart, and many ways she could fail herself and everyone around her. Love scared her with its paradox of longing and fear of getting hurt. She'd turn life into a cocoon to shield herself from love, but for how long? In and out of her mind, Rey still felt close, yet miles and miles away. A world apart. Should she emerge out of her cocoon now, delay it for later, remain forever hidden?

She reached inside her pocket and caressed the phone keys with her fingertips. Embracing love of any kind was risky, but maybe not as dangerous as giving up. And maybe that was love. Being vulnerable and allowing someone in so they could hurt you, but it could also open the door for them to give you everything.

♦

Silvia Villalobos lives immersed in the laid-back vibe of Southern California. She writes mystery novels and short stories. Her debut novel, *Stranger or Friend*, published by Solstice Publishing in 2015, was recently followed by her latest novel, *The Year of Secrets*. Her short stories have appeared in *The Riding Light Review* and *Red Fez*, among other publications.

Written in the Coffee Grounds

Sarah Nour

"Excuse me, can I get my fortune told?"

I looked up from the table I was wiping. A white girl in her late teens, slightly younger than me, sat nearby, holding out her coffee cup to show me it was empty.

I cast a brief glance around Bayt Alqahwah. We had just hit our summer afternoon lull, so there were only two other customers in the shop. My brother Ziad, who was working the front counter that day, was idly playing on his phone. Meanwhile, my sister Tasneem had been walking around with a full *dallah*, refilling coffee cups. She had stopped to chat with an old woman at another table. Neither of them needed my assistance, so I stuffed my rag into one of my apron pockets.

"Yes, of course," I said to the girl, taking a seat at her table. "Just let me have your cup and saucer."

She pushed the items across the table to me. Bayt Alqahwah was far from being the only Middle Eastern-themed coffee shop in Dearborn, but it was the only one that provided fortune readings. My siblings and I were well-trained in the ancient art of tasseography.

"Now I know why your cups are so small. That's the strongest coffee I ever had, and with the cinnamon and the cardamom you put in, it just tastes so good!" The girl babbled on in a caffeinated rush, her words running together. This was a common occurrence among customers who didn't understand our cup-size-to-caffeine ratio. "I'm not really used to that much caffeine all at once, you know, I've only ever had cappuccinos—I like the foamy milk at the top, and there's another coffee shop just down this block—"

While she went on, I swirled the cup's remaining contents from right to left. Then I placed the saucer on top of the cup and turned them upside down back onto the table.

The girl stopped talking just long enough for me to say, "We need to let it sit for a few minutes, so the coffee has time to drain."

It was a ritual I knew well, not only from my years spent telling fortunes but also from watching my parents and elder relatives perform the art. I'd started working at Bayt Alqahwah when I was fourteen. Now, six years later, I was managing the family business while my parents were away, with my siblings and cousins to pick up the slack whenever my classes at Henry Ford took priority.

The girl looked at my nametag. "Rhonda? Am I saying that right?"

"Randa."

"Oh, that's pretty. Arabic, right?"

"*Na'am*. That means yes."

The girl clasped her hands together in delight. "My name's Megan, and I love that your menu's in two different languages. I don't know Arabic, but it looks so pretty, like cursive letters! By the way, is it true that the name of this place is just House of Coffee in Arabic?"

I laughed. "*Na'am*. I know it's not that creative—"

"Oh no, I think it's great! It fits. You know, my friend Mateo told me about this Mexican place where the menu's in both English and Spanish, so I went there a few weeks ago and—"

My smiling and nodding were not insincere. The elder sibling in me found her babbling endearing. Normally, while waiting for the coffee to drain, I made conversation with customers by bragging that my talented sister painted all the landscape art displayed on the shop's walls. Tasneem's acrylic pieces included the snow-capped mountains of Lebanon, the sand dunes and rock formations of Jordan, and Elephant Rock in Saudi Arabia. But I didn't mind letting Megan talk. Customers appreciated being listened to.

When enough time passed for the coffee to drain, I turned the cup over and studied the patterns left by the thick, brown residue. Megan suddenly stopped talking, possibly assuming I needed quiet while I studied the patterns. I tried not to let the concern show on my face when I saw the broken circle around the coffee rim. It was probably best not to mention that first.

"See this vertical line here? It represents your goals, and it's thick and dark, which is a good sign."

"Oh, that makes sense!" Megan said. "I chose my college recently. I'm going to U-Mich in the fall, you know, the one in Ann Arbor? A lot of my friends are going there and, did you know, like, ten Nobel Prize winners went there too?"

"Sounds like a good choice. I have a few cousins who go to U-Mich."

I took another moment to study the patterns. A cross shape on the upper left side of the cup caught my attention. More toward the middle, there was a ladder shape near the rim. A kite with a long tail sat on the right, leading down to what looked like the number four etched into the residue. None of it looked too promising.

"See the ladder right here?" I said. "That means you're going to travel soon."

"Oh, yes! I'm going to Belle Isle Beach next week with a few friends. Thought I'd get in one last beach day before the summer ends, you know? It's going to be so much fun."

The hairs on the back of my neck stood up. I recalled recent news reports of disappearances at Belle Isle, specifically at the beach, but I knew that wasn't the only reason for my uneasiness. I'd been taught from an early age to trust my instincts, as I wasn't just a fortune teller. I was a *sahira*.

The word translated to witch, sorceress, or enchantress in English. But despite growing up speaking equal parts Arabic and English, *sahira* was always the word we used, even though my father, brother, and other male relatives were technically *sahir*. No other word felt right.

The abilities I'd had since birth, which I had honed throughout my twenty years of life, told me it was time to put them to use. I fixed my eyes on the bottom of the cup and channeled my magic toward the coffee grounds.

The patterns moved, forming images only I could see, as vivid as if I was there. Water rushing over a sandy shore. Megan in a bathing suit, running into the surf and swimming into deeper water.

Megan pulled under by black-gloved hands.

A scuba diver holding her underwater, one arm around her neck, the other around her torso.

Megan thrashing and struggling, air bubbles spewing from her mouth. Her movements slowing, eyes glazing over. Her body going limp in the diver's arms.

"Girl, you okay?" Megan's voice cut through my reverie. "You look like you're about to pass out."

I blinked several times, dissolving the vision, and clumsily placed the cup back on its saucer, using both hands to steady it. I swallowed and cleared my throat before looking back up at Megan.

"Don't go." My voice came out hoarse.

"What?"

I cleared my throat again. "Don't go to Belle Isle. It's not safe."

Megan's eyes widened. "Do you mean...?" She glanced around the shop before leaning in to whisper. "Those girls that went missing?"

I nodded.

"Is that going to happen to me?"

"Not if you don't go."

Megan's face paled, all traces of her caffeine-fueled exuberance seeming to disappear. "I'll—I'll go somewhere else. Let me just..." She picked up her phone. "I'll text my friends, let them know there's a change of plans."

As I stood up to leave, still holding onto the table for balance, Megan paused her texting and placed her hand over mine. "Thank you. I mean it. Thank you."

I nodded. "I'll clean up your table, don't worry about that."

I picked up her cup, saucer, and stirring spoon and made my way to the front counter, walking past Tasneem, who had sat down to read another customer's fortune. Hopefully, that one wouldn't be anything disturbing.

Once I was behind the counter, I set the dishware into the bin marked for dirty dishes, then knelt to open the minifridge we kept back there. I pulled out a bottle of water and sat on the floor, knees drawn up, with my back to the pastry display case. I swallowed a few mouthfuls before I realized Ziad was eyeing me with concern.

"*Shuu fi?*" he asked.

Ziad was eighteen but looked older, due to what he jokingly called his "terrorist beard." Two years prior, when our parents expressed concern about him growing it out, he responded, "Hey, I need something to take the focus off my nose. Have you seen the size of this thing?" This turned the conversation into a parental lecture about embracing our Middle Eastern features, which got Ziad off the hook about his beard. Though I shared my parents' concerns about him being a target for racism, I had to admit the beard suited him.

I took a deep breath, unclenched my fingers from around my water bottle, and motioned for Ziad to come closer before whispering, "I just saved a girl from being murdered at Belle Isle Beach."

Ziad's eyes widened. He knelt beside me and seemed to take a moment to absorb what I'd told him. Finally, he said, "That must have been intense. You okay?"

I took another swig of water, my nerves starting to settle. "I should be okay."

"You need a break? Take the rest of the day off?"

"I'm fine. Just give me a few minutes."

Ziad stayed kneeling beside me in silence. The soft murmurings of the coffee shop became a calming sort of white noise. I finished my water, stood slowly, and stretched my legs. Ziad got up too, leaned against the counter, and folded his arms.

"You want to talk about it?" he asked.

I fiddled with the lid of the water bottle while describing my vision to Ziad in a hushed tone, watching his face darken with uncharacteristic seriousness. I added, "I also saw the number four in her cup. I think it meant she would be the fourth victim."

"So that's what's been going on. The disappearances, I mean." He paused a moment. "You didn't see the killer's face?"

"If I did, I'd be hunting him down."

He smirked at this. "You know we don't operate that way."

I sighed in exasperation. "I don't mean killing him, Ziad."

"Hey, you're always lecturing me about the rules. Let me lecture you for a change."

That was fair, though I certainly wouldn't admit this to my smug brother. We stood at the counter while Ziad stroked his beard in contemplation.

"This is a gruesome question, but don't dead bodies float? Something about gas buildup when they start decomposing?"

I shrugged. "Ask Nadine. I'm sure she'd know."

I'd never expected that our cousin Nadine's morbid interests in true-crime podcasts and serial killer documentaries would be potentially useful.

"I'm just wondering why no one has found them yet."

"Could be any number of reasons."

Tasneem finished her own fortune reading, bid the customer goodbye, and joined Ziad and me behind the counter. She was a petite sixteen-year-old with large brown eyes and wavy brown hair, which contrasted with my own straight black hair. I'd been protective of her since her birth, gifting her all manner of defensive charms and amulets for every birthday, hence the hamsa pendant she wore. She rolled her eyes whenever I called her *binti*—my girl—though whenever I denied her anything, she was quick to pout and say, "I thought I was *binti*."

"That woman wanted lottery numbers," Tasneem told us with some amusement as she dispensed of the customer's dishware. "I told her it doesn't work that way."

Ziad shrugged. "Hypothetically it could."

"But we shouldn't," I said firmly, fully prepared to go into lecturer mode to distract myself from my disturbing vision. Using our abilities for monetary gain—whether for us or for others—went against the *sahira* doctrines our parents drilled into us.

"That's why I said 'hypothetically,' *ya hemara*."

Tasneem giggled at this insult as I mimed throwing my water bottle at Ziad's head. I turned away to conceal my amused grin and went to toss the bottle into our recycling bin. Hopefully, the rest of the day would be uneventful. I would take the boredom of the summer afternoon lull over visions of murder any day.

♦

Our last customer arrived only twenty minutes before closing time. Ziad was out on his break, Tasneem was washing dishes in the kitchen, and

I was placing chairs on top of the tables. When the man entered, I abandoned my chair duty and returned to the counter, hoping he'd take his order to go.

"Good evening, sir. What can I get for you?"

He looked ordinary, with a slender build and a blond combover. He wore a suit and carried a heavy-looking plastic shopping bag with both arms. I recognized the logo of a local sporting goods shop on the bag. Oddly, his shirt was buttoned tight halfway up his neck, when most men would leave at least one button undone. The buttons straining against his chest told me the shirt was too small for him. I could even spot a few chest hairs poking out between them. He couldn't have been comfortable.

The man slammed his bag noisily on the counter, startling me. "Whew, sorry about that, little lady," he said, offering a toothy grin. "Just had to set the darn thing down, you know? Anyway, I've heard good things about this place, and I thought, wouldn't this be the perfect day to give it a go?"

He rested his elbow on the counter beside his bag, collar buttons straining against his Adam's Apple. His raised eyebrow bordered on flirtation. My skin crawled. It didn't take *sahira* intuition to know this guy was no good.

"So, little miss, tell me something. Is it true you tell fortunes here? Are you a little fortune teller, huh?"

It took all my effort not to scowl at his condescension. "Yes, but you need to order coffee first. We read fortunes in leftover coffee grounds at the bottom of the cups. It's called tasseography."

"Ah, so that's how it works, eh?" His eyes flicked to the menu on the wall above me. "In that case, I'll take a small cup of black coffee, light roast."

He retrieved his card from his wallet. Just before swiping it through the card reader, he said in a lowered voice, as though confiding a secret,

"And when I say small, I mean the smallest cup you've got. I know your people like your coffee strong."

Your people?

To make matters worse, he winked.

"Pick a table. I'll bring your order when it's ready."

I hoped my tone conveyed just how much I wanted to kick him where it hurt. Apparently not, because he swiftly pulled out a business card.

"Here you go, little miss. As a token of my appreciation."

When I made no move to take the card, he dropped it on the counter and hoisted his bag away. He placed it under his table of choice and took a seat.

I spared the card a brief glance. Jonathan Dylan Hansen. The guy was a banker. No surprise there.

Luckily, we still had some warm coffee, so preparing his order took no time at all. I avoided eye contact when I brought him his coffee, nodded at his thanks, then resumed my end-of-workday chores. Once the chairs were out of the way, save for the one Hansen sat on, I swept the floor, not even glancing in his direction. He made no attempt to speak to me again. Maybe he had taken my hint.

I retreated to the back storage closet to retrieve the mop and bucket. Upon getting back to the shop, I stopped in my tracks, jostling the bucket and spilling a bit of water.

Tasneem, now finished with her kitchen duty, had pulled up a chair across from Hansen. He was chatting animatedly while she swirled the remaining coffee in his cup.

I deliberately made as much noise as possible, bumping the bucket against several table legs and allowing water to slosh onto the tiles. I willed Hansen to meet my eyes so he could read my silent warning. *Touch my sister and I'll kill you.*

Neither of them looked up, much to my irritation. Tasneem didn't have the instincts I had. She was still young and too friendly to distrust others. And was it my imagination or were Hansen's eyes on her neck? Was he looking at her pendant? Or did he have some kind of fetish? In times like this, I wanted to encase Tasneem in bubble wrap to keep her safe.

I noisily dunked the mop into the bucket and wrung it out just enough to ensure it made a slapping sound when it hit the floor. My mopping was sloppy as I made my way between and under the tables, and I never took my eyes off Hansen for long. Their conversation was light and casual, but Tasneem's smiling and nodding was becoming more tense. She picked up Hansen's cup and looked inside.

Suddenly, clear as a bell, I heard her voice in my head, scared and urgent. *Randa, you have to see this.*

I set the mop aside and opened my mind to hers. The vision I received was so intense, so jarring, I nearly slipped and fell on the wet floor.

Water, foam. Legs kicking. A young woman in a bathing suit, fighting, thrashing, air bubbles spewing from her mouth as hands pulled her under. Hands in black gloves. A scuba diver, one arm around her neck, the other around her torso, holding her close as the fight went out of her, as she lost consciousness. The scuba diver pulling the girl's limp body into deeper waters. A knife in his hand, her stomach slashed open, turning the surrounding water red.

I didn't want to see this. But once I opened my mind, there was no closing it, not until I'd seen what Tasneem needed me to see.

The diver was reaching into the incision, pulling it open, placing something inside. It looked like a dumbbell. The weight held her to the lake floor as blood spewed red from her stomach and faded pale pink into the water. The diver used the knife again, this time to saw off a lock of the girl's hair.

The vision faded. I rested one hand on a nearby table to steady myself, breathing heavily as I returned to the present. To Bayt Alqahwah. To Tasneem and the murderer sitting across from her.

Tasneem abruptly set the cup down and stood up. "I have to go—"

Hansen had the audacity to grab her arm to pull her back down.

♦

Sahira doctrine forbids using our abilities to do harm, except in defense of oneself or others. This situation qualified.

I channeled my magic toward the offending hand. *Crackcrackcrackcrack.* His finger bones snapped one by one in rapid succession. He pulled back with a yelp, but for good measure I snapped his thumb, taking vicious satisfaction in his resulting scream.

I went to stand in front of Tasneem. Hansen staggered back, tipping his chair over while cradling his injured hand. He looked at me with wide-eyed terror, face drained of color, as though I was a cobra poised to strike. Two buttons had popped off of his too-tight shirt, exposing part of his chest.

"Wh-What the fuck?" His voice came out strangled. "What was that? What the fuck did you do to me?"

I folded my arms. "It's time for you to leave, Mr. Hansen."

"What *are* you? How did...how—"

The front door opened and closed. Ziad had returned from his break. He strode over, shoulders squared, a hint of menace in his voice as he asked, "Is there a problem here?"

Hansen's eyes flicked between the three of us. He backed away slowly, cautiously, until he reached the door. Then he whirled around, pushed the door open with his good hand, and ran off.

"Randa," Tasneem said softly. "Look."

I turned. She had opened the shopping bag Hansen left on the floor. There were boxes of dumbbells inside.

I took a shaky breath and faced my siblings. "We need to do a ritual."

We discussed what to do and who would take care of which task. Ziad and I would gather the materials we needed while Tasneem called our relatives and got everyone assembled. We would need nine people. *Sahira* were always most powerful together.

Ziad and I made the drive out to MacArthur Bridge. We arrived late in the evening and parked near the shore of the Detroit River. I got out of the car and gazed at the bridge, where people drove to and from Belle Isle. How many of them had been to the beach? How many more would lose loved ones if our ritual didn't succeed?

I knelt on the ground and leaned over to fill my glass bottle from the river. Behind me, Ziad dug into the soil with a trowel, filling a cardboard box with a mix of mud and dirt. Once we finished our tasks, we silently returned to the car for the drive back.

The sky was darkening by the time we reached our uncle's house. I had barely uttered "*Marhaba*, Amo Asim" when he greeted us with his usual bear hugs. Ever the good host, he took the box and bottle we carried and ushered us inside.

Though Asim was technically our mother's cousin, we'd always called him Amo—Uncle—as a term of respect. A plump, balding man with three grown children, he had always treated us like his own. His home was a welcoming one, plus he had the space needed for larger rituals, so my siblings and I practically grew up in two houses: his and our own.

"Which of you is doing the incantation?" Asim asked, setting the supplies down on his kitchen counter.

"I am," Ziad said. Tasneem and I had agreed he was the best of us at reading Aramaic.

"You'll have to help me pick the right one." Asim looked sheepish. "I'm an old man. Even with my glasses, I can't read the words anymore."

I was about to head for the living room when Asim added, "Oh, I've contacted your parents in Lebanon. They send their blessings."

"*Shukran*, Amo," I said, embarrassed that I hadn't thought of that myself. I hadn't wanted to bother my parents during their mission to find new artifacts for ritualistic purposes. Sending blessings wasn't strictly necessary, nor did it always work, but it was a custom meant to foster connection between *sahira* separated by distance.

Leaving Ziad and Asim to their task, I entered the living room, where Asim's wife, Farrah, sat on the couch chatting with my father's sister, Najat. On the opposite couch sat Farrah and Asim's eldest son, Nadir. He was almost a decade older me and currently absorbed in his phone. Najat's teenage twin daughters, Nadine and Josephine, sat on the Persian rug, occupied with a card game.

Nadine, the first to notice me enter the room, leapt to her feet. "Randa! You met a serial killer? What was he like? Did he cry like a bitch when you broke his fingers?"

"Nadine!" Najat scolded.

I laughed and tucked Nadine's hair behind her ear. "Let's get the ritual done first. Then I'll tell you all about it."

Nadine pouted and sat back down. Farrah stood to greet me with a hug, while Josephine, the shyer twin, gave a smile and a small wave. Nadir looked up from his phone and grinned.

"Well done, Randa," he said. "I would have broken his fingers too."

I grinned back, glad for the support of a fellow eldest sibling.

"Where's Tasneem?" I asked, taking a seat beside Farrah and Najat.

"Downstairs, setting the altar," Farrah said.

"By herself?"

"She insisted. Said she was feeling inspired."

That didn't surprise me. An altar was a work of art, and Tasneem made her best art when left alone to her own devices.

Ziad entered the room carrying the bottle of river water and one of our family's ancient incantation bowls. The spell engraved inside it was in Syriac Aramaic—a language Tasneem and I were also taught but never quite mastered the way Ziad had. Asim followed behind him with the box of soil.

We heard Tasneem's footsteps on the basement staircase, and she emerged with her clothes caked in flour.

"I'm finished," she announced.

We all followed her to the basement. An enormous eight-pointed Star of Ishtar was meticulously drawn in flour on the tiled floor. In the middle was a perfectly proportioned circle. Lit candles sat at each point, the sole source of light in the dark room.

"It's perfect," I said.

Tasneem laughed. "Of course. I made it, didn't I?"

Ziad carefully stepped through the star and into the circle, where he sat cross-legged, placed the bowl in his lap, and set the bottle beside him. The remaining eight of us each took a handful of soil and spread it around the candles at the star's points. We then took our places at the points and looked to Ziad to begin. Josephine and Nadine stood to my left, Tasneem and Nadir to my right. Directly across from me was Farrah, flanked by Asim and Najat.

"Everyone ready?"

We nodded. Ziad took a deep breath, looked down at the bowl, and began reciting. The rest of us started walking, moving clockwise from point to point as he read.

The flames of the candles grew brighter and larger. The air in the room became heavy, making it more difficult to breathe. The more we walked, the more in sync we became. Group instinct took over. We sensed when it was time to change direction, so we turned in unison and walked counterclockwise. Smoke billowed from the candles, amassing on the ceiling like a dark cloud.

Ziad turned the bowl, voice rising as he read further into the incantation. He kept reciting as he opened the bottle and poured the river water into the bowl.

Finally, his voice reached a crescendo, the final words of the spell echoing off the walls, and the Star of Ishtar erupted in flames. We kept walking through the heat, and the flames died down as quickly as they came. The candles snuffed out as well, plunging the room into darkness.

I fell to my knees, gasping for breath, my head spinning and my energy drained. I heard my relatives collapsing as well, and Asim's hoarse voice asking if everyone was okay. There was no way to tell how long the ritual had gone on. It was like we'd crash-landed back on earth after being transported outside of time.

Someone found the light switch on the wall. Once my vision cleared, I saw the shape of the Star of Ishtar burned into the floor. The candles were reduced to pools of wax mixed with the burnt remains of the soil. The incantation bowl was empty. The water had dissolved.

♦

The next morning, I woke up on a couch, wrapped in a blanket. Nadine and Josephine were nestled in sleeping bags on the floor. I looked around the living room. Farrah, Asim, and Najat were having coffee on the opposite couch. Like me, they were in the same clothes they'd had worn the previous night. They looked tired and disheveled, as though having just woken up minutes before. The ritual had worn us all out.

"*Sabah al kheir*," Farrah whispered. "Ziad and Tasneem are sleeping upstairs. You only made it to the couch before you passed out."

I didn't even remember coming up from the basement. As Farrah poured a cup for me, I checked the news on my phone.

Bodies of Three Young Women Found on Detroit River Shore

Bodies Washed Up on Detroit River Shore Believed to Be Missing Women

Three Bodies Found on Shore Were "Sliced Open," Officer Says

Body Found on Shore Near MacArthur Bridge Identified as Missing

Teen Nicole Parks

Mutilated Bodies Found on Shore Revealed to Have Dumbbells in Their Stomachs

Family Claims Body on Detroit River Shore is Missing Daughter Kimberly Ramsey

Third Body Found Near MacArthur Bridge Identified as Emma Scott

Authorities Cite "Miraculous" Recovery of Three Missing Young Women as an "Anomaly"

News outlets were having a field day, both locally and nationally. What were the chances of three bodies, all missing persons, turning up together like that? The bodies were underwater too long for any DNA evidence to survive, but their families would have closure.

I found this headline while I sipped my coffee: *Anonymous Tip Leads Police to Alleged Belle Isle Killer.*

The mugshot of Jonathan Dylan Hansen barely resembled the put-together persona I'd seen at Bayt Alqahwah. Rumpled hair, pale face, that same fearful look in his eyes as when I'd broken his fingers. According to the article, police searched his car and found a duffel bag with scuba gear, a knife, and three locks of hair.

"Who called in the anonymous tip?" I asked.

"I did," said Asim. "Early this morning, just after the news broke."

I set my phone aside and stretched. We'd done well. Three bodies recovered and a killer apprehended. I drank the last of my coffee and decided it was a good day to keep Bayt Alqahwah closed. Some time off was well-earned.

"Are you finished, Randa?" Farrah asked. "Hand me your cup. Let me tell your fortune."

"No thanks." My tone was dry. "I've had enough excitement for a while."

Sarah Nour is a freelance writer based in Minnesota. Her poetry has been published in *Stone Path Review*, *Red Weather*, and *The Poetry Rag*. Her short fiction has appeared in *Northern Narratives*, *Wild Musette*, *Parakeet Magazine*, *Crow Toes Quarterly*, and other publications. Keep up with her work at www.sarahnourwriter.com

An Evening in Paris

Neil Millam Frederickson

THERE ONCE WAS A perfume named *Evening in Paris*, and Toby's older sister Claire kept a bottle of it on her bedroom vanity. The bottle was oval and deep blue, with a silvery cap. Even as an adult, Toby could recall the scent in the air when his sister got ready for a date. And now, decades later, he found himself in a cheap (tiny) hotel room in the City of Lights itself. All those decades later... It seemed like magic.

Toby was a man in need of a break, a change, a reboot, a jumpstart. His marriage of ten years had frozen into an armed truce devoid of communication. He vowed to double down and work harder, and perhaps even seek a marriage counselor if his wife Jane would agree to pay half the cost. She said it was a waste of money. She said she didn't want to spill her guts to some stranger who would sit in judgment on her. He had to admit it was a valid point.

Toby said they definitely needed a break. She agreed. He suggested a couple of weeks in Paris for a change of scenery that would let off steam. She said, "That sounds wonderful. Go to Paris for a couple of weeks." It took him a moment to understand she meant he should go while she stayed home.

Well, that *didn't work...*

Toby broached the subject to a colleague, Doug, at work.

Doug listened to the tales of shouting arguments. He swallowed the last of his chocolate-frosted doughnut and asked, "What are these big fights about?"

"Last night, it was about whose turn it was to take the trash bins out to the curb."

Doug laughed. "I thought it was about something important! I thought it would be about something like building a new house or having a baby. Trash bins? That ain't so bad."

"On the contrary," Toby replied. "It's worse."

Perhaps Jane was right. Two weeks might be just long enough to get a different perspective on their quarrels and work out some win/win solutions. On the other hand, he did not want to go on vacation alone. Eventually a former co-worker named Kory agreed to go along. They exchanged text messages about where to go and what to see. Toby obtained travel agency pamphlets and studied the options. Their schedule gradually took shape. Toby spread the pamphlets on his bed and examined the glossy photos. Euro-Disney—no, probably skip that one.

One pamphlet advertising the various boat companies traveling the Seine told of a legend. It was said that when a boat passed under the bridge spanning the Seine by Notre Dame, if a passenger tossed a coin into the air and made a wish before it fell into the water, this wish was sure to come true. Toby recognized the story as a common type of wish-fulfillment tale.

Unfortunately, just as he was trying to work out how to mend his marriage, he encountered Katrina, a friend from his college days. They met for coffee in a café they both remembered from the Sixties, since then renamed more than once. Time had been kind to Katrina. She was nearly as trim as he remembered, and still burned with the political concerns of their youth. As he gazed into her dark eyes, he felt fat and sluggish. He felt old.

Toby's expectations of what would happen vanished within the first five minutes when Katrina poured out the story of her divorce from an abusive husband. Toby drank in the details of her life: newly single, no children, a good job with comfortable pay. In short, no entanglements. A true reboot. It sounded like something from a movie on cable television. His pulse began to race.

They had coffee twice more, then went out for supper one night when Toby was able to fashion a lie to explain his whereabouts to his wife.

"We should do this again," Toby said as they paid their separate checks. One or the other of them said this every time they got together.

"Yes," Katrina replied, "we should do this again."

They stood in the parking lot of Perkins and looked at each other for a long time. The damp summer air draped over them.

This is how matters stood when Toby and his friend Kory flew to Paris. Their first two days in France, they took bus tours out into the countryside to see the great chateaux, including Fontainebleau, Versailles, Trianon, and Vaux le Vicomte. The following days, they climbed the Eiffel Tower and toured Rodin's studio, where they had the pleasure of watching workers clean the sculptor's most famous work, The Thinker, in the museum's yard. Toby took pictures of the Parisian streetcleaners in their green coveralls. As a lark, they had their hair cut in a real styling salon, where the stylist's assistant served them pastry and coffee while they waited.

Their final day would go to the museums—the Louvre and the Musée d'Orsay. This would involve a great deal of walking and standing on their feet. They decided to make the last event of their last day in Paris a restful boat ride on one of the famous Bateaux that carried tourists up and down the river, past the famous bridges and the Île de la Cité.

Toby prepared for the long siege of museum-viewing by loading his pockets with small candies for energy, and antacid tablets for the heartburn that would sooner or later show its face.

Their final day in Paris unrolled before them as their trip rolled up behind them. They began with the Musée d'Orsay: Monet and the water lilies; Monet and the haystacks; Manet and the luncheon on the grass; Degas' ballet dancers; Toulouse-Lautrec and the Moulin Rouge; Whistler's Mother. Toby drifted from one to the next, scarcely able to breathe. "I can't even tell you how I feel," he said to Kory. "These are paintings I studied thirty years ago. I know them but I don't *really* know them." He spread his hands in the air.

Outside again, they walked the ancient streets and crossed the Seine. A tourist boat moved slowly under the bridge and proceeded upstream. A guide spoke in a language that was neither French nor English. Toby remembered the pamphlet telling of the wish-making legend.

Toss a coin, make a wish before it hits the water, and it will surely come true.

Could such a thing be real? Absurd, fantastical! But no more so than the reality of being in the magical city of Paris, a place he had never dreamt of visiting. A place where almost anything might happen.

Now they went into the Louvre itself, and the sorcery continued. The sculpture of the Winged Victory, the Venus de Milo, the actual stele of Hammurabi, and finally, in a large, packed room, seen over the heads of a hundred (or perhaps a thousand) people, the witching Mona Lisa herself, who sent her smile straight to only him.

Hours later Toby and Kory limped out of the museum and stopped at a street kiosk for a snack.

Kory pointed at the menu. "What are pommes frites?"

"French fries, I think."

"I guess here they just call them fries," Kory joked.

It was time for their boat ride. With aching feet, they walked back over the river and made their way to the boat landing.

As the boat slowly left the landing, Toby and Kory moved to the railing on the port side. Toby could see the bridge upriver. It was the wishing bridge, the bridge of destiny. The fork in the road—or rather fork in the river. The moment was coming, the chance to wish for a new life with Katrina. No sooner had the thought arisen when guilt flooded over him. He imagined his wife at home, taking care of their dog and working at her job, doing things that a grown-up adult did every day. Yes, she was difficult to live with, but wasn't that the case with many marriages? Why should he expect anything better?

Still, there was Katrina, with her dark eyes and quick mind. Katrina, who actually listened when he talked. Katrina, who had more ideas in a week than he had in a year.

Which should he wish for, the *want-to* or the *ought-to*? He couldn't have both.

Now they were at the bridge and the ancient, mossy stones of the embankment were slipping by, slipping away from him.

Quick! Which do I choose? Jane or Katrina? What if I choose wrong?

Or . . . Or maybe . . . Or maybe he . . . Or maybe he could . . .

They were moving under the bridge and the lights of the boat illuminated the brickwork above their heads. It was now or never.

Toby yanked a silvery two-franc coin from his pocket and held it a moment as he took a deep breath. He tossed it into the air. The coin spun, the future flickered, and tumbled. Heads or tails, old or new, yes or no. He let out his breath in a rush. "I wish that love would come into my life."

He leaned against the boat railing, smiling, light as a feather. "Gotcha!" he said to the river, the bridge, to the boat. To the rest of his life.

♦

Neil Frederickson grew up in Okabena, Jackson County, southern Minnesota (population: 185). He is retired from a career with the federal court system. He now lives in Fargo, North Dakota, and belongs to a writers' group in Fargo, as well as another in nearby Moorhead, Minnesota.

The Calling

AL BAYNE

"WHAT IF THAT THING falls over? It would destroy our whole building," Mark says, using an X-Acto knife to slice open one of the half-dozen cardboard boxes they have yet to unpack.

"Don't be ridiculous. It's not going to fall over," Brett replies. "Can you hand me the knife?" He holds out his hand and waits for Mark to pass it to him, but Mark doesn't. His eyes are glued to the window, fixated on the gigantic water tower right outside of their apartment.

"Mark?" Brett says.

"Shit, sorry." He looks away from the window and finally hands Brett the knife. Brett grabs another nearby box with a label that has "living room shit" written on it in black Sharpie. He plunges the knife through the masking tape and rips it open.

"Seriously, that thing is nothing more than an eyesore. I promise." Brett removes a stack of DVDs from the box and places them onto their new TV stand, which he just spent the better part of an hour putting together.

"I know, I know. I just can't stop staring at it. It kinda freaks me out."

Brett shrugs. "We'll get used to it."

"Yeah. I'll get over it. It's just so...intense." Marks shifts his eyes back to the window.

"Hey, focus up. We gotta get this shit put away if we're having people over tonight." Brett finishes emptying out the box of DVDs, then stands up. His left leg has fallen asleep from sitting on the floor for so long.

"You're right. You finish in here, I'll work on the kitchen," Mark says.

Brett had been ecstatic when they found out there was a vacancy at 1632 Spruce Ave. Two bedrooms, in-unit laundry, and a second-story view of the river, all while walking distance from campus. Plus, the last tenants had vacated so abruptly that they left a big, plush couch and a large dining table. The only downside to the unit, even though Brett doesn't find it to be a big deal, is its proximity to Ash Valley's water tower. Sure, the thing is huge, and not exactly the most aesthetically appealing to look at, but it's not like it causes any actual problems. The tower itself is about double the height of their building, slender at the bottom, round, and bulbous at the top. The whole thing is white, except for the words "Ash Valley Welcomes You!" painted in deep maroon letters. There's a built-in steel ladder running up the side, all the way to the very top where there's a red light. The bottom of the ladder is fenced off. Brett wonders if the fence has always been there, or if they were forced to add it later because of people trying to climb it, like in *What's Eating Gilbert Grape*. Other than that, Brett has barely noticed it in the first three days of living there. The only time he even remembers it exists is when he's watching something on the TV, which is right in front of the windows that overlook the river and tower.

Two hours later, after nearly three straight days of unpacking, building furniture, and decorating, Brett finally finishes unpacking the last box. He stands in the living room and admires his work. The yellow and green lava lamp perfectly matches the Green Bay Packers flag tacked up behind the couch. The string lights Mark hung up make the whole room feel pleasant, which is a nice change from the sterile fluorescents they were used to in the dorms for the last three years. Overall, Brett is happy with the new apartment. It makes him feel independent, like he's finally becoming a real adult. Plus, now they have a place to hang out with their friends off campus.

Brett takes a seat on the couch and kicks his feet up. A couple of their friends are supposed to be coming over in a few hours, and he's already stocked up on beer and chips. He even found his old beer bong from freshman year when he cleaned out his boxes that had been sitting in the on-campus storage.

He clicks on the TV and scrolls through the guide, but nothing piques his interest. So he turns it off again. His eyes wander to the water tower, its massive circular head looming above him. The apartment is so close to it that he can't even see the entire thing from where he's sitting. It's windy out, and some of the trees have already begun to lose their leaves despite it barely being September. The partially naked branches tremble in the breeze like arthritic fingers. He wonders if there's a storm in the forecast.

Mark emerges from the bathroom. He's dripping wet, with nothing but a gray towel wrapped around his waist. He's leaving a trail of droplets behind him as he walks into the living room.

"Dude, did you even bother to dry yourself off?" Brett asks. "We're not in a linoleum-floored dorm anymore. We don't want unnecessary water on the hardwood floors. I don't know about you, but I'm planning to get that deposit back when we eventually move out."

"What were you watching? That singing was driving me insane, I couldn't take it anymore." He wipes at a bead of water trickling down his forehead. There's even a streak of conditioner left over in his hair.

"What are you talking about? I had the TV on for like two seconds, but I turned it off. There was nothing good on."

"Then what was that noise? Didn't you hear the singing?" He moves closer to Brett. He has a peculiar expression on his face, one that Brett doesn't recognize even though they've lived together for three years. He's seen Mark get angry, but this is different. His expression is mixed with genuine fear and confusion.

"Woah, dude. You need to chill. I didn't hear anything. I'm not sure what your deal is, but you need to relax." Brett stands up from the couch.

For a split second, it looks like his best friend might charge at him.

Then Mark snaps out of it. In an instant, his whole demeanor changes. His eyes widen as if he himself isn't even sure what just happened. "I'm so sorry. I don't know what's wrong with me. I think I'm just tired. But it's no excuse to be an asshole."

"It's fine, man. Moving is stressful. I think a little get-together tonight will do us some good." Brett sits back down. His heart is beating a little faster than normal, like he just walked up a flight of stairs or two. Mark disappears into his bedroom, then returns moments later with clothes on. He wipes up the water he tracked down the hallway, then retreats into his room without another word.

"Damn," Brett says under his breath. He hopes he's right, that a little time with their friends will help Mark calm down.

◦

"This apartment is so nice," Angie says, collapsing onto the couch next to Brett. They're almost done with their second drinks, and Angie is already starting to get extra touchy, not that Brett minds. He's been trying to get with her for the whole summer, and he has a feeling tonight might finally be the night. Angie leans her body against his, her head tilted slightly upwards. Her gaze drifts to the windows. "Woah, I didn't realize it's *that* close to the water tower."

"Isn't that the water tower that people have, like, jumped from?" Carter, one of their friends, replies. He takes a swig of beer.

Brett looks at Carter, his head slightly tilted like a curious dog. He's never heard anything about this, and he knows it's definitely not going to help Mark relax. "Not that I know of," he says. He tries to think of something, anything he could say to naturally change the subject.

"Wait, I've heard of that, too." Angie sits up. "My friend Cassidy from my statistics class grew up here. She said when she was in elementary school, kids would say it was haunted. You know, dare each other to go touch it and stuff." Angie sets her drink down on the coffee table, then kicks her feet up. "But that was a long time ago. Before they even built this building."

"Sounds like a bunch of kids being kids. I haven't heard anything about it." Brett stands up. "Does anyone need a drink? I have these really good seltzers. There are four different flavors."

Carter and Angie both decline, then return to talking about something else. Brett is just happy they've moved on from talking about the water tower.

Brett glances over at Mark to check on him. He's sitting on the floor, his back up against the base of the couch, still working on his first beer. He's scratched off almost the whole label on the bottle, resulting in a pile of tiny paper crumbles on the floor.

Brett returns to his seat next to Angie on the couch.

"What's up with him?" Angie whispers to Brett. Her mouth grazes his cheek and lingers there a moment longer than necessary, sending goosebumps down his body.

"He's fine. He's just been a little...paranoid." He grabs Mark's shoulder to get his attention. Mark's body jolts. His head whips in Brett's direction, eyes red and puffy. Even though he's looking directly at Brett, it feels like he's looking *through* him.

"Dude, are you okay?" Carter says.

"I don't...I'm not...what?" Mark replies.

Brett and Carter make eye contact with each other. Carter shrugs.

"I'll be right back," Brett says, handing his drink to Angie.

She grabs his hand. "Hurry back."

God damnit, Mark. I swear to God if you ruin this for me, I'm never going to forgive you.

"Can I talk to you for a second, Mark?" Brett says. He walks into his bedroom. Mark follows.

"Dude, what is up with you? I'm getting really worried." Brett shuts the door behind them.

"I don't know. I think I'm going crazy." He sits down on Brett's bed and throws his head into his hands. "I've been hearing this woman's voice all day. Sometimes she sings, other times she talks and says my name and shit. It's freaking me the fuck out, man."

Brett doesn't have a single clue how to respond. At first, it sounds so ridiculous that he's convinced Mark is kidding. It isn't until he lifts his head, tears in his eyes that Brett realizes this is serious. "Is this because of that bullshit Angie was talking about? It's just urban legends."

"No, I swear. I didn't even know about all that stuff. But it doesn't fucking surprise me." Mark fidgets with a small hole in the knee of his jeans. "I think I'm losing it, Brett. She just keeps talking and singing. It won't stop."

"What does she say?" This is all Brett can manage.

"She just says, 'Come to me' and 'Come closer, Mark' over and over again. Other than that, she hums. It's almost constant. It will stop for a few minutes here and there, but it always starts again."

"When did this start?"

When Mark hesitates again, Brett isn't sure if he's thinking or if he's too embarrassed to answer.

"I first heard it when we viewed the apartment a couple of weeks ago. I didn't think anything of it because it stopped as soon as we left. It started back up again on our first night, on and off. It gradually got more and more intense, and now it's constant. Am I going fucking crazy? I need help, man." He raises his voice at the last part.

"Shh," Brett says. "No, no. You're not losing your mind, okay? I think you're just psyching yourself out. Have you been sleeping? You look exhausted."

"You know what the craziest part is?" He completely avoids Brett's question. "Her voice gets louder and louder the closer I am to that stupid water tower."

Brett sighs. "So this *does* have to do with what Angie said about the water tower. I promise, Mark, it's not real."

"Stop it! It has nothing to do with Angie. I keep hearing this voice and I'm fucking terrified. Do you not understand?"

Brett doesn't know what he should say or do. Is he supposed to drive him to the hospital for a psych eval? That would suck, considering he's already two drinks in. Plus, Angie is finally coming on to him. He can't just leave.

He runs a hand through his hair and takes a deep breath. For some reason, as soon as Mark mentioned the water tower, he began to take him less seriously. Maybe it's because it makes something that already sounds crazy seem even more ridiculous. They're too old to get wrapped up in stories passed down by school kids. But still, Mark seems genuinely scared.

Brett takes a deep breath, attempting to compose himself. "Look. Why don't we just make it through tonight and see how you're feeling in the morning? Let's go out there and have a good time. If you hear the voice, just ignore it and move on. If you're still freaking out by tomorrow...well, then we'll have to figure something out. Okay?" He sits down next to Mark and throws his arm around his shoulders. "Everything will be fine. I promise."

"Okay." Mark wipes his eyes.

After a few drinks, Mark finally starts to loosen up. He's actually able to engage in conversation with Carter and even chugs a Natural Lite through the beer bong. By 10:00 p.m., he and Carter are both wearing a set of Virtual Reality goggles. Brett isn't sure what game they're playing, but judging by their movements, it looks like they're wielding lightsabers. They look so ridiculous that he and Angie are entertained by just sitting on the couch and watching them.

"They look so stupid," she says, laughing.

"They sure do."

"You know, I haven't seen your room yet."

"You think they'd even notice if we left?" Brett asks.

"Not a chance." She stands up and extends her hand. Brett takes it and leads her to his room.

She sits down on his bed. "What was up with Mark?"

"Oh, nothing. He's just stressed."

"I've never seen him like that." She leans against the headboard.

"I know. But he's clearly fine now. I don't want to talk about Mark anymore." Brett lies down next to her. Without any warning, she leans in and kisses him. He kisses her back, slowly at first. Her mouth tastes like beer and breath mints. He wonders if she popped one in while they were still sitting on the couch, as if she had been eagerly anticipating this moment as much as he had.

Angie pulls her shirt over her head and tosses it to the floor in one seamless motion. Brett kisses down her neck, nipping at her smooth skin, until he arrives at her bra. He unhooks it, revealing her perfect, goosebump-coated breasts.

"Damn, I've wanted this for so long." He kisses her again, his tongue slipping through her parted lips.

She pulls away. "Then what are you waiting for?"

"Nothing." He smiles and unbuckles his belt then, steps out of his jeans, then boxers.

He's wanted her desperately for four months now, imagining this moment so many times that it feels like another one of his fantasies, not reality. Yet, as he stands before her, half naked in his bed, he can't help but feel an aching sensation of guilt in his chest. A little over an hour earlier he was in this exact same spot while Mark cried in front of him.

He remembers Mark's eyes, glazed with fear, pleading with him.

"You okay?" Angie says. She slips her underwear down her legs and kicks them to the floor.

"Never been better."

Angie pulls him back onto the bed, on top of her. She twists her fingers in his hair, bringing him closer. The warmth of her bare chest against his melts the guilt. It doesn't take long before he completely loses himself in her before all thoughts of Mark have vanished.

Brett and Angie get dressed and return to the living room. Mark and Carter, their VR sets retired, are now watching *Stepbrothers.*

Angie pulls her hoodie back over her head, then nudges Carter's shoulder. "Hey, you ready to walk back to campus?"

"That's probably a good idea." He stands and stretches, then slips his shoes on. "Thanks, guys. That was fun."

"Yeah, we'll see you soon," Mark replies.

"It's pretty easy to find this place thanks to the water tower, huh?" Angie says.

"Exactly." Brett kisses her goodbye.

Once everyone is gone, Brett walks around the living room and gathers the empty cups and bottles. When he walks past Mark, he wonders if his eyes are really on the TV, or if they've wandered to the water tower.

"Hey, I'm sorry about my little freak out earlier," Mark says as if he could read Brett's mind.

"It's cool. I'm just glad you're feeling better. You are feeling better, right?"

"I think so." Mark scratches the back of his head.

"Well, good." But Brett isn't sure that he's convinced.

"I'm glad you and Angie finally got together. I was getting tired of that 'will they/won't they' thing."

"Oh, shut up." Brett tosses an empty Red Solo cup at him. "Well, I'm going to sleep. You should too."

"I'm right behind you."

Right as Brett gets into bed, he realizes he forgot his phone in the living room. He gets out from under the covers and walks back down the hall. Mark is standing by the window, close enough to where his nose is only a few inches away from the glass. Without thinking, Brett takes a few more steps as quietly as he possibly can, just close enough to the coffee table so that he can reach his phone. Then he goes back to his room and shuts the door.

◆

Brett wakes up from the natural sunlight spilling in through his new bedroom window. He rolls over to check the time, which is 7:28 a.m. He didn't sleep nearly as long as he expected to, but now that he's up, he's up.

He's delighted when he looks around his new room. It's at least three feet wider and longer than a dorm room, and it's all his. Before he swings his feet out of bed, something sharp digs into his side. It almost feels like a thumbtack.

It's a studded earring, silver with a round, pink gemstone. It must have fallen out of Angie's ear. Brett smiles and places the earring next to his phone on his nightstand. Maybe he'll invite her over tonight to come get it.

Like every morning, the first thing he does is make a pot of coffee. Mark is known to sleep in until well past noon, but Brett makes extra for him, anyway. He leans against the counter and waits for the coffee to brew. The bitter smell slowly starts to fill the kitchen. He uses his favorite mug, a red UW Ash Valley one that admissions gave to all the freshmen when they first moved in. He pours himself a cup, turns on the lava lamp, then clicks on the TV to watch the morning news.

Before he sits down, he notices something moving by the base of the water tower. He moves closer to the window and looks down. Someone is climbing the fence that surrounds the bottom of the ladder. Brett doesn't even have to see the person's face. He knows it's Mark.

He slams his mug onto the coffee table, spilling it in the process. He slips his shoes on and sprints out the front door, down the stairs, and onto the lawn. Without looking both ways, he runs across the street. Mark has hoisted his body over the fence and has now started climbing.

"Dude, what the fuck are you doing?" Brett shouts. "Get down from there!"

"I can't. I have to do this. I need to get closer." He climbs a few rungs higher.

"You're going to get hurt, Mark. You need to come down." Brett can feel panic rising in his chest like mercury in a thermometer.

"You don't understand, man. I can't stop," he sobs. He ascends two more rungs, then tilts his head back to look at the top of the tower. "I'm coming, okay?"

"Who are you talking to?"

"She's up there. I can't resist her anymore. It's too beautiful."

Brett's stomach churns.

Mark had seemed so okay last night after they talked. He was laughing and drinking and everything was normal.

"Look, Mark," Brett shouts, his head angled upwards at Mark. "I didn't really believe you last night, but I believe you now, okay? Just come down and we'll get you whatever help you need. I promise I'll be here for you, but I need you to come down."

"I can't...I just can't. I need to get closer." He sloppily climbs up a few more rungs, a little more than halfway to the part of the tower that starts to form its round head. The rubber toe of his sneaker slips against the metal, and he almost loses his footing.

Brett knows he needs to do something now, or Mark will get hurt. He reaches into his pocket for his phone. The only thing he can possibly think of to do is call 911. But his pocket is empty.

"Fuck, fuck, fuck." He looks around to see if anyone is nearby, but there's nobody. Not even a morning jogger or dog walker. He debates running inside to grab his phone but doesn't want to chance leaving Mark. "Mark, I'm not playing around. You need to get down." Brett begs the universe to send someone who can help him. A delivery driver, a mailman, *anyone.* But all that surrounds him are the trees, eerily still. The wind that had been ripping through them the day before has completely vanished. It's like they're frozen in their tracks, watching.

Brett cups his hands around his mouth and yells. "Come on, Mark, just get the fuck down!"

Mark doesn't respond. He climbs the last few rungs until he can touch the metal where it begins to curve outwards creating the bulbous head.

"I'm here," Mark shouts, and bangs on the metal. The thuds are deep, almost hollow sounding. "I'm here. Hello? Where are you?" He yells continuously, banging and banging.

"Stop it, Mark! Keep your hands on the ladder," Brett shouts up to him. But there's no way Mark can hear him. Here's making too much noise.

Mark reaches upwards with both of his hands like he's grabbing for something above him. His body tips backwards, and he falls.

Mark hits the ground with a deep thud. It's a noise that Brett will never be able to describe no matter how hard he might try. It's a sound that's so nauseating, so utterly repulsive, that Brett knows there's no way Mark will survive.

"Mark!" Brett screams. "No, no. Oh, God, no, please." He runs to

Mark and collapses next to him. Mark is on his back, his neck bent at such an unnatural angle that his temple is almost touching his shoulder. His eyes are open, but there's no life behind them. There's a trickle of blood dripping from his mouth, coating the blades of grass below.

"Somebody fucking help me!" Brett screams so loudly that his throat hurts. He grabs Mark's shoulders and shakes him, desperately willing him to wake up even though he knows he's already gone. Mark's head dips backward.

"Oh, God. I'm so sorry." Brett is now sobbing.

Mark still seems to be watching the water tower.

♦

Psychosis.

That's what the doctors chalked it up to be. A sudden, aggressive onset of psychosis and paranoia. Based on Brett's explanation, the authorities ruled his death as an accident. He wasn't thinking straight, too caught up in the hallucinations.

They said that when Mark reached upwards he may have seen something, something he could have been trying to grab onto.

They said he hadn't meant to fall.

Brett has barely slept in five days. Whenever he closes his eyes, he sees Mark's empty ones. Whenever he does manage to fall asleep, he's woken up almost immediately by the sound of Mark's body hitting the ground.

The bags under his eyes are so dark that he looks like a Tim Burton character. He can barely stand up without falling over because he hasn't been able to keep any food or water down.

The guilt is eating him alive.

Mark sat in front of him and cried, saying he needed help, and Brett still couldn't be bothered to help him. He could have prevented this, but he cared more about getting laid.

Now, the thought of Angie repulses him. He's been ignoring all her texts and calls, but that's because he's been ignoring everyone's texts and calls. His parents even offered to fly out and stay with him for a while, but he begged them not to.

He wants to be alone.

Brett has no clue what day it is. He knows it's been at least five nights since Mark died. Classes should be starting any day now, but he has no plans to attend. He doesn't even have plans to leave his bed. He wants to waste away in his sheets, in and out of consciousness, until he finally dissolves.

At some point, he hears someone pounding on the apartment door. He doesn't answer it. Instead, he closes his eyes and waits for sleep to claim him.

♦

"Hey, bro." Mark is sitting at the foot of Brett's bed.

"Mark?" Brett sits up. It's pitch-black outside. "But you're...how?"

Mark laughs, then smiles. "I know, I know. This is weird, huh?"

Brett nods, but he doesn't understand. There's a rational part of him buried deep beneath the exhaustion and stress that knows he must be hallucinating or dreaming, but another part of him knows this is Mark visiting him.

"I'm so sorry. I should have listened to you. I'm so fucking sorry," Brett says. "You're gone now, and it's my fault."

"I'm not gone."

"What do you mean? You're dead...your neck snapped. You're not really here." Brett doesn't know what's happening.

"But I am. I'm closer than you think." Instantly, Mark's entire demeanor changes. His expression sharpens, reminiscent of how he looked the day before he died when Brett thought he may lunge at him.

"Why are you here?" Brett asks. He suddenly feels terrified, like he wants to pull the covers over his head and hide like a little kid afraid of monsters in his closet.

"I came to tell you that I'm not mad at you. Even though you could have helped me."

"Why aren't you?"

"Because you're next." Mark smiles.

When Brett opens his eyes, it's daylight. He shoots upwards, his hair plastered to his forehead in a sheen of sweat.

It must have just been a nightmare.

For the first time in days, Brett feels like getting out of bed. When he lifts his comforter, a cloud of his own stench hits him like a ton of bricks. He peels his clothes off and walks naked to the bathroom. Now that he doesn't have a roommate, why does it matter? The shower hisses when he turns it on. Soon, the bathroom is foggy with steam, and he steps beneath the water.

The singing starts off quietly.

So quiet that he can barely hear it.

So quiet that it makes him laugh because his mind has to be playing tricks on him. He's paranoid.

It's the guilt.

But the singing gets louder. He turns the water off, not caring that he's still covered in soap. He needs to get closer to hear her melody more clearly.

He walks into the living room, water dripping down his naked body.

It's the most beautiful thing he's ever heard. It melts away his worries, his guilt, and fills his body with euphoria. It's as if he's flying, like his body is filled with pure sunlight. He walks over to the window, the song growing louder and louder in his ears, but it's not enough.

He has to get closer.

Al Bayne is originally from California but currently resides in Moorhead, Minnesota. After earning their Bachelor of Arts in Writing from Northland College in 2021, Al will be graduating from the University of Nebraska at Omaha with their MFA in Creative Writing in 2024. In addition to writing, Al works in an elementary school as a special education paraprofessional and also coaches lacrosse. Al is an artist, and one day hopes to write and illustrate their own graphic novel.

Beware the Grey Wolf

H. Ernest Coffman

It was late August, and the long, gray cylinder prowled through the frigid arctic waters, maneuvering around growlers, small fragments of ice roughly the size of a truck, and bergy bits, medium to large pieces of ice floating on the sea off the coast of Alexandra Land, a desolate island in the middle of the Arctic Ocean, and a million miles from anything. To a large ship, the three-foot growlers, lazily floating on the occan surface, are a nuisance, banging against the hull, sometimes denting them. Bergy bits, usually less than five meters, occasionally punched holes in ship hulls where the captains disregarded his speed.

The lone gray wolf, U-537, a Type IXC/40 U-boat, meandered around the ice floes, the captain constantly raising and lowering his binoculars, not wanting to damage his boat.

"I thought the ice edge wasn't supposed to be this far south this time of year," *Kapitanleutnant* Karl Wulf yelled down the hatch from the bridge into the control room.

"Normally, it isn't, Captain. The winter weather is early this year. That's why the Meteorological Service sent us out ahead of schedule," Doctor Artur Stein shouted back.

A storm of this magnitude so early in the season? It's going to be a bitch of a winter, Wulf thought as he slapped his arms around himself to get warm.

Clinging to one of the periscope masts, a lookout called out and pointed. "Twenty-five degrees off the port bow, Captain. Bluewater."

"Finally, a clear area," the captain muttered, putting the binoculars back to his eyes. "Come to 230 degrees. All ahead slow," he called over the multichannel submarine communication system.

The U-boat meandered slowly into a small cove off Alexander Land, a large island within the Franz Josef Land islands, north of Russia.

"*Jawohl, Herr Kapitän*. Come to 230 degrees. All ahead slow," the officer of the deck, or OOD, repeated while the Chief Engineer, or Chief of the Boat, relayed the message calling for all ahead slow.

"All stop. Change the watch and lookouts. XO to the bridge with me," the captain called down. Again, the order was called out throughout the boat. Winter was setting in early, and Captain Wulf didn't want any of his men getting frostbit, so he changed them out every thirty minutes.

The lookouts took a little longer to scramble up the hatch to the bridge because of the cumbersome foul weather gear and the heavy insulated arctic pants. Captain Karl Wulf pulled his collar up to keep the frigid air out and waited for his XO to climb onto the bridge.

"Clear to port, clear starboard, clear aft, clear bow except for ice floe," the replacement lookouts called out.

Water rushed and lapped along the submarine's hull. The diesel engines thrummed hypnotically with a reassuring vibration that everyone on the bridge felt in the soles of their feet. Cold salt air blew against the bridge and everyone standing on it, drenching them within minutes with the Arctic Sea.

"You've got to be kidding me. Those soldiers are going to live on that island in this weather," *Oberleutnant zur See* Ernst Addler, the XO, said as he pulled his gloves on.

"*Ja*. Makes you appreciate what we have," Karl said, putting his binoculars to his face.

"Someone in Berlin thinks this will be a wonderful place for a weather station? They must be out of their little Nazi minds." Addler looked around the bareness of the island and the solid white of the ice flow as it slowly crept towards them.

"Permission to come up?" a voice called up from below.

"*Ja*. Watch your footing, Herr Doctor. Ice is already starting to form on the bridge," Karl said.

Doctor Artur Stein stretched his arm out of the hatch, and the XO helped him up onto the bridge.

"Thank you," Stein said as he took a deep breath and coughed. "Excuse me, Captain. Being below for so long has clogged my lungs."

"You'll be all right in a few minutes, *Her*r Doctor. You'll get used to fresh air in a few moments," Addler said.

"So, Doctor, what do you think of your new home for the next few months?" Captain Wulf asked, handing him his binoculars.

"Grim looking, isn't it? We'll only be here until they deliver the automated meteorological unit, then it's back to Berlin." The doctor looked to the northeast. He didn't like the cloud formation coming over the extinct volcanic mountain. "That storm coming in," he said pointing to the dark clouds, "is going to be bad. It will be here in four or five hours. It will take us at least one to two hours to unload everything and another hour to build the shelters. I can hold off erecting the meteorological equipment until the storm has passed. If you can lend me a few more men, Captain, that would help."

Wulf maneuvered his submarine closer to shore. Finally, he dropped both prow and aft anchors, keeping the sub stationary while they unloaded the meteorological team's equipment and gear. With the extra men the captain gave the doctor, they had put the modular shacks together and had placed all the equipment where it was needed in under an hour.

◆

The last of the seamen returned to the sub, anchors were raised, and the sub slowly backtracked to open seas. The lookouts had rotated so fresh eyes were on top looking for growlers and bergy bits.

The storm had descended upon them with its full fury. Gale-force winds pounded the island with a wintery mix of snow, sleet, and rain. Wulf glanced at the ship's clock on the bulkhead. 0845, and over a half hour since they had left the meteorologist.

God help them.

As the submarine slowly made its way towards open water, the XO looked back at where they had been anchored and saw the ice flow moving in. "Nothing like waiting until the last minute to leave here."

"*Ja*, I couldn't let them stay on that rock without some shelter. Now I'm wondering if I made the right decision." Captain Wulf pressed the button on the bridge speaker. "Control, bridge. Speed one-third, maintain course 184. Otto, let me know as soon as the depth is thirty-five meters under the keel."

"Bridge, control. *Jawohl, Herr* Captain. Speed one-third, maintain course 184. Depth is ten meters and dropping."

The wind pushed the submarine forward, the temperature dropped, and the waves increased. The main storm was upon them. The U-boat rocked back and forth as the submarine moved out of the protected bay into the Arctic Ocean. Below was not much better. The violent corkscrewing, rolling, pitching, and the constant hammering of the waves on the hull trying to break in, cascading down through the conning towers hatch, made life almost impossible. The foul air, the stench of the overused toilets, the reeking of the bilge water, mixed with sweat and diesel fumes, was an everyday normality for the men who volunteered for the submarine service.

Wulf clenched his teeth. "Come on. Why is it when I want to dive there's never enough depth?"

Addler chuckled and pulled his collar closer to his neck. "Any time now, Otto," he whispered into his hands.

What seemed like hours was only a few minutes when the radio blared. "Bridge, control. Depth is thirty-five meters below the keel."

"Control, bridge, *Jawohl*. Lookouts below! Dive to thirty meters. Speed four knots."

By the time Wulf hit the dive button twice, the lookouts were already below, and the XO had disappeared down the hatch and was standing off to the side, waiting for Wulf to come down. The captain did a 360, ensuring he left no one on top. He slid down the hatch railings and stopped just below the hatch lid, pulling it down and dogging it. He then locked it while Addler pulled on the lanyard, keeping the hatch lid tight against the hatch tunnel. Everyone inside the steel coffin heard the rush of compressed air flowing back into their compressed air tanks. This allowed the cold arctic water to flow back into the ballast tanks and sink the sub. The vibrations of the engines ceased, while the noise of the hull compressing echoed throughout the boat as the water pressure increased. The boat tilted downward into the frigid sea. The quiet was deafening after listening to the diesel engines.

Twenty-four hours earlier, *Kapitanleutnant* Karl Wulf slid down the conning towers ladder and entered U-537. In every direction, fantastic mechanisms jutted from the floor, walls, and ceilings in a forest of technology - gauges, dials, pipes, conduits, speaker tubes, plumbing, valves, radios, sonar, hatches, switches, levers - every inch a protest against the idea that men cannot live underwater.

In icy seas, the overhead pipes dripped with condensation, freezing the necks and scalps of the crewmen. The only escape from the chill was in the engine room where huge twin diesel engines pounded out deafening metal symphonies. This created one-hundred-plus-degree temperatures with stifling humidity and caused hearing loss to some of its operators. Carbon monoxide produced by the engines chipped away at mental acuity, caused sleep disorders, and became the only recognizable flavor in whatever meal the chef could squeeze out of his postage-stamp-size galley. It was a grueling and claustrophobic condition under which these seamen waged war. This was the world Karl Wulf and all submariners lived in. This was the world they loved.

♦

"Hatch secure," Wulf called out.

The XO continued down the hatch, through the conning tower, until he hit the control room deck. Wulf was right behind him. A petty officer dogged the final hatch as two other petty officers took the dripping foul weather gear from the XO and the captain. Before Wulf could take a step, the smells hit him. Being on the bridge and breathing fresh air had rebooted his nose. The odors of fifty-eight men, diesel, and oil were overpowering. By the time he had dried off, his sense of smell was numb again.

"Captain has the control room," Wulf called out.

Lieutenant Otto Ebbe, the boat's navigator, stepped next to the captain. "Course is 184; ships speed is one-third. Depth is thirty meters. Batteries are fully charged."

Wulf nodded. "Thank you, Otto. Good job. You are now relieved. Go get some rest."

Captain Wulf stepped over to the chart table. According to the plot, they were heading southeast, away from Alexandra Land Island, towards the Barents Sea, then the Norwegian Sea, into the North Atlantic, then home to Bergen, Norway.

Addler stepped next to Wulf and showed him a piece of paper. "Our message to *Kriegsmarine* Headquarters stating the weather station has been set up on Alexandra Land Island."

Wulf nodded and signed the paper. "I'm glad this mission is over. Now maybe we can do what we do best, sink ships."

Addler smiled and went to the communications room and knocked on the steel hull.

Karl Wulf sat back and watched his men operate the boat. Each one was an expert in their particular job, making his submarine one of the deadliest weapon systems Germany had ever made. After an hour, the watch changed, and Lieutenant Smidt became OOD. Wulf went to get a couple of hours of sleep.

◆

"Captain! Captain, wake up." The voice was faint at first but grew steadily louder. Suddenly, there was a bright white light.

Wulf recoiled from its intensity. Instinctively he threw his hands up to block it while grumbling, "Turn off that damn light!"

"Sorry, Captain. A message from Admiral Dönitz for you, sir," Radioman Heinrich Albright said.

"If it's the standard orders from headquarters, give it to the XO," Wulf said, rubbing his eyes.

"The XO said I should give it to you as soon as possible," Petty Officer Albright replied.

"Just leave it on the table. I'll read it as soon as I get dressed."

"*Jawohl, Herr* Captain." The radioman left the sealed envelope on the small table and closed the curtain behind him. Only the XO saw the worried look on the petty officer's face. The message was unusual in that it came directly from Grand Admiral Dönitz himself.

Wulf rose from his bunk, threw water from his collapsible sink onto his face, and donned some warm clothes. He took off his red woolen plaid shirt soaked with sweat and condensation. Opening the small closet door, he pulled out another red woolen plaid shirt. This, too, smelled of diesel fumes, but he knew it was clean. For some reason, he just couldn't get warm since he had been on the bridge most of the day. Opening the sealed envelope, Wulf saw Addler's initials on the front, indicating that his XO had read it. He sat on his bunk and read the one-page message.

SECRET

Headquarters Oberbefehlsaber der Kriegsmarine
5 April, 1944
TO: U-537, Oberleutnant zur See Karl Wulf, Kapitän.
FROM: Großadmiral Dönitz, Commander-in-Chief of
the Navy,
SUBJECT: Special Order U-ED 437.5tta
MESSAGE: Proceed to U-Boat base Bergen, Norway,
most haste. See Kriegsmarine Flotilla Commander,
Fregattenkapitän Hans Clausz for further orders.
Disregard all other transmissions unless directed by
Grand Admiral Dönitz.
Signed: Grand Admiral Dönitz
1217-5555-11-2-0-ba-b-1

SECRET

Captain Wulf slid the curtain aside from his cabin and took three steps into the control room. Standing next to Addler, he handed the message to his XO. "What do you think?" Wulf asked.

Addler took a step closer to Wulf so no one could hear him. "If we change course now, we'll probably miss out on any stray ships out here. If we wait, maybe a half-day or a day, we just might add to our tonnage sunk."

Wulf nodded. One thing that every U-boat captain had in the back of his mind was that if you didn't perform or do your duty in sinking ships, you would be given a desk job or demoted. Wulf would make certain that didn't happen to him.

As if on cue, the curtain across the radio room flew open. Petty Officer Gerhard stuck his head out of the closet-sized room. The sonar man listened intently on the headphones as he swept the hydrophone 360 degrees around the U-boat. Just as the squalls can hide ships on the surface, sheets of rain pounding on the surface of the sea sound like a confusing static haze that obscures the sound of enemy ships. Gerhard raised his arm with a finger pointing up to let everyone know to be quiet.

"Captain, possible contact. It's hard to hear because of the storm above us, but I'm sure of it."

"This far out, they could be heading for Murmansk," Addler said.

"How long have we been under?" Wulf asked as he pulled on his cold-weather gear.

"Two hours."

"Keep your ears on it, Hans," Wulf called out.

"*Jawohl*, Captain."

"XO, bring us up to periscope depth," Wulf said as he climbed the ladder to the conning tower.

"*Jawohl, Herr* Captain. Bringing the boat to periscope depth," Addler called out.

Nothing about going to periscope depth is easy or stress-free. In the conning tower, Wulf rotated slowly three hundred and sixty degrees on his seat, eye glued to the eyepiece. He saw nothing but surging waves.

After several rotations, Wulf picked up the ship's phone and said, "Radio, conn, any contacts?"

"None, Captain."

"Surface is clear. Surface the boat. Lookouts to the bridge," Wulf called out.

As the sub rose, the ride became rougher when the huge waves above tried to push them back down. The boat tilted slightly upward, breaking the surface of the frigid sea. They waited until the submarine leveled out and began rocking on the rolling sea.

"The boat has surfaced, Captain," the COB called out.

"Up scope," Wulf called out.

Wulf stepped back as the long silver shaft rose. Waves caught the scope and tried to twist it. The control room shook. Wulf slowly spun around, looking through the eyepiece. Without warning, he clapped the focusing handles up and stepped back.

"Down scope! Hold on!" he yelled.

There was a big clang, and the sub shook when a large chunk of blue-white ice slammed into the side of the conning tower. The people standing on the starboard side of the sub's conning tower suddenly moved towards the port side as the conning tower dented inward.

"Officer of the deck. Take her down to twenty meters and test the periscope. If it's good, take her down to forty meters. We need to get rid of this storm. We'll come back up in another two hours."

Wulf went to the officer's wardroom for a warm meal. A steward handed him a bowl of sausage and potato soup. When the captain dipped his spoon into his soup something plopped into it. He flung the cockroach out and stepped on it. After taking another spoonful of sausage and potatoes, he opened the one-page message and read it again. Addler sat down across from Wulf, buttered a chunk of hard bread, and dipped it into his soup.

Wulf held up the message. "What do you think of this?"

Addler smiled. "A change of plans. It's odd that the admiral sent it directly to you, and it didn't come with the rest of the message traffic. They asked for no response. They want you for something, but what?"

"*Ja*. I guess I've put *Der Löwe*, The Lion, off as long as I can. I really did want to go to Iceland and sink a few ships. When we're done eating, we'll surface, recharge our batteries, and change course for home. Maybe if Poseidon is on our side, we just might find a stray ship to sink."

Two hours later, U-537 tried to surface again. "Bring the boat to periscope depth. Let's see if that damn storm is over," Wulf said as he walked into the control room.

"*Jawohl*, Captain. Bring the boat to periscope depth," the OOD called out.

Compressed air and water hissed throughout the boat as the submarine nosed upward toward the surface. The officer of the deck rotated the periscope multiple times inside the conning tower. Pushing up the handles on the periscope, he pulled down on the periscope lever, making the scope slide back down into its cradle.

"The storm is finally over, the sea is calm with no ice to be seen, but a heavy fog surrounds us, Captain," the OOD announced.

The submarine emerged from the dark cold depths. Water sluiced off her conning tower and decks and dripped from the 105-millimeter cannon mounted on the forward deck.

A seaman scrambled up to the conning tower ladder and popped the topside hatch, ducking his head as cold water dripped in. Lookouts followed next, all scrambling for their stations, followed by the XO.

"All stations call out," he commanded as he put his binoculars to his face, then stopped. "Captain, you need to see this."

Wulf climbed the ladder to the bridge.

"Damn. That must have been one hell of a chunk of ice that hit us," Addler said, looking at the damaged side of the conning tower.

"Maintain course and speed to Bergen," Wulf called down the hatch.

"*Jawohl*, Captain. Maintain course and speed to Bergen."

The sub ran for four hours at one-third speed, charging its batteries. "Bridge, control. Batteries are fully charged."

"Bridge, *Jawohl*. Batteries are fully charged. Maintain course and speed."

"Bridge, radio. One, possibly two contacts, 123 degrees, approximately fifteen thousand yards."

All binoculars turned towards the directions the sonar man gave them. Nothing but a bank of fog. No dark shapes, no movement.

"Bridge, control, anything?" Wulf asked.

"*Nein!* Nothing but thick fog, Captain."

"Lookouts, call out," the watch officer hollered.

"Nothing port, Nothing starboard, Nothing aft, Nothing on the bow."

"Bridge, radio. Contacts five thousand yards and closing."

The transparent veil of fog lifted only for a moment. The phantom ships appeared, then disappeared.

One of the lookouts called out uncertainly to the Officer of the Bridge. "Ships dead ahead!"

The lieutenant swung his binoculars around, overcompensating a bit as the unmistakable silhouette of a submarine hunter, followed by a large oil tanker, came into view. The other lookouts tensed immediately but kept their binoculars up and scanned their sectors furiously.

It was too much for Wulf. Before anyone knew it, the captain was standing next to Lieutenant Smidt. "Dirk, relieve the OOD so he can trace our movements."

"*Jawohl*, Captain," Smidt said as he slid down the hatch.

The XO called down to the control room. "Captain has the bridge."

Before anyone could reply, Wulf was giving his orders. "Lookouts below. Make ready tubes one through four!"

It was all he had. To land the meteorologist team on Alexandra Land Island with all their equipment, Wulf had to leave all his torpedoes behind except for the ones already in his four torpedo tubes. He was going to make the most of what he had.

Wulf racked his brain as to what kind of sub-hunter he was encountering. He would deal with the oil tanker after he dealt with the sub-killer first. Ever since his joining the *Kriegsmarine*, he had poured over the images of silhouettes and haphazard photographs in ship identification booklets for just this occasion. *Short ship, one stack, one four-inch, possibly five-inch gun on the bow. Flower class Corvette. Draft eleven feet.* He had only seconds before the lookouts on the Corvette would see them and blow him out of the water.

"Set depth five feet... Bearing mark... 123 degrees... Range... one thousand yards... Angle on the bow... five degrees... Speed, eight knots."

Where the hell is this guy going?

"Tubes one through four, ready, Captain. Waiting for a final solution."

Wulf didn't wait. "Shoot tubes one through four." It was a desperate blind shot. The three-thousand-pound weapon was ejected from its torpedo tube, accelerating from rest to over thirty knots in less than a second.

"Torpedo one away, torpedo two away, torpedo three away, torpedo four away," the XO called up to the bridge. The submarine shuddered as compressed air launched each torpedo from its tube.

Inside the control room, four stopwatches timed each torpedo. From the bridge, Wulf watched as phosphorescent wakes churned up by the torpedoes' propellers receded ahead of the sub, and the gruesome sewing machine-like noise faded as they raced toward their prey.

"Bridge, radio. All eels running hot and normal," Petty Officer Gerhard called out.

Wulf's heart raced as the wakes faded away and the two ships grew larger and larger.

"Right full rudder. Dive, dive." Wulf hit the klaxon twice, as men slid down the hatches, throwing themselves out of the way.

The inside of the sub was a mass of coordinated confusion as the men in the control room pushed themselves against the hard steel walls. This made way for men from the crew quarters and the engine room whilst they ran towards the forward torpedo room putting as much weight forward as possible. The captain held onto handrails in the control room trying to make his way to the periscope seat while the submarine dove toward the depths.

"Twenty meters, twenty-five meters, thirty meters," the COB called out. Then the first torpedo hit, the concussion rocking the submarine.

"Periscope depth," Wulf commanded.

The men acknowledged the captain's command and the helmsmen began to bring the sub back up. The long gray tube creaked and groaned as it strained to rise again.

Someone yelled, "Time," then there was an explosion. Wulf smiled at Addler, who smiled back. The seconds ticked on, and then they heard a thump. The third torpedo was a dud. Wulf bit into his fist.

The U-boat rose towards the ocean surface.

"Periscope depth, Captain," the COB called out.

"Up scope." Wulf rode the periscope up, and quickly scanned the surface, the waves idly lapping up against the periscope. He looked at the sinking ship, then turned to watch the tanker. The tanker had changed course. It was turning right into the last torpedo. It took everything Wulf had to stay calm.

"Come on ... Come on ..." he muttered under his breath.

Before Wulf saw the explosion, a cheer went up inside the sub when the crew heard it. The whole bow of the tanker disappeared when the torpedo ripped through it.

U-537 surfaced just as the Canadian Corvette broke in two and sank.

Wulf and Addler scanned the area then started to make their assessment of the tanker. Her bow was gone, and the ship was listing forward. Flames and thick black smoke bellowed up out of the gaping hole. The raging inferno sounded like a blast furnace. Every now and then, they could hear men screaming and hollering above the noise of the hellhole.

"Survivors in the water, starboard," the lookout called.

Neither Wulf nor Addler said a word as they watched the men desperately trying to save each other. All would be dead within minutes. If the oil and fire didn't kill them, hypothermia would. It was like a scene out of *Dante's Inferno*. Hot bright orange and red flames spewed out of the ship as if they were trying to reach the heavens. Endless screams rose while men, some on fire, tried to save themselves and others.

"We still have two torpedoes in the aft tubes," Addler said. "The ship could float for days burning like that. Might as well put it out of its misery."

Wulf almost panicked when he saw the ships come out of the fog. He had fired his torpedoes, hoping to hit something. With two last torpedoes, he took his time making a running solution. When he was satisfied with the solution, he fired the last two torpedoes into the crippled tanker, sending it to the bottom of the Arctic Sea.

"Remain on the surface. Charge batteries. Proceed at high speed to Bergen," Wulf said.

"*Jawohl, Herr* Captain. Remain on the surface, charge batteries, and proceed to Bergen at high speed."

♦

HMS Carrow

Deep inside the destroyer, Seaman Patti Donavan of the Royal Navy, HMS Carrow, a C-Class destroyer, bolted upright in his padded chair, startled at the sudden noise coming across his headset. He leaned towards the newly installed American SONAR device, his right hand turning the dial on the receiver while trying to get a clearer signal and hear the noise again. He touched a finger to his headset as if that would help him make sense of the sudden burst of sound. He sat up again, looked around, and snapped his fingers to get Chief Petty Officer Wallis's attention. Wallis frowned and stepped over to Donavan.

"What do you have, Patti?" Wallis asked, plugging his headset into the receiver next to Donavan.

Donavan looked up at Wallis. "Multiple explosions, Chief."

They didn't see it, but the horizon lit up like daylight when the Canadian Flower class Corvette blew up.

"There's a submarine down there, Chief." Donavan slowly turned the dial, trying to find it again. "It was there, and then it wasn't, sir. Nothing."

The Carrow was now going to General Alert and was heading full speed towards the burning ships.

◆

Wulf slid down the bridge hatch, past the conning tower, and into the control room. He made his way over to the navigator's table and waited until *Obersteuermann* Ebbe, his navigator, finished plotting the sinking of the last two ships. Putting his fingers on the chart, he quickly calculated how long it would take them to reach Bergen. They were entering the Greenland Sea. So close to home, yet so far away. He went to his small cabin to lie down.

Wulf was awakened by the klaxon going off and Addler yelling. Wulf was in his boots and in the control room before the XO slid down the ladder.

"Right full rudder, come to 186. Depth fifty meters. Rig for depth charge." Addler handed this foul weather gear to a petty officer. His commands were being repeated as Wulf stepped next to him.

"A destroyer coming from the direction of Iceland. One of those ships sent out a distress call before they sank," Addler said.

"Ship recognition book," Wulf called out. The book was handed to Addler, and he immediately started flipping through it.

"Here, this is it," he said, showing the captain the picture.

Wulf read under the photo of the ship. "C-Class British Destroyer. Continue dive to fifty meters. Rig for depth charge," the captain cried out over the intercom system.

Crewmen swung the heavy round watertight doors between compartments and dogged the massive clamps tight, sealing the men inside their tomblike pressure chambers. The U-boat slipped into the depths of the Greenland Sea hoping to hide from the British destroyer.

"Shutting main ballast tank vents," the COB reported, sealing the tanks.

The iron tube creaked as water pressure began to tighten itself around the submarine. The sub gradually slowed its descent until it leveled off at fifty meters.

The control room was quiet except for occasional reports and orders between watchstanders. Captain Wulf listened closely as the Radioman monitored the destroyer's pinging.

"Conn, sonar. Ship has turned. Fast propellers heading towards us," the sonarman called out.

Fifty-eight officers and men looked up, all listening, all praying that the depth charges would miss them. They all heard the splashes as death fell from the aft end of the destroyer. Each steel drum filled with two hundred lbs. of high explosives sank into the frigid waters of the Greenland Sea. Each man flinched when the detonator clicked. It exploded, sending its devastating concussion outward. Some say you never hear the bullet that will kill you. Not so in the submarine service. All heard the click of the detonator. All died together.

♦

H. Ernest Coffman is a retired United States Air Force Intelligence Analyst and author of two self-published action/thriller novels, and four short stories on Amazon. He is published in two anthologies including *Fark Fiction*, 2022, and the Fargo Public Library's Northern Narratives, 2023.

H_2O

BARBARA BUSTAMANTE

"In the beginning was the Word
And the Word was with God
And the Word was God." *
The Word created elements
From fire and light and love.
One hundred eighteen there was.

Two elements were attracted
To each other, a cute pair.
A perfect bond they made,
A gas, a liquid, a solid.
And the Word saw that it was good
And called it water.

The Word said let us create
A dance, a song, a story,
Each star and planet.

A universe In unison with the other one hundred
sixteen.
A world with time and space
And the Word saw that it was good.

The world saw the water's beauty
Its power to carve bodies fluid
Between mountains of solid rock.
How it creates a humble abode
To nurture and propel life
From birth to death and back again

The world spends its endless lives
To discover, test, and perceive
This simple substance in complexity
In chemistry and physics of
A substance that remembers.
To this, I live and dream and write.

*(Bible John 1.1)

A Matthew Trilogy

Barbara Bustamante

Catch of the Day (Matthew 13:24-30)

"Grandpa, grandpa, wait!" Akim ran down the path to the boat dock, hopping over the rocks and jagged tree.

Grandpa Alex, with rods, tackle box, and cooler in hand, grinned and glanced back. Akim caught up to him at the bench at the end of the dock.

"How about some fishin' before supper?" Grandpa Alex scrabbled through the tackle box for the right-size hook. "Here's one for you." He handed one to Akim.

Akim reached down for the old margarine tub for the bait. "What's this? No worms. What are these fish chunks?"

"My dad taught me to use rough fish for bait when nothing else works," Grandpa Alex replied.

They set their hooks and made the first cast. The two chatted while admiring the beautiful view of Minnesota's Lake Leona. The soft breeze made this warm Sunday afternoon enjoyable while a busy squirrel flitted from branch to branch in its search for food. Meanwhile, a family of ducks swam across the inlet on their way to the bank.

"Grandpa, this morning in church the pastor was talking about tares.

What's that?"

"In the Bible, Jesus tells the parable of the wheat and tares of a man who sowed good wheat in his field. While his men slept at night, the enemy sowed tares in the wheat field. The field grew with a mix of wheat and tares. His men asked if the wheat seed was good and how the tares got there. The man said the enemy did it. His men ask if they should pull the tares out. The man said, 'No, it will pull the wheat out with it. Let both grow together until harvest. Then I will tell the harvesters to bundle up the tares to be burned and gather the wheat into my barn.'"

"But what does this mean?"

"Jesus also said that the sower of the wheat is God, the field is the world, the good seed is the children of the Kingdom, the tares are the children of the evil one, the enemy is the devil, the harvesters are the angels, and the harvest is the end of the age. All of this explains the parable. The most important part is the verse, 'Let both grow together until harvest.' The word 'let' comes from the Greek word 'aphiemi,' which means to send away, leave alone, allow, or permit. One way to do this is by forgiving. To forgive is a 'win-win' way to love your enemies."

Akim looked puzzled. "I still don't understand what tares are."

"Well, let me tell you a story your great-grandpa, Leonid, once told me about tares from growing up in Russia. The fields in southern Russia grew very fine wheat. But there was a type of grass seed that grew with the wheat called tares. Tares is also known as darnel. When the wheat seed sprouts in the moist spring soil, the tares germinate, too, and look just like the wheat. It's best to get rid of a weed when it's young before the roots grow deep. But since you can't tell the difference you have to wait. At harvest time the tares are darker, poisonous, and bitter if made into a flour.

"There must be ways to kill it before it gets big."

"No, they didn't have weed killers or treated seeds to control weeds like we do here in Minnesota. So it was important to separate the plants at harvest. Then the wheat seeds could be saved for making flour or used for next spring's seeding."

"But, Grandpa, why did God make tares that are poisonous and don't taste good?"

"Good question. That's what I asked too, and Grandpa Leonid then said, 'They didn't just throw the tares away at harvest. Some were used to sow green lawns. But some were kept for a special reason. The tare seeds were used to make a bait for the big roach fish.'"

"What's a big roach fish?"

"It's a rough fish in Russia. Not a good eating fish and the dogs got sick from eating it. It was cut in chunks and used for bait to catch Beluga Sturgeon, known for its highest prized and expensive caviar."

"Wow! What a story!" Akim immediately felt a tug on his line that almost pulled him from the bench.

"Hang on there, you must have a whopper."

Akim steadily reeled it in.

"Be patient, take it slow, so it doesn't cut your line." Grandpa Alex reeled in his line to get the net ready.

After a couple minutes of letting the fish tire, Akim got the fish close enough to the dock to use the landing net.

"Look at that nice Northern."

Treading Troubled Water (Matthew 10:16-24)

"Come on, Duke, it's time to get the mail." Akim and his trusty black lab descended the steps from the side door of their home in the country. As they strolled down the gravel road, there was only the sound of their footsteps and the birds overhead in the trees. Through the canopy of trees arching the road, rays of sun dotted the path. Deep breaths of cool air helped Akim relax and meditate on the beauty of nature.

Akim cherished these peaceful walks since he and his wife, Julie, bought the hobby farm from old man Ackermann ten years ago. Since both had jobs in town, the fifteen miles to Wilma were an easy commute. It was a great place to raise their three children. But most of all, he loved the flowing artesian well that Mr. Ackermann's father had drilled eighty-five years ago. The well required only one pump to distribute the water through the house. Using gravity, the rest of the water flowed to the different tanks throughout the barn and outside to a larger tank that spilled out to create a creek to a pond a furlong away. The freshwater attracted a wide variety of birds and wildlife. It was not uncommon for deer or a moose to spend the spring in their groves of trees.

Akim removed the mail from the mailbox at the end of the driveway and leisurely perused the letters and junk mail on his way back to the house with Duke. His only distraction was a cute little gray squirrel stopping to get a glance of the approaching duo.

Once home, Akim started to fill the carafe for a pot of coffee. To his astonishment the water was slow. He went down in the basement and checked the pump expecting the cat had accidentally unplugged the pump, but everything was fine.

Like a man on a mission, Akim quickly exited the house, marched across the yard and firmly grasped the barn door handle, and opened the door. One huge step inside and he was shocked by water pouring at half pressure from the pipe. In anger and confusion, he strutted back to the house. Using the kitchen phone, he calls his neighbor, Jay, who lived a mile away.

"Hello, Jay, it's Akim. I'm wondering if you're having any water problems at your place. My well is only pumping at about half pressure."

"Mine has slowed a bit, but not half. I heard that old man Melvin had a total failure. I wonder what's going on. We've never had trouble like this before."

"You don't say."

"Melvin thinks it has something to do with Olson's buying up those four small farms by Buffalo Slough. He said that Olson got a contract offer to grow potatoes on his land."

"Have you heard from anyone else?"

"No, but get back to me if you learn more."

"Sure, Jay, talk to you later."

Akim grabbed the phone book to look up John Nelson's number at the county water management office. He dialed the number and explained the problem. John said he had heard some of the same rumors and would go out to Olson's place to check it out. John suggested Akim call back in a couple of days.

Akim quickly got ready for work and decided to pick up his coffee in town. On the drive, he thought about Bob Olson who went to his church, and all these rumors. What was he to do?

That night after dinner and once the children were asleep, Akim and Julie settled down to discuss the water problem. The worst outcome would require redrilling the present well -- and a flowing artesian well at that. At the least, it would cost $3,000. Even worse was the rift with a friend from church. Akim and Julie were shocked and in denial that their good friend, Bob, would jeopardize their friendship. They had been friends for a long time. Why would he do such a thing? They felt like they were up a creek without a paddle.

The next morning, John from the water management office called, informing Akim that the rumors were true about Bob's contract to grow potatoes. Growing potatoes requires two inches of rain per week to grow to the recommended size. The county's average rainfall was only two inches of rain per month. The questions were where Bob would get that much water and why he had chosen to use the aquifer over rivers and streams. With the popularity of these contracts growing, John agreed to call a meeting for all involved to settle the problem.

Jay was happy when Akim called back. Akim told him that John wanted Jay and Melvin to call him at his office for the details.

Akim sat quietly pondering how he would deal with Bob. Instead of discussing this over with his wife, Julie, he decided to ask his father. But talking to him was iffy. Some days his dementia was good and some days he wasn't. But he decided that he'd give it a try anyway.

The next day right before lunch, Akim decided to stop by the nursing home and have a visit with Dad. He had known Mr. Ackermann personally and how the well had been drilled, but Akim didn't know if Dad would remember. Dad had just gotten dressed for the day and when he saw Akim, he lit up. He was so happy to see Akim, which was a sign that this was probably one of his good days. When Akim sat down, Dad immediately wanted to know all about the kids and Julie and what they were up to. After discussing the kids and their activities, Dad pressed to hear about Julie, the 'cream of the crop' when it came to his daughters-in-law.

"How's the farm?" Dad asked.

"OK, but we're having problems with the well," Akim replied.

"There shouldn't be anything wrong with that well. I was there when they drilled it."

"But, Dad, that was sixty-five years ago and things have changed since then. You know Bob Olson who lives a couple miles away? He got an offer to grow potatoes for that big french fry company and, to grow bigger potatoes, they have to use lots of water. So he's been taking water from the aquifer and using it for irrigation. It's affecting everyone else's wells. Our water flow has decreased dramatically.

"That just isn't right."

"The big problem is that Bob goes to our church and he and I have been good friends for a long time. I don't understand why he would do this. I don't think that he knew that by dipping into the aquifer that it would affect everybody else. He just went ahead and did it. I haven't talked to Bob about it, but I really would like your help on how to deal with this."

"Well, you're between a rock and a hard place. I can understand why you would want to talk this out. First of all, what's most important is to realize that the water really doesn't belong to either one of you. This water is a gift from God. When it comes to Bob, he needs to be held accountable for what he did."

"Deep down I believe he's a good man, but there's a real big chance that he's being pressured by his own desire to make some extra money to make his and his family's life better. Sometimes people don't look at how it's going to affect others or their own relationship with God."

"Have you called the county about it?"

"I called John at the water management office. He felt it was necessary for all involved to meet to try to work things out. I learned that all the rumors were true about Bob. I plan on going to the meeting and to listen what the others have to say. But I feel anxious about doing the right thing."

"Doing the right thing can be a lonely road. Many will take the easy route, but easy isn't always the right way. Your friends may pick on you and steal what is rightfully yours. They will turn the tables on you and attack you from the rear. Be smart and honest and when the time comes, the Holy Spirit will give you the words to rebut."

With that, Akim hugged and kissed his father and quietly left the room.

The next day at the county water management office, John was preparing for the meeting in the conference room. There was a long rectangular table and chairs on each side of the room. John's chair was at the head of the table. He had a legal pad and a couple new pens in front of him. Melvin, the first to arrive sat on John's right. They chatted while waiting for the others. Jay arrived next and seated himself next to Melvin. Akim also arrived early and sat next to Jay. Just before the meeting was to start, Bob and another man in an expensive suit arrived and took seats on the other side of the table next to John.

John addressed Bob. "Who is this with you?"

"This is Ronald Marshall of the Imperial Foods Corporation," Bob said. "I've invited him to help answer any questions concerning my water usage."

"This meeting was set to discuss these matters privately among neighbors. I don't think it's appropriate to bring others in without my prior approval."

"I thought it was important to bring an expert in on these matters."

"That's for me to decide who to invite. But how versed is he in water management?"

"He knows what we're talking about."

"I'll allow him to stay," John said. "But if he interferes with any part of this meeting, he's out of here. Do you understand?"

"Yes, sir."

"Now, let us begin."

John read a prepared document explaining the complaints brought to his attention. Each farmer's complaint reported the issues and detailed evidence. When he concluded, he asked each farmer if they had anything to add. Melvin angrily elaborated on the extent of the damage to his well and the estimated cost of repair. Jay added several more details that weren't in the report.

Calmly observing it all, Akim was puzzled at Bob avoiding eye contact. Maybe his guest required his attention. Akim's mind kept wandering back to his father's advice - be smart and honest and let the Holy Spirit provide the words. What did this mean?

When Jay was done, John gave Akim the go-ahead to make his remarks. Akim opened his mouth to speak, but nothing came out. All eyes landed on him. Silence filled the room. At that moment he understood how the silence was the message. In the chaos of words and emotion, the Holy Spirit spoke.

John assumed Akim had nothing to say, so he addressed Bob. "How do you address these complaints?"

Bob discussed why the Buffalo Slough was an insufficient water supplier for the potato contract. Mr. Marshall interjected to supply statistics and offered the farmers reparations for the damage to the wells. But it was only for groundwater wells, not flowing artesian wells. When John heard this, he insisted that all wells be included. Mr. Marshall refuted the claim that that arrangement was not cost-effective. John then knew exactly why Mr. Marshall was there. John angrily asked Mr. Marshall to leave as his contribution to the meeting was disruptive. Bob followed him out. Akim, realizing that this was a personal attack and that nothing was going to be settled, sat and calmly waited. John asked if anyone wished to comment and, without further ado, the meeting was adjourned.

The next day, John called Akim. He had learned from the other farmers that their wells would be repaired by the corporation if they also agreed to a contract to grow potatoes. That left Akim out in the cold. John assured Akim that since his well was in the same watershed district as Lake Leona that his well would be included in any damage to the lake. In the meantime, Akim had to conserve his water as best as he could.

After supper that night, Julie and Akim sat drinking their tea.

"What more do you know about the well problem?" Julie asked.

"The other farmers get their wells repaired if they sign the potato contract. If it affects the lake, we have to wait for the courts to rule to get our well repaired."

"But that's not fair. We should all be treated the same."

"I know. Sometimes things don't turn out the way you want. Sometimes the rules don't decide in our favor. The rules aren't perfect; they don't make everyone happy. The rules are there for our safety. The rules are still there to prove our need for God. It's how we get justice."

In church the next Sunday, everyone noticed that Bob's family avoided Akim's family. Akim quietly sat and remembered the story of the wheat and the tares and the Holy Spirit's message.

Go Tell It On the Mountain (Matthew 18:21-35; 22:34-46)

The day the Federov family had long waited for had arrived - Grandpa Akim's ninetieth birthday party. Everything was planned. His great-grandson, Ben, would pick Akim up in Terrace, WA, and drive him to Camp Papoose, a mountain resort.

Ben arrived in his Jeep Wrangler at the log home of Akim's friend, David. Using a small step stool, Ben helped Akim into the comfortable truck seat. Instead of taking the ferry to the highway on the other side of the mountain, Ben chose a shortcut route up the side of the mountain using a paved single-lane alternate road. It would cut their traveling time in half. In no time, they were on their way.

In spite of the dark cloudy sky, the scenery was beautiful. They climbed the mountain, making many sharp hairpin turns. All of a sudden, graupel hit the windshield and bounced off the truck's hood. Around the next turn, a flash shower had created an ice patch. When Ben accelerated after the turn his truck spun around and headed off the road into a burned-out forest. The truck slammed into a dead tree which snapped and wedged itself under the truck's belly, making it immobile.

"Grandpa! Are you OK?" Ben exclaimed. "Holy crap, what happened?"

"You betcha, felt like ice," remarked Akim.

"I'll check it out." Ben jumped out and stumbled around the truck to check for damage.

Inspection complete, he climbed back inside, "We're going to need a tow truck." He reached for his phone. "What? No cell service. What do we do now?"

Akim leaned back in his seat. "Just wait. Someone is bound to come along."

"How long is that going to take?"

"Until they get here," Akim said. "They'll come - you'll see."

To change the subject, Akim asked Ben how he liked college. They shared their college experiences and laughed about some of the crazy things that some young people do.

"Grandpa, tell me about your life."

"Since we lived apart all of your life, we haven't had a chance to get to know each other and that I regret. But that has never changed my love for you and your family. I grew up in northern Minnesota where my great-grandfather migrated from Russia. My grandfather and I were very close. We weren't a religious family, but we had a strong faith in God. We'd go fishing and spend many hours talking about God. I remember when I learned that God, the Father, sent his Son, Jesus Christ to pay the price for our sins by dying on the cross. I was never the same after that."

"That must have been unforgettable."

"Indeed, it was and still is. You may wonder why God would do this. He loved us sooo much. He wanted to spend eternity with us, but we were flawed by sin. Being God, He knew all the questions as well as all the answers. As the all-knowing Creator of the universe, He wanted us to love Him with all our heart, soul, and mind and to love our neighbor as yourself."

"All this is fascinating. I've never heard it explained in this way before. I grew up playing a lot of sports and was involved with school activities. We never went to church and talked about God stuff. This is interesting, tell me more."

"After high school, I went to a community college while working in the public library, in Wilma, MN. With a liberal arts degree and promotions within the library I was offered a scholarship at an online university for a master's degree. Digital technology was needed for the library to succeed. I mostly worked from home, especially during bad weather."

"That's sweet how that turned out. So, I heard that you lived out-of-town. Right?"

"Yes, several years after Julie and I bought the hobby farm near Lake Leona my faith was tested. Neighboring farmers decided to use groundwater from their wells for irrigation. This damaged my well and our relationships with our neighbors. I learned how to listen to the Holy Spirit, which is not what I expected."

"That's amazing. How did you handle that?"

"God loves all of his creation including people. Period. But He's not too crazy about our behavior. We mess up more than we know. I needed to see my neighbors as God sees them - His dear children. It wasn't easy; they were stealing my water. In the end, I lost and had to drill a new well. But the broken friendships were a problem. Because God loves us, He justly gives us what we deserve when we sin. Eternal separation from God. When we regret these thoughts, words, and actions, He forgives us. In turn, He expects us to forgive our neighbor when they ask forgiveness. Not everyone is willing to pass the favor on. But it works and heals our brokenness."

"But isn't forgiving like letting someone get away with doing something wrong?"

"Nope, because forgiving is a gift of the heart. It's not ignoring the sin or letting it go. Forgiveness is like a two-sided coin – being forgiven and forgiving others. It's based on love. By knowing that God loves both sides, it's possible to see both sides. Forgiveness removes the responsibility to expect and make people change. It gives a fresh start to both the forgiven and the forgiver. It's a balance of good terms. No more tit for tat. You are free to be you and continue to love your neighbor as God sees them."

"Let me get this straight, if the world understood forgiveness, bad acts would end?"

"Not exactly. There's the issue of evil which is the absence of love. It's the thing that separates us from the love of God. The answer is Jesus. And since Jesus was true God and true human, His sacrifice of dying on the cross paid for our bad acts. In fact, the last word Jesus spoke on the cross in Greek, 'tetelestai,' translates as 'It is finished,' meaning paid in full. And ... Ben, I just can't get enough of this Jesus."

The two sat together for hours, sorting out the cures for the ills of the world. Ben and Akim hit it off with tears and laughter. But Ben was starting to wonder how long they would be stranded and asked Akim for any ideas to get them out of their mess.

Akim gazed out through the windshield to the dimming landscape of the river below. "You see the lights of Terrace below us?"

"Yeah, so what good is that?"

"Have you tried the headlights to see if they work?" Akim inquired.

"No." Ben tried the lights. They cast shadows around the dead stumps.

"Good," Akim said. "I have an idea. My buddy, David, showed me how to talk using Morse Code. Let's try a practice run and see if that works. Flash three short, three long, three short."

Ben flashed the lights in sequence.

"That's it. Now we wait until it's good and dark."

Wrapped up in blankets to keep warm, Ben and Akim used the code intermittently to try to communicate to anyone in town.

Meanwhile back in town, David finished his supper and settled down to watch TV, but something in the corner of his eyesight distracted him. He couldn't make out what it was. He asked his daughter for binoculars, but she didn't have any.

"Dad, I found a pair of Mom's opera glasses. Will that work?"
"Sure."

David went out on the front stoop but saw nothing. He waited a few minutes and he saw it again.

"By golly! That's Morse Code! Someone on the mountain is in

trouble. Call the police!"

Up on the mountain, Ben and Akim kept at it, but Ben was starting to doubt if it was worth it. All of a sudden, they heard a siren and saw colored lights shining around them.

When the policeman got to their truck, Akim asked him, "What took you so long?"

He replied, "Some old geezer called and claimed you were flashing S.O.S." The men's laughter could be heard down the mountain.

Using a jack and a winch, the policeman got the truck back on the road.

"We can still get you to your party. The retreat isn't far away," the policeman remarked. "I can escort you the rest of the way after I call ahead on our satphone. Will that work?"

Ben glanced at Akim for his approval. "Sure, lead the way."

After a couple turns, Akim said, "We've spent all this time talking about me, but I still don't know much about you. So, tell me about yourself?"

"Sorry, no disrespect, but it's your day."

The road leveled off at the top of the climb, winding around an open pasture.

"I'm a junior at the Boise State majoring in English," Ben continued. "I'm better at writing than driving as you can see. I'd be honored to share your stories about Jesus to the world with your permission."

"Ben, it would be my honor!"

◆

Barbara Bustamante started writing poetry in high school. Her love of words inspired her to write poetry and stories in the *Tales From the Frozen North* and *Welcome to Effham Falls*. She's retired, active in church, promotes mental health, and lives with her feline writing companion, Talon.

River Scofflaws

Tristan Duerr

"It's half past ten. They comin' or what?"

"They're coming. Cool yourself," I said.

"Cool me? Ya got me standing here in the middle of January, waitin' fer booze that's probably a block'a ice by now." Barry buried his hands so deep into the pockets of his trench coat they threatened to break the seams. I took a long drag from my cigarette, wondering if Barry was right.

"They'll be here soon." I let the smoke exit my lungs. The dim, orange glow of the tip was the only light source within view of the seemingly endless night, like the sun floating in the empty blackness of space. "Yeah? Bet the cops'll be here soon too. Then what?"

I rolled my eyes. "For a New York boy, you're jumpy, ya know that? Don't you boys do this sort of thing all the time out there?"

"Maybe that's why I'm so jumpy. Been behind the eight ball enough times to know when a job gets screwy." I took another drag from my cigarette and gave no response.

After another minute or so, Barry began to shake his legs to get some warmth back into them. "Let's just blow this place, alright, Edward? The buttons probably caught 'em on their way over here."

I looked at my wristwatch. 10:40 pm. Twenty minutes late. I was just about to admit he was right when I heard the slight rumble of a car approaching.

"There's our bucket." I took the last drag from my cigarette before flicking it into the snow, the lone star now dead. Two men hopped out of the car, the driver giving a nervous wave.

"Evening, gentlemen. Bring what we've been waiting ever so patiently for?"

"Yes sir, got most of it in the back trunk, a few extra bottles in the driver's seat."

"Good, and not a minute too soon," I said as we headed to the car's trunk. "My other half here was getting ready to bump you two off." My tone was somewhere between a threat and a joke.

"Sorry, sir, the bad weather made us have to move slowly, honest."

Barry played his part as the meaner half well, giving the two men a grizzled look while we opened the trunk. Someone in Canada would've seen an assortment of good drinks. But me, I saw liquid gold.

Wine, beer, bourbon, whiskey, and much more. A unique currency, once casually enjoyed by any American citizen with a few extra coins in their pocket, was now a highly sought-after luxury that had people paying a year's worth of rent just to have a standing area in an underground bar, and another year's rent to have the luxury to sit down.

You had people going blind from bad moonshine they'd brewed in their bathtubs, and government agents finding homemade distilleries in high mountain tops, and that's the least crazy thing people were doing. Alcohol hadn't been made illegal for medical purposes, so doctors became your next local bartender. Of course, they couldn't outlaw it for religious practices either, because what would the papers say to that? You'd have Father O'Malley preaching the good word on Sunday, give you a glass of wine for communion, then sell you a bottle out back on Monday for a 'generous church donation.' Wanna know the craziest item to hit the market? Dehydrated grape juice. It came with a very oddly specific warning not to leave it in your cupboard for more than a few days or it would turn into wine. Curiously enough, no shop could keep it from flying off the shelves.

All this was possible because the big boys in Congress got strong-armed into saying that alcohol was public enemy number one. Funny enough, once it was made illegal, our pockets were never heavier.

"That's it? You stiffin' us or somethin'?" Barry asked, seemingly disappointed by the quantity.

"Relax, Barry. This is the amount we ordered." I reached into my trench coat pocket, pulled out a few bills, and handed them to the men. "Two Cs, as agreed. But if you ever keep us waitin' like that again, I'll have my pal here break your hands with a wine bottle. That clear?"

The two men quickly nodded and helped us unload the crates. After we'd finished, they slowly drove off into the night, disappearing into the snowy darkness.

"This all ya ordered? Why waste time on a single trunk of booze?" Barry pulled out a cigarette. He cupped a hand around it but struggled to get the lighter going.

I reached over and lit it for him. "I bet in New York where ya got those big shipping containers right on the East Coast, you get all the booze ya want. Bet it's fancy too. Wine from France, whiskey from Scotland, beer from Germany."

"Alright, alright, get to the point," Barry said, before taking a drag. The smoke smelled rotten. Maybe the shit brand was responsible for his poor attitude. In my experience, treating yourself now and again tends to give you a brighter outlook on things.

"My point is that this ain't New York. It's Fargo, North Dakota. This ain't the Atlantic. It's the Red River, and this wine sure as hell wasn't made in Paris, where angels descend from the heavens and pour single tears into every bottle. It's Canadian. We take what we can get out here." In my opinion, the wine was fantastic.

"Why not just ship the better stuff out here?"

I wanted to bury my head in the snow and scream horrible obscenities that would've made my mother gasp. "Because the cost of doing so would be astronomical, not to mention all the buttons between here and there and all the other gangs who would lick their lips at a large shipment driving through the middle of nowhere."

Barry inspected some of the bottles. Seeing that most of them were Canadian made him visually upset. The pompous rich boy. "I'm gonna miss German beer."

I laughed. "Don't let the Canadians hear ya say that. Besides, I think their beer is lovely."

Barry and I delivered the shipment to a speakeasy located in downtown Fargo, right under the Fargo Theater. What interesting places these speakeasies were. There had no regulations, no rules. After all, you were already breaking the law. For the first time, you saw white men sitting right next to black men, women drinking in public next to men, black musicians performing for white crowds, and vice versa. The government attempted to use alcohol as a tool of segregation, but it only brought new social norms. I didn't mind too much, seeing enough things as I have. Things like what shade your skin was or what ya got between your legs seemed to matter a lot less. Besides, at the very least, it meant more clientele for us scofflaws, and the Red River was the vein that helped the alcohol flow through our little neck of the woods.

"You gonna head home?" Barry asked, stretching out a cramp in his hands he'd gotten from helping carry the boxes.

"Think I may stay for a drink or two. You're free to head out though."

He nodded, digging another cigarette from his coat as he left the speakeasy. I let out an exhausted sigh before I sat down at the bar table. Jazz music filled the air, people were laughing, and conversations of all kinds echoed like a dog pile of noise. I heard a woman talking about how her husband hasn't had a job in six months. I'm jumped by talk of a man who told of how he popped two fellas who flirted with his sister, then I heard the roll of dice and some unlucky shmuck who bet far more than he had any reason too. I picture what he's gonna tell his wife when he gets home. Maybe his wife will be the next patron here, complaining about how long her husband has been out of work. Maybe he's the husband of the woman I heard before. You got all kinds here, from those who are sitting on top of the world, to those who are picking up the crumbs. While some of the big speakeasies have high entry fees, this one relaxed on it a bit —if you count one hundred dollars being relaxed.

"What'll it be, Edward?" The voice of the bartender snapped me out of my thoughts.

"Give me Sidecar."

"Treating yourself today?"

"Something like that," I said when the bartender started to pour the ingredients into a shaker.

"Saw you and Barry bring in a shipment. Did things get rough?"

"Nah, just stayed out later than we planned."

He finished making the drink and handed it to me. I sipped slowly. The sweetness of the sugar-lined rim mixed with the roughness of the alcohol made for a satisfying drink.

"Perfect as always." I sipped again while the bartender cleaned out one of the glasses that had been sitting on the counter. "Hear anything down the grapevine?" While I was a mid-carder, I still wasn't privy to higher-up information. But say a higher-up got a little tipsy and loose with his words, eager to brag to some small bartender, well, was it such a crime to know a guy?

"Heard that a box job is next." The bartender looked at the glass in the light to make sure it was properly cleaned. "I'm assuming they'll use a bent car?"

"They don't wanna risk one of their rides getting impounded or spotted. Heard the buttons have figured out some of the big cheeses' cars. Don't wanna risk their cover being blown before the job even starts."

"They hitting a bank?"

"Nah, personal stash of someone comin' to town soon. Some Hollywood big shot, didn't hear who. Not exactly a bank, but still bound to have a lot of cabbage inside."

"Know where it's happening?"

"They'll be driving by the river before they reach the town. You'll be intercepting them along the way."

The river. It was always the damn river. Bosses wanted to have a chat, they fished by the river. Booze delivery? Meet them along the river. What was so special about the river?

"Why the river?" I asked. "Why not the woods, or somewhere more rural before he even gets close to here?"

"They didn't reveal that much. I don't like to pry too hard. If I do, they may think I'm a rat."

"The only person you're telling is a fellow criminal."

He chuckled, looking me dead in the eye. "Which is exactly why they're the last people I want thinking I'm a rat."

"Pretty smart for a barkeep."

"I'm only a barkeep because I'm so smart, Edward. When you go to a casino, you respect the one dealing the cards, not the factory that made them. When ya buy booze at an illegal bar, you ask the barkeep for what ya want, not the suppliers who brought it."

"Guess even the illegal bartenders keep the wisdom." I downed the last of my drink and he took the glass to rinse it out.

A week passed, and I was standing by the Red River with lungs full of smoke. I stared deeply into the rapids. The sound of the water sliding into the rocks hypnotized me like a siren from those old Greek stories. The burning from the smoke in my lungs was a stark contrast to the freezing winds. Even with my coat, I felt like tiny daggers were perpetually stabbing my body down to its bones. The orange glow from the cigarette tip burned bright, and the skies were completely covered in gray clouds, almost as if the sun had been swallowed.

"Eh, Edward, quit starin' off into space, would ya?" Barry tossed his cigarette into the snow and walked closer to the actor's car we had stopped. Some of the other boys were already interrogating him about his money.

Barry flashed about the fakest smile I'd ever seen. "Listen, buddy, I bet you're a real cake-eater down in those Hollywood clubs, but ya ain't gotta tease me with sweet nothins. So just tell me the code for the safe already."

"I already told you, I don't know it." The actor pleaded with tear-filled eyes while two of the men held him down on his knees.

The actor was chubby, wearing a roughed-up suit that in new condition would've put a middle-class man into the poor house. After the actor offered his excuse, Barry gave a slight nod to the men who instantly grabbed the back of his head and slammed it into the hard, ice-covered dirt. When the actor lifted his head, blood streaming out of his nose stained the small bits of snow on his face red.

"Aww, sorry about that, pal. Might not be the cats meowing in front of those cameras for a few days. Let's not make it weeks, eh? Tell us what the code is."

"I don't know. I swear!" The man said, blood flowing into his mouth.

I could imagine that iron taste, had to taste it many times myself. I wondered how many times the shmuck had tasted it. It'd be an honor if we had given him his first experience.

"My agent is the only one who knows it. He doesn't want me going on careless sprees." The actor whimpered.

"Oh, really now? Why you carrying it for 'em then, especially all alone out here?" Benny motioned to the two men again. They shoved the actor's face into the snowy dirt and each of them placed a few stomps to the back of his head before pulling him up again.

His nose was broken now, bending in three different directions, and blood flowed in a steady stream while a few drops spilled out from a few open cuts in his lip.

"Let me give it a try," I said, taking a final inhale. I let the embers consume the cigarette down to the bud before I flicked it into the snow.

"What are you gonna do, buy a coffee and compliment his movies until he tells ya?" Barry asked as I knelt next to the man.

"Something like that." I brushed the snow from the man's coat and straightened his tie. "Been rough? The acting I mean."

He didn't answer, simply nodded as he tried to keep his blood from entering his mouth.

"So you fell behind on your payments to us. It happens." I took out a handkerchief and wiped the blood off his lips. "Hell, I've come up short too. One time I was on a booze run, and a whole crate fell out of the car. A whole crate! The boss gave me an earful for that, gave me a mouthful of his fist too. I'm a fan of your films, ya know. Oh yeah, saw a few of them at the theater here in town. You still got it despite what they say in the papers." I looked into his tear-filled, green eyes, wondering if he got them shined somehow to look that way. Kinda like how you get your shoes shined maybe.

"Tell you what," I said. "You give us the code for that safe, I pull a few strings. We play some of your classics in the theater, we have you attend in person, get the papers, and a nice big crowd. We'll hang posters, the whole Hollywood treatment. Few nice reviews, you look all good for a smaller town, giving to the needy, and bam! You're the bee's knees all over again."

The man stayed silent for a moment before giving a slight nod. "Twenty-eight. Fifty-five. Twelve."

Another one of our guys tried the combo on the safe, and sure enough, it opened. More C's than I had ever seen in one place in my whole life. Well, that wasn't exactly true. I was used to seeing this kind of money in its liquid state, all nice and bottled with a pretty label. The beautiful river brought us money in all its forms. Maybe what makes it so special is that it flows north.

I looked at the man, smiled, gave him two playful pats on the cheek, and stood up, pushing another cigarette from the box. The two men holding him let go, looking disappointed that the fun was over. I slid on my black gloves, pulled out my revolver, and put a bullet in the side of his head.

I'd seen him die in a few of his films, but I bet he never felt like this. Guess his buttered nose was so busy sticking up in the air he'd never bothered to see the real thing. Shame, maybe he would've made more money.

"Dump his body in the river." I slipped off my gloves and dropped my gun. "Put on gloves, slide mine on his hands, and throw the gun in the river with him. If they ever find his body they'll think he did it himself."

The other men quickly did as they were told all while Barry looked at me in shock. I gave a light chuckle as I walked away from the river with him. "What? You think I got this job by being nice?"

"I don't know. You're just always so calm, always got that smile on your face, I just assumed that." He paused, trying to find the words. "You're only here because you were born into it by some family member."

I gave him a sideways glance. "The last thing I've ever had the privilege of is being born into anything of value."

We hopped into our car, and the engine hummed to life.

"I didn't plan on going that far. Thought he made us money. We give him exposure and twist a few arms to get him parties, and he gives us some of his revenue," Barry stated, confused.

"It was the deal, but he's been late on payments on multiple occasions. The only reason we gave him any slack was because he made us a killing. His career was in the toilet now though. He got beef with some other actors, word spread, and he could hardly get a part at all. Taking whatever we could from that safe was probably more than he'd make us in the next five years." I took a drag from my cigarette, letting the smoke fill the inside of the car before I rolled down my window a bit. "Besides, I'm a man of my word. Imagine the publicity he'll get now that he's dead. Theaters from here to both coasts will be chomping at the bit to show his old films to honor his memory and all that. After all, an artist's true value comes after they die."

Barry's eyes widened before he grinned, matching my own expression. "You're a sick bastard, ya know that? You'd fit in New York well."

"Ha! I'm flattered, but I'm not much of an ocean guy." I adjusted my rear mirror, glancing at the river one last time before we left. "I think I prefer the smaller joys here."

⬥

Tristan has always loved crafting stories and has expressed that love by writing and acting. He has published his own Anthology titled *A Collection of Madness* and has acted in many local theater productions. He also aspires to become a voice actor one day soon. When not getting lost in a good story you can find him sipping his coffee, and thinking of what else is out there for him to learn.

They Bite

Chris Stenson

Eight-year-old Timothy grabbed a couple of pieces of dry bread from the container and rushed outside. Halfway to the dock his mother's daily warning sounded in his head. "When you are on the dock, *always wear your life jacket.*" He shrugged, kept running, and skidded to a stop at the end of the dock. He glanced up just before his furry friend, Rex, bumped into him. Timothy teetered, caught himself briefly, lost his balance, and tumbled into the water. The dried bread flew out of his hand.

Timothy hit the water with a splash, plunging deep. He sputtered to the surface but couldn't kick his foot free from the tangle of weeds wrapped around his ankle. He panicked and tried to scream, swallowing a mouthful of water for his efforts. He sunk back down into the muck.

Rex barked.

Timothy fought his way back to the surface. "Mom! Help!" He tried to touch the bottom, but the muck was too thick, and he sank up to his knees.

Rex pranced and barked wildly.

Timothy reached for the dock. His fingers caught the edge, slipped off, and drove a splinter into his thumb. Blood seeped out of the wound. A small bluegill darted out from the safety of the shadows underneath the dock and nipped at his bloody finger.

"Ouch. That hurt." He pulled his injured hand away and grabbed the dock.

The water was alive. Aggressive small bluegills and sunfish had schooled around Timothy. They took turns nipping at his exposed skin.

"Rex...get Mom." Timothy's fingers started to slip. "Hurry."

The fish grabbed onto his red swim trunks and pulled. Timothy's precarious grip on the dock was slipping away. He kicked with all his might but couldn't dislodge the pesky fish. "Mom...Mom...help me," he screamed.

Rex barked and grabbed his shirt.

"Timothy," his mother, Beth, yelled. "I'm coming."

Timothy's heartbeat thundered in his chest as the weight of the fish became too great for him to bear. One by one, his wet fingers slipped. His thoughts raced. These were bad fishes. Were they going to eat him? He would never eat fish again.

Below him, the weeds disappeared. The clear blue water became darker and the surface got farther away. He was scared. His lungs would burst if he didn't breathe soon. A light appeared in front of Timothy. Suddenly, he was no longer scared.

"Grandma, is that you?"

"Yes."

"Where's Grandpa?"

"You'll see him soon."

"I'm scared. I should have listened to Mom."

"We know."

His grandma wrapped her arms around him, and her visage disappeared. Timothy sobbed, sputtered, and inhaled. Death cradled him gently in her arms as the fish dragged Timothy's limp body into the dark depths of the lake.

"Timothy. Timothy. Where are you?" Beth stood at the end of the dock, anxiety gurgling in her stomach. She bit her lip to keep from screaming and scanned the beach, waiting for her son to pop out of the water. Scared you, didn't I, he would say. Instead, a tennis shoe floated to the surface.

"No...No.... Mark, come quick!" Beth dove into the water, grabbing handfuls of weeds to pull herself deeper. She sputtered to the surface, took a quick breath, and dove back under. Clawing and kicking her way around the dock, she found no trace of Timothy.

Mark was standing on the beach when she resurfaced. "Beth, what's wrong?"

She stood and held up Timothy's shoe, but her legs gave out and she collapsed in a heap.

Matt lifted her. "Honey, what's wrong?"

"Ti..Tim...Our son is missing." She let go of the scream she had been holding in. "Our son is gone."

Later, lost somewhere in the depths of her grief, Beth stood at the end of the dock staring at everything and seeing nothing. Time and all movement around her moved in slow motion. Boats drove up and down the lake, searching. She felt sorry for the poor parents whose child was missing. Her husband came and stood next to her, pulling her into an embrace. Why was there such anguish etched in his eyes? Her heart ached for him.

"Oh, God." She trembled and shook all over. It wasn't somebody else's child. It was hers.

Several hours later, the rescue divers exited the waters of Turtle Lake. Their body language and the empty body bag told Beth all she needed to know. They didn't find Timothy. Tears streamed down her face.

Her husband, Mark, put his arms around her and pulled her close. "It's going to be okay," he whispered.

"It will never be okay. My baby is gone."

♠

Kevin held his mask, leaned backwards, and dropped over the side of his small boat. He popped to the surface and inflated his buoyancy vest. He attached his dive flag to the anchor rope, letting everyone on the small lake know that he was somewhere under the boat and they should keep their distance. As he floated, his heart raced with excitement and apprehension. He mentally went through his predive checklist and recalculated his bottom time. He was breaking two very important fundamental laws of diving: Never dive alone, and never attempt one hundred feet unless you have experience and your advanced open water certificate. He had neither.

Last weekend, while he was fishing, his depth finder spotted a deep hole around one hundred feet down. The locator also picked up something suspended off the bottom, either a giant fish or a large school of something. There wasn't enough detail, but he was eager to find out. He dove or snorkeled almost every weekend. The water was super clear but other than the various fish and the trash he picked up, he found nothing exciting. This was his chance. Most of the time he was alone. He knew this lake. His best friend, Darren, who was his dive class partner and a fellow junior at West Fargo High, couldn't join the dive today. Kevin decided going alone would be worth the risk. He let out air from his Buoyancy Control Device (BCD) and started his descent to the darkness waiting below.

Kevin glided down at a controlled leisurely pace, enjoying the clarity of the water and the abundance of small fish. He hit the thermocline at twenty-five feet and wished he owned a dry suit. He felt like someone dropped a bucket of ice cubes down his back. He overcame the momentary chill and a slight shiver with the help of Mother Nature. At thirty feet he stopped to check his dive computer and let his ears equalize. When he swallowed, his ears popped, and he was ready to continue.

As he dove deeper, the soft buzz of boats and jet skis fell silent. He floated at forty feet and was amazed by the silence and the vastness of the water surrounding him. He was part of a whole different world. Gazing upwards at the surface, he saw just a twinkle of brightness. He snapped on his underwater light and checked his dive computer again. He would need to pick up his pace if he wanted to spend any time exploring the bottom and the irregularities, he spotted on the depth finder.

The inky blackness enveloped Kevin. He reminded himself to slow his breathing. He was using too much oxygen. Small fish darted in and out of the light, their eyes glowing pinpricks. Shadows of larger fish, probably pike and bass, floated in the distance.

At seventy feet, he reached the bottom and shined his light on a large crater approximately twenty-five feet in circumference and eighteen inches deep. There were hundreds of large sunfish fanning the bottom. They acted like this was a giant nest. Didn't panfish normally spawn in the shallows? They ignored his presence until he was close to the edge, then they schooled together and swam straight at him. The largest, the size of a dinner plate, dashed at him and nipped at his legs. The fish clamped down.

"Ouch, son-of-a-bitch. That hurt." He could feel the welt already growing under his suit. They bite and bite hard.

Two more raced at Kevin. He pulled up his legs and, with fins extended, kicked at the approaching fish. Two more hard bites and Kevin had enough. He swam away before any more attacked. Once he was clear of the crater the fish left him alone.

Kevin glided near the bottom, trying hard not to disturb the muck that had accumulated over the years. After a dozen yards, the bottom started to slope downwards. The gradual decline became a dark and bottomless abyss. He had found the deep hole he spotted the previous weekend. He saved the coordinates in his dive computer and headed into the darkness.

In the dirty thirties, also known as the Dust Bowl years, when the water was low, companies had dug gravel out of the southern end of the lake until they hit a few springs, which flooded the lake with water. At the bottom of the pit, along an excavated wall of the long dead gravel pit, Kevin's light exposed unexpected color. He grabbed the object and yanked. A small pair of red swim trunks came out of the muck. Kevin's respiration and heartbeat quickened. He played his light over the expanse. Two white strings protruded from the silt. He pulled them and a tennis shoe slid out of the mud. He placed the swimming suit and the tennis shoe into his mesh dive bag. As his heartbeat thundered in his ears his excitement grew. The boy who disappeared had been wearing red trunks. Could these belong to him? Would he find Timothy?

Kevin swam faster along the wall, shining his light into all the nooks and crevasses until he reached a large dark hole five feet from the bottom. He swam up to the ledge. The entrance was littered with bright white stones.

Did Turtle Lake have an underground cave?

He was going to finally find something exciting and be a hero.

He kicked his way to the entrance and shined his flashlight inside the opening. The tunnel seemed to swallow the weakening light. What he thought were white rocks were bones, hundreds of human bones. He stopped. Two empty dark eye sockets stared at him from the floor. A skull's brown hair and flaps of skin waved in the current. The face looked familiar.

It was Timothy.

Kevin took a gasping breath. He didn't realize he had been holding it. His dive computer started to ding with the low oxygen warning, but he ignored it.

The current swirled and buffeted against him, tossing him around. A jet stream of water came rushing out of the tunnel like a freight train. Something big was coming. He pointed his light into the tunnel, illuminating two large eyes and sharp teeth. His fight-or-flight response kicked in. He screamed and headed straight to the surface, ignoring the loud alarm his dive computer emitted.

♦

Darren was concerned about his friend Kevin. Kevin liked to make rash decisions, never considering what the outcomes could be. He was too excited about diving into the deep hole he found at the lake. Darren wouldn't put it past his friend to risk his life and dive alone.

Darren dialed the number for the landline at the cabin. After a couple of rings someone picked up. "Is Kevin there?"

"No, he took the boat and went snorkeling," Kevin's dad said.

The hell he did.

Darren hung up and decided to go to the cabin. When he arrived, he found Kevin's parents lounging on the deck. "Hi. Is Kevin back?"

"No." Kevin's dad pointed towards the far end of the lake. "He must have found something interesting. The boat hasn't moved since you called."

"Where does he keep his diving gear?"

"In the back room. Why?"

Darren went to the backroom and found Kevin's dive gear missing. "He didn't go snorkeling. He's diving alone."

Darren ran to his car, grabbed his gear, and ran back to the docks. "Mr. Anderson, can you drive me to Kevin's boat?"

"Yes. Of course."

In minutes, they were at Kevin's boat, which sat anchored in deep water. The boat was empty, but at least the dive flag was out.

"Mr. Anderson, stay here. Kevin has been down a long time. You might want to call 911." Darren put on the rest of his gear and dropped into the water. He found the anchor rope and, hand over hand, pulled himself down.

A rush of bubbles exploded below him, and Kevin came up in a panic, all arms and legs. Darren saw unmistakable fright in his friend's eyes. He gave the hand signal to slow and stop, but his friend kept ascending at a rapid pace. He grabbed Kevin, but was shoved aside which knocked his mask askew and yanked his regulator out of his mouth.

Darren reinserted his regulator, adjusted his mask, and followed Kevin to the surface. As Kevin's father tried to pull his son on board Darren climbed into the boat and slipped off his tank and BCD. Pulling Kevin into the boat was like pulling up two hundred pounds of wet towels, all dead weight.

Kevin lay on the bottom of the boat, coughing up bloody, frothy phlegm. His eyes fluttered open and he spoke one word before falling unconscious. "Beware."

◆

Darla gave the thumbs-up signal to the driver. The boat rocketed forward and made a wide turn, skipping the tube carrying Darla and Jodi across the choppy water. The girls, who were cousins, squealed with delight as the boat picked up speed. Jodi glanced over the side as the boat slowed for the next turn. A large shadow seemed to be following the tube. She poked Darla and pointed. The shadow had disappeared. The two girls were whiplashed around the next turn, bouncing off the boat's wake.

Jodi's hands were slipping. Out of the corner of her eye she once again saw the large shadow that followed behind. If she had been in the ocean the first words out of her mouth would have been "Shark! Shark! Get out of the water," but she was in a small lake in Minnesota. She readjusted her grip and held on tight. Her unease grew though.

Figure eights, more body slamming, and wake jumping made the trip around the lake an adventure. Jodi's arms ached, and she didn't think she could survive another bone-jarring circuit. Their uncle drove the boat like he drove his car in Minneapolis--like a crazy man.

Darla squealed in surprise when the tube became airborne around the next turn and caught up with the boat. "I'm gone," she said and let go.

"No," Jodi screamed, but it was too late. Darla tumbled for a few feet before disappearing under the waves. Jodi scanned the water. The dark shadow below them was approaching fast. The buzz of the boats and the children's laughter suddenly stopped in Jodi's mind. The world became silent. The boat circled around to retrieve Darla. The *Jaws* movie theme filled Jodi's head as Darla lazily swam towards the tube.

"Hurry your ass up," Jodi said.

Jodi reached to pull Darla out of the water. With a smirk, Darla yanked Jodi off balance and pulled her into the water. Jodi let out a blood-curling scream as she hit the water. Panic erupted inside. She inadvertently sucked in a couple mouthfuls of water and wasn't sure if she would get on the tube before the large fish swimming below ate her.

Both girls scrambled onto the tube. Jodi slugged Darla in the shoulder. "Darla, what the hell is wrong with you? You almost drowned me."

Darla laughed. "Girl, you were freaking out. What the hell?"

Jodi opened her mouth to tell her friend about the dark shadow that had been following them but changed her mind. Darla would never believe it and would most likely make fun of her fears.

"Let's go in," Jodi told her uncle. She settled on the tube for the ride back to the cabin, however, she kept scanning the water for the dark shadow.

No sign of the giant fish. Maybe she had imagined the whole thing.

When they reached the shallow water around their dock, both girls jumped off and made for shore. After a couple of steps, Jodi felt a sting on the back of her thigh.

"Ouch!"

A couple of large bluegills circling nearby were protecting their nest and one had darted out and nipped her calf.

"Holy shit." Jodi got out of the water as quickly as possible. "They bite." She approached her mother, who was pulling weeds in the herb garden. "Mom, do you mind if I take a nap? Tubing wore me out."

"No, go ahead. I'll wake you for supper."

Jodi closed the door to the room she shared with Darla and inspected the painful welts the fish had inflicted. They looked like hickeys, painful hickeys. She lay down and hugged her pillow tight. Sleep never came. Her mind continued to be restless and the thoughts of a killer in the lake intensified. Nobody would believe her. She loved her cousin, but Darla could be cruel at times, making fun of her fears whenever possible. She needed proof of the large fish.

Jodi finally nodded off and when she woke, the house had become quiet and empty. She gazed outside and understood why. The family boat was not on the lift. This was her chance to slip away without being questioned.

Jodi dropped her paddle board in the water, slipped her phone into a waterproof bag, and paddled towards deeper water. If she saw the creature, she would get photographic evidence.

A school of small sunfish followed and took turns bumping into her board. She swatted at them with her paddle, but that seemed to intensify the attacks. What the hell was wrong with the fish? Larger groups struck hard enough to rock her small craft. A couple of times she had to concentrate to keep her balance. The swarm of sunfish multiplied tenfold. She slipped the straps of the waterproof bag over her head and took out the camera. She snapped two quick pictures and, as she focused for a third, the fish disappeared.

Something large rocked the paddled board, knocking her to her knees. Jodi's heart thudded in her chest. She glanced over the edge into large black eyes. The fish looked like no other fish she had seen before. It was at least four feet long, flat and oval. It didn't have a tail, only a dorsal fin. Its beak-like mouth seemed to be grinning. It was so odd-looking that Jodi thought the fish wasn't real. She grabbed her camera, but the creature struck the board, sending her into the water. The creature grunted before grabbing her by the arm and pulling her deep under water. She kicked and thrashed, but the creature never relinquished its hold. It continued to grunt until darkness and death took her away.

The board with the camera sitting on top washed ashore, but there were no signs of Jodi's body.

Two people missing—a child and a teenager—in two different lakes within miles of each other was no coincidence in James's opinion. Neither lake had any natural outlets. The bodies should have floated to the surface within two or three days, not simply disappeared. Turtle Lake was deeper and colder, but the young boy's body should have been found.

In the bed of his pickup, James flattened the map he studied. If these disappearances had happened around the 4th of July, he might understand, but they had occurred on ordinary lake weekends. Maybe he had to change his way of thinking, strip away the old and outdated, and upgrade his approach.

He would start by deconstructing each disappearance and study the lakes and their similarities. A few years ago, a man-made gravity fed outlet was installed in Turtle Lake and the water, through a pipe, made its way into the wetlands surrounding Long Lake and Lake Fifteen. Some geologists think that the lakes shared the same springs too. He would need to find out why these young people disappeared before the summer kicked into full swing. His gut told him this was just the beginning. There would be others.

A dirty blue sedan drove by and stopped suddenly, spitting gravel in a cloud of dust. A sandy-haired boy stepped out of the vehicle and, with long and purposeful strides, headed in James's direction.

"Are you James Underwood, head of the Clay County Search and Rescue team?"

"Yes, I am," James said. "How can I help you?"

"My girlfriend was the girl who disappeared on Long Lake…"

"That was your girlfriend?"

The boy nodded. His red-rimmed eyes showed his pain. He extended his hand. "My name is Darren Stevens."

James clasped his hand. "Nice to meet you. We haven't given up. We'll find her. I promise you."

The teenager rubbed his eyes. "I'm an advanced open water diver and have taken all my Divers Alert network courses, including rescue. I have night, deep water, and Nitrox certifications too. I want to help."

"How old are you?"

"Seventeen." Darren took a big breath. "My best friend is in a decompression chamber in Fargo. He dove Turtle Lake by himself." Darren ran his hands through his hair. "He found something that scared the shit out of him so badly that he shot up one hundred feet to the surface. I want to help you find them."

James scratched the three-day-old stubble on his chin. He could really use some help solving this puzzle, but a teenager?

"Okay, but if anyone asks, you're eighteen." James cocked his head. "Got it?"

"Got it." A small glimmer sparkled in Darren's eyes. "When and where do we start?"

"Now." James pointed to the depth chart of Turtle Lake. "Where did your friend dive?"

Darren pointed to the southern end of the lake. "This is the deepest part of the lake. My friend Kevin said that in the 1930s this end of the lake was almost dry. They hauled gravel and sand out of the lake by the ton until they hit a spring."

"'I'm assuming you have been diving in Turtle Lake?"

"Yes. My open water certification dive was there, and I've dived almost every weekend since. Deep and clear. Just a large bowl, with deep weed lines down to twenty-five feet."

"How about we meet at the public access tomorrow morning, say around nine?"

"I will be waiting for you with Kevin's boat. He has a state-of-the-art depth finder and graph. He always has it on. He should have pictures of what he saw that made him so excited to dive alone."

Darren and Mr. Anderson, Kevin's father, were waiting for James when he arrived at 8:30 am.

"Kevin's parents let me stay at their cabin last night. I downloaded the information from his dive that day and printed it out." Darren handed a stack of paper to James.

"I'm sorry to hear about Kevin's accident," James said, flipping through the sheets. "How is..." He abruptly stopped and stared at the papers before him. "What the hell is that?" He jabbed a finger at one of the pages. "That can't be right."

"I know," Darren said. "My thoughts exactly. There can't be something that big swimming in this lake."

"I'm sure there is a rational explanation." James swiveled towards Kevin's father. "How's Kevin's recovery coming along?"

Mr. Anderson shrugged. "He is still in the chamber, but his vitals are improving." He looked towards the lake. "I should be at the hospital with my wife, but I can't sit there and do nothing."

James started pulling on his wet suit. "We'll do a short reconnaissance dive, so I can see what's down there and later this afternoon we'll do a more comprehensive, targeted dive."

Darren nodded.

The morning was clear and bright with a few puffs of clouds scattered above. The lake was quiet except for a small fishing boat anchored on the north end. They loaded James's gear into the boat and headed out onto the lake. It only took a few minutes to reach the coordinates of Kevin's last dive. They dropped anchor.

"Keep close to me and watch my hand signals," James said. "We'll make a slow descent, take a few pictures, and make our way back to the surface."

"Okay," Darren said, licking is lips. His whole body trembled. He was anxious to start.

"Two things to remember. If you feel you are about to panic, slow down and talk yourself through it. Most people get in trouble diving because they do not take care of the little things right away, those little things snowball into big things, and then it's too late. You're dead."

Darren nodded. "I understand."

The pair dropped into the water and held onto the anchor line as they made their way to the bottom. James was surprised by the number of sunfish swimming below the deep weed line. There was nothing down here along the edges of the abandoned gravel pit. The fish seemed very interested in them, swimming just outside the range of their lights. They darted aggressively close, then backed away. Time and time again, fish grabbed onto his fins.

As they swam along the dark, silent, and foreboding bottom, James snapped as many pictures as he could. Large boulders dotted the bottom and the rough-cut walls. But soon, James motioned to Darren that their time was up and they needed to resurface. They ascended, making the allotted decompression stops, and reached the surface.

"There was something not right down there," Darren said. "The sunfish seemed ready to attack, like we were intruders."

"Let's get back to the house and download the pictures and see if we find anything that can help us."

At the surface, James and Darren slipped off their tanks and handed them to Kevin's dad, who then helped them into the boat. Darren finished taking off the rest of his gear and pondered the large shape they'd seen on Kevin's electronics. Could it have just been a giant school of fish after all? James and Darren silently settled into their seats for the quick ride back to the cabin.

"Has anyone on the lake complained about aggressive fish in the shallows?" James asked.

"At the last weeks TLIA board meeting, they discussed how aggressive the sunfish had become. Biting kids until they drew blood," Kevin's dad said. "And they weren't protecting nests."

They arrived back at the cabin and gathered around the laptop. James downloaded the pictures he had taken. One by one, they studied each of them.

"Here." Darren pointed to a dark fissure. "I felt a slight current, water a little colder." He took a deep breath. "I thought I saw eyes watching us."

"Have either of you heard of tunnels or caves associated with the area?" James asked.

Darren and Kevin's dad shook their heads.

James's cell phone rang. "Yes." He nodded. "I'll be right there."

"What's going on?" Darren asked.

"Grab your gear. A girl just disappeared on Lake Fifteen."

James and Darren loaded their gear and jumped into James's truck. They arrived at the lake in less than a half hour. Unloading the boat and stowing their gear on board took another ten minutes. James's phone rang as they were pushing away from the public access dock.

"The rest of my team will be here in thirty minutes or so."

James pulled up the depth chart for Lake Fifteen on the Minnesota DNR website on his phone. "This fish or creature or whatever it is will head to deepest part of the lake to finish feeding."

"Feed?" Darren's face blanched.

"Yes."

James drove the boat to what he thought was the deepest part of the lake. "We need to hurry. We have a small window to recover the body. The girl probably isn't alive."

"Where are we going?" Darren asked.

"To the lair of the monster."

The pair donned their equipment in silence and slipped into the water. Before putting their regulators in, James asked, "Are you sure you want to be a rescue diver?"

"Let's go find the girl."

Their search was fruitless. Even when the rest of the Clay County rescue team arrived, there was too much area to search. They had used up their bottom time and would have to try again the following day. A dejected James and Darren went back to Turtle Lake to regroup.

James and Darren sat on the deck and watched the sunset. James sipped a dark beer and Darren drank lemonade.

"In a closed body of water, how can a body just disappear?" Darren asked.

"I think that Turtle Lake, Long Lake, and Lake Fifteen are connected somehow. We need to find the tunnel or cave system that connects them."

A car door slammed and a few seconds later someone yelled. "Darren...anybody home?"

"We're in front," Darren hollered.

A middle-aged man neither one of them knew came around the corner of the cabin. "I'm sorry to intrude, but I'm a friend of Jodi's parents."

He handed Darren a small nylon camera bag. "They thought there might be a clue to Jodi's whereabouts on her phone."

Darren led them to the backroom and connected Jodi's camera to the monitor.

"Holy Shit," James said. "That's a sunfish, an ocean sunfish."

"What is an ocean fish doing in a landlocked lake thousands of miles from an ocean?" Darren asked.

"Only Mother Nature knows."

James laid the equipment they were going to use for the next day's dive out on the floor of the deck. He pointed to the tanks. "By using nitrox, rebreathers, and dry suits, we should be able to stay deep for two to three hours. Plenty of time to find some answers. We'll also be using full face masks with communicators, so we can talk to each other and the boat topside. We'll stay close and we will not take any unnecessary chances." James took a deep breath. "Darren, do you have any questions or concerns about the equipment or our objectives?"

"No. I understand."

"Don't stay up too late. We need to be sharp tomorrow."

Darren crawled into bed early, but sleep fought him at every turn. He couldn't clear his mind. Thoughts of the giant fish kept poking him awake. A restless sleep overcame him just before the sun peeked over the treetops. His phone's alarm sounded, letting him know it was time.

An egg sandwich and a cup of coffee were waiting for Darren when he walked into the kitchen. He grabbed his breakfast and joined James and Mr. Anderson on the deck. Nervous energy radiated from everyone, each of them lost in their own thoughts. What type of monster had Mother Nature unleashed on Turtle Lake? They would find out soon.

James and Darren went over their predive checklists in relative silence. Darren slipped on his wetsuit and his eyes grew big when James walked back from his truck with two six-foot spear guns.

"Can't take any chances," James said.

They loaded their gear on the Anderson's pontoon boat. As they pulled away from the dock, Darren noticed the schools of sunfish that normally congregated in the shallows were gone.

Shortly after they deployed the dive flag, both James and Darren were in the water. James spoke first. "Testing, Testing...One, two, three. Darren, can you hear me?"

"Loud and clear."

"Okay. Let's go.

They both emptied the air from their BCs and made a slow, steady descent. Fish of all sizes filled the water column. Every few minutes a group would make a rush at them. Northern Pike, with their bad attitudes and razor-sharp teeth, led the charge.

When they reached the bottom, the nest teamed with large and aggressive fish. They went way around, but several groups of fish made mad dashes at them nonetheless. James and Darren kept their heads on a swivel while they searched for the deep hole that Kevin had found.

Butterflies took flight in Darren's stomach as he hovered over the bottomless black hole. This was the same sensation he had staring into the abyss when he and Kevin dived the Caymen Islands. They were nearing the end of this mystery, and he had a gut-wrenching feeling that this adventure wouldn't end well. "James, I think we found it."

A cold-water current streamed slowly from the black maw. Somewhere thirty feet below them, the creature they came for was waiting for them. They were about to swim into the jaws of the unknown. Would they both make it out alive?

James pounded one of the long stakes into the mud that he had brought with him. He tied one end of the rope to the stake and the other to his dive belt. "It's now or never."

Darren nodded and when the silt settled from the stake insertion, he followed James into the darkness that their diving lights barely penetrated.

James grabbed his wrist. "Are you alright?"

"Yeah."

"Claustrophobic?"

"No."

"Stay close."

Darren expected the hole to be guarded, but there weren't any fish around. In fact, there wasn't any sign of life until they reached the bottom. White bones lay scattered in small piles everywhere. Darren's heart raced when he saw a white mesh bag partially buried in the muck. It was Kevin's dive bag. He pointed and called out to James. They found Timothy's red swim trunks and his missing tennis shoe inside.

"Keep an eye out for Timothy," James said. "This must be where the creature feeds."

Darren's mouth went dry. He turned in a tight circle, illuminating the walls with his flashlight. The composition was mostly gravel and a few larger stones, but as they neared one hundred feet the walls appeared to be composed of denser material. He wasn't a geologist, so he had no idea what the material was. There was an opening to their left, roughly six feet in circumference. A steady current of frigid water buffeted them in the face.

"James, where do you think this tunnel goes?"

"If I was to guess? Long Lake." James checked his dive computer. "We've been down an hour. We have thirty minutes left to explore before we need to head to the surface. James to surface, copy?"

"Surface, copy," Mr. Anderson said. "But I can barely hear you."

"We've reached our destination."

"10-4."

James uncoiled another rope and attached it to the entrance. "Do you want to go first?"

"Um...not really." Darren suspected this was where his friend encountered the monster and lost his marbles.

A large fish slid from the crevices and approached. James's breath caught in his chest. His dive computer chimed a warning. He saw a gleaming intelligence, sharp and cruel, behind the creature's eyes. They were in her world. This might have been a mistake bringing someone Darren's age with him. An alarm sounded as his anxiety built and panic set in. This wasn't going to end well. He closed his eyes and concentrated on taking slow and measured breaths. The alarm quieted.

Seconds passed. The water around him moved. He counted to three and opened his eyes. The fish filled his entire field of vision. Large, dark eyes studied him. The monster seemed to be licking its lips, ready to devour him.

"Darren." James yanked on the cord that tethered him to Darren, their signal to start reeling James in. "I found the monster."

Darren pulled with all his strength, but the rope must have been snagged on something. "James. Are you alright?" The rope jumped in his hands.

"No."

The creature attacked, biting off a few of James's fingers and crushing his hand. The monster tossed him against the wall before Darren was able to reach them. Darren leveled his spear gun, fired, and missed. He tried to chase the fish away, but the creature had other plans. It grabbed James by the shoulder and swam away. Bits of tissue and streaks of blood littered the water, leaving an obvious trail.

Darren followed the creature's trail into a large cavern. Crystals glinted on the walls. Large stalagmites touched the surface of the water. He felt like he had left his world and gone back in time to a scene from an Edgar Rice Burroughs book. He swam for a few minutes and shined his light into the darkness of the enormous cavern. The light stretched for a few feet before being swallowed. After a few frantic moments, he found James floating unconscious.

"Hello." The echo seemed to travel forever. "Topside, can you hear me?"

No answer came.

With no choices left, he carried James up to the nearest shore and laid him on the stoney beach. Darren took off his mask, then removed James's. The air was stale, but breathable. Dark shadows circled deep in the crystal-clear water. They weren't alone.

Darren shook James until he opened his eyes.

"Where am I?" James asked.

"On a stoney out cropping in a cavern or a spring, somewhere deep underground. My best guess? Somewhere between Long Lake and Turtle Lake."

James looked at his missing fingers, his mangled hand, and his face paled.

"He took a piece of you with him," Darren said. "Him and his friends are out there waiting, somewhere." Darren inspected his dive computer. "We have roughly twenty minutes to find a way back to the surface. I'm not sure which lake is closer."

James sucked in a painful mouthful of air. "The search and rescue team will come looking for us soon. When was the last time you radioed Mr. Anderson?"

"Not since we entered the tunnel."

"In my bag, there are several explosive devices. You need to seal this chamber. This creature cannot escape again."

"How?"

"Find the end of the cavern. It should eventually narrow. Place the explosive, set the timer, swim like hell, and hope the blast fills the gap." James grimaced and turned paler. "Exchange tanks with me and go back the way you came. Blow up that entrance. Go home."

"I'm not leaving you here."

"You must. For Timothy, for your girlfriend."

Darren sat for several minutes pondering his dilemma. After making his decision, he put his mask and helmet back on, grabbed the explosives and both spear guns, and slid into the water. The shadows in the water swam closer and followed, but never attacked. After ten minutes of swimming, he found the end of the cavern. Several tunnels branched off in different directions. Slowly and carefully, James talked him through how to set the explosives and the timer. Darren blocked out all of his emotions and just did what he was told.

The explosion rocked the cavern. Boulders and rocks rained down everywhere. Some splashed uncomfortably close. Darren's tank ran out of air about halfway back to James so he dropped the rebreather and swam hard. He resurfaced and gulped down air.

James eyes were closed, his breath raspy and shallow.

Darren nudged his shoulder. "James?"

"You did good. Finish the job," James whispered.

"The air is good. We can wait until help arrives."

"No. There are other monsters in here, and you can't let them escape."

"Okay."

The other monsters chased Darren to the tunnel that led back to the lake. He armed the explosives and set the timer.

"Good-bye, my friend," Darren said.

⬦

Darren was surprised that Mr. Anderson wasn't the one in the boat when he surfaced. It was the friend of Jodi's parents instead. The search and rescue team were nowhere to be found.

"Where's Mr. Anderson?" Darren asked. "And the rest of James's team?"

"Mr. Anderson never told me to call anyone. He asked if I would wait by the dive flag until you surfaced. He needed to leave quickly. His son took a turn for the worse and died."

Darren closed his eyes and cried.

♦

The ghosts of the summer never left Darren alone, his sleep dominated by drowned faces and frenzied screams. The missing visited his daydreams and James's ghost sometimes sat by his bed at night. None of the children were ever found. No explanation was given. Over time, people forgot. Darren avoided talking or answering questions about the disappearance of James and what they might have found. The pictures on Jodi's digital camera disappeared. When pressed, Darren did admit that they had found and entered an unknown tunnel, which had then collapsed. He had been able to escape, but his mentor and friend wasn't that lucky. The sand in James's hourglass had simply run out.

Sealing off the cavern seemed to have worked. No one else went missing that summer or fall. The menacing large dark shadow and the aggressive sunfish seemed to have vanished. Darren checked the news and social media daily, just to be sure.

The seasons turned. The leaves changed color and fell. The ice covered the lakes. Darren stood knee deep in snow and looked over the vast horizon of white and wondered if the monster was truly gone. In the spring, he'd venture back into the water. Kevin and James would want him to continue to live his passion.

Mother Nature was neither sweet nor forgiving.

♦

Chris is the founder and leader of the Moorhead Friends Writing Group.

His short stories have been published in the *Gates of Chaos, Horror Zine Magazine, Fear Forges* Spring 2023 edition. *Something Woke This Way Comes*, and two Moorhead Friends Writing Group anthologies. His dark fantasy novel, *Sins of the Mother*, will be published in 2024.

Lady of the Lake

Micaela Hallen

Based on the Lake Crescent Murder. Some of this story has been fictionalized, but the facts of the case have been told following history.

A GASP FOLLOWED BY the sound of a fishing pole clattering to the floor makes Louis turn around.

"What the hell—?" His brother grumbles.

"What is it?" Louis calls out. He reels in his rod, sets it in its holder, and walks to the stern where his brother stands stock-still.

"I don't know. It's large, wrapped in some sort of cloth and rope."

Louis reaches the back of their small fishing boat where his brother is staring out over the water. "What on earth...?" Louis says. "Quick, let's get it out of the water."

Louis turns around to get a set of gaffs to use. He hands one to his brother and they manage to pull the large floating object closer by hooking the ropes. Once they have it at the side, the brothers pull it up into the boat. They let it down with a loud *thunk*, and the item in question rolls away from them. The two stare at it, dumbfounded.

"Louis, does it look.... like a person?"

Louis takes a moment to answer. "I think we need to call the police."

Louis and his brother hurry to secure the item in their boat before steering the vessel to the first building they can find: the Washington State Trout Hatchery. When they reach the docks, Louis shouts at his brother to stay in the boat and jumps out. He runs up the path to the building and comes upon a man walking out the door.

"Come quick." Louis wheezes, trying to catch his breath.

"What is it?" the man responds, confusion coloring his tone. In his ten years of working in this managerial position, Fred has never once seen a man run up to him, fighting for air.

"We think we found a body," Louis says this so softly that Fred hardly believes his ears.

Fred tips his head back and laughs, his face coated in disbelief. "That's the most ridiculous thing I've ever heard. Must be a deer or something," he says in a disapproving tone.

Louis can only shake his head, still shocked by the discovery. "I swear on my life." He motions for Fred to follow him.

The two race back to the boat. The moment Fred sets eyes on the bundle of blankets, he sees a small piece of flesh peeking out. A cold shiver runs down his spine as if someone just dumped a cold bucket of water over his head. He turns his head away from the sight.

"Oh my God. It's.... it's really a person. I'll run and call the p —police. Be back in a minute." Fred turns on his heel and dashes back up to the Hatchery.

♦

They would later find out that the item pulled from the water was indeed a person. A woman. But here is where the story has a very unique turn of events. The tattered blankets and ropes revealed this woman had been in the water for a while, but when the police cut the ropes and unwrapped the blankets, they found her body well-preserved. Dr. Kaveney, one of the individuals who examined the body, stated: "I never saw a corpse like this one before. The flesh is hard, almost waxy. She must be nearly as large as when she went into the water. I'd say she is about five feet six inches in height and she weighed about one hundred forty pounds when alive."

The year was 1940 and this "Lady of the Lake" stumped almost everyone who came across her. After her body sank below the surface of the lake, over time, her fat turned into adipocere. What does that mean? When a body is exposed to anaerobic bacteria, that particular bacteria interacts with the fat inside the body, causing it to go through hydrolysis and transform into soap. This, combined with the freezing temperatures of Lake Crescent, mummified her body. But how had she gotten there? Who killed her and why? How long had she been under those frigid waters, waiting to be discovered and her killer to be brought to justice?

◆

"We've got a body down at the harbor of Lake Crescent. Some fisherman found her this afternoon."

Charlie, still half asleep after waking suddenly from his afternoon nap, grumbles an unintelligible reply.

"You need to get down here now."

"Okay, okay, I'm barely awake. Be down there in an hour." Charlie forcefully places the phone back on the hook. He rolls out of bed, gets some proper clothes on, and pours himself some coffee before driving out to the scene.

Charlie stands on the banks of the harbor in the unusually brisk air, unsure of what he is looking at. His tall, skinny frame leans with each gust of wind, making his grimace deepen. He takes slow, small steps in circles around the body, trying to see if he missed anything else. Unsatisfied, he lets out a long sigh and stops, tipping forward to take a sip of coffee. He scans the scene in front of him for the umpteenth time and his expression furrows in confusion.

Earlier when he had arrived at the Hatchery, he cut the ropes and removed the blankets, freeing this woman from her confinement. When his gaze fell upon her still perfectly preserved body, he was taken aback. He could see bruises that had bloomed across her torso, showing she was still alive when beaten. The worst of these were the marks encircling her neck, revealing she had likely been strangled to death.

What kind of sick bastard would do that?

"What the hell do you think happened here?" Ralph Smythe, the county's prosecutor, chimes in as he walks up to the others. Ralph's presence could be very intimidating to anyone who didn't know him. With broad shoulders, tall stature, dark brown hair, and a beard that rivals Santa Claus'. If not for his kind blue eyes, nobody would likely approach him on the street.

Upon hearing Ralph's deep timbre, Charlie turns around. "Hey, Ace, I was wondering when you would get here."

Ralph grunts at him while taking in the scene. "It would appear someone was trying to get rid of evidence. Looks like they did a good job of it too."

Charlie nods. "I'm having the body sent off to the medical examiner. Not much else we can do here."

"I suppose so," Ralph says.

With a nod and stiff goodbye to the other men, Charlie walks up the bank to his car. He sits there for a minute, trying to clear his mind of what he just saw. A face so distorted it didn't look human, but the rest of her body, like white marble, seemed perfectly intact. He couldn't shake the eerie feeling surrounding him as he drove away.

Harlan McNutt, a short, stout man in his late twenties, waits patiently for the body to arrive after the phone call he'd gotten from the sheriff. He had been given very few details, but one key thing Charlie mentioned was that he had probably never seen anything like this before. As a young medical student, Harlan loved how every death was unrepeatable, each victim with distinct qualities no other body could recreate. It intrigued him.

When the young woman's body finally arrives at the coroner's office, Harlan is ready to get to work. He slowly unzips the body bag. A fingerless hand pops out from under the polyethylene covering. Harlan pauses to appreciate the iridescent hue her skin has taken on before maneuvering the zipper down to her feet.

He carefully peels the bag off to the side, revealing the otherworldly corpse within. Harlan's stomach flips, and his blue eyes widen. He stares down at her body, wondering how this could have happened.

Harlan shakes his head, takes two long strides over to his table of instruments, and picks up a scalpel. His heart starts to beat excitedly as he makes the first cut of the Y, the blade sliding through her body like it's made of butter.

"How odd," Harlan muses, looking at the waxy substance remaining on his blade.

A shrill, yet masculine voice comes from behind. "McNutt, you need to take photographs before you cut."

Harlan turns around. Medical examiner Kaveney stands before him, looking stern.

"You know how procedure works. Don't screw this up." He continues giving Harlan a withering look.

"Oh shit. Sorry, you're right." Harlan sets the blade back down on the cold metal table. He proceeds to take pictures, from the bruises and ligature marks on her throat to her feet where all ten toes are missing.

Kaveney checks on Harlan once more before returning to his office, leaving Harlan alone to work.

Once Harlan is done getting his photos, he picks up his scalpel again, eager to cut into her and figure this mystery out.

He goes in for the second cut but stops. The room is quiet, too quiet. A preternatural silence fills the morgue. He nervously turns on the radio for some companionship. The voice over the staticky radio waves blurts out the latest news of the town.

That's better.

With the scalpel positioned down, he makes a second cut. Again, the blade slides between her tissues much easier than through typical postmortem flesh. Curious, Harlan gently presses into the woman's abdomen. A depression shaped like his hand remains. Eyes wide, he gasps at this unusual sight. Like putty, the flesh shifts, and he can scoop out a portion of her abdominal cavity. The substance somewhat hard but moldable.

"What the hell?" he utters, his mind racing with questions.

How could this be happening?

Harlan takes a small sample of the waxy material and brings it over to his microscope. What he sees is not a normal composition of cells.

He runs various tests with the help of Kaveney in an attempt to name what happened to this woman's body. Hours later, they have their answer. Her flesh had turned into soap.

"I've never seen anything like it," Kaveney comments.

"A professor I had in college mentioned something similar to this in one of his lectures. The person in question had not been submerged in a lake but was on land in a very wet and humid climate," Harlan replies, peering curiously at the unidentified woman.

How very peculiar this process would occur down in the deep waters of Lake Crescent.

Harlan continues the autopsy, finishing up with cataloging when he glances out the window. Night is falling. Shit, Harlan thinks. He had not meant to spend most of the day working. He meticulously puts everything back in its place. Lastly, he covers the body with a sheet and puts it onto a cooling board with the help of Dr. Kaveney. Once that's done, he grabs his bag and turns off the radio. Silence permeates the air.

"Goodnight, sir," he says to Kaveney as he hurries to the door. He swiftly shuts it behind him and walks home.

Harlan goes to church the next morning with his wife and spends the rest of his day trying to forget about the mysterious woman lying in the morgue. Despite his best efforts, as he lays in bed that night patiently waiting for sleep to take him, he can't stop seeing images of the woman's body. Her face is a blur due to all of her facial features being lost to decay and animals of the deep lake. When he does finally drift off, his sleep is restless, nightmares plaguing him. He wakes in the early morning with sweat dripping from his brow. After trying and failing to get back to sleep, Harlan gets up, dresses himself, eats a piece of toast, and writes his wife a note before heading out into the misty cool morning.

Once back at the morgue, Harlan pulls out Jane Doe's body and continues to work on her. The woman in question no longer has fingers or toes to help identify who she is, so he moves on to the next best thing, her teeth. He carefully opens her mouth and finds a partial dental plate.

This could be just the ticket to finding out who this woman is.

Harlan checks his watch. It's just after seven-thirty in the morning. He decides that it's best to wait a couple of hours before calling to alert anyone else about his finding. He gets to work cleaning the partial, ensuring the debris from the lake is removed. After that task, he makes a mold of her remaining teeth to compare to dental records. By the time he finishes up, it's after nine o'clock. An acceptable hour to call someone, he thinks.

He rings the sheriff, hoping to update him on his discovery. The phone rings and rings with no answer. He waits another thirty minutes before trying once more. Finally, Charlie answers on the fourth ring.

"Hello, Sheriff Kemp here."

"Hello, this is Harlan McNutt calling from the morgue. I may have found something to help us identify the victim from Lake Crescent."

Kemp's voice rings out. "Hell, that's great news. I'll be straight over."

"Okay, I will—" The phone clicks, signaling Kemp has ended the call.

Harlan goes back to work, sewing the body back up. He's almost done when the buzzer goes off, letting him know someone is at the door. He removes his gloves and washes his hands thoroughly before walking over to the door to greet the sheriff.

"Hello, Charlie. Thanks for making your way down here. I'm hoping this will be enough to identify the body," Harlan says excitedly.

"I hope so too," he says, coming over to the counter. He shudders at the sight of the young woman's ghastly pale skin in stark contrast to the dark table below her. He turns away and spots the item in question. He grips it between his thumb and index finger. "It's fortunate you found this. Did you figure out why her body appears so unnaturally preserved?"

"She's one of the most peculiar cases I've seen. Her body appears mummified due to the process of saponification. I couldn't find much else. No old injuries to help identify who she was." Harlan watches the sheriff examine the dental bridge.

"Very good, very good. I'll bring it back and show Ralph. Hopefully, we will get some answers soon. If you discover anything else, please call the office."

"Yes sir, I'll let you know immediately if there's anything I missed."

"Okey dokey, I'll see you around, kid," Charlie says with a salute of his finger. He walks back out the door to his next stop.

♦

Charlie walks through the door of the prosecutor's office and calls out, "Top of the morning to you, Ralph!"

Ralph gets up from the desk, his face distorted into an almost pained expression. "Good morning," he replies, dark shadows brooding under his eyes.

"Didn't sleep well either?" Charlie chides.

"No. I must've slept wrong. Everything hurts today." Ralph's annoyed tone signals Charlie not to irritate the man any further.

"Harlan, one of the medical students at the morgue, has been working on our Jane Doe. He had me come over this morning to get a partial to help identify the body." Charlie pulls the bridge with six gold teeth out of his pocket and sets it down on Ralph's desk. This seems to put Ralph in a better mood.

"This is great! Exactly what we need to identify our victim. I've already started compiling a list of missing women from the last few months. I figure you can help me go through them."

Charlie nods. He makes his way over to an open desk and grabs a handful of papers. He proceeds to rifle through the stack dated 1939, taking note of any women in the area who went missing and remained that way. There weren't many and, by late afternoon, the two have narrowed their search down.

Charlie reads through a file on Marion Steffens, a young woman from Chicago. She had gone missing in Olympic National Park in September 1939. Her description and clothing when she disappeared were similar to the woman found.

Standing up, he takes long strides over to Ralph's desk. "Here, I reviewed this woman's file and she seems to be a likely candidate."

Ralph lazily holds his hand out for the file in Charlie's hand. "Good stuff, I'll make some phone calls to her family and see what I can find out." With that, he picks up the phone, squinting at the number typed onto the page in front of him.

Charlie walks back to his desk and continues to review the missing person files. He casually listens to Ralph, who seems to be conversing with the missing woman's mother. "Oh, she had a prior neck injury? Broken vertebra, got it."

Shoot, this information pretty much rules her out since the medical examiner has not found any injuries to their victim's spine.

Once Ralph gets off the phone, he comes back over to Charlie's desk, tossing the file down onto it. "Another dead end. Mark her file- very low probability."

Charlie lets out a sigh. "Damn, I was hoping we had figured out Jane Doe's identity. Well, let's get back to the search."

The office remains fairly silent for the afternoon, except for the occasional humming coming from Ralph. That's when the phone rings, startling both of the men. Ralph quickly scoops up the phone in his meaty hand and holds it to his ear.

"Prosecutor's office and Port Angeles PD, this is Ralph speaking."

Charlie strains to listen to the conversation. First, an annoyed huff comes from Ralph's lips, then a chuckle before he sets the phone back down.

"That was Kaveney. He thought Harlan had already told us how long the body had likely been in the water but, clearly, that was an oversight. Turns out she's been in the lake for over two years."

Charlie's mouth drops open upon hearing the news. "No shit, I would have pegged her being there under a year for how good the body looks. Have you looked back that far yet?"

"No, I'm currently looking through cold cases from earlier this year.

Who knows, maybe they're wrong about how long she was in her watery grave."

The pair continue to work well into the evening, going through paperwork and making calls. Charlie glances at his watch, noting it's almost seven.

"Well, I better get home. My wife isn't too happy about me working on her birthday," Charlie says. He gets up from his chair and stretches.

"Ahhh, I suppose you're right." Ralph sets his stack of files down and stands up. Charlie shuts off the light at his desk and they exit the office together. Ralph takes his keys and locks the door before turning back to Charlie.

"G'night, Ralph. See you tomorrow?"

"Yep, have a good night now, and say happy birthday to Beth for me."

"Will do." With a tip of his head, Charlie walks off to his car, frustrated by the lack of answers in their latest case.

It is now September 2, 1941, over a year after our Jane Doe was discovered in the glacial waters of Lake Crescent. During that time, Sheriff Kemp had sent letters to the surrounding states with a description of the woman and pictures of the unique dental bridge. Regardless of his efforts, he isn't any closer to solving the mystery of who this woman is. Yet another cold case to put with the others, collecting dust in the back of the filing room.

But this Tuesday is very different from the last fifty-eight odd Tuesdays since their victim floated up to the surface of a lake famous for never giving up its dead. Charlie receives a letter from Mr. Edgar Thompson, a gentleman who works for the culinary alliance of Port Angeles. He tears open the envelope and pulls out three pieces of paper.

In the letter, Mr. Thompson states he had seen the sketch of the missing woman (attached to the back) and believes it to be Hallie, a waitress who had vanished almost three years ago without her employment papers, never to be seen again.

Eagerly, Charlie goes over to Hollis Fultz, one of their local investigators who specializes in cold cases.

"Eh, I got a tip on a case from almost a year ago." He holds out the letter to the young man.

Hollis looks up from his typewriter. Taking the letter, he reads it quickly. "Just when we thought there wasn't any hope," he utters. He gets up and walks into the file room. Eventually, he finds what he is looking for and an exhilarated pulse flows through his veins. There's no feeling quite like when an unsolved case gets life breathed back into it.

Back at his desk, Hollis tears the rubber band off the binder full of documents and starts to read through them. After some time, he finds the small file with Hallie's name on it. He makes several calls to family, friends and finally, a couple of dental offices she visited to see if either of them knows anything about the bridge found in her mouth. After that is done, Hollis makes copies of the photographs of the partial found in their victim's mouth and mails them to the dental offices. Now it's a waiting game to see if either can positively identify the person it belongs to.

A week and a half later, a dentist from Faulkton, South Dakota, finally calls back.

"Hello, this is investigator Hollis Fultz with the Port Angeles PD."

"Er, hello," comes the voice before static takes over the other end of the line.

"Damn it, I knew we should have spent the budget on new phones." Hollis proceeds to smack the end of the phone with his palm.

"Hello? Is anyone there?" a voice blurts out from the earpiece.

Hollis quickly puts the phone in the correct position, cradling it between his ear and shoulder. "Yes, I'm here. Who am I speaking with?" he inquires impatiently.

"My name is Tom Hager. I am calling in regards to a missing woman."

Fultz's ears perk up at this. "Our Jane Doe from Lake Crescent?"

"That's the one. I received a call last week from your office asking if I could help identify this missing woman. I got the letter today, the one you sent to me regarding the unique dental bridge found in her mouth. One look at the picture and I knew I had made that for a young woman by the name of Hallie Spraker."

Hollis's eyes widen, his hands flying across the desk to find her file. "Thank you so much for calling back and helping us with identifying her." He finishes his conversation with the man and feels his heart flip in his chest as he sets the phone down.

Holy Shit, did I finally figure out who our famous Jane Doe is?

The next day, Charlie and Hollis drive out to the cemetery in the early morning. A half-hour later, they stand in the biting autumn air, staring down at the two boys working hard to remove the dirt and exhume the body of their Jane Doe.

"It's nothing short of a miracle that the man from the restaurant saw your missing woman posters and that led us to this moment. You said a friend was coming out to help identify her?" Hollis asks.

"Yeah, a friend and old co-worker, Carrie," Charlie responds, his gaze resolute.

Not long after Charlie says those words, Carrie arrives at the cemetery. They greet one another and make small talk while the boys make short work of lifting the casket from its shallow grave. Before they open it, Charlie prepares Carrie for what is about to happen and then they lift the lid clean off.

The moment the top is gone, Carrie looks as if she is going to faint. The pungent smell of formaldehyde and earth hits their noses. Charlie watches her from a couple of feet away as she bravely takes a step closer, eyes scanning the hardened flesh. The body looks almost exactly like it had the day it was found.

"It's her. I'd recognize that dress anywhere. It's one of her favorites," she utters before turning away, tears pouring down her cheeks. "It's good to finally know. We always wondered."

♦

Once they confirmed their Jane Doe was indeed Hallie Illingworth (previously Hallie Spraker), they had to figure out what happened to her. Over the next couple of weeks, Charlie and Hollis worked with a few other officers and the new prosecuting attorney, Max Church, to collect information and, more importantly, evidence for her case. By the end of October, Fultz and Charlie had their suspicions about Hallie's husband, Montgomery Illingworth, known better as Monty. He was well known for being a notorious character around town, a corrupt man who didn't appear to care for anyone but himself. Neighbors and co-workers described him as an angry drunk who liked to blame everyone else but himself for his problems.

When Charlie calls Monty and questions him about the disappearance of his wife, his response sounds rehearsed. "I was at a party in Port Townsend, celebrating the upcoming holidays. My wife had to work, which is why I went alone. I recall coming home late on the morning of December 23rd and finding a note saying my wife had left me. She was going back home to the Dakotas. I thought that was for the best since I had filed for divorce days prior. We were getting into a lot of fights, and she hated my partying ways. I figured when she left, she never wanted to hear from me again. I didn't realize she was missing. Swear to God."

Fortunately, Charlie had been sheriff of the area for many years and was no fool. Both Hollis and he saw right through Monty's bullshit and investigated further, looking for that one scrap of evidence they so desperately needed to take him down. Talking to neighbors, friends, and family, they started to draw a picture of the man Hallie had married. They didn't have enough evidence to convict him just yet, but if a jury could be convinced beyond a reasonable doubt, they might have a chance.

But Monty Illingworth was nowhere to be found. It wasn't until October 26, 1941, that Port Angeles PD tracked down Monty at a residence in Long Beach, California, and brought him back to Washington to be interrogated. After questioning him further, prosecutor Max Church got Monty to contradict what he had previously said to them. Monty now claimed he had last seen Hallie on December 22nd, saying she went to work and, upon returning home, they got into another horrible argument. He left the apartment and went out to the bars to cool off and when he returned home late that night, Hallie was gone and he never saw her again. After incriminating himself even further with more lies, they officially arrested him, charging him not long after with second-degree murder of his wife Hallie Illingworth.

Over the next five months, Sheriff Kemp, Hollis Fultz, and Prosecutor Church, among many others, worked on gathering evidence for the upcoming trial. Fultz and Charlie diligently combed through notes from the medical examiner on the autopsy, pictures, files, and more. Despite only having circumstantial evidence, the two of them knew he had done it and were determined to prove it, one way or another.

It's February 24, 1942, and the trial of Monty Illingworth is commencing. Judge Atwater's voice booms out over the courtroom. "We will start the proceedings now."

The prosecution starts with their character witnesses, knowing they need to convince the jury what a terrible husband and person Monty is right away.

"We call Mrs. Evelyn Brown to testify," Max Church calls out.

Someone helps an elderly woman to stand and, with the support of their arm and her cane, she walks up and sits on the witness stand to the left of the judge.

"Mrs. Brown, you lived at the same apartment building as Monty and Hallie Illingworth in December 1937, correct?" Max asks.

"Yes, that is correct. I lived next door to them for over a year."

"Thank you. Can you please tell me about the night of September 25th?" Max continues.

"Certainly. But first I want you to know that Monty is well known for being an angry drunk. A complete arsehole if you ask me. I recall that night in September very well. Monty and Hallie were yelling at each other, and I heard her shrieking, begging him to stop hitting her. I thought he was going to kill her then. I've never heard someone scream like that... It made my blood run cold. I went over to check on her and she answered the door, saying everything was fine, but I knew in my heart everything was not. I could see a bruise sprouting across her cheek and her eyes —she looked terrified. I called the police. I didn't know what else to do. She wouldn't accept my help." She lets out a sob and covers her face. "I wish I had done more, gotten her out before... he hurt her."

"Thank you, Mrs. Brown, that will be all."

Judge Atwater clears his throat and takes a drink of water, watching Evelyn leave the stand after the defense denied having any further questions.

"I will now read two police reports filed in the months leading up to Hallie Illingworth's disappearance." He looks around the room, eyes settling on the members of the jury. "On October 8, 1937, the police were called in regard to a man with a bleeding head wound lying on the ground in the apartment entryway, unconscious. When officers Briant and Swanson arrived, the man in question was woken up. He became violent, trying to hit the officers and yelling at them to leave him alone. Upon hearing the noise, his wife Hallie exited the apartment they lived in together and told him to come inside with her and sleep it off. The man walked down the path, stumbling around, speaking profanities. When he got to the door, he knocked into his wife so hard she fell. She told the police over and over: 'It was just an accident, claiming she was not in harm's way and thought he just needed to sleep.' The officers told her to call if she had any other issues and left the premises."

Judge Atwater sets down the piece of paper and collects the next report, the only sound in the courtroom being the shuffling of these papers. He starts to read the next statement.

"Our next report dated November 17, 1937. Officers Broswell and Clemmings went to the apartment where the Illingsworths lived at the time in regard to a domestic violence call. Upon arriving at the scene, they discovered a woman beaten severely. Her left eye was bruised and marks were present on her neck, as if someone had attempted to choke her recently. Despite all their efforts, the woman (Hallie Illingworth) did not press charges against her husband (Montgomery Illingworth). The officers left their information with the wife, Mrs. Hallie Illingworth, in case she needed any further assistance and left the premises." The Judge finishes and a hush falls over the room. A dismal quiet of those pondering what poor Hallie had to endure at the hands of her husband, Monty.

Prosecutor Church stands up from his table and turns his darkened eyes upon Monty and the jury. "We will now call our second witness, an old friend and co-worker of the deceased to testify on behalf of these reports."

The woman who came to ID the body at the cemetery gets up and walks down the row of benches and up to her chair next to the judge.

"Identify yourself for the court and tell us of your connection to Hallie Illingworth," Judge Atwater orders.

Her eyes flick up at him before looking out into the crowded courtroom. "My name is Carrie Thompson. I used to work at the Lake Crescent Tavern with Hallie. I was another waitress there."

"Thank you. Continue." Prosecutor Church walks her through testifying, first asking her about the days after November 17th.

"Hallie showed up to work looking rather unsightly with bruises marring her body. She could barely do her job due to the injuries but, despite this, she wanted to work anyway. She wanted to be away from Monty."

After she finishes her testimony, Church asks her to identify the clothing found on the dead body once again. Carrie positively identifies the green dress as one Hallie wore frequently.

"Thank you, Mrs. Thompson. You may go back to your seat now," Church says, motioning to the rows of benches behind him. She gets off the stand, giving the jury a teary-eyed look as she goes.

"We have heard compelling testimony today, from character witnesses and police reports. I am adjourning the trial for today. We will start again tomorrow at nine sharp." Judge Atwater bangs his gavel, making it official.

Over the next week, evidence is presented, refuted, and some determined inadmissible. Just when prosecutor Church thinks all is lost, Sheriff Kemp finds evidence that will tie Monty directly to the crime. The rope used on Hallie matched one Monty had borrowed from his old employer, Mr. Earl Enos at Port Angeles Distributing Company. Charlie had sent the rope fibers earlier that month to be tested, and the results finally got back during the trial, showing an exact match to the ones used to hogtie the victim. *They have their smoking gun.*

Once Max Church presents this evidence, the trial wraps up rather quickly. Judge Atwater sends the jury to deliberate and four hours later, they reach a verdict.

The moment one of the members announces their final judgment, the courtroom erupts into cheers. Montgomery Illingworth is found guilty of second-degree murder.

The members of Hallie's family, friends, and people of the town finally have their closure.

◆

Hallie Illingworth, now famously known as the 'Lady of the Lake', had her justice. Four and a half years later, Monty Illingworth finally paid for the crime he had so callously committed against his wife. To quote the newspaper article in the San Francisco Examiner, from May 24, 1942: "She rose, not to catch an enchanted blade but to bring the sword of justice to the man who murdered her four years before." Lake Crescent is famous for not giving up its dead, but Hallie somehow got free of its clutches and gave her loved ones the answers they needed. Her story will always be remembered, not only for the unique embalming of her body through the process of saponification but for the amazing, strong woman she was, a woman determined to hold her murderer liable for his crimes.

Sources:

1. https://morbidology.com/the-lady-of-the-lake-hallie-illingwor th/

2. https://www.historylink.org/File/8599

3. Newspaper: San Francisco Examiner, May 24th, 1942 https://www.newspapers.com/image/458762685/?clipping_i

d=26983367&fcfToken=eyJhbGciOiJIUzI1NiIsInR5cCI6Ik
pXVCJ9.eyJmcmVlLXZpZXctaWQiOjQ1ODc2MjY4NSwi
aWF0Ijox Njk5OTIyODI5LCJleHAiOjE3MDAwMDkyMjI
9.zj9LMBc2Q70fQdEtWRDOoNfZorLn5YNrfOyOQQVfv
Hk

4. Newspaper: Daily News. August 9th 1942
https://www.newspapers.com/image/434345234/?clipping_i
d=105368386&fcfToken=eyJhbGciOiJIUzI1NiIsInR5cCI6I
kpXVCJ9.eyJmcmVlLXZpZXctaWQiOjQzNDM0NTIzNC
wiaWF0IjoxNzAwMDgwMjkyLCJleHAiOjE3MDAxNjY2O
TJ9.cpf6opfolhjupevbX3k0DjvuajKJPMW5_lMdIlZgSCg

5. https://www.sciencedirect.com/topics/medicine-and-dentistr
y/adipocere

6. https://www.findagrave.com/memorial/20841050/hallie-bro
oks-illingworth

💧

Hi, I'm Micaela Hallan and you just read my first published work. Thank you! I've always been interested in True Crime stories and I stumbled upon Morbid, a podcast, back in 2019 when driving home from my family's cabin in Minnesota. The Lady of the Lake story immediately caught my attention. Being a girl obsessed with lakes, I was amazed by the unique phenomenon of saponification and how it led to Hallie floating back up to the surface of the lake to catch her murderer. I hope you enjoyed my version of events mixed in with the real facts of the case. Please listen to a podcast on it if you want to hear more!

Minnesota: Home to Lakes, Rivers, Streams & The Loon

Eileen Tronnes Nelson, CP

During the months from May to October, Minnesotans' response to, "What are you doing this weekend?" is "Going to the Lake!" However, they usually do not disclose which of the "Land of 10,000 Lakes" in Minnesota they mean. They just say, "Going to the Lake." Minnesota is known to have 11,842 large lakes of ten acres or more and hundreds of small lakes. If all basins over 2.5 acres were counted, Minnesota would have 21,871 lakes.

Lake properties are owned by people with a variety of incomes. Today there are multi-million-dollar homes built on the lakes and many rustic screen-door cabins as well. The lake places are a family focal point and are often passed from generation to generation.

Minnesota is home to one of the country's great outdoor regions, the Boundary Waters Canoe Area Wilderness, which has over one million acres within the Superior National Forest.

Lake Superior is the greatest of all the Great Lakes. It could hold all the water from the other four Great Lakes combined, plus an additional three Lake Erie's. If Lake Superior were emptied of all its water, the whole of North and South America would be covered in one foot of water.[1]

MOORHEAD, MINNESOTA BEGAN ON LAND FORMED 14,000 YEARS AGO

The City of Moorhead is on land that once was the bottom of an enormous glacial lake. Formed about fourteen thousand years ago and existing for nearly four thousand years, glacial Lake Agassiz (named for a 19th-century geologist) was larger than the combined area of the current Great Lake: Its one hundred ten thousand square mile area covered parts of northern Minnesota, the eastern part of North Dakota, and much of Canadian Manitoba.[2]

When Lake Agassiz drained as the last ice age ended, the Red River Valley emerged from the lakebed. The silt-heavy soil from the lakebed was excellent for farming and became the region's most precious resource once full-scale settlement began.[3]

Native Americans inhabited the Red River Valley for centuries before Europeans first set foot in the area. French and British traders traveled along the Red River of the North and its tributaries in the 17th and 18th centuries, mostly for the purpose of obtaining furs to sell in Europe. This trade continued into the 1800s, with a few hardy individuals settling down to live their lives in the Red River Valley. Large-scale white settlement did not begin until after the American Civil War, when a railroad was built from Minneapolis to the Red River of the North.[4]

MINNESOTA GEOLOGY

The story of Minnesota begins with geology. Invasions of a great salt sea laid down the strata in which oil and other mineral deposits are found, and, later, fresh-water rivers formed strata. Erosion, caused by wind, water, and glacial ice sheets, shaped the surface of the land, leaving what is now Minnesota as part of significant physiographic provinces of

Minnesota: Central Lowlands and the Great Plains.[5]

For hundreds of millions of years, Minnesota was intermittently covered by a salt sea stretching from the Gulf of Mexico to the Arctic. Sediments carried into the sea by flowing water was deposited on the bottom and slowly compacted into strata, or layers of sedimentary rock made up of clay, shale, sandstone, and limestone. During the long periods when the sea withdrew, the exposed surface was eroded. Thus, the strata are thicker in the deeper parts of the basin, covered longer by water, than they are in shallower parts or outside it.[6]

At the beginning of the Cenozoic Era, or Age of Mammals, some seventy million years ago, the ancient sea withdrew for the last time, and all other rock formations were laid down in fresh-water rivers and lakes or by glacial ice sheets. Large rivers eastward from the Rocky Mountains, carrying huge quantities of gravel, sand, and clay. They dropped much of this material on Minnesota, turning from side to side to build an extensive alluvial plain and leaving behind scattered lakes, rivers, streams, along with trees and shrubs.[7]

GUNDY THE TRICERATOPS SKELETON AT BARNES COUNTY HISTORICAL SOCIETY MUSEUM, VALLEY CITY, NORTH DAKOTA

Gundy is one of the horned dinosaurs that lived in North Dakota during the Cretaceous Period, sixty-five million years ago. It had three horns, grew to lengths of twenty-five feet, and weighed as much as eight tons. Her skull is 5 ½ feet long and 4 feet wide and was almost 95 percent complete in its fossil form. She is about eighteen feet long.[8]

Valley City's Mike Triebold, of Triebold Paleontology, discovered Gundy in 1992 on private ranchland in the Hell Creek formation deposits of Northwestern South Dakota. Triceratops comes from the Greek language, with 'tri' meaning three, 'keras' meaning horn, and 'ops' meaning face. The Triceratops was a plant-eating (herbivore) dinosaur.[9]

MAMMOTH TUSK UNEARTHED MAY 2023

In May 2023 at the Freedom Mine near Beulah, North Dakota, a seven-foot-long mammoth tusk was discovered by coal miners. The miners unearthed the tusk from an old streambed, about forty feet deep. Experts estimated the tusk to be ten thousand to one hundred thousand years old. A subsequent dig at the discovery site found twenty bones, including a shoulder blade, ribs, a tooth, and parts of hips. It is likely to be the most complete mammoth found in North Dakota. Mammoths once roamed across parts of Africa, Asia, Europe, and North America. The Freedom Mines discovery is rare in North Dakota and the region, as many remains of animals alive during the last Ice Age were destroyed by glaciations and movements of ice sheets. Mammoths went extinct about ten thousand years ago, according to the Geologic Survey. They were larger than elephants of today and were covered in thick wool.[10]

WATERSHEDS

"A watershed is an area of land that drains or 'sheds' water into a specific waterbody. Every body of water has a watershed. Watersheds drain rainfall and snowmelt into streams and rivers. These smaller bodies of water flow into larger ones, including lakes, bays, and oceans. Gravity helps to guide the path that water takes across the landscape.

Not all rain or snow that falls on a watershed flows out in this way. Some seeps into the ground. It goes into underground reservoirs called aquifers. Other precipitation ends up on hard surfaces such as roads and parking lots, from which it may enter storm drains that feed into streams. Watersheds can vary in size. A watershed for a tiny mountain creek might be as small as a few square meters. Some watersheds are enormous and usually encompass many smaller ones. The Mississippi River watershed is the biggest in the United States, draining more than three million square kilometers (one million square miles) of land. The

Mississippi River watershed stretches from the Appalachian Mountains in the east to the Rocky Mountains in the west. Thirty-one U.S. states and two Canadian provinces fall within the Mississippi River watershed. Watershed management is a term that describes the use of land, forest, and water resources in ways that do not harm the plants and animals living there. Watershed management may include goals and processes such as reducing the amount of pesticides and fertilizers that wash off farm fields and into nearby waterbodies. Watershed management is closely linked to conservation."[11]

MINNESOTA HAS EIGHT MAJOR WATERSHED BASINS & EIGHTY-ONE WATERSHED DISTRICTS

In 1955, the Minnesota Legislature authorized the creation of watersheds through the Watershed Act. The intent of the Act was to develop water management policies on a watershed basis because water does not follow political boundaries.

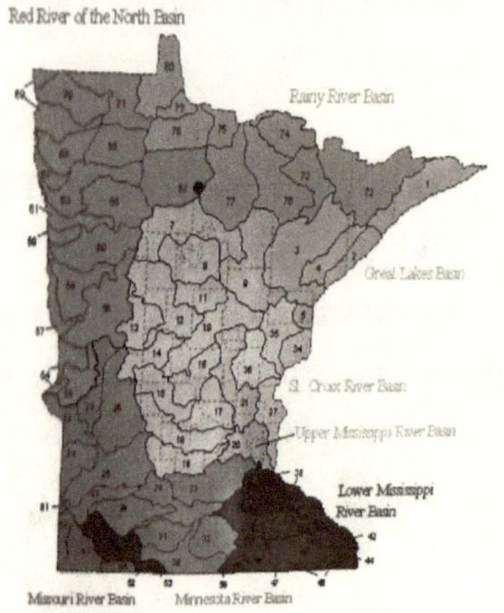

RED RIVER VALLEY: BOTTOM OF LAKE AGASSIZ

The Red River Valley begins at Lake Traverse near the South Dakota border flowing north to Canada and eventually draining into Hudson Bay. The Red River Valley extends eastward into Minnesota and westward into North Dakota for thirty or forty miles from the Red River of the North. This Red River Valley is commonly known as the "Bottom of Lake Agassiz," a flat land lying eight hundred to one thousand feet above sea level and sloping down toward the north. Pembina in North Dakota is seven hundred ninety-two feet above sea level. The rivers in this region drain into Hudson Bay.

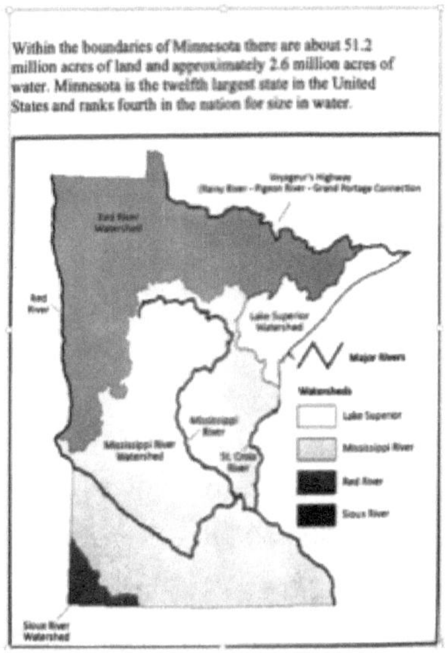

EBB and FLOW OF RED RIVER OF THE NORTH

The Red River of the North is the border of Minnesota and North Dakota. During April 1997, the existence of Moorhead was threatened when the Red River of the North and its tributaries, swollen with the moisture of a wet autumn and a heavy winter overflowed in the worst flood on record. It seemed that cities along the Red River of the North might come to an end.

In 1996-1997, I was living in Grand Forks, North Dakota, during the blizzards and the devastating flood of 1997, when there was a mandatory evacuation of all residents of Grand Forks, North Dakota, and East Grand Forks, Minnesota.

The flooding occurs because the water in the Red River of the North is still frozen in the north during the spring, and the water flows from the south to the north towards the damming occurring from the frozen water. Water spreads out of the riverbanks over the flat land—like a tabletop. The land is so flat I was surprised the water could keep rising.

The following information on the 1997 Flood Timeline is from the Grand Forks Government website.[12]

◆

1997 Flood Timeline

April 1997

4th - Blizzard "Hannah", the region's eighth blizzard that winter dropped an additional six inches of snow. "Hannah" also brought freezing rain that left over 300,000 Red River Valley residents without power.

4th - The Red River officially reaches flood stage at 28 feet.

8th - ND Governor Ed Schafer activates the National Guard to help with the flood fight and blizzard recovery.

14th - The Red River rises to 44.43 feet.

15th - The Point Bridge closes between Grand Forks and East Grand Forks

17th - The Red River rises to 50.96 feet.

18th - Grand Forks orders evacuation of Lincoln Park Neighborhood.

18th - Evacuation of the Riverside and Central Park Neighborhoods.

18th - The Red River raises eighteen inches in eighteen hours to hit 52.62 feet.

18th - The Kennedy Bridge is closed cutting off Grand Forks from East Grand Forks.

19th - Water is four feet deep in downtown Grand Forks.

19th - The Grand Forks Water Treatment Plant fails.

19th - Grand Forks orders evacuations of all areas east of Columbia Road.

19th - A fire is reported in the Security Building in downtown

Grand Forks. The fire eventually damages or destroys eleven buildings throughout three city blocks.

22nd - The Red River crests at 54.35 feet.

23rd - The Red River begins to recede.

May 1997

8th - Altru Hospital reopens.

12th - Altru Clinic reopens.

19th - The Red River falls below flood stage (28-feet).

August 1997

City's Public Schools resume classes using rented facilities that include two churches, one hundred relocatable buildings, the National Guard Armory, and a portion of two high schools.

1997 - 1998

About 850 properties are purchased by the city through a voluntary buyout program designed to remove structures from high-risk flood areas.

August 1998

The Grand Forks Herald newspaper opened a new $4.3 million building on the site of its former office devastated by both flood and fire.

January 1999

A new elementary school, named Phoenix to mark the city's rebirth, is built to replace two longtime elementary schools (Belmont & Lincoln).

October 1999

A $16 million commercial office complex built by the city opens in the heart of downtown. Known as the Corporate Center, this two-building complex replaces virtually all the commercial office space lost in the fire. The buildings provide about 100,000 square feet of office space.

January 2000

A new $20 million county office building opens. The building improves citizen access to government agencies by co-locating them under one roof.

June 2000

Town Square, an outdoor gathering place in downtown Grand Forks, opens for public use.

June 2000

Officials break ground for a $409 million flood protection project for Grand Forks and East Grand Forks.

February 2001

The $80 million Alerus Center opens.

October 2001

The $104+ million-dollar Ralph Engelstad Arena opens.

Summer 2002

King's Walk Golf Course, a $6.8 million Arnold Palmer Signature championship course, opens to the public.

June 2004

Lincoln Dr. Park is completed and dedicated. The park occupies the site where Lincoln Elementary School stood prior to the flood.

January 2007

The flood protection project is functionally complete.[13]

NOTE: THE FARGO MOORHEAD FLOOD DIVERSION PROJECT IS CURRENTLY UNDER CONSTRUCTION.

MISSISSIPPI RIVER HEADWATERS

The mighty Mississippi River begins its winding journey to the Gulf of Mexico as a mere 18-foot-wide knee-deep river in Itasca State Park in Minnesota. From here the river flows north to Bemidji, where it turns east, and then south near Grand Rapids. It will flow a total of 694 miles before working its way out of Minnesota.[14]

Within the park, people enjoy walking or floating on inner tubes the first half mile of the river, which meanders at a slow 1.2 miles per hour during the warm summer months. In the winter, you can still see the water flowing over the rocks, as warmer spring water keeps the area ice-free at the headwaters.[15]

The iconic headwaters are a must when you visit Itaska State Park. The historic marker dates to the 1930s and indicates the Mississippi River's total mileage of 2,552 miles. Since then, the river's course has been shortened and altered by flooding and channeling. Every summer canoeists leave Lake Itasca to begin their river adventures, with hopes of reaching the Gulf of Mexico over 2,318 miles away.[16]

MINNESOTA DEPARTMENT OF NATURAL RESOURCES

The Minnesota Department of Natural Resources began in 1876 as an organization responsible for the preservation and running of all the natural resources in the state. It oversees taking care of water resources, fish and wildlife, forests, trails, parks, leisure areas, and leisure trails of the state. All the mineral resources are monitored by the Minnesota Department of Natural Resources, in combination with its forestry and wildlife.[17]

Six Divisions of MN Department of Natural Resources

Ecological and Water Resources, Enforcement, Fish and Wildlife, Forestry, Lands and Minerals, Parks and Trails.

The Fish and Wildlife Division's main responsibility is to make sure all wildlife and fish within the state are preserved and protected. It is also responsible for the issuance of fishing, hunting, trapping, stamps, wild rice harvesting, trail licenses, commercial licenses, snowmobiles, watercraft, ski passes, horse passes, registration of leisure vehicles, and permits for water-related projects within the State of Minnesota.[18]

The water-related division monitors projects that impact Minnesota's water resources and are regulated by a variety of state, local, and federal agencies. In many cases, a permit is required from one or more of these agencies before proceeding with a project.[19]

LOON THE MINNESOTA STATE BIRD

The common name "Loon" is thought to have originated with early European settlers in North America and is based on an old Scandinavian word *lom*, meaning "lame" or "clumsy," referring to its awkward movement on land.

Loons are often referred to as feathered fish because they spend much of their lives underwater or on the surface of the water. They touch land only at birth, during mating, and while nesting.[20]

The limiting factor in loon habitat is not the presence of people, but rather the availability of safe nesting locations undisturbed by people and free from predators such as raccoons and skunks. In addition, they need clear water (because loons hunt by eyesight) and the availability of small and large fish.[21]

With more than 11,000 large lakes and hundreds of small lakes, Minnesota has more loons than any other state in the continental United States—about 12,000 loons.[22]

Only one or two pairs of loons occupy an area of about two square miles. The resident loons defend their territory against all other loons, thus keeping the population density down. Loons can live up to 30 years.[23]

Endangering the loons are monofilament fishing line, coastal water threats, mercury poisoning, and lead fishing sinkers.[24]

The male loon is generally larger than the females. It is difficult to distinguish between the sexes unless they are sitting side by side for comparison.[25]

Most birds have hollow bones. Loons have mostly solid bones, making them heavier than other birds of similar size. The added weight increases their specific gravity, which makes their bodies ride lower in water and decreases the amount of energy needed to swim underwater, where they spend much of their time during the day.[26]

The adults have deep red eyes. The eye color appears red in daylight because the eyes reflect the red part of the spectrum of sunlight while absorbing all the other wavelengths of light. However, due to the properties of water, most red light is filtered out, making the eyes appear black when underwater. Against the black head plumage, which may make the eyes invisible to prey and help camouflage the loon's presence. Loons can see extremely well underwater, which enables them to see the prey.[27]

Loons can submerge gradually without diving headfirst like ducks. Loons can surface slowly or with just their heads showing above water. Loons also surface stealthily, with just the top of their heads and nostrils showing, to take a breath and head back underwater again.[28]

To take off, loons need to run across the surface of the water. Facing into the wind, they back up to get a long stretch of open water. The distance required to take off depends upon the wind, but up to five hundred feet is needed in a calm wind. Shorter distances are necessary when loons are flying into a headwind.[29]

Young loons practice taking off and landing around August. The young loon practices takeoffs and landings five times in one hour. After each test flight, the loon swims back to the opposite side of the lake to face the wind and try again.[30]

Loons are designed to land on water. When landing on a lake, loons hold their wings very high over their backs to avoid clipping a wing on a wave on the surface of the water, resulting in a crash landing.[31]

Loons cannot take off on land. Some loons land on large, empty parking lots, mistaking them for the flat open surface of a lake. When a loon is on land, it is unable to take off. The oversized feet are so far back on the body, they are excellent for propelling during swimming, diving, and chasing fish, but they make a loon awkward when on land. Loons cannot walk the same way as ducks, swans, or other birds of similar shape. Instead, a loon will push itself along, dragging its breast on the ground while its feet prop up the rear. Even though a loon must push most of its body along the ground, it can move quickly on land and may use its wings to help push when needed. A land-bound loon needs to be captured and transported to a lake large enough to facilitate takeoff.[32]

The loon is an iconic waterbird. The striking black-and-white breeding plumage and deep red eyes of the Common Loon befit its elegance and grace. Loons have a white necklace around their necks. Loons are physically amazing, with large powerful feet that propel the birds underwater at speeds fast enough to overtake fish. They have wings capable of carrying them thousands of miles to wintering grounds and back again with the changes of the seasons. The call of the loon catapults our memories to a time at a lakeside.[33]

THE LORE OF THE LOON'S CALLS

Loons communicate with calls to other loons. The loons have four basic calls.

The Wail Call of the Loon.

Loon Preservation Committee. Listen to the Wail Call. https://loon.org/the-call-of-the-loon/ (last accessed Dec. 18, 2023).

The wail is an all-purpose call that expresses a loon's desire to be closer to other loons. It means, "Where are you?" or "Come here!" Wails are also given when a loon feels anxious or threatened.[34]

The wail rises and falls in pitch and often sounds like the howling of a wolf. Wails have three forms. The one-note wail is a single unbroken note that does not change. The two-note wail begins on one note and moves quickly to a second note of higher frequency. The three-note wail adds a third, higher note to the two-note wail.[35]

Wails are used to call to mates and family members. After hearing a wail, loons often swim toward each other.[36]

The Loon's Tremolo is a Laughing Call.

Loon Preservation Committee. Listen to the Tremolo Call: https://loon.org/the-call-of-the-loon/ (last accessed Dec. 18, 2023).

A peculiar laughing call of the loon led to the phrase "crazy as a loon." There is physical evidence that the laughing call is comprised of two overlapping notes. An alarm tremolo is given when a loon is feeling threatened or is threatening another bird. This is the most common call people hear because loons give it when they are approached by people.[37]

The Loon's Yodel is A Warning Call.

Loon Preservation Committee. Listen to the Yodel Call: https://loon.org/the-call-of-the-loon/ (last accessed Dec. 18, 2023).

The yodel is a danger or warning call given only by male loons to announce and defend territory. Yodels are used in aggressive displays and encounters and are given most often when loons are nesting and raising young. Loons in Minnesota have the highest voices. Males may strike another posture during yodels known as vulture position or vulture stance. A male will rear up high in the water and crooks his neck while delivering the call.[38]

The Loon's Hoot is a Contact Call.

Loon Preservation Committee. Listen to the Hoot Call: https://loon.org/the-call-of-the-loon/ (last accessed Dec. 18, 2023).

The hoot is a short, single call note, usually given by family members nearby. Considered a contact call, the hoot permits individuals to keep in auditory contact while they look for fish, scan for danger, or watch for other loons. Hoots are also given when an adult approaches a group of other adult loons for a social gathering.[39]

Chick Calls by Baby Loons.

Loon Preservation Committee. Listen to the Chick Call: https://loon.org/the-call-of-the-loon/ (last accessed Dec. 18, 2023).

Baby loons communicate in the same way that other baby birds keep in touch with their parents with soft peeping calls. Loon chicks three to four months of age deliver wails and tremolos that are indistinguishable from adult loon calls.[40]

MIGRATORY LOONS
ABOVE THE WATERS OF THE CENTRAL FLYWAY

Loons gather in large migration groups during late summer and early fall, but they migrate individually. Adults leave in autumn a few days to several weeks before the young. Loons migrate anytime during the day and rarely at night. Most leave at first light before the sun comes up and fly throughout the day, landing just before it gets dark after sunset.[41]

Differences between autumn migration groups and social gatherings include time of year, activities, and group size. Autumn migration groups may include juveniles, while social gatherings do not. Surveys on important staging lakes such as Lake Mille Lacs in Minnesota show that, just before autumn migration, loons gather in very large groups of up to five thousand adults and juveniles.[42]

During migration, loons take a day to a week to rest and feed. Recent studies show birds migrating out of the upper Midwest stop at Lake Michigan for a few days before heading toward the southern states, where they rest and feed at large reservoirs. While most loons in the central part of North America around the Great Lakes region migrate to the Gulf of Mexico to spend the winter, some winter along the eastern coast of Florida. Loons in eastern states usually winter along the Atlantic coast from the Carolinas to Florida.[43]

With the arrival of the loons each spring on their lakes, the season starts anew. Just as they have done for thousands of years, loon adults establish or re-establish the pair bond and get to the business of choosing nest sites, constructing a nest, incubating eggs, and attending to the needs of the young. It is a natural cycle of life that brings a certain comfort and calm to the world. Loons are gentle and patient with their babies yet find time to socialize with other adult loons. They are extremely good-looking birds with many highly specialized adaptations, making them unlike many other birds. Their sounds have become a calling card for true wilderness. They are endearing birds that have captured the hearts of people at their lakes, fascinating us now as they have for thousands of years.[44]

Looncam 2023

https://loon.org/looncam/

Loon Preservation Committee's LoonCam Live. The broadcast is live from loon nests in the Lakes Region of New Hampshire from May through mid-July. During the LoonCam season, short clips of interesting activities around the loon nest are published on the Loon Preservation Committee's YouTube Channel. It is a good way to catch up on what has been going on. The following playlist from the 2022 season includes archived clips from both Looncam 1 and 2 – sorted by most popular topics.

Eileen C. Tronnes Nelson, CP®, Family History Research Award for "Advancing Genealogical Skills," Heritage Education Commission, Moorhead, MN, converted from a Keynote document, Settlers in America: from Norway & Sweden & too large for publication as one book, thus divided into 4 eBooks & a paperback on Amazon. The subtitles: (1) "My Genealogy Techniques May Assist You," (paperback & eBook); (2) "A Customized Itinerary Independent Travel," (eBook); (3) "Photographs Traveling in Norway," (eBook) (4) "Photographs Traveling in Sweden" (eBook). The fifth publication is a paperback & an eBook: (5) "Eleanor Thompson Asphyxiation & Marie Wick Murder & Gummer Trial" (Books 1-5 in a series of 8 books). Publications in 2 anthologies, *Tales from the Frozen North* ("Blizzard in North Dakota March 2-5, 1966") (2022) & *Welcome to Effham Falls: Tales from a*

Small Town ("Where is Effham Falls? People & Places of the Arrowhead Region") (2023). https://amazon.com/author/eileentronnesnelson

---

1. *Top 10 Reasons People Love Living in Minnesota.* MNR News Aug. 25, 2023. (Dec. 18, 2023).

2. Shoptaugh, Terry (2004). *Images of America: Moorhead.* Charleston, SC: Arcadia Publishing, 9.

3. Shoptaugh, 9.

4. Shoptaugh, 9.

5. Robinson, Elwyn B. (1966). *History of North Dakota.* University of Nebraska Press: Lincoln, NE.

6. Robinson, 2.

7. Robinson, 3.

8. *Gundy the Triceratops*, Barnes County Historical Society Museum, Valley City, ND (last visited Museum Dec. 19, 2023).

9. *Gundy the Triceratops*, Barnes County Historical Society Museum, Valley City, ND (last visited Dec. 19, 2023).

10. *Coal miners in North Dakota unearth a mammoth tusk buried for thousands of years,* (last accessed Jan. 7, 2024).

11. National Geographic, *Watersheds.* (last accessed Dec. 21, 2023).

12. *1997 Flood Timeline* (last accessed Dec. 21, 2023).

13. *1997 Flood Timeline*. Grand Forks Government. (last accessed Dec. 21, 2023).

14. *Mississippi River Headwaters*, MN Department of Natural Resources. (last accessed Dec. 18, 2023).

15. *Mississippi River Headwaters*, MN Department of Natural Resources. (last accessed Dec. 18, 2023).

16. *Mississippi River Headwaters*, MN Department of Natural Resources. (last accessed Dec. 18, 2023).

17. MN Department of Natural Resources. (last accessed Dec. 18, 2023).

18. MN Department of Natural Resources. https://www.dnr.state.mn.us (last accessed Dec. 18, 2023).

19. MN Department of Natural Resources. https://www.dnr.state.mn.us (last accessed Dec. 18, 2023).

20. Tekiela, Stan (2021). *The Iconic Waterbirds*, Adventure Publications: Cambridge, MN, 34.

21. Tekiela, 27.

22. Tekiela, 28.

23. Tekiela, 28.

24. Tekiela, 28, 36, 39, 40.

25. Tekiela, 44.

26. Tekiela, 51.

27. Tekiela, 55.

28. Tekiela, 88.

29. Tekiela, 91.

30. Tekiela, 91.

31. Tekiela, 95.

32. Tekiela, 95.

33. Tekiela, 11.

34. Tekiela, 101.

35. Tekiela, 102.

36. Tekiela, 102.

37. Tekiela, 105.

38. Tekiela, 106-107.

39. Tekiela, 111.

40. Tekiela, 112.

41. Tekiela, 143.

42. Tekiela, 143.

43. Tekiela, 143.

44. Tekiela, 157.

Fear - On the Water's Edge

Dennis Kooren

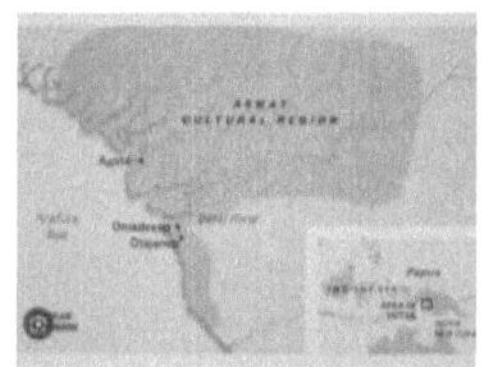

A map of
Indonesia with
Asmat highlighted

Permit me to take you on a special journey back in time, to a place the world left behind, and a place our modern world does not understand. A world apart, and a world away.

My work as a geographer, as well as being a nephew to a Catholic priest with missions among the Asmat in West Papua New Guinea, drew me to this island in the late 1980s. I have been returning regularly ever since. The island became like a second home to me, and an escape from our modern world.

Asmat rests on the southern coast of West Papua New Guinea. Indonesia controls the western half of Papua New Guinea to include

Asmat. The Papuan culture (Budaya) of New Guinea is vastly different from the Budaya of the rest of Indonesia. New Guinea is also the ancestral home of the Aborigines of Australia.

The Asmat had been left alone for thousands of years with no outside influence until WWII encroached on them and introduced them to our outside world. The missionaries who had been established in other sections of New Guinea were forced into the area after the Asmat started raiding outside villages in search of metal and other minerals that the outside world possessed. What they found were people different from what the world had painted.

Viewed as a warrior race, the Asmat built much of their culture on family and revenge. A glimpse into their lives is like a glimpse into human nature. These people with their simple existence have taught me a lot about humanity, good and evil, and faith.

They see things in a simple clear light and are not afraid to show it in very demonstrable ways. They laugh easily, cry easily, and do not hide their thoughts. They are people of the tree. Trees are their existence. To this day, believing they were drummed into life from a tree, they seal the skin of their drums with their own blood. Their best carvers also hold as high a position as the chiefs of the villages. It is through this sense that the land and the people become one. Asmat! True people of the true land.

The Asmat build their villages on the outside curve of a river so it is easy to see if an enemy is approaching to seek revenge for the taking of a life by them or their ancestors. They have escape routes set up into the jungle behind them, where only they know the area and can easily attack anyone searching for them.

Living in the world's largest rainforest tidal swamp, the Asmat's only way to travel is by canoe.

The Asmat welcomes visitors with a ritual war representing good and evil. The visitors coming to the shore represent the good, the people on land, the evil. With arrows and spears flying close to the canoes, the ritual war begins. We are eventually allowed onto shore. The good has won out, and we are welcomed into the village. A huge welcoming celebration ensues but during this celebration, there are always one or two people tasked to represent the evil still lurking in the shadows. Their job is to instill fear, so they taunt you, pretending to throw their spears at you and twanging the bowstrings off the ends of sheathed arrows pointed at you. I asked my uncle what I should do on my first greeting, and he calmly told me to ignore them, because if I didn't, there would be ten or twenty more people doing the same thing.

This is a picture of what fear does in a very real sense. Even though good has prevailed, evil propelled by fear lurks in the shadows. If we give into that fear, we start seeing only the fear.

Much of their Budaya was based on this fight between good and evil. They lived their lives encircled by it. This culminates in a very intense spirituality, in many ways similar to what our Native American community possesses.

Housed within the culture was the concept of an eye for an eye. They believed that if someone from their village was killed by another village that death had to be avenged or the evil spirits would haunt them. This gave rise to ritualistic fighting between villages, which in turn helped prevent them from becoming part of the modern world.

Life

This is just a little slice of life in the largest tidal swamp in the world. Asmat comprises over seven thousand square miles and is home to the largest mangrove rainforest in the world. No roads exist there. The only way to get around is by river or flying into a select few tiny airports built up out of the mud.

Called "The land of mud and unlimited impossibilities" by the missionaries who have been there since the 50s, this nearly impenetrable swamp is home to tens of thousands of the most fascinating people on earth. Drawn there by the bounty of the rivers and rainforest, they have established a life unlike any other on earth.

It is such a fascinating area that it draws in world explorers to this day. The most well-known among them was Captain Cook in the late 1700s, who felt he was being attacked by their welcoming ceremony and advised that people stay away from these fierce warriors who were cannibals and headhunters. One more recent explorer in the early 60s was Michael Rockefeller, who was there collecting artifacts and carvings from the coastal areas and met an untimely death because of a Dutch soldier's actions decades earlier.

In our time working with the Asmat people, we welcomed in crews from National Geographic, the Smithsonian, Sony Pictures, and others, which included "A World Away" by television station WCCO. Asmat represents a land and a people frozen in time, virtually unchanged for thousands of years. This was a favorite spot of the famed psychologist Margaret Mead as she delved into human nature.

Unless one spends time living among these special people, it is impossible to fully understand how they have survived in this harsh environment for thousands of years. It is only through working together and sharing that this was accomplished.

I fell in love with their simple way of life and found that the only way for me to be able to return was to use my geography degree from North Dakota State University and set up a specialized geographer-centered travel agency called Geographical Connections Inc. I kept the agency in existence until 9-11 happened and the travel world turned upside down.

There are no orphans in Asmat and as a result, I was adopted into a number of Asmat villages and given special names in each of them, usually after a past family member. This practice helps keep that person alive in one's mind. They would share their bounty of food and shelter with me.

For close to fifteen years, I escorted small groups of explorers in and out of the jungle so they could witness and experience what I did. Eventually, I was also able to bring in most of my immediate family to share the experience.

A welcoming Celebration

*An Asmat warrior tasked to
represent fear.*

Travel

As stated earlier, it is never easy to get in and out of Asmat. Special permission is also needed to enter the area without a walking paper or "Surat Jalan", which is a special permission slip signed and stamped by a special government official.

Guides are often necessary to assist in getting permission, and they are indispensable while traveling throughout Asmat. It is very easy to get lost in the intricate river systems and travel through the jungle lining the river's edge is nearly impossible. Over time, I established a very close working friendship with a young guide named Andre Liem. Even though he was not Asmat himself, he has a love for them as I do. He was, however, born and raised in West Papua New Guinea with great connections to the Asmat people who would act as our guides while traveling through different sections of Asmat.

On my first trip there it took almost two weeks to get into Asmat and a week to get out and back home after our visit. The final leg was on a small single-engine Cessna. We traveled from the north side of the island through the tall mountain ranges of the island's central backbone and then flew over the huge tidal swamp for over an hour before landing at the small airstrip built close to the mouth of the river. After all that, we still had an hour of boat travel. This all had to be done early in the day because the mountains would cloud over in the afternoon.

Stopping the Eye for an Eye

The Asmat were cannibals and headhunters, based on revenge and power. Because cannibalism is strictly taboo in our modern culture, the Asmat had to stop this ritualistic practice. The Indonesian government threatened to shoot people if they did not stop and forbade the practices leading up to this.

The missionaries had a better way of encouraging the people to stop this practice. In most all Christian beliefs Christ gives of himself in Holy Communion. He strengthens us through the water and wine. In the Catholic tradition and many Protestant traditions, He places himself into the bread and wine. This is called the Eucharist.

The Eucharist fits into the Asmat tradition like a piece in a jigsaw puzzle. By killing a member of a warring village, they would take on the attributes of that person. This was such a strong belief that the village who lost that member would recognize this in the person who took the life. Christians believe Christ gives himself to us as a sign of his love for us and for others. His strengths and love become ours.

Since Christ gives of himself, the Asmat would no longer need to kill to gain the powers of others. The jigsaw puzzle becomes complete. This revelation helped stop the fighting almost overnight.

Protecting the Asmat culture weighed heavily on the minds of a number of the missionaries. The bishop of the area and my uncle were anthropologists. They had seen the damage that outside cultures had done to our Native Americans and vowed this should not happen to the Asmat.

The missionaries encouraged the government to allow the Asmat traditions (minus the killing). They even started a fantastic museum for the people to showcase their traditional art, carvings, and feasts in Agats, the capital city of Asmat, and the only real link to the outside world. St Thomas University in St Paul, Minnesota also houses a large collection of the famed Asmat art and carvings, courtesy of the missions and the Asmat themselves.

The Fantastic Journey

One of the largest river systems in Asmat is the Unir River system. It hosts some of the area's largest villages. Many villages had been fighting each other for centuries. This was also the river system where my uncle had his villages.

The bishop of Asmat was to host a huge celebration on this river system to finalize the end of the fighting within that area of Asmat. I made a point to attend this special ceremony with a small group of tourists and it turned out to be an adventure that many would only dream of.

Because this celebration was set way upriver close to the mountains in the Asmat tidal swamp, we needed to land in one of its most remote sections called the Senggo-Brazza area. To this day, some people there still live in tree houses for protection. Because of difficulties getting permits and flights into the area, we were delayed and forced to travel through a maze of uncharted rivers and channels through the tidal swamp overnight just so we could reach our destination before the celebration began the following morning in Munu.

This was extremely dangerous on many fronts. If our guides took the wrong channel or river in the dark, we could end up stranded on a dead-end stream when the tide went out. With huge tidal swings over fifteen feet, this could easily happen. Other possibilities were even more dangerous. The rivers were filled with logs, fallen trees, and branches. If we hit one of these it could take out our motor. Going through the small cut-across channels would require lifting the boat across fallen trees and logs. Huge saltwater crocs and pythons also call this home, so getting out of the boats could be dangerous.

We had two boats in our entourage. The first held the local guides and a motorist. The second and heavier boat carried our small group of explorers. This way the guide boat broke trail for us.

It took little time to get our bags off the small airplane and transferred to the boats. We were shortly on our way. Being just south of the equator, we had around twelve hours of daylight and close to twelve hours of darkness. With the sun directly overhead, sunrise and sunset were short-lived.

The first few hours of our journey were in the daylight on a large river traveling at a good speed through the near impenetrable rainforest tidal swamp. It was special to see and hear so many birds and small animals. It is impossible to describe the beauty of a flock of rare black cockatoos and the sounds of the jungle and the birds of paradise hidden within.

The mountains above Asmat rise to over sixteen thousand feet. The tallest is Puncak Jaya at 16,024 feet. It is often covered in snow, and its rivers flow down into this huge tidal swamp of the shallow Arafura Sea. There are no rocks in the Asmat tidal swamp, only mud. The waters are brackish, hosting a mix of salt and freshwater aquatic life. It is quite common to find jellyfish, dolphins, and sharks far upstream. The high tides cover the jungle floor, and the low tides expose the mud and occasional higher ground, often built up by a bird called the jungle chicken. On the large river systems, it is possible to get a glimpse of the mountains towering above these sea level, mainly mangrove, swamps.

Once the sun set, our pace slowed. We could no longer easily see the logs (or crocs) floating in the muddy river. The flashlights came out. Their feeble light guided us through this maze. With the daylight beauty gone, the nighttime beauty took over. Silhouettes of trees in the moonlight guarded our path. The rarest among them are the firefly trees. Fireflies congregate on certain trees there and they lit up like huge Christmas trees, blinking on and off and becoming visible for miles. They were welcome beacons as we slowly traveled in the moonlight. Nature is very special.

This all started changing when we headed into the smaller cut across rivers and channels. It became a struggle to find the right path. I remember having to backtrack a few times when the guides decided we were on the wrong channel. Oftentimes, parts of these channels were only ten to twenty feet wide and easily blocked by a fallen tree.

We struggled for what seemed like an eternity but was actually only a few hours that we spent trying to get through the small channels, often slowly sliding over sunken logs and moving tree branches out of the way so we could pass. Memories of being caught on the wrong channels in daylight started going through my mind. To this day, I am totally amazed at our Asmat guides who knew the way through this treacherous swamp that has claimed so many lives in the past.

To my amazement, once we got out of the crossover section of the journey and onto a larger river, one of our small group of five broke out a bottle of Kahlua in celebration. We all happily partook in it in celebration. It was still dark, but the extremely treacherous part of our journey was now history, and we could again see the starlit jungle silhouettes on the opposite bank.

Once it became light, we were able to travel at a faster pace. I was familiar with the river we were on. It was the Unir where my uncle's villages were. Munu is his largest village and second most remote. Avemu was a couple of hours upstream.

My uncle had told me a few years earlier that I would never be able to sneak into the village to visit him without the grapevine alerting him. As we drew closer, I could hear the villagers shouting that Dennis had arrived and he was not alone! We were able to sneak up on both him, the villagers, and the bishop for this special once-in-a-lifetime Celebration of Life.

People from the entire Unir river system made it up to this very special celebration. They were former enemies, now working to forge new friendships and stop the fighting between them that had gone on for millennia. In fact, it was so deep rooted, the upstream villages spoke a different dialect of Asmat than the downstream villages.

Bishop Sowada knew the importance of keeping this celebration within Asmat tradition as did my uncle who the people called Wasan.

Hundreds of us sat on either side of the church, which was made into a facsimile of a *jeu* or gathering house. Family fireplaces lined either side. In the center, Bishop Sowada had evenly spaced a number of spears and placed them in the board edges of the floor. Each spear represented a village. During the service he broke each spear over his knee, signaling the end of the fighting for that village. The Asmat fully understood the meaning, as this was a piece of their culture.

After the service, the huge celebration began with much food and many games. People danced and drummed into the night. The spirit of the people was alive and well and it continues to this day.

May we all find a way to put our vengeance and jealousies aside and live in peace.

♦

Dennis Kooren sitting behind
the imbedded spears at the
celebration

Dennis Kooren is a Geography graduate of North Dakota State University. His former travel company called Geographical Connections Inc. allowed people to take part of expeditions into some of the most remote regions of the world. Married to Karen (Riskedahl), they have three children and six grandchildren. Dennis and Karen enjoy retirement, visiting the children, along with the lands and peoples of other unique areas of our world. This memoir is his first publication.

Letter to our Readers

www.ingramcontent.com/pod-product-compliance
Lightning Source LLC
Chambersburg PA
CBHW032117310726
48972CB00001B/263